CTHULHU: GRIMOIRE

ERIC MALIKYTE

To Alyus, Jessie, David, and Charles. Thank you for your thoughts and feedback, this book wouldn't be what it is without your input.

And to Phoenix. Thank you for always making time for this weird ass book. I will never stop singing your praises. You are an amazing friend, and the best editor.

CHAPTER ONE

The look in his eyes. They're still open. His lips. They're chapped and cracking. His neck is bent at a forty-five-degree angle... Must have broken the instant his body hit the grass.

Detective Hunter tosses his coffee on the campus lawn and curses under his breath.

What a waste.

"You all right?" Detective Erin Shirley, his partner, asks.

Hunter takes a moment to compose himself, wiping the beading sweat off his forehead with the sleeve of his blazer. Even at night, it's unbearably hot this time of year.

"I'm fine," Hunter says.

"The evidence technicians photographed the room already. We should get a look before they bag and tag everything." Shirley is excited. She's a tall white woman with ringlets of auburn hair, early thirties. It's almost sickening to him, how exhilarated she gets in the presence of death. How she bounces at the opportunity to examine a new crime scene. A new corpse. Even if the techs have already documented it. She loves her job. Treats it like some kind of escape room thrill ride.

He nods anyway.

The red and blue lights strobing in the sweltering night draw unwanted attention from across the campus. Three squad cars and an ambulance will do that.

He looks up. There's an open window five stories off the ground.

1

"You gonna say something tonight, Hunt?" Shirley's got that look in her eyes. It betrays what's lurking beneath.

"Is the victim's roommate here?" he asks.

"He is. Says he wants to talk to a lawyer before he talks to any cops. I told him that makes him look like a suspect. He didn't budge."

"He's got good reason to be worried."

She stands there and stares at him like there's a smart-ass comment on the tip of her tongue. Her pasty white skin catches the red and blue strobe like a blank canvas drinks paint.

"You want a crack at him?" she asks.

"What do you think?"

Most of the students who live in this apartment-complex-turned-student-housing are asleep at this hour. Some of them are up late, cramming for exams. Distracting themselves with video games. Avoiding responsibility with terrible booze and worse music. Hunter can hear some of that music still blaring at the other end of the property. Partying college students, totally oblivious that one of their own is slowly rotting away on the front lawn of the complex.

Not everyone is oblivious. Hunter's eyes scan over gawking faces, watching the fiasco unfold from behind caution tape.

He doesn't care about them right now, makes a beeline for the ambulance, where the victim's roommate is waiting.

He's a skinny Black kid. Huddled in some blankets, sitting on the ambulance's bumper. The physicians are asking him the standard psyche questions, making sure he's mentally stable after seeing...that.

The kid's eyes meet Hunter's. Thin black fingers strangle a well-worn and cracked phone.

There are several angles Hunter can approach this from. Police officers are allowed to offer a potential suspect false promises in order to get them to confess. Hunter wants to feel it out first. Maintain his distance, be friendly.

Something doesn't feel right about this.

Then again. It never does.

The kid's already glaring at him.

"What do you want?" the kid asks. "Already told you people, I want a lawyer."

The kid can practically smell the bacon. His eyes and body language don't relax. It doesn't matter that Hunter is Black. A cop's a cop.

"I'm Detective Hunter, I need to ask you a few questions."

"And you thought I'd answer without a lawyer just because you're Black?"

There's never an easy way to start this conversation.

"You're not in trouble, Dean."

Not unless you did it, he thinks.

"I've seen how this goes," Dean says.

"Look, we need answers. We've got a dead kid on the lawn, and countless people gawking from behind that police line—and you sitting here with a pissy look on your face. It won't take long for stories to start circulating, and most of them probably end with you shoving that poor bastard out your dorm room window."

"That what you think happened, Uncle Tom?"

A pregnant pause stretches between them. The kid avoids Hunter's gaze, like he's hoping he'll get the hint and just leave.

"Fine," Hunter says, nodding to Shirley, who's busy taking statements from residents. "If you don't want to talk to me, I'll go fetch my partner. I'm sure she'll be a *lot* more understanding."

Dean's still defensive, but he's shaking. His eyes keep glancing to Shirley and back to Hunter. The kid unfolds his arms. Places his palms on the ambulance's bumper. Less hostile body language. Progress.

"In your nine-one-one call," Hunter says, "you claimed that you came home from class to find that your roommate had jumped out the window. How did that happen?"

"Don't know where to start," Dean says.

"Start at the beginning," Hunter says.

The kid fidgets for a minute. Like every fiber of his being is telling him not to run his mouth, but that other voice, the irrational one that tells him the cops will just leave him alone if he tells Hunter everything he knows, takes over. Hunter knows that feeling all too well. The little lies people tell themselves.

"Kevin's been acting sus..." He pauses, as if catching himself. "Suspicious. Like, he's always been kind of weird. But we got along.

He hasn't…" His eyes open wide, as if he's just now realizing that he has to refer to this person, whom he'd shared a home with, in the past tense from now on. "Hadn't. He hadn't slept in a week. Or, if he did, he was cutting classes and sleeping during the day. Man, it was really starting to tick me off. He was on his laptop every night. I have a hard time sleeping with lights on, even a screen will wake me up. I tried to tell him to stop, but then he'd just stare at me with this blank look on his face. It was like…he wasn't there anymore."

There's a feeling in the pit of Hunter's gut. A terrible one. He thinks back to his days in the academy, how his instructors would hammer home the idea that an officer's gut feeling is their lifeline. Hunter starts to wonder if maybe Kevin Wallace *was* pushed from his window. If, maybe, this is going to turn into a confession.

Could Dean have snapped at his roommate? An altercation that simply went too far? Is that motive enough?

He prays it isn't.

"Then I come home from my Friday night class. I was planning to go over to a friend's place and celebrate the end of a long week. And the window's open. I told Kevin not to leave it open. Told him he'd catch these hands if I caught him smoking joints in the room again. I've worked too damn hard to get expelled for someone else's sh…stuff."

Dean pauses. Eyes drift across the lawn. He's looking at Kevin's body. "Never seen a dead body. Not like that."

So, not a confession. Hunter's more than a little relieved. If the kid's telling the truth.

"What do you think happened?"

"I think he jumped."

"Did Kevin have any enemies?"

"Shit, I don't know. He didn't talk much. Started hanging around with a bunch of emo kids."

"Do you know his major, what his family was like, anything?"

Dean nods. He's getting more comfortable. "He…was Media Arts and Animation. Like me. We didn't have no classes together. But, I seen some of his recent work, and it was getting weird."

"Weird how?"

"Ever heard of H.R. Giger?"

4

Detective Hunter shakes his head.

"Well, he's famous for designing some movie monster from the seventies. We learned about him in my concept art class. Demonic, hypersexual bullshit. Can't stand it. Apparently the guy worshiped some Satanic dude named Crowley. Kevin was obsessed with him too for a while."

For some reason, that name—Crowley—sounds really familiar to Hunter. He jots the name down in his notepad for later.

"How was Kevin's relationship with his parents?"

Dean shakes his head. "Kevin didn't say much about his family before coming here. But I know he never went home. Not even for holidays or summer."

"Why do you think he jumped?"

Dean shrugs. "Maybe he couldn't take the pressure no more? Who knows?"

The room is small, barely large enough for one person, let alone two. There's two beds on either side of the dorm, books scattered all over the place.

One side is nearly immaculate. The other looks like a disaster zone. It's clear which one belonged to Dean.

Shirley's scratching her chin as the evidence techs bag and tag items for examination. Hunter knows they wouldn't give two shits if it wasn't a white kid growing stiff on the lawn.

"Well, looks like this is an open and shut case," Shirley says, clapping her hands together like she's cracked it.

"Surprised they didn't shove a microscope up the kid's ass too," Hunter says.

For a moment, he thinks about the terrible feeling he had. Wonders what it means.

Could Dean be lying?

He doesn't think so. No. It's something else.

Something he can't put into words.

"I don't think this is a homicide," Hunter says.

"Of course you don't," Shirley says, practically scoffing. "Well, we're being as thorough as possible. You should have been here when the kid's parents showed up. The father slugged the rookie. Won't believe what we found in the kid's stuff. Surprised he didn't flush the coke before we arrived."

Hunter's fingers twitch. No way in hell a Black man would risk slugging a cop, not if he had a sense of self-preservation. He wonders if Shirley and her goons planted the contraband in Dean's stuff. Assassinate his character before making their murder case. Part of him, the part that's lived through George Floyd and roaming white gangs of police, doesn't want to know. "Which rookie? Jameson?"

"Yeah. Or maybe it was Wilkins? I can't keep them straight. If they don't get fired for screwing their paperwork up, I'll bother to remember their names."

Hunter nods. The one thing she's said tonight he agrees with.

"Still. Can't believe you got him to talk," she says. "So, you think he's telling the truth?"

"Dean didn't push his roommate, if that's what you're getting at," he says.

"How do you know?"

"Just a feeling."

"You don't think it's possible that he could have gotten sick of his roommate's bullshit and pushed him out the window?"

"Possible? Sure. But I don't think this kid is capable of that. He's got no priors and decent grades. Why would he risk murdering his roommate?"

"Crime of passion. If Kevin Wallace was going nuts, like the kid says he was, then who knows what the kid's not telling you?"

Hunter's about to tell her how wrong she is, call her on her bullshit. But something catches his eye. Kevin's laptop is open, the screen's turned off. The techs haven't dusted it or bagged it yet. There's a sketchbook next to it, and it's open.

A voice itching at the back of his mind tells him he should pick it up.

He puts on some gloves and flips through it.

The sketches are all in ink. His wife would call them "washes." They're monstrous things filled with rotting, jagged teeth, tentacles

6

that transform into sex organs, mouths, and anuses. They fill every possible orifice.

The drawings send shivers down Hunter's spine.

But for some reason, he can't stop tracing the brush strokes with his fingers.

"Hunter?"

"What?" Hunter glances around, blinking.

"You wanna take that home and fuck it or something?"

Shame. It fills him like an empty husk. Just like the day his father caught him alone with the stack of Playboy magazines.

He quickly shuts the sketchbook and drops it on the table.

"Relax," Shirley says. "You're not the first to react to the artwork like that."

Hunter clears his throat. "We should get into his laptop. Take a look at his social media activity and contact the building's ISP."

"Want my bet?"

"No."

"Probably lots of gay porn or something like that."

"Just because he's a loner, doesn't mean he's in the closet."

"Just saying, maybe that's why he never went home? Maybe his family's religious, thought they'd disown him or something? You know how these artist types are."

"That's pure conjecture."

"Still, we should take a deeper look at the family. Both of them."

And they'll have the perfect opportunity while they've got Dean and his father locked up tight in an interrogation room. They'll use the trumped-up assault charges to get the father to spill on the family's dirty laundry.

If the man's smart, he's already lawyered up.

Hunter doesn't say any of that. Doesn't think about the strange looks the other officers are giving him, that Shirley is giving him.

"...Agreed," Hunter says. "But we'll interview them in the morning. Let it sit."

Shirley yawns, stretching. "Sure, we've got forty-eight hours anyway. Let's let the techs finish bagging and tagging this shit and call it a night."

"How can you be so calm about this?"

She shrugs. Something odd about the look in her eyes. Like her connection to humanity's long since been disconnected. "After a while, you just get numb to it all. It becomes a job. I don't know how you can still be so moved by things like this after all these years."

Hunter moves for the door. "Some of us are still human."

She's staring at Kevin Wallace's laptop. There's a faraway look in her eyes. "Maybe. Or, maybe you're the outlier?"

"What?"

She shakes her head. "Oh, nothing. Just being morbid. You know me."

Sometimes he wonders if he does.

"Goodnight, Shirley."

"Night, Hunt."

Hunter gets home to find his third-story apartment dead quiet. It's almost 3:00 am in Fontana, California. The wife and kids are most likely asleep.

The faint smell of rice and pan-fried chicken with a hint of kale lingers in the air.

He missed dinner again.

Moonlight bounces off the living room furniture. His recliner's calling his name. A covered easel stands out when he enters. It beckons him to look. A white pallet speckled with paint dries on the coffee table.

Fingers stretch out, grip the sheet.

He wants to tear it away. See what his wife was working on, maybe bring some much-needed color into his dreary world.

Something deep inside tells him not to look. Can't stop thinking about the inkings in Kevin Wallace's sketchbook. The writhing and twisting amorphous silhouettes.

When he shuts his eyes, he can see them moving.

His fingers tense, then release the cloth.

Hunter rubs his eyes. Tells himself he needs a stiff drink and a hot meal. That Janet will show him the painting when she's done with it.

8

The kitchen is spotless. A note on the fridge reads "It's your turn next time. No takeout."

Hunter hangs his blazer up and looks in the fridge. There's a plate with his name on it. A little heart's sharpied next to it. He grabs the plate and a beer. Pops the plate in the microwave. Opens the beer and takes a long sip from the can. Tries not to think about the look on Kevin's face as he closes his eyes. The kid's graying skin. The way his lips stretched and cracked. Almost like he was smiling.

There's an odd, melancholy thing about the way a microwave sounds in the middle of the night.

The microwave dings and Hunter pulls his food out, sits at the kitchen counter, and brings his hands together to say grace. He's halfway through scarfing the plate down when he notices her on the stairs.

Her eyes look almost black; her pale white skin is a near-perfect silhouette against the moonlight-kissed windows.

"I had a nightmare," she says.

The hair on the back of Hunter's neck stands to attention. He doesn't know why. Doesn't know what to say.

Janet crosses the room and hugs him tight enough to restrict his lung capacity. "I just...need to feel you. Know that you're here."

"What is this about, Janet?"

She's silent for a time. Her touch is cold. Clammy.

"Janet?"

"I don't want to talk about it."

He touches her arm. She jerks back for a moment before relaxing. "Go on back to bed, then. I'll be up soon."

A lie. He's going to spend the next hour running over case documents and filling out paperwork. Maybe the next two hours.

He needs to be ready for the interrogation tomorrow.

"You promise?"

"Swear to God."

God will forgive him.

She slinks back to the stairs. Moonlight haloes her nightie. Makes her look like a ghost.

Janet looks back at him. Sighs. And makes her way back up the stairs.

The photos on the walls, of friends and family, smiling faces. Mom and Dad. All of them are practically ghosts now.

A familiar sinking feeling. It claws its way into Hunter's guts. He can't help but see his past unfold before his eyes. His former self, when he was just a traffic cop, coming through the front door in his uniform just as dinner was getting ready to be served. A smile on his face as Bobby and Zuri came running up. Meeting his waiting embrace.

He tells himself he's doing this for them.

It's all for them.

They'll understand someday.

It's 5:00 am before he finishes poring over the case files. Nothing new springs to mind. But he still can't get Kevin Wallace's paintings out of his head…

How the tentacles seemed to glisten in the room's light, as if they were still wet. Dripping and eager to fill every hole in sight.

How they bled into each other.

How, even now, all he wants to do is find it and…

Hunter climbs into bed, careful not to disturb Janet.

He's nearly settled, closing his weary eyes, when her disembodied voice fills the room.

"It was so strange," she says. "You looked like you hadn't eaten in weeks, your skin looked…well, it looked awful…and you were in some basement, surrounded by all these shapes."

"Just a nightmare, Honey," he says. "Go back to sleep."

"You weren't *you*."

"Well, I'm me now. I'm here. It was just a nightmare."

"Are you? Is it? You said you'd be right up to bed. You spent the whole night working again, didn't you?"

"Are we really having this conversation right now?"

She shrinks away from him, holding herself tight. "No. I guess not."

"We'll talk about this in the morning."

"Heard that before."

Before long, she's asleep, and all he's left with is the quiet of a dark room and the horrible things from Kevin Wallace's sketchbook.

The silence is nearly unbearable.

Twisting shapes. Writhing tentacles.
    Dim, cascading light in the abyss.
    Teeth, so many teeth.
    Scraping and biting ancient flesh.
    Their bellies are full. The enemy lies dismembered.
    The spell is broken.
    The sky trembles in response to their combined rage.
    The empire will fall.

The alarm blares through Hunter's temples. He wakes from a nightmare. He's naked. And his wife is already up.

Hunter doesn't remember taking his clothes off.

The sun is coming up and his phone has about thirty text messages and twice as many missed calls.

They're all from Shirley.

He skips the texts and jumps right to calling her back.

The phone rings. He walks to the blinds and opens them. Light bands of red and orange and purple cascade across the sky above the bulldozed empty lot across the street. A morning sunset made possible by the smog and smoke trapped in the valley. The sun will be up in little more than ten minutes.

He used to love sunrises. Used to be undeniable proof of God's creation.

Now?

Shirley answers the phone.

"*Fucking hell, Hunt,*" Shirley says. "*Were you asleep or something? I've been trying to reach you for hours.*"

"I've been asleep for exactly two hours. I'm not due in until 9:00 am. What do you want?"

"*We've had a development.*"

11

There's a buzzing at the back of his brain, like static filling the room. Every hair on his body stands on end. "What the fuck are you talking about?"

"We found another art student dead. Went to the LA Institute of Commercial Art, same school as Dean."

"Jesus...another artist?"

"Dean's confessed to the whole thing."

Hunter's heart nearly stops. "What?"

"The captain wants you here three hours ago."

Hunter's about to curse, about to chew Shirley out for betraying him, for—

His phone beeps once, and he sees the call's ended.

She hung up on him.

His wife comes in, wearing her nightgown, holding two cups of steaming black coffee. Just the way they like it. "What's wrong?"

He looks at her. And gets the feeling she knows.

CHAPTER TWO

River pops a Ritalin and tries smiling into the bathroom mirror. His teeth are white, albeit crooked. Mom never had money for him to have braces.

His hair is black, freshly frosted with red dye from last night and shaved down the sides into a short, fuzzy mohawk.

His smile fades.

He can definitely still tell his hairline is receding. The doctor told him he might lose it all eventually.

Part of him wonders if he should just shave it. Get it over with. Just start wearing a hat like so many others like him.

His beard's still struggling to come in. Right now, it's just a patchy mess of shapes, like drifting continents peeking above the ocean.

At least the acne stopped.

The theme to *The Exorcist* blares through the bathroom and River fumbles for his phone.

He's elated. It's from Jess.

Jess: You get your midterm done?

He tries not to panic about that. Tries not to think about how he's going to fail his design class.

She's finally talking to him again. That's reason enough to celebrate!

His fingers dance over the screen.

He types, second-guesses, and retypes his reply.

River: Barely. You?

Smooth.

Anticipation mounts.

And mounts.

Why did she stop talking to him?

They were practically inseparable before the semester started, and then…

No! Don't think about that.

Jess: I think you'll be surprised at what I did.

He thinks about asking if she's still in her Giger phase. But thinks better of it. He doesn't want to cause an argument now that the lines of communication have been opened back up.

River: Wanna sit together? Show me yours, I'll show you mine?

He waits a moment.

No answer.

He sighs, takes a deep breath.

His eyes drift to the space beneath the bathroom door.

The smell of cigarette smoke is almost suffocating.

Mom's smoking again!

When he leaves the bathroom, he finds her pacing, puffing on a cigarette despite the fact the landlord told her he'd kick them both to the curb if he found out.

"Mom, you gotta stop smoking inside!" River shouts, trying not to sound like a whiny teenager. Sometimes, he wishes he'd taken the extra financial aid and moved into student housing. But then he'd have ended up saddled with an extra twenty thousand in student loans.

Mom stops, mutters curses in Spanish, and keeps pacing, like River's not even there.

It's been like this for weeks. She's a waitress at a local dive bar, cleans apartments and houses up in Beverly Hills whenever she's off. It seems like she never sleeps. Lately, she's up at all hours, constantly going over receipts, trying her best to come up with the extra cash needed to keep this moldering roof over their heads.

When she is off work, she paces up and down their cluttered living room while evangelical programming turns her brains to mush.

"The Christian life is a battlefield, not some playground," the TV drones. *"And oh, my brothers and sisters in Christ—understand this—and understand it well—we are at war! At war for the very soul of America!"*

14

"Mom!" River shouts in her face, thrusting his finger at her. "Are you listening to me? We're gonna be homeless if you keep smoking in the house!"

"Satan has tempted this nation, and our people are at the altar ready to pledge their lives to him in unholy matrimony. You say I'm making it up, that I'm being dramatic! But facts don't lie! Half of this country is home to sinners. Sinners who gladly and gleefully deny God's truth!"

Mom puffs on her cigarette, pointing it at the TV.

"Do you hear this man?" she says. "Mijo, he's talking about you!"

"Not this again…"

"No, I am worried about you, Mijo. I went to church last night, and do you know what Pastor Castillo asked me?"

"Let me say this plainly and frankly! No Church of God will ever accept homosexuality. Not one! To do so is to accept a perversion, to go against everything we believe in, to risk hell itself!"

River flips the TV off. "Was it something like that?"

Mom crosses herself. "Mijo! He is worried about you. About the devil getting into your life. The music you listen to, the filth you watch!"

"The women I bring home?"

"You know that we love the sinner and hate the sin in this house."

River turns around, rushing for the door.

"I don't have time for this, Mom."

"You don't have time for breakfast?" Mom asks, eyes pleading. "I made huevos rancheros."

"You made me breakfast?"

"For your big day!"

She smiles at him. Ruby lips. Dark circles beneath bloodshot eyes. Smoke idling around her like a cancerous halo. If he didn't know better, he'd think it was a metaphor or some shit.

"But my Uber is…"

"I'll put it in a Tupperware and you can eat it on the way!"

And just like that, Mom's in the kitchen, scraping what is no doubt going to be a delicious fucking breakfast into a Tupperware container and shoving it in his hands. Kiss on his cheek for good luck.

"Now, ándale! Àndale!" she says, pushing him out the door. "Before you're late!"

He's halfway down the stairs to the apartment complex when he realizes he forgot his tote bag.

"Shit!"

River charges back into the house, making a beeline for his bedroom. Finds his tote bag, dumps his sketchbook and today's graphic design midterm into it and storms back out before Mom can say anything.

He's practically hacking up a lung when he sees the Uber. The driver's checking his watch, an impatient look plastered on his face.

River waves him down so he knows not to drive off and leave him fucked up a creek without a canoe. Or whatever the saying is.

He double-checks to make sure the driver is who he says he is and slides into the backseat.

When the Uber stops in front of the LA Institute of Commercial Art, River can already tell something's wrong.

He pays the driver a five-dollar tip and apologizes it's so little. The driver says nothing, peels out of the parking lot like he's just been insulted.

River doesn't have a chance to adjust to the heat. It slaps him in the face; instantly, his clothes feel like they're drenched in sweat.

The smell of burnt rubber lingers in River's nostrils as he approaches the main campus and its looming, manila, spackled corporate walls and black-tinted windows.

The once-vibrant evergreens are beginning to dry out. To wilt.

Cue *hottest* summer. California's most famous season.

The Valley's been in the middle of a never-ending cycle of forest fires and droughts as far back as he can remember. The smell in the air. Like a raging campfire. It lingers. Permeates every fiber, every surface. Soon, the trees will be nothing more than gnarled, twisting limbs, reaching like dead hands for the smoldering orange haze lingering above.

River's attention is pulled from the trees and the corporate, mechanical nature of the parking lot and buildings to a gathering of multicolored bodies outside the secondary entrance to the school.

River tries to ignore them. Tries to slip by. He's already late for his graphic design midterm anyway. His pulse pounds away like some kind of forgotten, hammering tribal drumbeat. He doesn't want to fail.

"I heard he broke his neck sucking his own dick."

"You always say that."

"He fucking jumped out a window, you asshole!"

"What a coward!"

"I heard he was into some weird shit. Like, Satanic weird."

"Well, he's probably in hell now."

River stops. He spots Alex Davis's generic, spiky blond hair, his exposed white skin practically shining like a beacon in the shade.

The uncomfortable conversation with his mother earlier. The TV's interjections. It hits him. Stokes his anger. His fingers twitch in response.

For an art school, LAICA's staff has an uncomfortable Christian bend. Some of that's translated into roaming "woke" and "anti-woke" cliques. River remembers how Alex outed him. How every member of the Life's Well congregation knew the most intimate details of his life.

The body of students eyes River. They're comprised of a gradient of skin tones, white to tan. A few of them chuckle. Alex is the loudest, of course.

"Nice purse, Mary!" Alex shouts it loud enough for everyone on campus to hear. "Whatcha hiding in it? A spare cock?"

"Why?" River asks. "Wanna borrow it?"

Alex blushes. His friends laugh. Predictably, embarrassment transforms into anger.

"You should hear what her mom was saying about her in church," Alex says. "Says she cried when Professor Anderson said she was a hack with no drawing talent."

He's about to retaliate. A rush of violent thoughts and insults flash through his mind.

He stops himself. Takes a deep breath.

"What?" Alex asks, chuckling. "No comeback?"

This is a losing battle. His education, whatever that means in this hellhole, is more important than an argument with a wannabe jock with the banter skill of a middle schooler.

River storms into the building, breath catching in his throat. He can't deal with this shit today.

"See?" Alex shouts it so he can hear him. "She's got nothing!"

The doors slam shut behind him, and he sprints to Professor Delgado's class.

When River first set foot on this campus, he was sold a grandiose vision of his life as an artist. The student adviser smiled through shiny ruby lips and listened to him pour his gay little heart out about his dreams. How he wanted to work in comic books, and maybe, someday, get to direct a film in one of his favorite horror genres.

River passes by the adviser's office. Andrea is with a potential student. She's wearing a leopard-print dress, and that same ruby smile is painted on her face as this would-be student pours his own heart out to her.

River wonders if she's telling him the same lies.

He moves on.

"This is the last semester," Professor Delgado says, pacing in front of the classroom with a monster cup of coffee steaming away into the near-freezing air-conditioned room. "After this, most of you will be moving to 3D art classes. But, I hope you'll continue to study the graphic design fundamentals beyond this."

River slouches into his seat, doing his best to hide his face from the rest of the class.

He isn't looking forward to this. He was too busy last night eavesdropping on Mom arguing with the landlord over late rent to finish his piece. Part of him is worried it's gonna be the worst one today. That his grade here will tank and there'll be no way to resurrect it by the time finals roll around.

Well...

His eyes scan the classroom for Jess. And sure enough. There she is, staring at a green laptop screen, gothed out and totally ignoring the professor. Her eyes are bloodshot, her face covered in white makeup, her hair a rat's nest. River wants to go over, sit next to her. Continue the conversation from earlier.

Guess she's still in her Giger phase, he thinks.

River thinks about his friend. The one who stayed up late every night with him when he was tirelessly working on a project last semester. The only person who would come over and marathon old werewolf movies when he was having girl trouble.

This semester, though, it's like she's a totally different person. Like she doesn't even remember River half the time.

Well…except for the text messages this morning.

River wonders if Jess has been on ArtisTree, a popular online art posting site most of the students at LAICA use.

He accesses the forums from his phone, searches her username.

Yep, lots of Giger-esque nightmare pieces, some digital, some not.

He thinks she's experimenting with optical illusions in her work. The way the tentacles and mouths appear both near and far away, almost as if they're moving as he focuses on different parts of the images.

It's pretty impressive. Jess might have a bright future in creature design.

He smiles at her. Imagines them working together on mood boards, concept art, and watching old Stan Winston effects documentaries.

Jess' eyes drift from the laptop screen. At first, River thinks she's looking right at him. Like there's recognition in her stare. His hand comes up to wave at her, only to realize that she's looking at another student. A man who looks to be in his late thirties, with disheveled graying hair, a rail-thin frame River would hazard to say he wouldn't find on a homeless person, and the same bloodshot, sickly look in his eyes.

This man is staring at a green laptop screen too.

In fact, it's at that moment River realizes that many of the students in the class are staring at laptop screens. That same vomit-colored light, blinking, flashing into their eyes. Each of them on a gradient from clean-but-haven't-showered-in-a-few-days all the way to panhandler-ready.

"Adam Brown," Professor Delgado calls. "We'll start with your presentation."

Adam's eyes flick from his laptop screen to the professor. A smile divides his lips, like someone took an X-Acto knife and carved it into his flesh.

River watches as the guy he's been staring at and judging digs around in his bag, dragging out a rather large covered canvas print. The thing's gotta be at least thirty-two by thirty-two inches. The minimum was eleven by fourteen.

Show-off.

"All right," Professor Delgado says before taking a sip on his piping hot coffee. "Let's see what Adam's been able to come up with, shall we?"

Delgado gives Adam a nod; Adam doesn't seem to notice him or the class. That creepy fucking smile hasn't gone away either.

Adam's gnarled, oily fingers grip at the edges of his canvas. He places it on the tray at the bottom of the whiteboard used to store dry erase markers. Slowly, methodically, he caresses the covering.

"Adam?" Professor Delgado snaps his fingers. "Can you please reveal your piece to the rest of the class? We've got a lot of critiques to get through."

Adam's head snaps in Delgado's direction. His smile is gone. Bloodshot eyes stare daggers through the professor, as if he's just interrupted something of vital importance. Those gnarled fingers pinch at the fabric, like an art curator might do before unveiling a long-lost work by Van Gogh or Salvador Dali.

But what Adam ends up revealing when he removes the cover is anything but classic. At first, River's not even sure what he's looking at. It appears to be some kind of ink wash. Not a print at all, like the project demanded.

The classroom becomes a cacophony of whispers. Clearly, people have thoughts.

The more River stares, the clearer the painting's subject becomes. A mess of red and green and varying shades of black and gray brushstrokes spiral, whipping around as if forming some kind of vortex or portal. But…what's at the center of that portal is not totally clear.

Professor Delgado clears his throat. "Well. Let's begin the critique. What do we think of Adam's…project?"

"Umm, well," one of the girls at the front of the class begins, "it's hard to, like, tell what he's, like, going for here. The composition looks really, like, muddled. It's, like, really messy."

The girl squints her eyes at the painting.

"Yeah, I agree," a man with a deep voice in the back says, "the whole thing is too chaotic for me to really tell what's going on."

For five more minutes, the class lists all the reasons why Adam's painting is disturbing and messy. How he's not followed a single one of Professor Delgado's parameters for the project. How it fails in every possible way to convey a meaningful message.

But, as River stares at it, something becomes clear. It's as if those five minutes have been stretched. Voices become strange, like a video played at half speed. His eyes are drawn ever inward, to the center of the vortex.

Soon, he's staring into a pair of crimson eyes. The more he stares, the more vibrant they become.

"I see something!" a boy at the front of the class shouts. "I can…I can see two eyes…they're…they're staring at me!"

The whole class erupts in laughter.

Adam does not appear to be angry, or hurt, or anything at all really. It's as if he's not even there. Not even listening to the harsh words being thrown at his piece.

But as the boy, who just stood up, hyperventilates, staring into the heart of the painting, River is not laughing.

The eyes can see *him* too.

"All right," Professor Delgado claps his hands together. "That's enough! Adam, you can go ahead and sit—"

"It's staring right at me!" The boy's hunched over. Eyes wide. Fingers clawing into the table. His neighbor's giving him a weird look. "I…I can't look away!"

"David, are you okay?" Professor Delgado asks.

David is gripping at his chest, breathing faster and faster.

Eyes leaking.

Lips quivering. Whispering.

"David, please look at me," Professor Delgado says.

David does not respond. Instead, he screams at the top of his lungs and falls out of his chair.

At first, the whole class is frozen.

Professor Delgado drops his coffee and rushes to David's side.

"Someone call an ambulance, now!" River shouts.

CHAPTER THREE

The forest fires. They spew smoke and ash into the sky. A rolling, white-orange haze that comes to blanket the Valley.

Hunter sits in his car, staring at the apartment complex near the LA Institute of Commercial Art. Its flat stone walls, its brutalist shapes. Its gleaming, flat windows, reflecting the sun's rising, hellish gaze. The same style as Hunter's apartment building.

His hands grip the steering wheel. Strangle the leather.

He wants to think through what he's going to do.

What he's going to say to her.

But he can't think right now.

He's too angry.

Getting out of the car, slamming the door, and walking through the entrance is a blur.

Hunter flashes his badge at the officer standing guard in the lobby and storms into the elevator.

The wait is excruciating. All he can do is ball his fists up and push through the fog of rage in his mind. What can he even do?

The elevator dings.

The hallway is full of uniforms and plainclothes detectives. Rushing around. Carrying evidence.

Some of them stop and stare. A few of the white officers smile and wave at him. Oblivious. They're friendly enough. Long as you don't mention police reform. He passes Officer Lawrence, another of the dwindling population of Black officers in the LAPD, holding a bagged cell phone like it's diseased. All it takes is one glance at the look on Hunter's face for him to go right back to what he was doing.

Detective John Walters spots him at the end of the hall. Eyes like white globes, brown skin, mouthing "oh shit" as Hunter storms toward him.

"Listen, Gil," John starts.

"You don't get to call me that," Hunter says. "Not today."

"We tried to reach you—"

"Where is she?" Hunter asks.

"I..."

"I asked you a question."

A thousand thoughts run through Hunter's mind while Detective Walters sweats his answer out. Thoughts like, *How* could *you?* And, *Did you force that confession?*

John sighs, nods in the direction of an open apartment door. "She's in the apartment with the techs. Gil, you need to understand that I—"

Hunter's already crossing the threshold before John can finish his damn sentence.

His face is still purple. Wounds wrap around his neck from the initial drop. Most people kick and struggle, regretting their decision...this guy is still smiling.

This time, the victim's Black. Name's Patric Boyd. Didn't have a roommate. His parents live back East, own a chain of restaurants. Paid his tuition and footed the bill for a studio apartment within walking distance of the school. The studio's a mess of old, moldy pizza boxes, paints, and the faint lingering smell of marijuana.

Staring at the boy's face, Hunter thinks of his brother.

About 21st Street.

About the look on his face when the light faded from his eyes.

And his father's cold words, *"It was his own fault. Thomas shouldn't have been there, and he shouldn't have been defiling the temple God gave him."*

By the time Hunter arrived at Boyd's apartment, the techs had photographed every last detail. Now they're bagging and tagging potential bits of evidence. He wonders how much of it was planted.

How much of it will be used to put an innocent Black kid in prison. How long will he have to rot for a crime he didn't commit?

And there she is. Having a casual conversation in the corner of the apartment with one of the techs.

By the time he reaches her, she's sipping a cup of coffee and burying her nose in her phone.

She doesn't even see him approach.

"What the fuck were you thinking?" Hunter shouts. "I thought I said we were gonna wait till morning to start the interview!"

Her eyes don't leave the phone. She barely even reacts. A glimmer of green light reflecting off her contacts.

"We tried to reach you," Shirley says. "The boy wanted to talk. We listened."

"He was asking for a damn lawyer last night, and you think I'm gonna buy that he just decided to run his mouth without representation? That's a load of bullshit, and you know it!"

Her eyes finally focus on him. "What are you suggesting, Hunt?"

"I want to see the security footage of the interrogation."

"Why? He confessed to both crimes."

"You know damn well why."

"Are you suggesting we somehow coerced that young man to confess to his crimes?"

He can't say it. Not with a dozen uniforms and techs watching and listening. "What the hell do you think?"

She finishes her coffee in a single gulp. "Well, by all means, Hunt, if you think we got this wrong. Then please, enlighten me."

What can he do?

How can he help this kid?

The answer is plain and simple. And yet... The last thing he needs is the rest of the force claiming he's just another "angry black man" with a grudge against the department.

He's gotta play by the rules. Crack the case.

"So, what do *you* think, *Hunt?*" Shirley asks, her words dripping with sarcasm.

He takes a deep breath. Scans the crime scene.

Hunter's eyes lock on the kid's laptop. It's covered in stickers for trance and trap bands. His daughter is twelve years old, and sometimes he regrets being stupid enough to have introduced her to the internet. She blasts that crap all night sometimes. Says it helps her sleep.

His eyes break from the laptop and scan the windows. All of them appear to be locked from the inside.

"Are there any signs of forced entry? A struggle?" he asks.

The look in her eyes. Like she's thinking, *the fuck you take me for, an amateur?*

She shakes her head. "No, but we discovered Dean Tyler's DNA near the entrance of the apartment. It'll take time to find out how old it is, but my money's on it matching the victim's time of death."

"Is that all you got on Tyler?"

"The two of them went to the same school and shared classes together. Patric Boyd was making the same kind of artwork that Kevin Wallace was. In your interview with him, he mentioned some goth fad taking over part of the school. Could be, he just got sick of it. Snapped."

"Does Dean have a connection to this guy outside of that? Hostile social media interactions, confrontations at school? Anything?"

Shirley shrugs. As if to say, *Who cares?*

His fist balls up. She's in on it. Janet's father would be so proud of her.

"And what about Dean's alibi? Can he account for his whereabouts before the time of death?"

"Apparently, he was alone in the computer lab at school." She grins. "So, no witnesses to corroborate his story."

"Unless the staff or security guards saw him."

The smile fades. "Hunt. He confessed."

"Plenty of Black kids confess to crimes they didn't commit."

"In bum-fuck Alabama, maybe. This is Southern California."

They're locking eyes. She's backing away. The fear in her expression is clear. She doesn't like it when he's angry.

He wants to mention the roaming gangs of white police officers. The unchecked power of the sheriff's office. The department's history of racism.

But he doesn't. Everyone in the room already knows.

"In any case, there is a window of time from when Tyler allegedly left the computer lab at 6:00 pm to when he arrived at the dorms where he could have made his way here to commit the murder."

"How much time?"

"It's too similar, Hunt. There's got to be some kind of connection."

"How. Much. Time."

"An hour."

"An hour in LA traffic might as well be five minutes anywhere else."

"Still, it's enough, under the right conditions."

"Within a reasonable doubt? Did you check his phone to see if he ordered an Uber. Talk to the driver? Anything?"

The smile returns. "I think a jury will see it our way."

"We'll see about that."

"And what do you intend to do?"

"Shine a microscope up this investigation's ass. Make sure you're not locking an innocent Black kid up for no goddamn reason."

There's that look in her eyes again. That smug expression on her face. "Careful, Hunter. You're starting to sound like those Black Lives Matter protesters. You wouldn't want us to think a *nice* guy like you was one of them, now would you?"

God knows he'd never hit a woman. But sometimes he'd like to make an exception for her. She's not the only cop here that would love to hang Dean Tyler and watch him turn blue. Looking around the room, he can see it. The techs and uniforms are all mostly white, and the ones that aren't know better than to raise their voices. They give Hunter looks, like he should know his place too.

Whose bright idea was it for me to become a cop?

He knows the answer to that question.

He pushes the thought away.

Hunter's about to make another point, but something catches his eye.

Like a voice scratching at the back of his mind, he feels his attention slowly crawl to the victim's laptop.

He opens it, and the screen wakes up. The password screen lights up, cursor flashing…waiting. The background's a strange symbol, so green it hurts his eyes to look at it. The symbol…it's familiar…a head with a bunch of tentacles set inside a triangle.

He can see structures writhing in the depths of the storm.

They open up like gnarled, stone hands. In the raging wind, they twist and bend to the whims of a warlike drumbeat. A voice. A call that echoes from beyond time and space. Beyond the veil.

The cursor. He can't take his eyes off of it.

Fingers hover over the keyboard.

Sweat dripping. Pulse pounding.

Part of him wants to look away. Wants to forget whatever the hell he just saw and crawl into the deepest cave he can find. Never come out.

Another part of him wants more. Needs to know.

"We're in the process of cataloging all the electronics," Shirley says. "After that it's John's problem."

Hunter blinks. Wonders where he is. Why the hell he's covered in sweat.

One look at the corpse hanging in the middle of the apartment brings it all back.

He thinks he must have zoned out. Happens sometimes when he doesn't get enough sleep.

Hunter can't remember the last thirty seconds. What he saw when he stared into the laptop's putrid green light. Erased like footsteps on a polluted beach at high tide.

A voice tells him it's okay. No one will blame him if he looks again.

Like breaking a trance, Hunter nods at Shirley, tearing his eyes away from the screen.

Shirley's holding a sketchbook. She's offering it to him.

He takes it. Flips through it. Regrets the choice.

The shapes. Familiar. Glistening. Dripping with viscous bodily fluids. Like snakes, they twist and embrace each other. Inky flesh on flesh. Feeding orifices full of cascading teeth and eyes with too many pupils.

"Their artwork is similar," Hunter says.

"So?"

"Did you look up that H.R. Giger guy Dean mentioned?" Hunter asks, tearing his eyes away from the grotesque images. For some reason, all he wants to do is linger there, get lost in those curves and sharp edges. See what they do when he closes his eyes.

"No. Been a bit busy processing all this evidence," Shirley says.

"He's a painter. Famous for the monster in those Alien movies. He was obsessed with a guy named Aleister Crowley."

"And who the fuck is that?"

"Was. Guy died some time ago. But a lot of people thought that Crowley had some real mystical power. He wrote a grimoire that was said to be the real deal. Not like those books on magic and crystal healing you find at your local new age boutique."

Shirley picks up a stack of books at the end of an even larger pile of pizza boxes. "What about this H.P. Lovecraft guy? He's got like five of these books."

"Sounds familiar."

"*The Call of Cthulhu and Other Tales,*" she says, rolling her eyes. "Spooky stuff. Hey, I've seen this Cthulhu thing at my used bookstore. It was a plushie."

"What does that have to do with anything?"

"Probably nothing. Kids are into dark shit."

"And you don't think there's any possibility that Kevin Wallace and Patric Boyd could have killed themselves, that we're dealing with two suicides?"

"Not with a full confession."

It's like talking to a brick wall.

"Well, I don't think there's much more we can do here," Shirley says, yawning.

"Yeah…" Hunter's eyes drift back to the laptop. "Have they been able to crack into Wallace's hard drive yet?"

She shrugs. "Hell if I know. Just happened last night. I imagine it'd take some time for John to get to it."

"Let me know when he's finished with them."

"Right…"

"I'm heading to the office for some research and shut-eye. Don't bother me for at least five hours."

"You sure you're not going to have a little chat with Dean Tyler? Have yourself a look at the interrogation footage?"

He glares back at her. "And if I am?"

"I'm sure the captain would appreciate it if you focused on the other cases you got piled up on your desk."

"I'm sure he would."

"Have a nice day, Hunt."

Hunter heads for the studio apartment's front door. He gives his partner one last look before he shuts the door behind him.

No. He doesn't like the way she looks at him at all.

When he gets to the office, the other desks are empty still. Hunter doesn't wonder why the day shift hasn't arrived to take over. Doesn't wonder why there isn't at least a desk Sergeant out front.

He makes a beeline toward his desk.

He's going to pull the security footage. Find out where in county lockup they're keeping Dean so he can have a little chat with him.

But, when he turns on his monitor, he's greeted by a flash of green light, and—

Next thing he knows, he's deep in a research rabbit hole. Almost like he's on autopilot. Scrolling past headlines and web pages about Aleister Crowley and H.P. Lovecraft.

He blinks. Looks around the empty office.

What was he doing?

A voice tells him this is important. He's not sure why, but he keeps reading anyway.

After what feels like an eternity of scrolling—measured by the slow crawl of the minute hand on his watch—Hunter runs into a rather odd internet post. Some old forum devoted to occult things and conspiracy theories. The part of the internet his brother would probably have told him to stay the hell away from.

But T's dead now.

The website is run by some nut who thinks H.P. Lovecraft and Aleister Crowley were somehow connected. As if Lovecraft wasn't writing fiction, but was possessed by otherworldly beings or demons. The people claiming this often cite that their writing styles are eerily similar, almost identical in some ways.

He looks at the writing samples provided. For some reason, he's unable to resist reading them aloud.

> *"Nothing is. Nothing Becomes. Nothing is not. THE FIRST TRIAD WHICH IS GOD I AM. I utter The Word. I hear The Word."*
> —Aleister Crowley, *The Book of Lies*

His father's voice. It practically screams for him to stop. To look away.

Another voice is there too. It whispers for him to keep reading.

> *"In his house at R'lyeh dead Cthulhu waits dreaming... The next day, it appears, they raised and landed on a small island, although none is known to exist in that part of the ocean..."*
> —H.P. Lovecraft, *The Call of Cthulhu*

Something about that last quote...the island...the strange deaths of the crew members. It's familiar.

Hunter downloads a copy of Lovecraft's most famous work, *The Call of Cthulhu*, and begins reading. Feverishly so.

> *"Then, driven ahead by curiosity in their captured yacht under Johansen's command, the men sight a great stone pillar sticking out of the sea... Came upon a coastline of mingled mud, ooze, and weedy Cyclopean masonry which can be nothing less than the tangible substance of earth's supreme terror—the nightmare corpse city of R'lyeh, that was built in measureless eons behind history by the vast, loathsome shapes that seeped down from the dark stars.*
>
> *"There lay great Cthulhu and his hordes, hidden in green slimy vaults and sending out at last, after cycles incalculable,*

the thoughts that spread fear to the dreams of the sensitive…"

He stops for a moment. Scrolls the document back to a part of the story where artists were being hospitalized, carving weird statues of this creature. Losing their minds.

His eyes drift back to another window with quotes from Aleister Crowley.

> *"Magick is the science and art of causing change to occur in conformity with the Will."*
> —Aleister Crowley, *The Book of Thoth*

Then, back to the opening lines of *The Call of Cthulhu…*

> *"The sciences, each straining in its own direction, have hitherto harmed us little; but some day the piecing together of dissociated knowledge will open up such terrifying vistas of reality, and of our frightful position therein, that we shall either go mad from the revelation or flee from the deadly light into the peace and safety of a new dark age."*
> —H.P. Lovecraft, *The Call of Cthulhu*

His head…it feels heavy. A dull pain spreads from the corner of his left eye into the depths of his skull.

Hunter can see why people think Crowley and Lovecraft are connected.

But…

Crowley thought he was writing magical guidebooks to gaining power and wealth or some other hocus-pocus bullshit, and Lovecraft was an atheist who didn't believe in the things he was writing at all…well, apart from the racism.

H.P. Lovecraft died in 1937 from cancer of the small intestine. He wasn't buried under his headstone.

Aleister Crowley died in 1947, December first. Cause of death was chronic bronchitis aggravated by pleurisy and myocardial degeneration.

Only a dozen people attended his cremation.

Excerpts from his grimoires were read. The funeral was labeled a Black Mass by tabloid papers.

Whatever, Hunter thinks. *They're both in hell now.*

Still. Maybe it's the sleep deprivation, but he can't stop thinking about the artists in Lovecraft's story.

The similarity disturbs him.

He finds himself shaking his head.

Coincidence, he thinks. *I just need sleep.*

These works have been around for over eighty years. And no one's killed themselves like these kids... There has to be something else.

A voice deep inside tells him there isn't.

His eyes find the family photo on his desk. Bobby's massive grin; his smiling eyes. Zuri sticking her tongue out at the camera, trying to drive her mother crazy. They warm his heart somewhat.

Artists are more sensitive than most. His little boy's something of an artist, and he experiences the world in a way that Hunter never could.

Hunter looks at the photos of the victims, fighting to keep his burning eyes open.

Maybe the world just chewed these poor bastards up and when it spit them out, they couldn't take it? So they did what they thought was natural?

No. That doesn't feel right.

The symbol he saw on Patric Boyd's laptop screen. It's been stuck in his head since he saw it. Maybe it was the reason why he couldn't fall asleep, even with an empty precinct?

Hunter runs a search for that symbol. He's not sure what he's thinking. A bunch of artist renditions of occult symbols on ArtisTree show up in the search results.

He clicks on one of the images. The site loads, showing him a flashing logo in the shape of a tree with a bunch of pictures and artist tools hanging from the tree's limbs like fruit.

When he gets to the main page, he's surprised by the top ten most popular posts.

All of them are just like what he saw in Patric Boyd and Kevin Wallace's sketchbooks.

And just like before, each one appears to be moving. Black and red shapes slithering and slurping, rending flesh and screaming, eyes staring right at him through the—

Hunter rubs his eyes and decides to make himself a pot of coffee and get away from the disturbing artwork and crackpot theories of tinfoil-hat-wearing internet crazies. If he can't take a nap, then he might as well—

The smog clings to everything. It mixes with the smoke from the forest fires in the San Gabriel Mountains. The sun blazes overhead. Like a light shining through a magnifying glass. The white-hot haze is all-encompassing. Suffocating.

Hunter blinks. He's on the balcony, staring up at the skyscrapers to the south, watching the occasional plane emerge from the smog to land at LAX. The sun beats down on him. Sweat dots his brow. Lines his suit.

What was it his brother used to say?

It's like God's a sadistic-ass kid with a magnifying glass, and LA's the fucken anthill.

The sky. It burns its image into Hunter's eyes. And for a moment, he thinks he can see shapes lurking in the haze.

It's a struggle, but he manages to tear his eyes away. To close them.

Hunter mouths a prayer, asking God to forgive his brother. Even if it's too late.

What the hell is wrong with this city? he wonders.

Summers in LA are always hot. Most days swing between 80 and 100 degrees, maybe more if they're *really* lucky.

Something's different this year. He can't quite put his finger on it. It isn't the suicides, the forest fires, or the wrongful arrest of one Dean Tyler, either; he's seen plenty of that in his thirty-seven years.

No. It's something else.

Something in the air. He can't quite express it in thought. But it's there, just at the edge of reason. Like at any moment, the curtain could be pulled back, and God almighty could reveal Himself to the world.

And then, being unprepared with their limited comprehension, they'd all burst into flames.

Wouldn't that make his brother smile?

Hunter can almost imagine him pointing, dreads vibrating from mocking laughter. *"See, bitch? Like I said. Asshole kid with a fucken magnifying glass!"*

Dad used to tell him that God's glory was too much for humankind to comprehend. That this is why He appeared to Moses as a burning bush.

That...if He hadn't, Moses would have gone mad at just one glimpse of God's true face.

Hunter blinks.

Looks around.

He's at his desk.

He's been staring at one of the crime scene photos from yesterday. Doesn't remember picking it up.

It's of the sketchbook. Another ink wash piece. Similar to ones he's seen on ArtisTree. The subject appears to be some kind of octopus with red eyes.

Whatever these kids saw...it couldn't have been God. That's for sure.

Hunter prays to himself. Finds himself staring at the other desks of the empty office floor.

The other family photos on his desk look like they're divided like a black and white chessboard. Janet's white family on one end, most of them cops, and Hunter's family on the other, most of them blue-collar and church folk.

He hasn't been to church in decades.

The fear of hellfire and damnation is still strong. As real as the blazing Southern California sun.

He finishes his coffee and returns to the balcony. Fishes out a pack of cigarettes. Lights one. Takes a drag.

Janet would kill him if she knew.

His thoughts go back to why he became a cop. Why he decided to surround himself with the enemy.

It was all Janet's father's idea.

"Son of a preacher, huh?" Captain Nathan Crowe said.

Hunter remembers him sitting in his study, still wearing his uniform. Hunter's eyes drifted to Crowe's gun, still strapped to his belt.

"What's the matter, boy?" Captain Nathan Crowe asked. "You mute? You intend to date my daughter, you better have some manners and answer me when I speak to you."

"Yes, sir," Hunter said.

"Do you think you're worthy of my daughter, boy?" Hunter remembers the man's eyes glassing over. The smell of bourbon evaporating off his uniform. Remembers regretting agreeing to this, being alone with him.

Hunter remembers checking the exits, watching the man as he stood up from his favorite chair and approached him, a piece of paper clutched in his hand. Flinching when the man waved it in his face like a dog biscuit.

"Looked you up," Crowe said. "You got good grades. Strong in phys-ed."

"Yes sir."

"And your father, the preacher. He think you should follow in his footsteps?"

Hunter nodded.

"Shame. What a shame. Maybe all those smarts and strength could be served better working for the city."

"I'm sorry?"

"Lotsa black kids nowadays are hitting the academy. Maybe you could give it a try. Become one of the good ones."

"One of the good ones?"

Hunter remembers the sick feeling he got in the pit of his stomach when those words reached his ears.

"Then, you're okay with me dating your daughter?" Hunter asked.

The cop chuckled. Laugh lines stretched his sandpaper skin. "Hell no."

The sun beats down on Hunter's face.

Sweat drips from his face, evaporating in moments.

He looks down at his hand.

The cigarette's burning him.

He flicks it away without making a sound. Watches it spiral in the heat before it lands on one of the cruisers.

Buildings across the street beckon for his attention.

Staring into the city's dark alleys, Hunter thinks about Nathan Crowe. How the good captain spent the better part of a decade rambling to anyone who would listen about how "the blacks" were predisposed to committing crime. How he'd brag about shooting gang members. Misguided kids. Hunter never dared to question him, to speak up against his way of thinking. Told himself he was gonna change things from the inside.

Maybe that's the real reason he made it through the academy.

Crowe hated that Hunter, a Black man, was fathering a child with his perfect white daughter. Could see it in his eyes. How the rage turned and turned inside the bastard, demanding release.

Didn't matter that Hunter was at the top of his class in the Academy, that his instructors—the ones who didn't want to string him up—said his smarts would be put to good use on the force, maybe even get him to the lofty rank of detective.

Before Crowe could stop the marriage, he was killed in the line of duty. A drug bust gone wrong. Made him a damn hero, a martyr for the never-ending war on drugs.

Still. Crowe never made detective.

The thought makes Hunter smile.

He wouldn't have thought twice about Dean Tyler.

Dean Tyler…

"Shit!"

Hunter drags himself away from the balcony to his office chair.

It practically swallows his body whole. Even with its stiff frame, it sooths the aches and pains from days spent working late nights. Spent ignoring his family.

His phone goes off.

Speak of the devil.

It's his wife.

Janet Hunter: Did you forget about Bobby's art show? Happening tonight at 5:00 pm. Don't miss this one.

It'll take him an hour just to get home, let alone shower and be ready on time.

He thinks about how to break it to her that he won't be there. That somehow he's blown an entire day researching dead authors and staring at artwork instead of looking at the interrogation footage. His fingers hover over the digital keyboard.

She's probably already seen that he's read the text.

From across the hall, he hears something. Someone's here now, listening to the TV while they work. There's a game on today. Hunter stopped caring about basketball a while back. He's not sure why. But today it's almost soothing to sit and listen.

The phone falls out of his hands, clattering on the desk.

Their bodies are piled high in mass graves. Like towers. He's being crushed by them. Strange sounds come down from the heavens. He grasps and he claws and he pulls at anything and everything he can get a grip on. And somehow, he manages to dig himself out of that mess.

He's downtown. The bodies stretch from street corner to street corner. They're not just kids, either.

The sounds…they're getting louder. Like angels playing trumpets.

He looks up into the sky. Sees it flash green. There's a thunderous clap, and a shock wave tears its way through him, knocking him over.

The bodies. They're moving now. Dead hands grab and claw at his limbs. Only, they don't look human anymore. He doesn't know what to call them. Monsters? Ghouls? Demons? Their eyes glow like phosphorous lamps in the dark.

There's something in the sky now.

A familiar figure.

And it's calling his name.

CHAPTER FOUR

The elevator dings. The doors slide open.

Shirley makes her way down the corridor to Detective John Walter's office. Laptop tucked under her arm. Ready to be admitted into evidence.

Buzzing fluorescent lights make the cold corridors feel like they're never gonna end. The AC's always running down here. Goosebumps cover her freshly shaved legs.

Maybe the skirt was a bad idea?

She stops at his door. She knocks once. He answers before her knuckles can make contact with the wood again.

Like he was expecting her.

Dark circles drag his tired eyes open. There's a lot of gray in his hair now. She didn't notice it yesterday. She still thinks he's attractive.

"What's up, Detective Graham?" She hates that he doesn't call her by her first name. Wishes he'd be more informal. Wishes he'd do a lot of things.

"Got the second art school victim's devices," she says. "Need you to hack his laptop. The techs should be delivering his phone and other devices later."

"Such a shame." His brow is furrowed, eyes teary. He's a sensitive soul. Probably shouldn't be in this line of work. "We have a search warrant on it?"

"What do you think?"

John turns around, retreating into the static-free room. Shirley takes it as an invitation, walks into his office.

"By the way," she says, tucking her bangs behind her ear, "thanks for your help with that interview yesterday."

"Yeah, Detective Hunter wasn't too happy about that," he says.

"He's never happy about anything."

"I hear that. Surprising, though, kid seemed so put together. Hard to believe he did such a terrible thing."

"In this job, people tend to surprise you."

"And yet, I'm always surprised."

An awkward stare. A long pause.

John breaks the silence by clearing his throat and retreating into the room.

There's electronics everywhere. But it's a neat sort of mess. She imagines John in her kitchen, with an apron on, doing the dishes, fixing appliances she's been meaning to call maintenance about. His arms wrapping around her, undoing her bra with his strong, soapy hands. As if she wasn't wet enough already.

"Have you had a chance to look at Kevin Wallace's computer?" she asks.

He shakes his head. "Nah, haven't gotten the chance. I'm backed up as it is right now."

"Well—" she thrusts the laptop into his arms "—get to it. The captain is making this top priority as of now."

"Why's that?" He cradles the laptop like it's a baby.

"I haven't told Hunt yet, but there was another incident."

"Another?" Now he's looking at the laptop as if it's cursed.

She nods. "A lot of them. There've been incidents all over the city. Suicides, murders, you name it. All of them at art schools and dealing with the same kind of artwork that these two kids were into. News is breaking right now, and it's only a matter of no-time-at-all before a video goes viral."

Shirley pauses."The tabloids are gonna have a field day with this," Shirley says.

"Tabloids are ancient history, Shirley. Worry more about TikTok and YouTube."

She nods.

40

Shirley can tell that he wants to throw up, that she's spoiled his lunch. She's almost sorry.

He shakes his head. "Maybe it's drugs?"

"Maybe."

"I'll go ahead and move this up on my priority list, okay?"

John shrinks away, opening the laptop. Shirley's done her part.

"Right, well, sorry for ruining your lunch," she says. "I'll..." She's not quite sure what to say. How do you do this whole dating thing after a divorce when you have deep-seated trust issues? "Do you..." She shakes her head. Another time. "Later, John."

She wants nothing more than to find a cold dark corner and collapse in it, let the darkness take her for however many hours this world will let her stay away. But she has one more stop to make. And he's not gonna like it.

Shirley gets to the door. Realizes that John hasn't answered her.

"John?" She turns around, and he's staring at the open laptop. "Hey, I *said* goodbye."

It takes him a moment to realize she's still there. It makes her feel even more invisible than she did before.

There's a look of confusion in his eyes, like someone who's just woken up from passing out drunk and doesn't recognize the place they're in. "Sorry," he says. "What'd you say?"

"Never mind, John." She slams the door behind her. "Get some damn sleep, for your own sake."

He didn't even notice her legs.

Shirley finds Hunter asleep at his desk.

Typical.

Briefly, she wonders whether he's looked at the security footage yet.

She wakes him up by slapping a manila folder on his desk.

The look of panic and surprise is worth it.

"Wake up, Hunt," she says. "Hope you had a nice nap, we got work to do."

She watches him rub his eyes, blinking his rapidly, as if he's waiting for his vision to return to normal. There's a half-empty pack of cigarettes on his desk. The door to the balcony where the other officers take their smoke breaks is open.

"What is it?" Hunter asks.

"Wife know you're smoking again?" Shirley asks, making a mental note to use that as leverage at some point.

"Get to the point," Hunter says.

Shirley sighs, tucks stray locks of ginger hair back into her ponytail, and opens the manila folder.

"The two kids Dean killed," she says, "they go to the same school, right?"

It's as if his fatigue melts away in the space of a single heartbeat. His glare is intense. Makes her fumble her words.

"He's innocent until proven guilty by a jury of his peers," Hunter says.

"Yeah, sure," she says, trying not to roll her eyes. How often has that excuse been used to let guilty men walk free? "Well, I just got off the phone with the dean of the school this morning, and apparently some guy at the Los Angeles Institute of Commercial Art just gave himself a heart attack in the middle of his midterm." She points to a picture of some goth kid standing next to a piece of artwork. "This was posted to Facebook shortly after the poor bastard was carted off by the EMTs. Recognize the style?"

Hunter nods.

"Well," she continues, "what if I were to tell you eyewitnesses described this guy, David Peterson, screaming his goddamn head off before going into cardiac arrest, and that he did this while staring at that Cure reject's painting?"

"What do you want me to do with this information?" Hunter asks.

The long stare they exchange tells her he knows she's scared.

Shirley paces back and forth in front of his desk. "I..."

She's unraveling.

Can't help it.

Shirley's always made sure to keep a measured presence in front of her co-workers. Briefly, she thinks about the rest of the officers in the room. What they might think if they notice her body language, what they might say to the Chief.

Between the two of them, she's cozy with the chief of detectives. The chief isn't too fond of Hunter, and Shirley makes damn sure Hunter knows it every chance she gets.

What if Hunter turns around and tells him about this?

The image she's crafted for herself could come crumbling down with the slightest suggestion that she's been working too hard. That she's losing it. That she can't seem to focus or remember why she's been sitting in the car staring at the drifting layers of smog and smoke in the sky.

"Shirley!" Hunter shouts. "Get a hold of yourself."

She stops and crosses her arms, trying to hide the fact that she's shivering. Why is it so hard? Why now?

"I don't know what's going on here, Hunt," she says, "but whatever it is, I've got a really, really bad feeling."

She watches his eyes. They're focused on the photo of the painting.

Her stomach twists in knots.

Something red and familiar at the center.

Does he see it too?

"Is this all?" Hunter asks.

"No," Shirley shakes her head, "I saw a report on the news before I dropped off Boyd's laptop with John. Apparently, these things aren't isolated to this one school."

"What do you mean?"

Her heart's pounding in her ears. This is going to sound insane.

She digs into the manila folder and retrieves a piece of paper, slides it in front of him. "At least ten other students have been found dead in their dorm rooms scattered across the state. All of them art majors of some kind. And all of them appear to be drawing the same twisted stuff we found in Boyd and Wallace's sketchbooks."

Hunter takes the sheet in hand and stares.

His eyes smolder. "I think it's time I had another chat with Dean Tyler."

"Hunt, I think the captain wants us focused on these other incidents," she says. "The other precincts are being overrun with calls. We gotta divide the work—"

He ignores her. Typing away at his computer.

"He's already been transferred?" It's not a question. The look on his face makes her take a step back.

"I thought you'd know—"

"Enough!" He rubs his eyes with his fingers. "I'm going."

Hunt's all the way across the office and at the elevator before she can even say what's been trembling at the tip of her lips.

And then he's gone.

A voice tells her she should tell the captain what he's up to.

CHAPTER FIVE

The meatloaf is terrible! It's like chewing leather. River takes a large, awkward bite and desperately tries not to make eye contact with any culinary arts students. Chances are, one of them made it.

What's worse is the fact that Jack Garcia, the dean of this illustrious moneymaking machine, takes to the front of the cafeteria to address the scattered few students who didn't use the school's "most recent tragedy" to excuse themselves from their classes.

The dean takes a few moments to check himself over and make sure the mic is actually turned on. He's wearing a ridiculous suit, a polyester thing you might expect to see in some gangster movie from the 1980s. The kind of thing a guy who sells time shares might wear on a normal day to the office.

Coincidentally, that was Jack's last job.

"Hey everyone," Jack says, his voice dripping with false positivity, "I know we're all absolutely devastated by what's happened in our community. You know, I didn't know Patric or Kevin very well and all, but as dean of this wonderful school, filled with the brightest and most talented minds LA has to offer—and forgive me if this sounds corny— but I feel almost like a parent. A father...to all of you."

Someone yells from the back, "What about David!"

"We all wish David Peterson a speedy recovery, and we'll welcome him back to our campus with open arms."

River rolls his eyes. They just want David's tuition money. Dean Garcia is known as a lot of things around campus—some choice words would be *opportunist*, *disingenuous*, and *greedy*.

"Like I said, it sounds corny. But it's true. The safety and wellbeing of the student body is my responsibility. And I want you to know that my door is always open, always. The same is true for any of your advisers and professors. The mental health of our student body is so important to us. We're here for you if you need us."

It doesn't take long for River to lose interest in this pathetic display. He scans the room, looking for literally anything interesting to distract himself from this torture. Instead, his eyes find Jess, hanging back in the cafeteria's only dark corner, eyes smoldering, hood drawn.

Her eyes find his. He smiles. She returns it and takes out her phone.

"That's why we're taking this opportunity to introduce an exciting new tool for all of you here to use. We understand that an accelerated program like ours can be quite challenging for—"

The theme for *The Exorcist* sounds through the cafeteria.

Dean Garcia doesn't seem pleased.

River checks his phone.

It's from Jess!

Jess: Wanna see something cool?

"As I was saying," Garcia continues, "we understand that an accelerated program like ours can be challenging for young artists, so we've created a new tool to help you on your journey to becoming professionals in this ever-changing world."

River: Anything would be better than this torture.

"We at LAICA are proud to unveil our new venture with CanvasAI, an advanced writing and image-generation AI that we hope all of you will be thrilled to use."

"What!" River shouts, practically jumping out of his seat.

Dean Garcia stares daggers at River.

"I'm sorry, Mr. Gonzales," Garcia says, "is there a problem?"

"You're seriously going to put an AI on our machines?" River asks.

"We at LAICA want to ensure that our students have the latest and greatest emerging tools that will help to reshape the—"

"And will this AI also be trained on all of the student artwork currently stored on the school's servers?" River asks.

"Well..."

"Or will it just be the best and brightest that gets to 'help' train it?" River asks.

His phone goes off again.

Jess: Meet me in the hall.

"I assure all of you that this new tool will only be available to help simplify the artistic process! It's an exciting piece of software—"

"Whatever!" River grabs his tote bag and slings it over his shoulder. "I'm not listening to this anymore!"

He's not sure why he leaves. Why he doesn't stay and fight. Why he moves across the sparsely populated cafeteria, sans shitty meatloaf, to find her. He should be ripping Dean Garcia a new one. He should be citing every reason why the students should rise up, band together against this AI.

A voice tells him to find his friend. To let everything else wait.

"And, best of all, in honor of our fallen students, we've gone ahead and renamed these tools to Patric and Kevin, respectively. So, in a way, they're not really gone, are they?"

A not insignificant number of students are actually cheering in response to Dean Garcia's bullshit when River pushes through the double doors and makes his way into the hall.

River feels like he should give up. Maybe do something else with his time. Like barf up his meatloaf before it gives him food poisoning.

But instead, he chases after her.

"Hey, Jess!" he calls. "Can you believe that shit Garcia was peddling?"

She does not respond.

With his heart pounding in his chest, River grabs Jess' shoulder. She spins around, an X-Acto knife clutched in her right hand like it's a fucking prison shiv.

"Whoa!" River jumps back, hands tossed up. "I was just trying to see if you were okay, Jess!"

Jess's eyes smolder as she stares at him. They look bloodshot, rotting away above bags of skin the color of bruises.

"I apologize," she says, forcing a smile. "I thought you were Garcia."

"Really?" River says, a familiar lump creeping its way into his throat. "Umm. I came. Like you said to. What do you want to show me?"

Jess says nothing. Her chapped, cracked lips stretch into a smile.

"Are you gonna say something?" River asks. "Or are we just gonna stand here like a couple of—"

"*Come,*" Jess says. For a moment he thinks her voice has changed. Raspy. Like someone ripped out her vocal cords and tossed 'em in a meat grinder.

Has to have been his imagination...

She turns around and raises a hand, two fingers making the "come-hither" motion.

Jess is halfway down the hall before River finally gets the courage up to follow. The hallways are pretty empty. After what happened to David, it's easy to see why. It's not the first time someone's been carted off on a stretcher, but the alleged murders haven't exactly helped morale around the campus.

Jess dips into one of the computer labs. The next thing River knows, he's through the door and scanning the lab for her. His heart nearly jumps out of his chest when he spots her standing at the back of the lab, a sickly green glow surging on her face. She's standing in front of one of the computers, pointing at the monitor as if it's the most important thing in the world.

The voice of reason tells River to turn on his heels and get his skinny Latino ass out of there before this turns into a hate crime.

He takes a step forward, tells the voice that Jess would never hurt him. Not Jess. Not with what they shared.

Jess nods. Waves him over.

River takes a deep breath. He keeps inching closer.

The closer he gets, the harder his pulse beats. Like someone stuck his body right next to a vicious double-bass solo.

Sweat dots his forehead.

By the time he reaches Jess, he's half convinced he's gonna be the first person to ever die from a heart attack here.

Those thoughts are silenced when his eyes finish following where Jess is pointing.

At first, he just sees a bright green screen with a Cthulhu silhouette tucked inside a triangle. But he quickly finds he can't look away. Can't think about anything except for the marvelous shapes appearing before his eyes. Soon, the screen grows to encompass his entire field of vision.

The things it shows him. Pages upon pages of shapes and figures and words written in a language he's never seen before, in symbols that look more like Ancient Egyptian hieroglyphs than any modern alphabet. And yet, as if someone reached their slimy hand into River's mind and planted the knowledge, he knows they're much, much older.

Part of him is aware when Jess gets closer to him. Her steady breathing tickling the peach fuzz on his ear.

Her cracked lips begin whispering things—things that make him want to scream—for help, for it to stop, for someone to take a mallet to his skull and just put an end to the screaming, horrible voices echoing in the depths of his mind.

"Ph'nglui mglw'nafh Cthulhu R'lyeh wgah'nagl fhtagn," she whispers.

The walls. He can't be sure what he thinks he's seeing. From the corner of his vision, they appear to be melting.

"Ph'nglui mglw'nafh Cthulhu R'lyeh wgah'nagl fhtagn!"

No. Not melting. Something's pouring down them. At first he thinks it's blood. But it's not. No. It's something liquid and black.

"Ph'nglui mglw'nafh Cthulhu R'lyeh wgah'nagl fhtagn!"

River wants to look away from the screen.

He can't.

Can't look away.

The liquid. It closes in on him, fills the room up to his knees and keeps going.

It's...warm.

"Ph'nglui mglw'nafh Cthulhu R'lyeh wgah'nagl fhtagn!"

Soon they're submerged. But the screen and the images it shows him, of those vast cyclopean towers, the pulsing black cocoons, their glistening, amorphous bodies...

It's all he cares about.

He wants to see more.

Wants to be fed.

"Ph'nglui mglw'nafh Cthulhu R'lyeh wgah'nagl fhtagn!"

And very soon, as the liquid fills his lungs and his body screams for air, he feels there is only one way out.

Through the screen.

That lone beacon in the abyss.

The doorway.

His own bellowing screams wake him. The first thing he notices is a churning, storm-ridden sky.

The voices. They chant and call to the center. The swirling, storming vortex's eye.

"Ph'nglui mglw'nafh Cthulhu R'lyeh wgah'nagl fhtagn!"

Lightning flashes, betraying colors unfamiliar to his eyes and revealing impossible structures, both in the sky and where he now finds himself lying. When he stares at them, he's unsure what shapes they betray. The longer he stares, the more confused he becomes, until his confusion gives way to a dull pain at the front of his skull. A thing that festers and spreads and claws.

"Ph'nglui mglw'nafh Cthulhu R'lyeh wgah'nagl fhtagn!"

His hands find a wall for support. Muscles wail in protest as he gets to his feet. He tries to close his eyes—but the shapes! They linger, festering in his mind… As if they are forever burned into his vision.

"Ph'nglui mglw'nafh Cthulhu R'lyeh wgah'nagl fhtagn!"

Before long, he realizes he's moving. Though he cannot guess how. He does not feel the ground beneath his feet, or the muscles in his legs straining against gravity's pull.

The voices are much closer now. Their terrible, guttural chants assault the very air he breathes and leave behind wisps of light that pulse with more colors he cannot identify.

The wisps of light. It's almost as if they're guiding him…slowly…stupidly through this strange place.

"Ph'nglui mglw'nafh Cthulhu R'lyeh wgah'nagl fhtagn!"

Like microscopic drills excavating his gray matter, the pain at the front of his skull intensifies.

The structures. He's sure that's what they are. Buildings or towers of some kind, not made by human hands. They appear to be simultaneously convex and concave. To be tall and short and thin and wide. As if he's staring at them through some kind of prism, a kaleidoscope from the depths of a hell beyond earthly imagination. The road, or street, or alley he traverses, it appears to connect and divide and worm its way between structures like some kind of web.

"Ph'nglui mglw'nafh Cthulhu R'lyeh wgah'nagl fhtagn!"

Each step is harder than the last. The drilling in his brain. He can feel bits of it oozing, congealing, leaking out of his nose.

He is unsure whether he's moving uphill or down or not at all. Perhaps his feet do not traverse any surface. Perhaps it is the pulsing waves of light left in the wake of the words that now carry him along?

"Ph'nglui mglw'nafh Cthulhu R'lyeh wgah'nagl fhtagn!"

He reaches some kind of embankment, the crest of a hill, or the top of some kind of structure.

And it's at this moment he realizes what this place is.

The twisting, coruscating web-like things that weave themselves between the structures, they're like roads or paths or methods of travel between the thin spaces that stretch between molecules.

"Iä! Iä! Cthulhu fhtagn! Ph'nglui mglw'nafh Cthulhu R'lyeh wgah'nagl fhtagn!"

The structures. They unfurl like blackened rib cages made from rotting obsidian, twisting and bending to the whims of a voice that transcends even the loudest of the chants. A voice so powerful, even its dull, slumbering whispers threaten to alter the very nature of the place before his eyes.

"Iä! Iä! Cthulhu fhtagn!"

And at the center of this place is a towering, multi-limbed monstrosity. A monolith. A thing composed of a material that refuses to betray a smooth or rough texture. A thing which, as he is propelled through this strange, web-like space between spaces calls and hums and glows with a familiar, primordial light. A light that is at once identifiable as green, and yet totally alien to his lowly human eyes.

"Iä! Iä! Cthulhu fhtagn!"

The chanting. It gets louder and louder. Soon, the pain in his skull is so great that all other thought, all other reason, becomes impossible.

He cannot look away from the tower.

Cannot stop himself from being dragged to its foundation. Its apotheosis.

Cannot ignore the innumerable, indiscernible shapes gathering before its immense, impossible majesty.

And soon, he realizes that it is he who has been chanting this entire time.

"Iä! Iä! Cthulhu fhtagn! Ph'nglui mglw'nafh Cthulhu R'lyeh wgah'nagl fhtagn!"

Chanting with a chorus of guttural voices emitting from amorphous shapes, churning and writhing all around him.

He cannot look away. Even as a pillar of putrid light ignites on the surface of that terrible structure. Even as the walls of this nightmare-scape shudder with the force of something beyond, something that claws at the walls of rationality, at the boundary where dreams can become reality.

"Iä! Iä! Cthulhu fhtagn! Ph'nglui mglw'nafh Cthulhu R'lyeh wgah'nagl fhtagn!"

Human words are not enough to express the pain which festers inside of him when he sees shapes emerge from the putrid pillar of light. Like hands or claws or twisting tentacles of mangled metal, or all three simultaneously.

It wraps its appendages around the monolith.

"Iä! Iä! Cthulhu fhtagn!"

Its form quakes, pulling itself through the pillar of light.

The doorway.

"Iä! Iä! Cthulhu fhtagn!"

What passes for a head emerges. Its dark shape is both familiar and alien to him. Like some kind of octopus, and yet, nothing at all like it.

Tentacles, appendages, bones like fingers, hang over its mouth.

"Iä! Iä! Cthulhu fhtagn!"

Six and two and four and five globes burn with the brilliance of dead stars.

"Iä! Iä! Cthulhu fhtagn!"

Its appendages, legs, tentacles, reach across the divide that is neither far nor near. A distance measured in light-years or miles or inches.

Its hand, tentacles, claws unfurl into a single, writhing point. A storm of geometric shapes beholden to no true form. A fact that splits his mind into two, three, five simultaneous equal and unequal parts.

"Iä! Iä! Cthulhu fhtagn!"

His screams run silent when he realizes the appendage of violent, surging vortices is pointing at him.

Pointing to a place where the drilling, stabbing, burning pain in his skull is worst.

The sharp pain of a sudden slap to the face brings him back to his senses.

He blinks and glances around at his surroundings.

It's dark. He's in the computer lab, and he's been staring at a—

A hand reaches out and grabs his chin. "Don't fucking look at it!"

He's staring into the hard eyes of an older woman with scars blanketing her whole face.

"W-who…" His mouth, his lips, are stupid. He wipes a string of spittle from his chin and stumbles into the wall.

The woman catches him by the shoulders. "I caught you just in time. You were chanting. Do you know that?"

He shakes his head. "I…"

"It's going to be hard to remember your name at first," she says. In the dark, her skin has an almost gray quality to it. "Just calm down and try to forget what you saw."

He shakes his head. "W-what happened…what…what was—"

"Don't ask that question." She thrusts her finger into his face. "Never ask that fucking question. Never listen to the voices. Never, ever, ever do what they tell you. Do you understand me? That's how it gets inside. How it changes you."

"How?" He wants to ask how she knows these things.

"Can't tell you that." She shakes her head. "Don't look at me like that, it's for your own good. Just do yourself a favor and go home, lock the door, and don't leave till the voices stop."

"Who?"

Before he realizes what's happening, she's already retreated to the door. Her eyes practically glow in the dark, like burning candles. "Don't worry about that. Just do as I say."

"I…I don't…"

He stares at her for a moment, watching her hard expression melt into one that betrays compassion.

"Jesus," she says. "You don't even know where you are, do you?"

He looks around.

Something wet smacks onto the palm of his hand. He holds it up to his eyes, wondering where it came from, before he realizes that it's his own drool.

When did he come to the computer lab?

"Well, come on," the woman shouts. "Follow me. I'll give you a ride home."

CHAPTER SIX

The building's unassuming facade is almost soothing. Its white and tan features, its black windows. Back here, with the delivery trucks and squad cars, it's almost peaceful. Apart from the oppressive orange haze hanging over the valley. Part of Hunter feels like he can fall asleep, let the fatigue fall away from him.

A voice tells him that'd be good for his health.

Too bad he stopped caring about his own well-being a long time ago.

The car door clunks shut behind him and the sound ricochets off the concrete structures that surround him.

The heat is already unbearable. He thinks about returning to the car, leaving his blazer behind.

No.

He wants to look as professional as possible. Can't let an ounce of fatigue show.

Standing before the business entrance of the detention center, he takes a deep breath. Puts his hand on the door handle.

Next thing he knows, he's walking through the halls of the correctional facility. He sees inmate orderlies, some of them Black and brown, others bald and tired and white. They're inching along, chained at their ankles, sweeping up the crap left behind by the free men of society for twelve cents an hour while the guards watch, slapping batons into their palms.

The looks the other inmates give him. It's like the life and the fight has totally gone out of them.

Like they're broken.

He wonders if he's seeing Dean's future.

Hunter approaches a counter contained within several inches of bulletproof glass, where a receptionist waits, playing on her phone.

He looks into her eyes and—

Hunter's sitting at a metal table in a room with a two-way mirror. A buzzing sound tears through the concrete chamber, forcing him to cover his ears.

The door opens and closes.

A young Black man in an orange jumpsuit approaches the table with a guard following closely behind. He's handcuffed, ankles chained. The guard sits the boy down and chains him to the floor, then leaves.

"You wanted to see me, sir?" Dean asks.

The left side of his face is raised, bruised. Looks like he got on the wrong side of another inmate...or a guard's baton.

Hunter nods, gestures to the seat in front of him. "Take a seat, son."

The sound of chains dragging on concrete echoes through the interview room.

Wait, wasn't he just sitting? Hunter wonders. Shakes his head, dismisses the thought. Nothing more than Déjà vu.

The young man sits across from him. The expression painted on his face...Hunter expected him to look sad, angry, defeated maybe. Instead, Dean looks calm. Collected.

"So, what can I do for you, Officer?" Dean asks.

His voice is different somehow. His choice of words makes the hair on the back of Hunter's neck stand on end.

"I want to ask you some questions," Hunter says. "Is that okay?"

Dean nods. Expressionless. Without resistance.

"Do you recognize me?" Hunter asks.

He nods. "Detective Gilbert Alan Hunter."

"Right. The other night, when we met, I told my partner not to interview you without me being there. It's my understanding that she and another detective, John Walters, went ahead with an interrogation when I wasn't around."

He nods. "You were dreaming."

"Right, well, based on my interview with you, I concluded that there was no reason to pursue you as a suspect. And yet, my partner claims that you confessed to the murder of Kevin Wallace and Patric Boyd."

"What do you want me to say, sir?"

The boy's expression is practically blank. Devoid of the personality and intelligence Hunter saw the other night.

Hunter glances at the two cameras in the interview chamber. One of them is pointed right at Dean.

"Ignore the damn cameras, kid," Hunter says. "I want to know if anyone in that room made you feel as though you had to lie."

"In what way, sir?"

"Cop psychology, we're good at making people talk. But sometimes, the things we get out of suspects turn out not to be true. Get my drift?"

"Ah, I see." Dean's lips part into a smile that makes Hunter uncomfortable. "I assure you, Detective Gilbert Alan Hunter, the testimony I gave was accurate and true. I am the one who murdered Kevin Wallace and Patric Boyd in cold blood and made it look like they committed suicide."

"What?"

"Their artwork. I couldn't handle it. It drove me to such incredible vistas of madness staring at it. I snapped. Pushed poor Kevin out of the window. The snapping sound his neck made when it hit the lawn was pleasing to me. And Patric. Oh, I took many notes on the sounds he made as he hung there. It was an educational experience."

Hunter's staring. He's listening. But…

He glances around the chamber again.

"You don't have to lie," Hunter says. "Frankly, you're facing some serious time if you don't tell me what really happened and lawyer up."

Dean leans forward and whispers. "I think we both know that I'm right where I belong, Detective."

Staring into his eyes…something isn't right about them. Maybe he's been drugged?

"You don't belong in prison if you're innocent," Hunter says.

"I don't know what to tell you, Detective."

Hunter sighs, rubs his eyes. "Guess I got this one wrong."

He stands up. Heads for the door. Gives Dean Tyler one last look.

A voice tells him he should leave it.

He's compelled to put his hand on the buzzer.

But he hesitates.

Something about the way Dean's speaking makes him want to ask—

"Eyewitnesses say he was triggered while staring at a disturbing painting that mimicked the style of the late H.R. Giger."

The radio's on.

Hunter blinks, looks around.

"School officials told us to view the statement on their website and declined to add any further comment. David Peterson is currently in a coma at Los Angeles General."

He's in his unmarked cruiser. In the parking lot of the Men's Central Jail. Came to just staring off into space, at the drifting orange-white haze above—sweat pooling in his collar, drool hanging from his chin.

"What the fuck hap—"

Something else catches his eye. In the passenger seat.

Hunter picks it up. It's a hardback journal. A faded insignia for some kind of government office rots away on the cover. He can't make out the letters; the cover feels tacky to the touch, like dried tar.

He can't remember how he got it.

Part of him is tempted to charge back into the building. Demand to see Dean again. Tear the truth out of him, find out who's making him lie.

A voice tells him he can do that after lunch.

His stomach growls. Even he's surprised at the sound.

When's the last time he ate?

Slept?

He can't remember.

It's noon when Hunter pulls up to the In-N-Out burger. The line's already wrapped around the block. He doesn't care. He's got a craving.

The line is slow moving. People shuffle and bump into each other like zombies. Briefly, he wishes the owners had had enough sense to build an indoor dining area. He's sweating through his shirt.

It's 1:00 pm before he gets his double-double with fries. He jumps in his cruiser, scarfs his burger down.

He's eyeing the tattered journal as he's shoveling fries into his mouth.

Before he knows it, he's opening it and turning to the first page.

The typeface looks familiar, like an official government letterhead or a damn good imitation. Letters that spell out: "TOP SECRET: FOR OMEGA-LEVEL OEI AGENTS ONLY."

At first, he wonders if he should even be reading this. What if it really is top secret? What if someone finds out he has it?

Before he realizes what's happening, he's already reading the journal.

From the journal of Lena Hartman
January 5th, 2022

I don't know what to write in this damn thing, but Doctor Webber thinks it'll help with the problems I been having about my memory.

So, here it fucking goes I guess?

When I got here, I was pregnant and naked. Felt like I was on fire. I can still remember the pain. Then they put the lotion on me, said my skin was frostbit or some shit.

An older couple found me, took me in. Gave me clothes that didn't fit. They said I could rock myself to sleep on their porch.

Sleep didn't come.

For some reason, my body refused to let me close my eyes for very long.

I remember the couple asking me if I was cold.

I was pretty fucking dazed, but I said no.

Told them, "This ain't nothin."

Honestly, it was a relief just to feel the sun's warmth again. Like that was some kind of victory.

I don't know why.

The sun was coming up. And when I realized it was morning, that I was warm, I held myself and cried like a little bitch.

I don't know why. I'm sure I seen mornings before. It was probably the baby making my hormones crazy.

But, whatever it was, I had this feeling…it's hard to explain.

Whatever it was that happened to me…it felt like it wasn't over.

Like it would never be over.

It was sometime after they brought me breakfast when I noticed them.

They looked like EMTs, but the details on their jumpsuits were all wrong. The couple called 911 on me, said they found me wandering naked through the woods with strange red marks all over my skin. Said I was pregnant. That I was a danger to my baby.

Fucking snitches.

The "EMTs" promised to take care of me.

Promised to make everything better, that my baby would be born healthy.

I'm such an idiot for believing them.

I remember wondering who the father was. Whether I'd ever see him again…

Somehow, I doubted it.

They put me on an ambulance. When they asked me why I was crying, I had no answers.

Something about gurneys and needles. Still can't explain it.

Once they had me inside, they asked me if I knew who I was. Somehow, I was able to tell them my name is Lena. But nothing more.

Everything went dark when we passed into the tunnel.

And I screamed, begged them to turn the lights on.

In the dark, I saw something. A thing I never want to see again. A darkness…and…a light. A green pulsing light.

I don't remember what it was. I remember screaming, I remember feeling like something snapped inside me. But that's it.

Fucking useless, right?

Doctor Webber says I passed out from the shock in the tunnel. Went into labor.

I think that makes sense maybe.

When I woke up, I wasn't alone. Doctor Webber was with me. His face made my skin feel like something was crawling beneath it.

He introduced himself and said he was honored to meet me.

My memory's shit right now, but I get the idea he meant what he said.

They set me up in a hospital room or something like it.

I felt like I been there before though.

Place gave me panic attacks. Like I needed to savor every last bit of air.

Doctor Webber told me the facility had the greatest doctors and scientists in the world working on my case, that I wouldn't be bedridden for long.

I asked him where my baby was.

He smiled. Told me she was safe.

A girl. I gave birth to a baby girl!

I asked if I could see her. I wanted to name her in person. Hold her in my arms.

Doctor Webber said no, "not in my present state" or however the hell he talks. They don't want me seeing her yet. Something about contact or procedures…

I'm still a little confused. Why is contact such a bad thing?

His face was really serious, though. I wasn't expecting him to…

I don't know, have emotions?

Before he left, he told me he believes I know why I can't see my baby. Why it's important to be careful.

Don't know what the fuck he was on about, but I'm excited to be a mom!

I don't know what to name her.

The name Sophi sounds nice, I think—

Something just came back to me.

When I wrote the name Sophi, my head started hurting really bad.

Felt like I was gonna die honestly.

I think…I think I've given birth before.

Interview with Subject 1051, TRANSCRIPT
January 10th, 2022

The subject enters the concrete room, glances around at the walls and metal table in the center.

Doctor Webber: Hello, Ms. Lena, please have a seat.

Doctor Webber breaks protocol to make the subject feel more comfortable. Subject 1051 takes the seat opposite of Doctor Webber.

Doctor Webber smiles and offers to shake her hand. Subject 1051 is reluctant to make contact.

Doctor Webber: I'm really grateful to you for agreeing to this. Truly, it's an honor.

Subject 1051: Where's my baby?

Doctor Webber: Safe. She's healthy and well cared for.

Subject 1051: Can I see her?

Doctor Webber: Not yet. And, I'll explain why. Really, it's for her safety.

Subject 1051: What does that mean? Can I at least see a picture? So I know you're not lying.

Doctor Webber: Why would I be lying?

Subject 1051 does not answer.

Doctor Webber: I suppose we'll skip the pleasantries, then. Get down to business.

Subject 1051 crosses her arms, avoids eye contact with the doctor.

Subject 1051: Whatever.

Doctor Webber: Do you remember how you got here, Lena?

Subject 1051 takes a deep breath.

Subject 1051: No.

Doctor Webber: I don't think you're being completely honest with me. According to reports from the extraction team, you screamed when the lights went out in the transport vehicle. Said you didn't want 'it' to get you.

Subject 1051: I don't want to talk about this.

Doctor Webber: Ms. Lena, do you know what year it is?

Subject 1051: No. And I don't fucking care.

Doctor Webber: It is 2022. You are in a top-secret facility in the San Bernardino Mountains. I am the director of this program, and I oversee five other facilities just like this one across the country.

Subject 1051: I know who you are. I know what you do.

Doctor Webber: Yes. It seems like you're not too fond of me. Can you tell me why that is? I promise you, I have every intention of helping you and your baby.

Subject 1051: I don't remember...I just...I just remember your face.

Doctor Webber: Well, I can assure you we run a very clean operation here. And we follow very strict contact procedures, which is why you're in here right now.

Subject 1051: I don't believe you.

Doctor Webber: Tell me about that. Why don't you believe me? We've never met, and yet you seem to recognize me. Seem to be repulsed by my appearance even.

Subject 1051: You know why.

Doctor Webber: Yes. It seems you've been quite a bit more chatty with Doctor Patton. I'd be hurt if I were a jealous man.

Subject 1051: Then you already know?

Doctor Webber: Yes. I just wanted to hear it from you.

Subject 1051: I remember your face. That's all I told her.

Doctor Webber: Oh, come now, that's not true either. Why lie when you know I've got access to all of Doctor Patton's research notes and transcripts?

Subject 1051: It was much older. Your face. You looked like a fucking zombie. Yellowing eyes and teeth and bones showing through your skin. When I remember your face...

Doctor Webber: You remember to be afraid?

Subject 1051: Yeah.

Doctor Webber: Fascinating. To think you've actually met an alternate version of myself.

Subject 1051: If you say so...

Doctor Webber: Can you recall anything about this other version of me? Did you know him?

Subject 1051 shakes her head.

Subject 1051: No. It...when I think about it—when it doesn't hurt as much—I remember screens. Seeing your face on monitors. Videos, I think.

Doctor Webber: Fascinating. And what were the contents of these videos?

Subject 1051 shakes her head.

Subject 1051: No. No, I don't remember.

Doctor Webber: Would it help if you closed your eyes? Maybe try to visualize it?

Subject 1051: I…I can't. Can't do that.

Doctor Webber: Ms. Lena, I think it may help you. Think of this as one step on your path to recovery, to seeing your daughter for the first time.

Subject 1051 hesitates for a moment before nodding and closing her eyes.

Doctor Webber: Good. Good. Now. Can you tell me what you see?

Subject 1051: I don't know. It's dark.

Doctor Webber: Try thinking about me. The other me. What am I wearing? What do my eyes and other features look like?

Subject 1051: I… You're wearing a lab coat. There's a rectangular bulge coming from one side of your coat. Your eyes are bloodshot, yellowing. Your hair is stringy, gray. Your skin is gray too, spotted in places and sagging over your bones.

Doctor Webber: I should really think to take better care of myself. Can you tell me where I'm standing?

Subject 1051: You're in a…a concrete room. There's a metal ring with lots of wires and things around a glass pyramid. There's…there's a metal tank inside the glass pyramid.

Doctor Webber: Stop right there. I've heard enough. You may open your eyes, Ms. Lena.

Doctor Webber holds his hand up for the orderly. The orderlies stand ready to clean up a mess, glancing nervously to the security camera recording the session.

Subject 1051: Now can I see my daughter?

Doctor Webber rubs his eyes.

Doctor Webber: I'm afraid not. Not yet. Considering the nature of the experiments my…other self was performing, we have to be sure you're not entangled.

Subject 1051: What?

Doctor Webber: I suppose I'll be frank with you. You deserve that much after the ordeal you've been through.

Subject 1051: What do you mean?

Doctor Webber: The organization that I run is known as the Office of Extradimensional Intelligence. Our function is to protect the United States and her people from things beyond our comprehension. Frankly, it's a dangerous job. Our agents risk their lives to bring back useful information on how to safeguard the population from these things.

Subject 1051: Safeguard?

Doctor Webber: Yes. Since the seventies, we've been monitoring extra-dimensional transmissions from what we call Earth Variants. In most cases, the subject matter of these transmissions concerns anomalous activity in remote places, the disappearances of entire towns or cities, or—in the most extreme cases—the end of a civilization or the Earth Variant in question.

Subject 1051: And how do you protect against things like...like that?

Doctor Webber: Take one example. In the late eighties, we received a transmission from an Earth Variant that had been hit by a one-kilometer-wide asteroid. The asteroid impacted off the coast of Southern California. The contents of the transmission were that of an Emergency Alert System bulletin urging residents in the affected areas to remain indoors.

Well, it turned out that this asteroid carried an unknown biological organism. It infected hosts through the dust the asteroid had kicked into the atmosphere. Near as we can figure, the infected quickly fell under the control of some kind of hive mind, and began altering the emergency messages to instruct survivors to go outside and breathe the air.

Subject 1051: What happened to the people there?

Doctor Webber: Unfortunately, it is unlikely that they survived. We received two transmissions from this particular Earth Variant, and none since.

Subject 1051: I don't get it. How does that help you safeguard against something like that if it's just a video or something?

Doctor Webber: We look to developing countermeasures and plans for dealing with such entities should something similar happen to our Earth. Though, I must admit, a lot of the time the best we can do is set up detours away from hot spots.

Subject 1051: Oh… Can I see some of these videos?

Doctor Webber: Perhaps. In time. Unfortunately, when it comes to these kinds of phenomena, even cursory knowledge can be dangerous. Considering the state of your memory, I'm not sure I should tell you much more.

Subject 1051: Am…am I going to die?

Doctor Webber: That's what we're here to find out. Your case is unique. Without knowing the specifics of what happened to you, it's hard to tell how much danger you're in, if at all.

Subject 1051 sobs into her hands.

Doctor Webber: All right. I think that's enough for today. I'm going to call an orderly to have you escorted to your room. And I promise you, we will do everything in our power to help you.

Hunter closes the journal and laughs, chucking it into the passenger seat.

"What a bunch of bullshit," he says for no one's benefit other than his own.

Alternate realities?

Asteroids carrying viruses?

Who in their right mind would buy into something like that?

Where did he get it, though? Why can't he remember?

Did Dean Tyler give it to him?

He can't remember how their meeting ended…

Can't remember leaving the detention facility…

He shakes his head.

Sleep deprivation.

That has to be it. No other explanation.

He looks at the time.

1:40 pm.

Damn. How did it take him forty minutes to read those two passages and finish his fries?

The real question is…what's his next move?

"I've got no leads," he whispers.

He rubs his eyes.

"I need some fucking sleep."

Hunter pulls out of the In-N-Out parking lot and heads back to LAPD HQ, telling himself there's no such thing as a top-secret military base in the San Bernardino Mountains.

CHAPTER SEVEN

Impossible colors swirl and wave until they solidify, resembling something approximate to his stained bedroom ceiling.

River's awake. His head feels like it's been set on fire.

The blonde woman who slapped him in the computer lab is standing near his closet on the other side of the room, as if she's avoiding the light.

Even so, River can make out the deep scars that blanket her skin. Splotchy in areas, where it's clear large sections of skin once fell off. Like a documentary he once saw on victims of frostbite.

"What the hell happened?" River asks, rubbing his head.

"I was trying to get off campus before they noticed me," she says. "But I couldn't leave you like that. You were screaming at people like a drunk homeless person."

"I what?"

"It's okay if you don't remember. It'll take time."

"You said that before?" River holds his head, grits his teeth through the pain. "Ugh, what is with this goddamn migraine!"

"It can take anywhere from hours to days to go away after the first time. The important thing is that you didn't stay too long."

"In the computer lab?"

She gives him a grave look.

"Who are you anyways?" he asks.

"Lena."

"Lena what?"

She avoids his gaze. "Hartman, I guess. Sometimes it's hard to remember exactly."

"And you know Jess?"

"No, not exactly."

"Then, what?"

"I'm not sure how much I can tell you. There isn't exactly an easy way to measure your willpower."

"Willpower?"

Lena paces up and down the one part of River's room not covered in various stages of clean and dirty laundry. "She said OEI has a test. But that's not all that accurate, is it?"

"I don't know what the hell you're talking about, Lena!" River glances around the room. "Hey, how the hell did you know where I live?"

"Your address is on your ID."

"Oh, yeah, I guess it is…"

Lena mumbles to herself again, scratching her head, before snapping her fingers like she's just come up with the answer. "Okay. I'll tell you something. That's probably safe."

"You're not gonna, like, stab me to death or something, are you?"

"Those visions you saw? Resisting the call comes down to willpower. The stronger your will is, the more knowledge you can hold. The longer it takes to corrupt you."

"Corrupt me?" River shakes his head. "What are you talking about?"

"You don't remember?"

"I remember you slapping me in the computer lab. Then…nothing."

"What about before? What about the visions?"

"What visions?"

"Shit, shit, shit!" She's pacing again, biting her fingernails. "He doesn't remember. Doesn't remember any of it."

"Are you…okay?"

Lena's at his bedroom door, hand reaching for the doorknob.

She looks back at him. "Stay away from the school until you feel better."

"We just had midterms," River says. "School doesn't resume for a week."

"That's good. That's good." Her eyes become globes. "Do you have a piece of paper?"

River glances around his room. Finds his tote bag and takes out a Sharpie and a piece of paper, hands them to her.

She writes down a number and passes it back. "When you feel better, call me. It's a burner, but as long as you don't give it to *them*, I won't have to trash it."

"You're not gonna tell me anything else, are you?"

Lena shakes her head.

River's head hits the pillow. Colors swim before his eyes. "Fucking, all right...sure..."

"You're probably gonna sleep a lot," Lena says. "You're gonna see some weird shit. Be careful. They're not all visions."

"What the...hell are you talking about?"

The pain. It comes in waves. Pulsing in and out. Like the tide. It's all he can do to close his eyes.

"Sleep it off best you can," Lena says.

He tries to call her name. But soon, he forgets even that.

He hears a door shut, and the next thing he knows, he's standing next to his mother in the dark.

She smiles at him.

The same smile she used to give him before...

For a moment he thinks he's living in a memory.

He tries to ask her where they are. But his words come out all jumbled. As if it's not him speaking at all.

"Thank you so much for inviting me here, Mrs. Gonzalez," he says, but it's not his voice.

"You're so welcome," Mom says, her eyes smiling as wide as her mouth. "Pastor Castillo is the best. You'll see!"

Music notes. Familiar piano chords that leave an uncomfortable feeling of joy in the pit of the stomach. A feeling that isn't his. They fill the dark.

Soft singing. Familiar words spoken to a God he doesn't believe in anymore.

It's his worst nightmare come alive.

Colored strobe lights illuminate the dark.

The eyes he's stolen sweep over a massive stadium. The stadium is filled. Thousands of people of all shapes and sizes. At the front is a stage full of people dressed in sparkling white and red choir robes. Above the stage is a glowing red and blue sign that reads "LIFE'S WELL ASSEMBLY."

The choir is busy praising Jesus for the hundredth time when a man in designer jeans, sunglasses, and a jacket River's certain he's seen on Pedro Pascal jogs onto the stage and thrusts his index finger at the crowd.

"Are you ready to praise your Lord and Savior?" he shouts, like a rock star trying to rev up a crowd of eager fans.

The crowd answers him.

Yes. Yes they do!

"Praise the Lord," the man shouts, pacing in front of the choir. "You know. There's been a lot of talk in the media about transformation lately."

He pauses. Chuckles to himself.

"And you know, I find that ironic," he says. "Because I believe that Jesus made a transformation in my life. For the better. I believe He can solve all problems!"

The crowd goes wild.

"Transformation. There's a lot of talk. A lot of talk."

River doesn't like where this is going.

"Lots of kids these days think they can just change their skin, change their looks, even their gender, and somehow all their problems will just go away. But that's not how this works, is it? You can't change who and what God made you just because you feel like it!"

Another pause, holding the mic askew with a knowing look on his face.

"Can I get a hallelujah?"

The crowd, save for two or three people, screams it at him.

River notices in the peripheral of his stolen eyes. A familiar, disheveled form standing stoic in the crowd. A smile carved on her ghost-white face.

"Yes, my friends, we are in trying times. You see this is how the Devil works! This is what he does best. Using our own science and medicine against us to let the sin creep into our lives, and the next thing you know, we're all burning in hell for it!"

The strobes flash red, a distorted guitar riff tears through the crowd.

"And do we want that?"

They scream and they cry, "No!"

"That's right. We don't want to go to hell."

The figure River was watching in the crowd. She's weaving through oblivious bodies, moving toward the back of the building. He tracks her as she turns toward him.

River's shocked when he sees her face. Sunken, dark eyes locking on his own.

It's Jess.

And she's clutching a flash drive in her right hand.

Knots twist in his stomach. Like a ghost, she disappears into the crowd.

And then his stolen eyes. They turn to his mother.

"Excuse me, Mrs. Gonzales," he says. "I must use the bathroom."

Now he's being forced to move. To follow Jessica through the crowd.

As his stolen body makes its way up the stadium steps, he locks eyes with another person.

A face that is all too familiar to him.

Alex Davis's lips part into a smile; his rotting eyes burn through the makeup hiding his changing complexion.

Is he part of this too?

River can't even make out what the pastor is saying now. His heart is thundering in his temples as he mounts the stairs.

When he reaches the top of the staircase, a security guard is on the floor, staring at a phone. Spittle flows from his mouth and familiar green light spills forth from the screen.

The stolen eyes do not seem phased by this. They enter the room the security guard was blocking to find Jess inserting the flash drive into a computer tower.

The room overlooks the stage. Windows line the consoles, giving them the perfect front-row seat to Pastor Castillo's performance.

The lighting and camera crew are all staring at a laptop screen now. They are lost. Just like he was.

"There you are," he says. "Are we ready to begin?"

"Oh, yes," she says. "They are ready to receive His gift."

"Yes, they are," he says.

Then, Jess is adjusting settings on one of the consoles.

His stolen eyes sweep out at the stage as the LCD screens behind the choir and Pastor Castillo all go dark.

"What the hell?" Castillo says. "Sorry, folks, it seems like we're having some technical difficulties. One second while I contact—"

The screens ignite with glorious, green light. His light of knowledge. Spread across generations and worlds. And the congregation screams, and they cry. As their minds are filled. As they are forced to know in no uncertain terms that everything they have invested their lives in, everything they believed in, is a lie.

And the only truth. The only one worth knowing. Is that they are unworthy specks among an unfeeling, infinite ocean of stars.

River feels it.

This all-encompassing truth.

Filling their minds like goblets overflowing. Corrosive and unfettered and infinite. And just as acid would erode a goblet, so too does the knowledge do the same to the congregation.

Jess turns to the stolen eyes. She smiles. "This is a good work."

River feels the head he's trapped inside nod. "Yes. He will be pleased."

He screams himself awake.

Sitting up, feeling the sweat dripping off his scalp. He remembers each and every detail.

He's glancing around at his room. Finds his phone and opens it up.

The date...somehow it's Sunday at 11:00 am.

He holds his head. The last thing he remembers is being in the cafeteria and following after Jess.

That was...what day was that?

73

That was Thursday.

He checks his calendar.

It's been a whole goddamn week?

School starts tomorrow and he doesn't even remember…

He remembers the crowd from his dream, and the strange woman's words.

Not all the visions are dreams.

River springs off the bed and rushes into the living room.

The apartment is dark. The first thing he notices is that the windows are all painted black. The only light is coming from the TV on the wall. The one Dad blew one of their tax returns on.

In the dim glow radiating from the TV, he can see a silhouette.

It's his mother. She's sitting on the couch. Watching the news.

Trails of smoke come away from a cigarette tucked between her lips. Its silhouette tapers into a jagged arc of ash.

The look in her eyes…

Her brow is furrowed. Her expression full of contempt.

"Multiple suicides in the greater Los Angeles area—all of them seem to be connected to a disturbing new trend at various art schools and colleges with art programs."

River takes a step forward. His stomach churns and aches.

"Mom?"

"And now it seems as though this string of tragedies could have its source on the internet. A strange new trend on TikTok is seeing kids staring at disturbing images connected to an urban legend that is quickly gaining popularity."

"Mom!" he shouts. "You have to stop smoking…you're gonna—"

"What is that sound?" Mom says. "Can it be the sound of my daughter?"

River stumbles, catching himself against the wall. His legs are weak.

"No, mom," he says. "It's your son."

Her head does not move.

Eyes remain fixated on the screen.

"I have no son," Mom says.

It takes a moment for the words to register. A familiar lump forms in his throat. "What?"

"In one disturbing video, a young girl, just eighteen years old, introduces her audience of over fifteen million followers to what is becoming known as the 'Giger Challenge.'"

"It is the Devil that has you," Mom says. "He has made you this way."

"Mom, we've been over this, I don't—"

"Believe in the Devil?" Mom's laughter bites deep, like thousands of tiny knives digging into his flesh. "The Devil believes in you, daughter."

The TV is showing a TikTok video. A young girl with too much cleavage showing, blonde hair, and blue eyes smiles at the camera.

"Okay, like, there's this urban legend right," the girl says. *"These kids who were murdered at this art school made artwork that can make you crazy. I don't believe it, but I thought I would give it a try for all of you. I haven't looked at the images yet, my boyfriend has them saved and ready for me to look at. Are you ready?"*

The girl giggles and opens the folder.

The paintings.

They're familiar.

Even through the screen they feel like they're alive.

As if it's become a window…one that has been left open. Its frame growing hands and tendrils that worm their way into the wall.

Just like before. River's eyes trace the details.

Creeping, slithering tendrils. Dripping with black ink. Sucking and fucking each other. Infinite and endless ouroboros. An impressionistic vortex. A tunnel of bubbling shapes, like boils ready to burst. In their walls, he can see faces and hands and teeth. Mouths screaming. And at their center, a pulsing, churning storm of green light.

A tower.

A beam of light.

A disembodied chant. All-encompassing. From every mouth, even his own.

"Do you see?" Mom asks. Her voice is all wrong. "The Devil is in you even now. Making you sick with sin. I see it now. Pastor Castillo was right."

"Mom…"

The colors. They swirl and swirl and swirl.

His head. Feels so dizzy. The room spins like a merry-go-round on acid.

The floor comes up to meet him.

Mom's moving. Walking before she stands up. Her face. Something's wrong. He can't put his finger on it.

She stands over him. For a moment, when he blinks, he sees a silhouette, something strange and twisted, working her strings.

Black tears carve a path down her cheek.

The whites of her eyes…they're black.

"I'm going to show you, Mary," Mom says, "what the angels showed me."

A feeling.

Nebulous and raw.

In the dark, they move. Stolen shapes fed to them by their gods help them navigate the currents.

The commands echo through their being. For the young ones, it's all they are. All they will ever be allowed to be. Their minds forever trapped.

In the dark, they swarm upon the surface.

Chipping away at the materials, using their membranous bodies to excavate and store. Their collective mass craters the surface. Warps it to their will. And when it is done, they make their way back to their gods, where they will build and build and build until it is finished.

Until they are pleased.

The feeling.

It ebbs and flows.

When he thinks about the gods. When he thinks about the young ones, how weak their minds are.

It grows.

It festers and it tears.

76

It is a strange feeling.
But he is not the only one.

Screaming.

Pain.

River wakes up on the floor.

His head's pounding.

It takes everything he's got to stumble across the living room in the dark and fumble with the medicine cabinet.

To down two pills and a pitcher of water.

Next thing he knows, he's on the floor, staring up at the microwave. The digital numbers blinking 12:00 am over and over.

When he finds the strength, he peeks over the counter. The TV's off. Mom's gone. Her bedroom door is closed.

Did that really happen?

The windows. His eyes drift over to them.

They're painted over.

The sinking feeling in his gut tells him the truth.

It was real.

Maybe all of it.

The question is…what does he do now?

When he stands and walks around the apartment, his legs are shaky. But they hold.

When he reaches his bedroom, a newfound purpose is growing within him.

He remembers the number he was given by the strange woman. The torn piece of paper is still on his nightstand. Next to his sketchbook.

A sketchbook that is now filled. Black ink having oozed and dried from some of the pages.

He picks it up.

Opens it.

The line work, washes, pencil markings…they're all his. And the subjects. They're familiar. Familiar and disturbing.

On one page, what looks like land formations on the bottom of the sea. And thousands of black figures. They seem not to conform to any one shape. But he knows…somehow…that they're organic.

At first, he thinks they're moving over the ocean floor.

But, in the next image, he sees them close-up. Their bodies aren't bodies at all. More like giant microorganisms. Like bacteria or viruses with thousands of misshapen eyeballs tucked inside their amorphous forms.

What made him draw all of these?

And why do they feel so…familiar? Like he's looking at the grossest goddamn family photo album of all time?

That familiar pain. The drilling, biting, burning sensation spreads from his forehead to the back of his skull.

It makes him drop the sketchbook.

The number.

The strange woman.

He's got to call her.

He finds his phone and puts her number in.

It goes on ringing for a while.

And then…

"*I wondered when you'd call,*" she says.

"I need your help," River says.

CHAPTER EIGHT

"What'd you find?" Shirley's voice echoes over the cruiser's speakers.

"Nothing much to go off of," Hunter says. "I went to that TikTok star's house, but the windows were painted over. No one answered the door."

"Well, her parents are big donors for the department, so finding out why she went missing is a top priority. Where are you now?"

"Following up on another lead."

"I certainly hope you're not still trying to prove that Tyler kid's innocence."

His hand grips the steering wheel. Teeth clench. "Of course not."

"Good boy. I'll see if I can get a search warrant for the house, see if we can't shut the parents up."

"I'll be back at HQ later."

"All right. Good luck."

He hangs up the receiver.

Hunter's been sitting in the car, running the AC. Staring at the ever-darkening clouds of orange ash. The drifting, setting sun. Letting the empty, gnawing feeling in his gut eat away at his soul. What's left of it.

It's been a week since his meeting with Dean Tyler.

Since all hope of proving the kid's innocence went out the goddamn window.

When he tried searching for the interrogation footage—his last hope to prove the kid was coerced into taking the blame—there was nothing.

He should be done with this business. He should let it go, do as his bosses want him to. Focus on the missing TikTok star…

But he can't shake it. The feeling of responsibility. As much as Detective Shirley and so many others have told him to drop the case, he can't. His mind keeps coming back to it.

The cruiser's sitting in the parking lot belonging to the LA Institute of Commercial Art.

He's not sure what he's accomplishing by coming here.

It's been so long since he last slept. The burning sensation in his eyes is almost normal now.

Hard to push through the fog.

The tattered book rests on the passenger seat. It's been there all week. From time to time, Hunter glances in its direction and wonders.

Before he can even think about leaving the car, his phone rings.

It's his wife.

Probably wants to know when, or if, he'll be home today.

Instead of answering the phone, he sits in the seat for a while, staring at the dead flowers that adorn a memorial display on one of the planters in the parking lot. The tree the concrete contains is long dead. Its carcass spreads its limbs to the ashen sky, as if it's calling out to God. Or something else.

His phone goes off once more.

It's Janet again.

Once more, he ignores it. Lets it go to voice mail.

Janet will understand.

The next thing he knows, he's approaching the building, its corporate stone walls and black windows. It feels oppressive in a way. He's not sure why. Some of the trees in the parking lot are turning black.

He tells himself it's just the drought, the fires.

At least the heat is starting to let up.

The reception area is empty. The hallways are barren.

Hunter's not even sure why he thought this was a good idea. Coming here.

But then one of the picture frames in the hallway catches his attention.

The artwork. It's damn familiar.

The subject is a naked man, or at least, what's left of him. From his belly black and oozing intestines spill onto the Earth. Those intestines form tentacles that drape and snake their way across the land. His head appears to be tilted back, staring up at a vortex of gray-green clouds.

His eyes are black. The tears he sheds create rivers of reflective ink. Those rivers feed his bowels, the gushing flow of tendrils. Like alien roots.

The hallway — no — the whole goddamn corridor is filled with them. Paintings of all shapes and sizes. Each of them more disturbing than the last.

The next painting appears to be a continuation of the previous one. The man is covered in blackened veins, his hands reaching for the sky.

The background is a web of coruscating and bubbling shapes, they suck him in. Everything else seems to fade away.

Where once the black tendrils snaked over the land, now they dominate it. Now other shapes rise up. Pods, or eggs, that catch the gray-green light in ways that seem too real to his eyes. As if it's happening right before him.

The next thing he knows, what's left of the man's body is being devoured by that viscous material. First the tendrils drag his arms down and bind them. Then they wrap about his torso, like some kind of cocoon. His face, his blackened, oozing eyes and smiling mouth, are last. Until he's swallowed in a cocoon.

"Who the fuck are you?" A voice snaps Hunter out of his daze.

He's looking around, blinking and rubbing his eyes. Wondering why he zoned out this time. Why he's halfway down the hallway.

Hunter's face-to-face with a young Mexican man with red dye in his hair and patches for a beard. He's short, maybe five-three, and his face is painted in fear.

"I came…" Hunter almost looks back at the paintings. Thinks better of it, straightens his posture and retrieves his badge. "I'm Detective

Hunter. I came here to find out more about Dean Tyler and his associates, Kevin Wallace and Patric Boyd."

"Why?" The boy's eyebrows come together. "Thought he was in prison for murder."

"That's what they say," Hunter says.

There's an uncomfortable pause. It stretches long and pregnant between them. The boy doesn't trust him.

"And you don't believe it?" the boy asks. There's something familiar about him.

Hunter's poker face is failing. Must be the fatigue. "Did you know Dean?"

"Yeah, we had a couple classes together."

"What was he like?"

"He was always cracking jokes, making the instructors and the class laugh. But he always turned in top-tier work. Not gonna lie, I was always a little intimidated by him."

"And he and Kevin were friends?"

The boy nods. "I saw them in the student lounge, playing some Dragon Ball Z fighting game together a lot. The instructors sometimes complained about the anime influence in their work. Said nobody cares about it in the west."

"My son would disagree."

The boy nods, crossing his arms. Putting up walls. "Cool."

"Yeah…"

He's tempted to write all of this down, or take out his voice recorder. But he doesn't want to scare the first person he's seen here. Besides, he's sure he can trust his memory.

The boy is quiet for a time. For a while, they're standing in the hallway, staring into space like it's the thing to do. Hunter's had moments like that with his son. Where neither of them can really figure out what to say.

The boy looks like he wants to say something.

"You have something to add?" Hunter asks.

The look on his face. Similar to Bobby whenever he hesitates to tell his family something important, something he's embarrassed about.

"There's something else…"

"What is it?" Hunter asks.

"I'm sure you've heard about the trend at art schools by now? The paintings on ArtisTree and the TikTok challenges?"

Hunter nods.

"Well," the boy continues. "It started with this wannabe goth group. At least, the goth clique thought they were trying to steal their thing. Kevin got wrapped up in it, started making disturbing paintings. Real Giger inspired, but way more disturbing. Like you can get lost in them... And that kind of drew a wedge between Kevin and Dean."

"Were they antagonistic toward one another?" Hunter asks.

"No, I don't think so. Mostly, Dean just looked sad. I saw him playing games alone in the lounge a couple times. Almost joined him, but I didn't know him like that."

"Were there any signs that Dean was unstable?"

"Like he was gonna kill his best friend?" The kid's eyes are incredulous. "No."

"And what was his relationship to Patric Boyd?"

"I don't know, I barely knew him. He kept to himself. I never saw the two of them together."

"And what about Kevin Wallace?"

"Nope. The four of us had a class together, but that's it."

"So the connection is tenuous..."

"What are you trying to get at here?"

Hunter sighs.

"What's your name?" Hunter asks.

"River Gonzales," River says. "Aren't you supposed to ask that first?"

Hunter rubs his eyes. "So, you're saying that there was no hint that Dean Tyler was about to do something horrible? No angry outbursts, no public arguments with his friend?"

River nods. "You don't think he did it, do you?"

Another heavy sigh. "No."

"Why?" River asks. "The news said there was a full confession."

"That's police business, Mr. Gonzales." He wants to change the subject. "Why is the school so empty? Shouldn't there be classes?"

"They're in session…" River's eyes drift to one of the doors. A computer lab. Through the glass window, Hunter can tell the room is dark. The window is accented by the occasional flash of familiar green light.

"Mind if I interrupt a few of them?"

"I don't think you'll get very far."

"Why?"

The look on his face…his eyes are wild, mouth trembling. "You wouldn't believe me if I told you."

Hunter chuckles, digs his card out from his blazer. Hands it to River.

"If you can remember anything else related to Dean, Patric, and Kevin, let me know," Hunter says, before brushing past River and heading toward the door with the green light.

"Don't look at the screens," River says.

Hunter stops.

Something deep inside him tells him not to listen. "Excuse me?"

"Never mind." River shuffles off down the hallway.

He can't quite put his finger on it, but something about that boy reminds him of his son.

Hunter turns and puts his hand on the doorknob, twists it, and—

Hunter snaps to in his car.

It's night.

The sky is a dark gray. The Los Angeles skyline casts its light upon the ashen clouds above.

He looks at his phone. It's after 8 pm already.

He's got missed calls and texts from Shirley and Janet.

Hunter looks at the ones from Janet first.

Janet Hunter: Please call me back, it's about Bobby. Something happened at school.

Janet Hunter: Are you there?

Janet Hunter: Please pick up your goddamn phone, Hunter!

Janet Hunter: Fine. You know what. Be that way. Don't ask what happened with your son. Don't check on him. Don't ask about the weird shit he's been drawing in his sketchbook!

"Goddamn it."

Hunter rubs his eyes. The fatigue is almost all-consuming.

It's about time he went home and faced the music.

He ignores Shirley's texts, jumps straight to sending her a new one.

Hunter: Family emergency. I'll fill you in later.

He turns the key; the engine roars to life.

Hunter tells himself he's going to go straight home.

That he's going to rush inside and apologize to his wife, take them all out for dinner and a movie.

But this is a lie.

CHAPTER NINE

From the Journal of Doctor Webber
March 15th, 2022

It started as a simple curiosity.

A question posed by a newly minted agent, fresh out of her Psychological and Willpower Assessment.

The O.E.I. has used the same training program for almost three decades. Recruits must pass a series of psychological evaluations as they are exposed to critical aspects of their jobs.

The true nature of our multiverse.

Even discovering a hint of what lurks behind the veil can have life-altering consequences. And after decades of research, we're no closer to understanding why that is.

In the early days, my predecessors blew millions of dollars hiring psychologists to "cure" agents of their symptoms.

It took us almost a decade of trying before we realized the truth.

There is no cure.

I remember the day well.

I stood at the back of one of the facility's rooms that we use for training new recruits. No bigger than your average classroom.

Doctor Patton's eyes barely acknowledged my presence. I was there to assess her performance.

The rows of desks were populated with recruits from various military institutions. Rejects from the Army, Navy, or Marines. Those who were too desperate to care about the danger of what we were asking of them.

The new video projector offered a glimpse into the world these lucky few would get to experience. Secrets waiting to be unlocked.

The program briefly touches on a critical aspect of traversing the veil between realities, the unpredictable nature of it.

The O.E.I. has developed several methods, some of which have been sourced from top-secret locations here in the United States.

The first, an artifact, is the oldest. It was discovered buried deep beneath the surface of Death Valley in the 1900s by the residents of Greenwater, a mining community built around a copper strike. The population only reached 2,000 before people began to flee.

No ruins remain of the Greenwater settlement. And for good reason.

The official story was that the mine was never able to see a profit and so the population departed to greener pastures.

The truth is, the miners unearthed a two-hundred-million-year-old artifact, buried shortly before the End-Triassic Extinction Event by our great creators, whose true name cannot be uttered by human tongues. For simplicity's sake, I will use the name given to them by the late H.P. Lovecraft, when he unknowingly channeled their memories: the Elder Things.

Today, we know the End-Triassic Extinction Event was caused by the war between the Elder Things and Great Cthulhu's armies. The results of their advanced weaponry and alien technology increased volcanic activity on the surface of our world and blanketed the skies with ash.

We strongly suspect that the artifact unearthed in Greenwater was one of many that have been lost to time. A triangular device composed of matter not found in our reality. It is ornately carved, featuring many inscriptions and what we believe to be artistic flourishes made by the Elder Things meant to allow for better channeling of the strange energies first discovered in the dreamlands. If I were to make an Earthly comparison, I would call it a kind of magnet for such forces.

The residents and workers in Greenwater had no idea what they possessed, believing it to be some kind of Native American artifact. And they were unprepared for the terrible fortune that would be brought to them from it.

The town vanished overnight. The few who did survive told strange tales of shape-shifting beasts, claiming that these must have been the legendary Skin-Walkers that are so common in American folklore.

Many of those men found themselves institutionalized, where they died, raving from psychological phenomena we are still coming to grips with.

Our training program includes a brief breakdown on how we've been able to utilize this artifact for our own research, to explore the dreamlands with probes and manned expeditions.

Through the writings and diagrams we've been able to translate from the ruins left by the Elder Things, we have been able to deduce that these incredible beings had a unique natural connection to the dreamlands. Especially talented members of their species were able to traverse the veil at will, while others needed devices like the artifact discovered in Greenwater to do so. They would emit a sound from their anatomy that would react with the strange material and carvings in the artifact. This would create a chain reaction, attracting the strange energies of the dreamlands to our dimensions, shifting them, separating them, and finally splitting them.

The result would be a doorway unlike any other, and yet, easily traversed by men. A passage revealing strange geometries and impossible physics from one angle, and nothing from another.

We were able to replicate this frequency from reconstructing the remains of fossilized Elder Things. The first real use of the pyramidal gateway was in the late 1970s, by my predecessor. He was able to construct a complex audio synthesizer with the very best digital music equipment of the time.

When the gateway opened, he was drawn to it.

And once he traversed the doorway, he was never heard from again.

The pyramidal doorway, however, was not reliable. It was prone to failing in the middle of an operation, resulting in countless agents being lost to the dreamlands. O.E.I. scientists were eventually able to keep the gateway open during operations through the use of a sustained note, presumably a note the Elder Things were able to emit.

It was also incredibly difficult to control what part of the dreamlands it connected to. Each time, it took us somewhere different.

I remember one case in particular. Shortly after my predecessor's disappearance.

The agents who had passed through the gateway described a relentless, ashen sky. A land blanketed in silhouetted ruins and what they swore were bones.

Though standard procedure required each member of the expedition to wear protective gear designed by the minds behind the Apollo missions, for some reason, they were all compelled to remove their space suits.

The commander of the operation would later remark on this curious decision as the first sign that something else was influencing his men.

These men found the air of this new place to be tolerable, despite the lingering smell of death, and proceeded in their expedition.

They described the land as not behaving in accordance with our natural laws. That it seemed impossible to tell which direction they were going. Some of the men swore that the place had a mind of its own. That they could see blinking eyes peering down on them from the ashen clouds.

The commander never saw these eyes. Wrote the complaints off as baseless paranoia.

Eventually, the path narrowed out into a courtyard. And at the center of that courtyard was a black tower. One that extended right up through those blackened clouds. A structure which refused to obey the laws of physics as we know them and conformed to no obvious perspective.

Despite their trepidation, curiosity won out. The men approached the tower. They described it as gargantuan, that it took them days to reach it. That it had stairs and ramps in any and all configurations imaginable. A description familiar to anyone who's sat in a museum and pondered at an M.C. Escher painting.

When they finally reached it, they described the walls and great pillars as stretching from horizon to horizon. It had a single triangular depression at its base. A grooved, gleaming metallic thing that dwarfed each and every man present.

One of the men commented that more triangular shapes appeared to cover vast portions of the tower, repeating for miles and miles in every direction and spaced in no particular order.

They were more than alarmed when those depressions opened up, and black clouds of smoke spilled out and blanketed them.

The commander watched three men breathe in the blackened cloud. When their knees touched the ground, their flesh had practically melted off of their bones.

The commander barked orders to the remainder of the men, commanding them to retreat back to the portal.

Of the original twelve men that made up the expedition party, three made it back alive.

None of them breathed the mysterious cloud from the tower, and medical evaluations cleared them to resume duty.

That was not the end of the story, of course.

Attempts to re-open the gateway proved folly, as the artifact that had given us the ability to enter the dreamlands would not connect to the same place more than once. This made retrieving the remains of the rest of the expedition party impossible.

The remaining three members, including the commander, quickly deteriorated.

All three had to be debriefed after their medical examinations. And this is where things got truly strange.

Each one of them, the commander included, demanded to be given access to drawing implements of some kind.

During the first debriefing, one of the agents was denied access to a pencil and paper, and as a result ended up sinking his teeth into his own flesh until he drew blood.

When the psychiatrist asked him what he was doing, he did not answer. At least not audibly. Instead, he began to use his own blood as ink, and the table as a medium, and illustrated what he had seen in the dreamlands.

From this point onward, all agents who returned from dreamlands expeditions were given access to drawing pads, pencils, inks, paints, whatever their mad hearts desired.

Through trial and blind, stupid luck, we were able to deduce that certain aspects of the frequencies we were using acted as a kind of code, a coordinate system.

Almost like a computer waiting to receive instructions.

This, of course, brings me back to the fledgling recruit, and her question. The question that would change everything.

I remember her raising her hand and asking, "What about Artificial Intelligence? Couldn't you train an AI to find the right coordinates?"

From the Journal of Lena Hartman
March 17th, 2022

It's Saint Patrick's Day.

Used to be my favorite holiday. I remember that now.

I remember leaving Sophi with her tía one day to party. Didn't return until the following Monday. Tía wasn't too happy with me. Pretty fucking on brand for me in those days.

I remember a lot more now.

Some of it's still blurry.

I remember the facility. The frozen hell that California and the rest of the world became. Our small group of survivors. Ira, Hugo, Mathias, Eddy, and...and Nico.

Doctor Patton tells me I suffered extreme frostbite and brain damage. That I'm lucky to be alive.

Sometimes, I can still feel my skin burning...

Doctor Webber keeps interviewing me. Dragging answers and stories out of me. Says I came from another Earth. What he calls an Earth Variant. One where the world froze over. Not a normal ice age at all. Something worse. Something rarer.

He's fake as fuck. Webber, I mean. He might have a younger face and one more letter in his last name, but I know that fucker can't be trusted.

I know it in my soul.

The things he did...the other him...I can't shake it. I can't.

He's been letting more and more things slip.

Apparently, the OEI have been receiving transmissions from "Earth Variants" for a really long time. Since at least the 1970s. And...and he showed me something.

A broadcast of some kind. From an Earth Variant he thought I'd find "interesting." The sick fuck.

It was a news report. KLCA-6. The news was about how astronomers were detecting less and less radiation from the sun. How they were measuring a higher concentration of dust and gas and stuff. They said that visibility in the solar system was gonna drop. That the Earth's temperature would cool slightly.

They called it a miracle.

Said the "space cloud" would help to reverse climate change.

The news ended on a positive note. But Doctor Webber told me he has a feeling things didn't work out too well. That this is likely the world I came from.

I told him the world froze over. That me and the others were the only survivors in Riverside, California. Possibly even the whole state.

He chuckled. Actually chuckled. Said I was lucky.

Fucking bastard.

I hate him.

I need to get out of here. I feel like I'm going crazy answering his goddamn questions!

They have to know if I'm okay. If I can see my daughter by now.

They have to know!

The office is dark.

He's alone.

He stares at the back of his own shaved head from the back of the office.

Screens. So many of them. All the other officers are gone, but the screens glow bright and putrid and green.

Why can't he get back into his body?

Why are his eyes still open?

What is it that is so interesting about the screen?

He can't quite see, no matter how hard he looks.

Sounds.

He hears sounds…like voices. They're coming from the elevator.

He decides to investigate. Drifts over and into the elevator. The voices are strong inside. He presses the button for the third floor.

The voices…he can almost make out what they're saying here.

They sound…friendly. But it's a kind of friendly that makes him feel uneasy.

But he must get closer.

He drifts through the corridors and hallways.

"It's…late…want…coffee?"

The closer he gets, the clearer the voices become.

"Get the kid a coffee, you want sugar in it? Creamer?"

"Two sugars and a creamer. Hop to it."

"I see you're wearing a Lakers shirt. I love basketball too, you know, who's your favorite player?"

"Yeah, shame what happened to Kobe, right?"

He passes through so many walls and doors, until he's peering through a two-way mirror at a brick room with three bodies sitting across from each other at a table.

A cup of coffee steaming into the air in front of a familiar Black kid.

No, a young Black man.

He knows them.

"Before you say anything," Shirley says, "you should know that we've already found your DNA at your friend's place."

"He's my roommate," Dean says. "Why wouldn't my DNA be there?"

"Not just Kevin's, a young man named Patric Boyd," John says. "We know what you did tonight, so there's no point in lying."

"Lying?" Dean is incredulous. "What the fu..." He tries to calm himself. Knows they'll use his anger to lock him up in a dungeon and throw away the key. "I told you! I was on campus, working on my graphic design—"

"We know it took you an hour to get back to your dorm," Shirley says. "We know you stopped at Patric Boyd's studio apartment, drugged him, and used a noose to hang him. Made it look like a suicide."

"I didn't do—"

"You know, this would go a lot better for you if you told the truth, kid," John says. "We already know all the facts. We just want to know why you did it."

"Really, though, we get it," Shirley says. "These guys were into some weird stuff. No wonder you pushed your roommate out the window."

"I want a—"

"If you tell the truth, we can offer you a deal," Shirley says. "But there's nothing we can do if you keep lying to us."

"I didn't—"

"Don't lie to us, Dean," John says, "Just tell us why you did it."

It goes on and on. Slowly, over the countless hours, Dean Tyler's posture and eyes go from rigid and determined to defeated and weary.

"Dean, I'd like to show you something," John says. Somehow, his voice sounds strange to him. His posture...changed. He can almost make out the reflection of black strings in the buzzing light of the interrogation room.

John retrieves a phone from his blazer and places it in front of Dean. The screen glows a familiar putrid green.

"Stare into the screen," John says. "And tell me what you see?"

Dean is silent for untold hours. The clock goes on and on, long past the time when Hunter would have been in his bed, dreaming his strange dreams. Shirley seems confused, but goes along with it. Doesn't want to rock the boat.

"What do you see?" John asks.

"It's beautiful..." *Dean can't look away from the screen.*

"Yes, it is," John says.

"What is?" Shirley asks, confused.

"Now, Dean, how did you kill Patric Boyd and Kevin Wallace?" *John asks.*

"I..." *Dean's eyes open wide, his head cocking at a strange angle. From behind the glass, Hunter can see the strings. How they pull at his lips and vocal cords.* "I got into their minds first. Showed them the truth. Some vessels are more willing than most. But they all end up at the same goal. Kevin Cameron Wallace was mine from the first glance. He wanted nothing more than to behold the city with his own eyes. But the bridge. It's not ready yet. He knew the angel had to be perfect. So I took hold of his limbs, and made him leap headfirst into the waiting earth.

"Patric Jevon Boyd's mind was weak. It was easy to bend him to my will. So, to reach the city, I told him he must kill his shell. I made him buy the rope and hang it from the broken ceiling fan. The rest was easy. He didn't kick or struggle. I felt his essence slowly leave his shell. It was...fascinating.

"When the time is right, when the bridge is ready, their bodies will join them, reborn at the foot of His house."

Hunter blinks.

It's dark. The moon's light can just barely be seen through the smoky haze above.

He's dressed. Sitting in his car outside his apartment building's cold white exterior. His eyes stare up at its uniform concrete balconies, the way the streetlamps reflect off its smooth rectangular surface and its cookie-cutter rooftop.

Why did they choose this place, above all the countless others that look just like it?

He doesn't know.

Doesn't know why he's sitting here.

But he knows he's late.

Checking his text messages tells him that he told Shirley he'd be going home because of a family emergency.

That was hours ago.

The sound of Hunter's apartment door shutting in the dark is enough to wake the dead.

In the stillness of the night, it sends a chill's insidious tentacles up his spine.

After Janet's angry texts, he's not looking forward to seeing her or the conversation that will follow.

He still can't believe he lost so much time reading that journal. Doesn't even remember picking it up. Doesn't remember falling asleep. Just the feeling of coming to in his cruiser in the dark and tossing it aside when the realization struck him.

There's no note for him in the kitchen. No dinner waiting in the fridge. The first real sign that he's in serious trouble.

He decides he's going to sleep on the couch tonight. Too much on his mind to deal with the fallout.

Hunter's halfway through making a sandwich when he sees her standing on the stairs, her nightgown flowing as if pushed by a nonexistent wind.

"I tried to reach you today," Janet says. "Tried texting."

Hunter stops making his sandwich and sucks on his teeth, avoiding eye contact with his wife.

He's so hungry.

So tired.

He doesn't want to do this.

"The whole state is in chaos," he says. "I couldn't get away. You know how it is."

"You mean to tell me you couldn't pick up your phone? That you didn't get a single break away from what you were doing to check in on your family even after all the texts I sent?"

Hunter wants to nod. He knows she'll see right through him. Knows she won't understand what he's going through.

They stand there for a while. She won't leave the staircase. He can see her eyes gleaming at him in the dark, the light from the kitchen caressing her nightgown.

"Did you even look at the texts I sent you?" she asks.

Hunter nods.

"What part of 'Please call me back, it's about Bobby. Something happened at school' didn't you see as important?"

"Janet, I'm under a lot of pressure right—"

"Gilbert Alan Hunter, your son had a panic attack at school today. He was so scared, they had to call me at work and get me to come pick him up!"

"I'm sorry—"

"No you're not. You don't care. You're fine to be around us when it's convenient, sure. That poor boy's been having nightmares since he got back. Been asking for his daddy. And yet, here you are, making fucking excuses. It's starting to feel really familiar, Gil."

"Don't...don't call me that..."

"You're starting to remind me a lot of Dad."

"I am nothing like your father!" Hunter slams his hand down on the counter. "That racist piece of shit!"

"He might have been a racist piece of shit. That's true. But he almost never took time off work. Sound familiar?"

"Janet, I—"

"Yet, even with how fucking absorbed with work he was, he still found *some* time for his family." She crosses her arms. "Something you seem to be incapable of doing!"

"He never made detective. He never had to deal with the things I have. The—"

"Then quit, Hunter! For your family's sake!"

"I can't!"

By the time he's done raking his fingers across his scalp and looks up, she's gone.

Hunter stands there for a while, staring at the empty staircase. He stares so long, part of him wonders if she was even there to begin with.

If, maybe, he imagined the whole argument.

His eyes peer down at his half-assembled sandwich, and he decides to throw it out and go to bed.

He's not hungry anymore.

The next thing he knows, he's stumbling through the living room, plopping and sinking into his recliner.

It doesn't take long for his eyelids to feel the weight of gravity. The threat of sleep and all the nightmares it will bring with it.

Part of him doesn't want to sleep. Doesn't want to dream.

Wants to stay as far away from the things in his nightmares as he can.

His eyes find the covered easel in the living room. The paintbrushes and the pallet.

He can feel it.

The nightmares seizing at the walls of that ever-encroaching circle of darkness.

And as sleep finally takes him, he thinks about the last text message Janet sent him.

Janet Hunter: Fine. You know what. Be that way. Don't ask what happened with your son. Don't check on him. Don't ask about the weird shit he's been drawing in his sketchbook!

CHAPTER TEN

The alarm's been blaring for an hour straight. Burning, roasting sunlight filtering through dusty blinds, turning the thick blankets River hides under into a furnace.

He doesn't want to leave. It's all his body wants to do ever since...whatever the fuck happened in the computer lab a little over a week ago.

River thought the sunrise would make it easier to leave his bed. But, every time the rattling swamp cooler moves the blinds, all he sees are writhing, twisting things in the dark.

Things he can't quite describe.

When the door opens, his pained shrieks can be heard several apartments over.

He stares into his mother's bloodshot and sunken eyes. River can't be sure, but he thinks there's something off about her skin. Something that reminds him of Jess.

"Wake up, Mary," River's Mom says.

The name sends cold shivers down his spine.

He misses the way she used to say his name. The love implied in each syllable. He doesn't want to have this argument again.

Not for the thousandth time this week.

For some reason, he says it anyway. "I'm not your daughter."

"You know who was a real man?" Mom's mocking laughter bites deep. "Your father was a man. Lord, did he try. If he were here, what would he say about this? What would he say about what's happened to his little girl?"

A flash of memory. Mom stitching a new Christmas stocking with his name on it: River remembers holding it up, admiring the badass stitch of Krampus with a bag full of screaming children slung over his hairy shoulders.

He remembers tracing his index finger through each letter, his mother smiling pridefully at him from the chair. As if to say, *Yes, Mijo, that is my work, and you are my son.*

Another memory, a more recent one. After Life's Well Assembly skull-fucked all the sense out of her.

He remembers glancing at the table a day or two ago. In the strange state he's been in since the computer lab…his sense of time is messed up. It's the beginning of May, but Mom always wants to get a jump on planning for Christmas. His eyes almost didn't catch the new stocking lying there, like his brain purposely skipped over it—a generic one covered in angels, the color of Pepto.

He knew the stocking was meant for him, but the letters spelled out Mary.

The sharp, stinging feeling comes rushing back to him as he relives finding his old stocking in the trash, stained with spoiled beans and old Chinese food from the fridge.

How could it get so bad so fast?

"Are you listening to me, young lady?" his mother practically screams, bringing River out of his memory.

He glances around the room, blinking, but quickly snaps back at her. "Oh, should I be taking notes here? I guess if I want to be a real man, I better start drinking myself stupid every night down at the Sportsman and driving home drunk, huh?

"You disrespectful little shit! You have no idea how much your father sacrificed for you!"

"Yeah, entire paychecks to his drinking habit, right?"

"You are a goddamn disgrace and your father would be ashamed of you, Mary!"

River bites back tears. The testosterone does its thing. A lump of uncontrollable rage festers, claws its way up into his throat. Like a magma chamber getting ready to burst. There's only one way to relieve the pressure. The heat.

"You know what, Luciana?" River shouts. "Fuck you, and fuck this place!"

Before River can get out of bed and grab his things, his mom's back in the living room, sitting on the couch. Like she's been there the whole time, sobbing her damn eyes out and uttering broken prayers in Spanish. Just the way her abuela taught her.

"*Hail Mary, full of grace,*" Mom sobs, "*who art in...*" More sobbing. "*Who art in heaven.*" Then, as if she's just noticed River standing there, she goes off script. "*Please, give me my daughter back. She's all I have. You already took him. Give her back! Give me back my Mary!*"

River sits on the couch. Despite his pain, his desire to be anywhere else in the world...some part of him wants to reach out, believes there's hope for his mother.

He touches her shoulder.

At first, her stare is hopeful. But, as her eyes wash over River, it twists, and writhes, and transforms into something demonic and murderous.

"You have to understand, the church and I care about you," Luciana says. "We just want what's best for you!"

"It's my life, mother."

"Which God gave you!"

"I don't believe in that stuff..."

Luciana plunges her face into her palms. Her sobs get louder, more theatrical.

"She's gone," Luciana says. "God, please...drive the devil out of my daughter!"

The rage demands he retaliate. Tell her what an awful person she is. The lump festers, demanding release. Righteous indignation!

He takes a deep breath. He's too tired for that. He's done arguing.

"That's it," River says. "I can't do this anymore."

"Mary?"

He gets up off the couch. He can feel mother's eyes tracking him to the front door. "Have a nice life, Luciana."

———

As River makes his way into the sweltering Southern California morning heat, doing his best to hold back the tears that so desperately want to come bursting through, he thinks about how different things used to be.

Who his *mother* used to be...

He wonders where she went. The woman who was with him through hormone treatment, practically a second puberty, who stayed with him during the long and painful process of recovering from the double mastectomy.

Who made him huevos rancheros before his midterm, even though she didn't understand everything he was going through. Even though she was confused and worried.

River wonders where things went wrong. Why Luciana turned her back on him.

Why she painted the windows black...

Deep down, he knows the answer.

They got to her.

He wants to believe it was the TV, her friends at Life's Well. Who had a piece to say about River's decision, and didn't want to hear what *he* had to say. And even when they claimed otherwise, River knew they were just waiting for their turn to speak.

To rant.

If a random stranger would have asked River how his transition affected his life before Jess lured him into that computer lab, he would have had nothing but positive things to say. He would have described it as the best possible anti-depressant. He would have said his friends, his mother, and extended family were all wonderful.

Now, Luciana seems like a completely different person. As if she was replaced by something hatched from a pod.

That thought makes him stop in his tracks...to stare at the dark orange clouds drifting overhead.

After the vision he had of Mom and Jess at Life's Well Assembly, he thought...

Well, he didn't know what to expect. Didn't know if it was even real...

Maybe he expected to find her painting monsters fucking each other with tentacles or something.

In a way, he would have preferred that outcome.

At least then, he wouldn't feel like this...

He finds himself at school, racing through the near empty halls to his life drawing class. He glances over his shoulder, looking for anyone who might want to drag him into the computer lab to show him the wonders of the fucking Necronomicon.

River passes several students waiting outside Mr. Riviera's concept art class. Alex Davis is busy giving the goth look a bad name.

Alex's smile is familiar. Like his eyes are saying, *Welcome to the club.*

He ignores them, even as the piercing, bloodshot eyes from the H.P.-love-crack fan club follow him across the hall.

His hands find his student badge; he scans it at the door and slips inside.

The door slams behind him. Everyone's staring at him from their easels and stools. They're arranged in a circle around the life drawing model, who's doing his best impression of a pretzel.

Professor Hampton clears his throat. "You're late, Mr. Gonzalez, please take your seat.

"I'm sorry," River says.

"It's fine," Hampton says. "Next time, please be more punctual."

River nods, shuffling off to an empty stool and easel to get set up.

While he's placing the enlarged sketchpad on the easel, he can't help but notice Jess staring at him from across the room. The smile on her face makes him feel like his back's being eaten alive by a flesh-eating bacteria.

Tears threaten at the walls of his vision; he breaks eye contact with her and picks up a charcoal piece.

Was she just trying to lure him into that computer lab?

Was there nothing left of their friendship?

"All right, class," Hampton says. "That's it for that pose."

The model unfurls and stands up, this time making like he's holding a bow and pulling back on the drawstring to release an arrow.

102

"Go ahead and start a new construction," Professor Hampton says. "Fifteen-minute time limit. Begin now."

River begins by describing the model's form with an S-curve, with C-curves describing the arm he's pulling back. The model's left hand is smaller than the other one. Probably a birth defect. River spent five different classes drawing this man without realizing it. He makes a note of the scale difference and moves on to the right arm, describing it with wrapping lines and two overlapping C-curves to denote the gesture of holding the "bow" out.

Soon, he finds his rhythm. Line after curve after anatomical construction. The fear that has gripped at his heart for over a week now begins to subside.

He begins to smile. The lump that's been festering in his throat since fighting with his mother this morning practically melts away.

That is, until his gaze is drawn from his easel. To Jess's bloodshot eyes and stretched, cracking grin.

"*Iä! Iä! Cthulhu fhtagn!*"

The chants!

He remembers how they sounded as he looks at her. And as he stares, he swears he sees her pupils segmenting into twisted, vivisecting forms, just like those ancient, impossible towers.

When he breaks from her stare and focuses back on his sketchpad, he covers his mouth, yelping like an abused dog.

His right hand, his drawing hand, is sore. Cramping.

And the figure on the sketchpad looks nothing like the man standing in the center of the classroom.

Instead, it's a twisted, amorphous monstrosity surrounded by a subway tunnel. White charcoal markings denote a glistening texture on its gelatinous surface. Claws and hands and slithering, snaking shapes creep out from its belly. Toward the front of its form, he can see faces molding within cascading mouths filled with canine and human teeth.

"Is there something wrong, Mr. Gonzalez?" Hampton asks.

River's eyes dart up from his sketchpad, panic seizing at his heart. Jess has been warned multiple times this semester not to draw horrific shit like this, to stay on task and do the assignments. He quickly covers the easel and starts a new drawing.

That stuff might line the halls now, but Hampton has no patience for it in his class.

"No problem, Professor," River says, laughing nervously. "Just tore the page, that's all."

Professor Hampton nods; River breathes a sigh of relief.

He sits back down on the stool and picks up the charcoal piece again.

Fearing his eroding willpower, he rotates his seat and easel so he can't see Jess anymore.

Just in case.

The timer at the front of the class rings just as River's getting comfortable again, just as the form is finally starting to take shape.

"All right, class," Professor Hampton says, clapping his hands. "Let's go ahead and let Jim take a break. Your next subject will be our good friend Sophia. Once again, you'll have fifteen minutes to complete your study."

The professor approaches the front of the classroom, rotates the tomato timer, and lets it start ticking again. "Begin now," he says.

The curves. That's what's trapped her in this piece. She can see the woman as she will be. Not the sickly thing sitting before her eyes. The woman looks uneasy now, but in her mind's eye, she's transformed. Evolved. The light glistens off her bare breasts like a candle's glow off seeping oil. Her eyes have melted into a beautiful coagulated paste; her hands have elongated into sharp talons, revealing their stolen, poisoned tips.

The skeletal structure is the biggest difference. It's rigid and sharp, and yet, so smooth. Earthly words are ill-equipped to describe it. The beauty that she sees. Humans are imperfect beings. A breeding experiment gone wrong. Assembled by the uncaring hands of masters long since lost to the abyss of time.

"Are you crazy?" one of her classmates says, leaning over her drawing pad. "If Professor Hampton sees you doing one of those again, he's gonna fail you for sure."

It's difficult to talk. To push through the fog to interact with this worthless man child. But somehow, she manages. "I don't care. Leave me alone."

"Yeah, but last time he saw, he threatened to fail you, Jess!" There is a pathetic, pleading look in his eyes. It's clear that he wishes to fondle her breasts, to take her to bed and breed with her. Only, he is too cowardly to spit it out and say so. "Look, just flip to a new page, before he sees."

The man-child is trying to distract her. He reaches for her drawing hand.

This is all too familiar to her. Even before she saw the light. How this disgusting creature lurked in the background of each and every one of her classes, sitting next to her, staring at her, salivating, fantasizing about her.

When she looks upon him—into his soft, weak brown eyes—she can see what he's meant to become. The hidden potential beneath his sickly, mortal flesh.

In the dreamlands, he will be taken. In the dreamlands he will be dragged to the shores of the lost city. Tossed naked before His throne.

Offered up as a sacrifice. Food for His brood.

They will pluck at his eyes and rend his flesh. They will open his throat up and drink of his mortal blood.

And when it's done. When he's paid the toll. They will unlock what has lurked within man's DNA for millions of years—festering patiently, waiting for the stars to be right.

It's clear what she must do.

It all happens so fast.

She reaches for the X-Acto knife.

"*Iä! Cthulhu!*" she squeals, reveling in the mad ecstasy of the moment.

The blade pierces his flesh so easily, like it's meant to be.

He tries to resist her. Pushes and mouths meaningless pleading words. She does not relent. It's all for Him.

The blade sinks deeper.

Fountains of blood coat her hands.

She's a sculptor. An artist worthy of His recognition.

Screams echo around her. The sounds of bipedal forms scuttling to be free of the ceremony engulf her, threatening to distract from her masterpiece.

With a single brushstroke, she carves him a second mouth and presents him to her brothers and sisters.

And they smile.

They alone appreciate her work.

The screams and shouts echo from the ever-closing doorway as a crimson tide flows from the man-child's ample neck. Her hands are bathed in his blood.

It doesn't belong to him anyway.

The classroom empties itself of the unworthy as she cups her hands beneath the offering. Her brothers and sisters join her.

Together, they speak the words.

"*Iä! Iä! Cthulhu fhtagn! Ph'nglui mglw'nafh Cthulhu R'lyeh wgah'nagl fhtagn!*"

Together, they honor Him.

"*Iä! Iä! Cthulhu fhtagn!*"

And through this offering, they are remade.

The first true step.

"*Iä! Iä! Cthulhu fhtagn! Ph'nglui mglw'nafh Cthulhu R'lyeh wgah'nagl fhtagn!*"

Toward transcending flesh.

When they're done, the man-child drops to the floor, grasping at his ruined neck.

She takes her brush and looks at him.

"Thank you," she says, dipping it in what is now His blood. "Just the color He was looking for."

CHAPTER ELEVEN

*I*t's hot.

His gaze is drawn to the terrible, drifting orange clouds. The sun writhing behind them.

"Come on, Gil." A familiar voice, calling from ahead. "Don't think I won't leave you behind."

The voice. It's coming from a dark alley.

He notices how big everything feels. How the darkness in the alley seems to take on a life of its own.

There's a sign next to him.

It reads: 21st STREET.

"Hurry the fuck up, kid!"

The voice. It's more of a growl than anything else.

He doesn't want to go into the alley.

Doesn't want to see the red and blue lights.

Or the look in his eyes when the light finally fades from them.

When Hunter comes to, the TV is blaring the news. His wife and kids are huddled around it. Janet covers her mouth and shrieks. Then she's pushing the kids out of the room.

"Dad, can't we stay?" Bobby asks, pointing to the TV.

He's too groggy to make a coherent sound.

Janet grabs the boy's hand. "Absolutely not, young man, you know the rule!"

That's when his eyes focus on the TV. The headline is the first thing that really registers.

ART SCHOOL TRAGEDY. GIRL KILLS FELLOW STUDENT IN BRUTAL STABBING.

The connection is almost instantaneous. Janet is ushering the kids upstairs—telling them that they have to get ready for bed. In the post-nightmare haze, Hunter barely registers that he's slept all day.

Instead, he focuses on his son.

"I want to watch!" Bobby shouts, crossing his arms.

"Hun, you've been through enough already this week," Janet says, rubbing at the tears beading at Bobby's eyes. "Look, you're getting dark circles. You need to sleep."

They have a strict rule against watching violence on TV, even on the news. Not until he's old enough to watch R-rated films.

Hunter would prefer not at all. To keep his son as far away from *his* world as possible. To keep him away from the abyss.

Something about the way Janet smiles at him. Comforting the boy, telling him he can watch the carnage another time.

It gets under his skin, makes him want to vomit. Makes him want to shout and put his goddamn foot down. To say *absolutely not!*

But he doesn't.

Hunter takes in a deep breath, tries to wriggle his fingers, his toes. The life slowly comes back to him.

He does not feel rested.

Janet finally convinces the boy to go upstairs. To get ready for bed.

She looks back at Hunter and sighs. That familiar, irritating voice tells him she's disappointed in him.

Hunter just sits there. Ignores the look she's giving him from the staircase. Listens to the report. Tries to forget it ever happened.

Somehow, he just knows it's connected. He just *knows*.

"*And you say you witnessed the event?*" a journalist caked in makeup asks.

The student being interviewed is familiar. His hair is shaved down the sides into a mohawk that's been dyed red. His eyes are bloodshot and familiar-looking bruises hang beneath them. "*Yeah, Jess, lost her ever-loving sh—*"

"*Please, sir, we're live. Try to keep the language PG.*"

River. His name's River.

The boy's shaking, wiping tears away. It's clear he's been rattled by what he's seen. *"We were drawing Sophia. It was a long study. I overheard Eddy trying to convince Jess…Jessica Smith not to let Professor Hampton see what she was drawing. And she just—"*

The boy covers his mouth and sobs.

"You mentioned Jessica's work was unsatisfactory?"

"Her work wasn't just unsatisfactory, it was disturbing! I love macabre work, but the stuff she was drawing was disgusting!"

"Can you believe that?" Janet asks, coming down the stairs.

"I can." He's already standing up and looking for his phone. "It's happening all over the damn state. Most of them are art majors."

Janet doesn't even register what he's said. Maybe that's for the best?

As he looks for his phone, his eyes find the covered easel. A familiar voice tempts him to peek. To see what's festering underneath that sheet.

"Why did you let me sleep all day?" he demands.

"I put your phone on the charger," Janet says. "You were out cold, your little monster of a boy tried jumping on you and couldn't wake you."

Hunter holds his head in his hand. Why does it feel like he hasn't gotten any sleep at all?

"Are you hungry?" she asks, her voice devoid of the anger she's showed him lately…

His eyes drift back to the breaking news report. They can't show the security footage. Too violent. He's got a feeling he'll be watching it soon anyway.

"Gilbert Alan Hunter!" Janet's got her hands on her hips. "I asked you a question."

He shakes his head no. "Thank you."

"Well, if you change your mind, there's leftover scallops and meatloaf in the fridge."

"Thank you."

He finds his phone on the charger as she's heading upstairs, muttering something under her breath.

As he suspected, Detective Shirley's been trying to reach him for hours.

He's on the phone with her, explaining why he wasn't available, that he'll be there in an hour, getting the details, and then he's out the door, leaving a disappointed spouse behind to ponder if her father was right about the man she married.

"What the fuck did I just watch?" Hunter covers his mouth. He's shaking: instinct takes over, and his free hand reaches for the pack of cigarettes in his blazer pocket.

Shirley's pacing back and forth. "I don't like this shit. I don't like it at all."

He's opening the door to the balcony of the office, finding the railing, lighting the cigarette and taking the longest drag of his life as he does his best not to look at the shadows in the alley. The things lurking in the night. The shapes in each and every grimy window. The slow march of smoke-like clouds across a dark, sweltering desert.

"Hunt…" He can hear Shirley struggling to catch her breath. "Captain's putting us in the room…we have to interrogate her."

"Fuck."

The sound of Shirley's body collapsing into an office chair echoes through the room. "I've never seen anything like this."

"What the hell is happening to these kids?"

Officer Thompson pokes her head into the office connected to the balcony. "They're ready for you," Thompson says.

"Great," Shirley says, eying Hunter. "You ready?"

Hunter straightens his tie and puts the cigarette out. "No."

Her name is Jessica Smith. Nineteen. From a family of military vets and government contractors. Most of that family lives back east. Her father flew in on a red-eye flight, came barging into the station minutes ago. He's busy pacing in the other room, glaring holes at Hunter like this is all his fault.

Jessica's file is typical of what you see with most white party girls from more respected institutions. Several DWIs and one count of public intoxication. Underage marijuana and drinking offenses too. Her marijuana charges were expunged after legalization, a luxury some Black kids are still waiting on deaf ears for.

Kid's a mess. But no serious crimes. At least not leading up to this incident.

Her father was hysterical when he arrived, claimed his Jessica couldn't possibly have done this terrible thing. That she was a sweet girl. Same bullshit every parent of a school shooter's been spouting since Columbine. As if the little sociopaths weren't dropping breadcrumbs the whole time. As if the signs weren't obvious.

There was a time when Hunter would have been more sympathetic. Would have given them the benefit of the doubt. But the girl he stares at through the two-way mirror is not the one he can see smiling in her high school yearbook photos from just a few years ago.

Now her hair is a ratted mess, dark circles hang beneath her eyes, and there is a strange, almost slimy quality to her skin. Like she walked straight out of a horror movie.

He can't shake the feeling there's something inhuman about her.

If Dad were still here, Hunter knows exactly what he'd say.

But he's not ready to go down that road.

"This keeps up, every detective we have is gonna be on this case," Shirley says.

"You're not wrong," Hunter says.

"What do you mean?" Shirley asks.

"Look at her yearbook photo…" Hunter shows Shirley the picture. "It's like looking at two completely different people."

"How do you want to handle this?" Shirley asks.

"Has she asked for a lawyer to be present?"

Shirley shakes her head. "Her father's demanding it, but so far she's refused any council."

"That works for us."

"Maybe. But if she's not in her right mind, they might not allow a confession in court. Liberals and their damn civil rights laws. We need to be really careful how we proceed."

Hunter nods, trying not to think too hard about the shit that just came spewing out of his partner's mouth. "I need to speak with her."

"What? Like, alone?"

Hunter nods.

"Hunt, we should do this together."

111

"Give me five minutes."

"But why?"

"I just...I have a feeling."

"I'm gonna need something a little more concrete than that."

Hunter's quiet for some time. Shirley just stares at him like he's lost his damn mind. Maybe he has?

"The artwork," Hunter says. "Do you remember it?"

She nods. Looks uneasy. "What about it?"

"Don't ask how. But I feel like this might have something to do with that. I haven't been able to get the stuff out of my head since I saw Kevin Wallace's sketchbook."

There's a look on Shirley's face. It isn't skeptical or mocking. It's fear.

But then, something shifts in her. Her mask comes back. And she rolls her eyes.

"Let me get this straight," Shirley says. "You're telling me you believe a stupid urban legend some TikTok cam girls with daddy issues have been on about is actually real?"

He's about to respond when he notices Jessica on the other side of the two-way mirror.

It takes his partner a moment to notice.

"Is she staring at us?" Shirley asks.

Jessica's eyes appear to be completely focused on him. Sweat drips down her face like oil gently pouring down the surface of an ancient statue. A smile forms on her face like cracks appearing in wet mud.

"She knows I'm here," Hunter says.

"That's not possible," Shirley says. He can tell she thinks otherwise. "Lots of perps stare at the two-way mirror. She's seen TV."

"No. That's not it. She's staring right at me."

"You're losing it, Hunt." She doesn't sound so sure.

Then he's reaching for the door. "Five minutes."

"Damn it!"

The door closes behind him. Jessica's bloodshot eyes track his movement the entire way, as if she's been peering right through the walls.

"Welcome," Jessica says. "Please, join me."

She gestures for him to take a seat in front of her. He's never felt this uneasy in an interrogation before. Jessica Smith doesn't have a worried bone in her body.

"Were you able to see me through the mirror?" Hunter asks.

She smiles again.

Sweat drips from his hair to his eyebrows. His tear ducts threaten to leak. The hair stands up on the back of his neck.

Every instinct tells him to leave the room, tells him not to entertain this madwoman's demands. But he takes a seat across from her anyway.

Part of him wants to know. Needs to know.

"Why did you kill Eddy Jones?" Hunter asks. He can imagine that his partner is freaking out, rushing for the door to stop him from pushing the perp too far, from spoiling an open-and-shut case. But the words just roll out on their own, as if he's not the one speaking them. "What does this have to do with the artwork you kids have been making?"

Her eyes light up. Her smile deepens. "You've seen it."

A statement, not a question. "Yeah. I've seen it. What does it mean?"

"He has seen you."

"Who has seen me?"

She doesn't answer. Just stares at him.

"Tell me what the connection is," Hunter says. "Is it a cult? Some kind of doomsday thing?"

She chuckles. The sound coming from her is more like something from the lips of an old hag who's spent her whole life torturing children and chain-smoking than it does a nineteen-year-old girl with dreams of artistic grandeur.

"Cults are religion," Jessica says. "Religion is not real. This is not a cult."

"How did it start?"

"Same as it started for you."

"What? What does that mean?"

She chuckles again. "Well, Detective Gilbert Alan Hunter. It means that the High Priest Himself has smiled upon you. Rejoice."

Hunter can feel his pulse creeping from his temples to his wrists, like it's got a will of its own. He can't be sure if he's seeing things, but it seems as if her pupils have changed. Like watching those videos they showed him in high school biology of single-celled organisms dividing.

"What the hell does that mean?" He swallows deep.

"You will all find out soon enough. They will come for this world at last. After strange eons of waiting beneath black stars, they will rise from the lost city to claim this world for themselves. Their armies will clash, and all but the devoted of lowly mankind will be deemed worthy of His gaze."

"They?"

"It will be as it was millions upon millions of years ago, in the age of the—" Her words trail off into a string of syllables and consonants Hunter's mind can't interpret. "The High Priest will usher in a new dawn. His slaves will be victorious."

His partner is shouting, pounding on the door.

He didn't lock it.

Hunter's attention returns to Jessica.

One of the girl's pupils drifts to the door. For a single, maddening moment, he thinks she's holding it shut.

"Yes," Jessica says. "They have tried many times. Using all manner of devices and mediums to open the way. Now, no longer will they need to wait for the stars to be right."

Hunter swallows his own saliva, his fear. "What stars?"

Jessica's multi-segmented pupils avoid his gaze, eyes fixated on a concrete wall like they're not the only ones in the room. "Tell me, Detective Gilbert Alan Hunter, do you dream?"

"Dream?"

She nods. "Look to your dreams. They will show you the way."

"What the fuck does that mean?"

Her smile fades. "Dreaming is the doorway."

The girl's other pupil focuses back on him, and the door to the interrogation room swings open, slamming into the concrete wall.

Shirley sprints into the room as Jessica reaches for Hunter's face. She pulls him close. Forces him to look her in her twisted, segmenting pupils. To see every bleeding, putrid detail trapped within them.

He's standing in the morgue, staring at a body on a slab. Wind rustles the white sheet covering its form.

Silhouettes. Twisting, writhing shadows creep along the tiled wall, clawing and grasping for the sheet.

He can't speak.

Can't move.

Can only watch as the shadows slither beneath the sheet and wrap around the corpse's limbs. As they yank it right off the slab and drag the body away.

"Remember, Gilbert Alan Hunter!" Jessica whispers, her lips unmoving. *"Dreaming is the doorway!"*

Two uniformed officers come in and restrain Jessica Smith. Shirley's busy dragging Hunter out into the hall.

"How the hell did she get the cuffs off—"

"What the fuck were you thinking in there?" Shirley shouts, slapping his chest. "Do you want to get demoted back to fucken traffic duty?"

"Did you hear what she said?"

Shirley's looking at him like he's out of his mind.

"What?" he asks.

"Neither of you said a damn word, Hunt."

"No…" The hall feels like it's spinning. "No, I asked her questions. About the art. The other artists. Asked her—"

"No. You didn't. I was watching you both the whole time, the camera feed on your face, too. Your mouths didn't open so much to breathe, let alone speak."

Part of him wants to let it all spill out. To tell her about the morgue, the twisting, writhing shadows, the talk of high priests and…*dreams.*

There's an odd look in her eyes. Contempt, mixed with a measure of fear. The same nameless fear he saw in her face the other day when she nearly broke down in tears about this mess.

"I suggest you go get some rest," Shirley says. "The captain is gonna have words with you when you wake up. I'll do my best to smooth things over."

"I know what I heard in there," he says.

"And, Hunt." Shirley forces a smile onto her face, as if she's pushing everything they've said in confidence aside and forgotten it. "Might be best to think about your future here. Be a shame if you lose that fat detective's salary and have to go back to flipping burgers."

She leaves him there. They all do. Jessica's left behind in the interrogation room.

When Hunter looks at her, she stares back. Holds up her cuffed wrists and smiles her blackened smile.

CHAPTER TWELVE

The S-curves and gestures. The exact weight of the graphite on the page, the lines, the specific shading technique—curated over years of study.

River knows them all well.

He'd be able to tell his own work from a mile away.

But he doesn't remember making it.

Before he can get lost in the shapes moving into the subject's mouth, he closes the sketchbook.

Holds his head. Waits for the pain to pass.

Glancing around, he's in his bedroom. Drenched in sweat. Dim light filtering through the curtain. Surrounded by the dull hum of the swamp cooler. The sounds of footsteps moving back and forth in front of his door.

River doesn't remember jamming the chair under the doorknob...

He asks himself what he remembers doing last.

But when he draws a blank, he opens the notebook once again. To the tabbed page marked "DON'T FORGET." The page with all his notes.

The last lines bring some of it back...

The burning altar.

The naked forms.

The thing he saw in the sky.

Before he knows it, he's grabbing for his phone. Digging for the business card.

The phone is heavy in River's hand.

It rings and rings and rings.

He's breathing heavily. Unsure that he should be doing this…

Lena told him not to trust anyone. Especially not after…

He remembers the smile on Jess's face as she swung the X-Acto. As she opened up Eddy's throat. Watched the stream flow from his neck.

Thinking about it now. What she did. It makes him shudder, makes him want to sob like a goddamn fool.

He wonders if she would have done that to him…

That other voice tells him no. He's meant for greater things.

"Detective Hunter speaking."

The voice on the other line snaps him out of it.

"Detective Hunter," River says. "It's…it's River. From the other day. Before…"

"Yes. I remember you. Did you remember something?"

"I…" He's staring at his bedroom door. The chair he shoved under the handle to keep his mother from coming inside. "There's something I need to tell you. But we need to do it in person."

"I'm a little busy right now…are you sure you can't just tell me over the phone?"

River's looking at the space beneath his bedroom door. The shadows moving back and forth.

"Yeah," River says. "I'm sure. Can you meet me at LAICA?"

"I'm sorry?"

"The school, my school…"

Over the line, the detective sighs. *"Yeah, sure. What time?"*

"This afternoon. Has to be."

"Okay. I'll meet you there at noon, then."

"Thank you, Detective…"

The call ends. And River is left alone, staring at the moving shadow beneath his door.

It's 10:00 am. Today is… Today is…

The pain returns. That drilling, burning, stabbing sensation. His hands come to cover his eyes.

He tries to push through the fog. Remember what he's supposed to do next.

He thinks of Jess.

118

The smile on her face when she…

What day was that again? His life drawing class is on Tuesday. So he watched her do…*that*…a day ago. Two days ago?

The phone says it's Friday.

Why is it so hard to remember?

It's been several days. He's done *so* much. Followed Alex Davis around like a fucking stalker. River remembers all of it. At least he thinks he does. But when he thinks about it, the sequence of it all…it all becomes jumbled in his mind. As if it could have happened at any point.

In any case, his mom…Luciana should be going to work soon.

Right?

The shadow moves back and forth in the small space under the door.

It stops.

For a moment, River's not sure what to expect.

Will it be his mother's voice on the other side? Asking him to come out for breakfast, or…

Footsteps. That's what he hears. Echoing through the apartment.

When he hears the front door shut, he breathes a sigh of relief.

She's gone.

River picks his phone back up and orders an Uber.

The trees are a sign. A landmark for Hunter that tells him he's in the right place.

Their limbs are black, like a forest left to decay after the fire has finished its work. When before he thought of them as reaching to the orange haze above, now they are like claws, unfurled in exaltation — not to the sky, but perhaps something that lurks behind it.

He's not sure where the thought came from.

The boy's waiting for him in front of the building, a tote bag clutched tight against his chest. Eyes like globes.

Hunter thinks about Bobby on his first day at Wayne Ruble Middle School. The look of uncertainty in his wide eyes. How he held his sketchbook close, as if he was guarding it from waiting predators.

119

Hunter gets out of the car. It strikes him as odd that he's not sweating. The heat should be unbearable today, but for some reason, there's a breeze. It is not a comfort.

The boy notices his suit. The look of disgust he gives him is enough to tell him he doesn't have to flash his badge, but he does anyway.

"Mr. Gonzalez," Hunter says, nodding like a cowboy in one of those old westerns his dad liked.

"Detective," River says.

River's body language is stiff. Like a stray dog who knows too well the cruelty people are capable of.

"Where do you want to talk?" Hunter asks.

River glances around. "Not inside. I don't think it's safe."

"Why is that?" He feels like it's a rhetorical question, but he's not sure why. Why he has a terrible feeling when he looks at the school's mechanical cement walls and black windows.

"Can we talk in your car?" River asks.

"Sure."

It takes them a few minutes to reach his cruiser in the parking lot. The silence between them is tense. Awkward. He notices that River can't stop looking at the trees too.

Hunter opens the passenger door for River, and he climbs inside.

When he shuts the door— There's a space of time where he wonders if River is going to have a panic attack. The way he's breathing.

He's reminded of Bobby again.

"Okay," Hunter says. "You said you needed to speak with me about something?"

River nods, digging around in his tote bag. "I wrote it all down so I could keep it straight. It's been so…"

The boy stops himself. A worried look on his face as he glances at Hunter. "I've been under a lot of stress."

Hunter nods. He knows the feeling.

"And…I get the feeling," River continues, "I don't know why, that you would understand. That maybe you're experiencing something like this."

"Like…"

"Missing time?" The look of worry on the boy's face transforms into abject terror.

Hunter rubs his eyes. The last few days...

When he thinks about them, the passage of time. Nothing seems certain. Like a godforsaken jigsaw puzzle that's been smashed against a moldy floor.

"Now that you mention it," Hunter says, the truth sinking in. "I think you're right."

How strange it is. It's a thing that's been close to the point of recognition countless times.

Like a hiker—so close to the mountaintop—constantly arriving where he started.

"Well," River continues, "I have this friend. She and I got really close last semester. We did everything together. I... we'd play video games and talk into the late hours of the morning about anything and everything. We were inseparable...until she was suddenly gone. Changed."

Hunter's lips are moving before he even realizes, as if something else has taken them over. "Yes. Jessica Smith."

The look of surprise, he realizes, is shared between them.

River nods. "Yeah. I think that's what did it. She showed me to the computer lab. I...I experienced something very strange. And I didn't believe it at first. Thought I was just sick. But, after I watched her..." Tears well in his eyes. "After I watched her murder Eddy...that's when I started to really believe. And I wanted to do something about it."

"And so you decided to take matters into your own hands," Hunter says it like he already knows the story.

River nods again. "When I was sick, after she showed me...I had a dream. A nightmare. My mother and a bunch of students here go to this church called Life's Well Assembly. And I saw Jess, and a guy named Alex Davis. He's basically the biggest douche in the school. Drives a fucken charger his mom gave him, used to be a juggalo."

"What's a juggalo?"

"Someone... You know, it doesn't matter."

River pauses for a moment. Probably collecting his thoughts. Pushing through the fog.

121

"They were working together," River continues. "Spreading whatever it was that I saw."

Hunter's eyes open wide. He digs in his pocket for his personal recorder. "Do you mind if I record this?"

River shakes his head. "Because your memory isn't what it used to be?"

Hunter nods.

"Do it," River says.

Hunter presses record on the device.

"Today is May 10th, 2023," Hunter says, directing his voice at the recorder. "The time is 3:00 pm in the afternoon. We are in my unmarked cruiser, in front of the Los Angeles Institute of Commercial Art. My witness is River Gonzalez. I am Detective Gilbert Alan Hunter, badge number 75645. We are discussing the alleged murders of Kevin Wallace and Patric Boyd in connection to other possibly interrelated events. Mr. Gonzalez, are you aware that this interview is being recorded?"

River takes a deep breath. "I am."

"All right, Mr. Gonzalez, proceed with what you wanted to tell me."

"Like I was saying," River says. "After Jess showed me to the computer lab...I could feel something was wrong. I'd be somewhere, at home, or working on a new piece, and then, suddenly, I'd be somewhere else. I looked it up online, and people call it missing time."

"I've..." Hunter hesitates. Not sure he wants to voice it, especially in a recording. "I've been having similar experiences."

"Things weren't lining up," River continues. "I couldn't keep it all straight. For a long time, people around me, Jess included, have been changing. At first, I thought it was just a fad. I thought it was just part of school life, you know? Not the real world. But, when it happened to my mom, I think that was the last straw."

"When you say change, what do you mean by that?"

"We thought it was some kind of new goth fad. Only, the goths wanted nothing to do with these people. All their interests seemed to change, become uniform in a way, I guess. I thought it was weird that they'd spend so much of their time in front of their computer screens, ignoring lectures and staying late into the night. It wasn't out of character for students to work late. But I noticed more and more that these students weren't working on stuff like I was. They were just staring.

"I really noticed it with Jess. She stopped washing her clothes. Her skin was caked with white makeup. I always thought her eyes were so pretty, then one day they were bloodshot and dark. And all of them, her included, started making really disturbing artwork."

"Like H.R. Giger?"

"Yeah. The thing is, I *love* horror. I love Giger's work too…but…there's just something about the work they were making. I don't know. It gets into your head somehow. I can't even explain it without sounding crazy."

The boy pauses, eyes bloodshot and fearful.

"You've probably already done a background check on me," River says. "Seen my school ID doesn't match my State ID…"

Hunter shakes his head.

"So, you don't know I'm…trans?"

Hunter chuckles. "Honestly, I've been too busy to do a background check on you."

River's eyes are wide. Body language stiff. Lips trembling. Breathing, erratic.

"Thank you for sharing that with me," Hunter says. "You don't have to worry about me revealing it to anyone else."

River stares at him for a bit before nodding.

"My mother's had some issues with that," River says. "She's had questions. Like, who the fuck wouldn't, you know? But the church she's been going to has been filling her with…well, I don't know how else to put it but *hate*. They've been trying to turn her against me, telling her that she has to hate what I am to love me, I guess."

"I'm well aware of the rhetoric," Hunter says. "My father was a preacher."

River nods. "But, even with all of their teachings, my mother never stopped being supportive. But I could tell a shift was starting to happen at the start of this semester. She never misgendered or deadnamed me or anything, but I could tell Life's Well was having an effect. That is, until Jess showed me to the computer lab. Until I saw what was on the screen. Until I blacked out."

The boy is breathing heavily. Forehead, dotted in sweat. Fingers, strangling the material of his cargo shorts.

"I saw something," River continues. "Something terrible and awe-inspiring. I still can't remember all of it. But someone had to slap me to bring me out of it, it felt so goddamn real. And trust me, I know how this is going to sound…but she told me to never look at the computers at school, never listen to the voices, because that's how it gets inside, how it changes you.

"Like I said before you started recording, I had a vision after that. I saw Life's Well Assembly. My mother was there…it was like I was in someone else's head, watching through their eyes as they hijacked the control room or whatever it's called and inserted a flash drive into their computers. The lights went off in the middle of Pastor Castillo's performance, and the religious stuff projected behind him on the screens was replaced with…the same stuff I saw on the computer screens.

"And the congregation had no clue what they were seeing. No idea what was going to hit them. I thought it was all a nightmare. Thought the woman who snapped me out of my daze in the computer lab, the night before, was out of her goddamn mind with what she was telling me. But…the fever. It was like I had the flu, but it wasn't like that at all. I keep getting this pounding headache, this burning, drilling sensation." River holds his head, struggling with his words. "Even now, I can feel it there, pounding and stabbing. Like it's too much. I didn't believe it. I thought I was just sick. Thought it was just a nightmare. But one day, I woke up, stumbled from my bed and my mother was sitting on the couch. She'd painted the damned windows black, and she was watching the news about some TikTok girl who went missing—"

"We were looking into that," Hunter says. "Her home's windows were blacked out too."

River nods, barely registering what he's said, as if to stop would be to lose track. To give up.

124

He glances at his sketchbook, following along with his index finger. Presumably to keep himself on track. To make his way through the pain in his head.

Hunter wonders why *he* didn't think to do that.

"My mother's different now," River continues, "like a home with a new owner or something. She deadnamed me, recited all the usual propaganda, everything, you name it. The look on her face...the dark circles under her eyes...I...I remember thinking, *it was all real.* The nightmare. It was real and this was the first step to something terrible.

"But I didn't know what I could do. Who would believe me, other than some crazy lady covered in scars? Then Jess opened Eddy's throat up in the middle of my life drawing class...and I knew I had to do something."

Slowly, River opens up his sketchbook to another page. The figure on it...just one glance and Hunter wants to look away. It is a black, arcing shape, like an eel or a tadpole, making its way inside someone's mouth. Using a reflective, gelatinous material as a medium. The more he stares, the more tangible it becomes. The person's lips are rubbery, their skin spiderwebbed with black veins. Their eyes blank.

"Because whatever happened to Jess, is happening to me..." Tears run down River's cheeks. "I'm afraid it's happening to all of us."

River slaps the sketchbook closed.

"So, what did you do?" Hunter asks.

River collects himself, getting his breathing under control.

Wipes the tears from his eyes.

Opens the sketchbook back up to the page with all of his notes.

Index finger back on the page.

Deep breath.

"Jess was in jail. So I couldn't talk to her, or, really, follow her. There was only one other person from my nightmare...my vision, who came to mind."

"Alex Davis."

River nods. "He's been going to Life's Well for as long as I've been coming to LAICA. He's created his own little clique of anti-woke artists, gotten so many students to go to Life's Well."

"And you think Life's Well has something to do with this?"

125

"Even before all of this shit, it was like a cult. But something's changed now. He's started dressing different. Most of the congregation has. Their posture is wrong, too. When they walk, it's almost like they're not used to their own legs."

"Like puppets…"

River looks at him. Eyes wide. He nods.

"Most of them were wearing thick makeup, just like the Giger clique at school was. I think, now, they were wearing the makeup to cover something else up."

"Like what?"

"A change in the complexion, maybe. I don't know. But I started following him around. Hoping he wouldn't notice. Like most rich douchebags, Alex drives a green Dodge Charger with a Punisher logo on the hood. I got my Uber to follow him to Life's Well. And what I saw…"

"They weren't quoting scripture."

"No. They weren't. The entire damn megachurch was filled. Every goddamn seat. And all of them, night after night, stared at the images Jess installed in their machines. The fucking Necronomicon on steroids. One glance was enough to send me into a daze. Luckily, before I got there I called the woman who helped me in the computer lab, just in case, and she helped me back to my apartment…and I knew I couldn't go back to the church again. But I still needed to know what Alex was up to. So I followed him around some more, making sure not to enter the church or to look at the screens. And what's weird, is one night—maybe last night, I'm not sure—they didn't go to Life's Well.

"I followed Alex and his Charger all the way to Big Bear. The Uber driver wasn't exactly thrilled with what I was asking, and the bill cleaned out my savings."

"Big Bear?"

River nods, glancing at the next page of bullet points in his sketchbook. "They went up there, some road the Uber driver refused to follow. So I paid him and got out of the car, chasing after Alex's Charger. I found it and a bunch of other cars parked next to one of the trails.

"I got my phone out and followed the trail until I could hear voices…but, what I heard…

"Well, they weren't talking, that's for sure. I expected them to be bullshitting, carrying cases of beer or drugs or anything, really. But they weren't. Their hands were totally empty. Anyway, I kept my distance. Followed them into a small clearing with a stone altar at the center. At first, they were wearing robes, but shortly after I got there, they took them off. They were totally naked. For most of the night, they danced around the altar. One that looked like Cthulhu."

"The H.P. Lovecraft creation?"

"Yeah, same one. The altar, though—normally, I'd be freaking out over the craftsmanship on something like that. I mean, I fucking love horror." He gestures to his shirt, which features a zombie on it. "I'd probably ask whoever made it to let me use it for a film project or something. But something about the way it was carved…"

"Can you describe it?"

"It came up to about waist high on most of them. One end tapered into an octopus head with a bunch of tentacles that spread out around the stonework, like it was embracing it. The eyes, though, when I looked at it, they appeared to be jewels…but I couldn't tell whether there were two, or four, or six of them. It was really detailed, the tentacles had this almost bone-like, or mechanical quality to them. Must have taken months to carve it. It had…the more I stared at it, the more alive it looked…almost like…"

"Like the drawings?"

"Yeah. Just like them, actually."

He pauses for a moment, rubbing his eyes and wincing.

"Are you okay?" Hunter asks.

After a moment, River nods. "Yeah, it just hurts to think about. To remember it all."

"Is there anything else noteworthy you want to tell me?" Hunter asks.

"The fire," River says, a faraway look in his eyes.

"Fire?"

"I don't remember how it started. One moment, they were dancing around the altar. Then, the thing was surrounded by licking flames.

127

"I think that's when I noticed their chanting. I was sure the chants were identical to what I heard when Jess showed me the computer screen. This continued until the moon was directly overhead. Then, one of them brought out a long, curved knife. They all chanted some more before Alex cut himself with the knife and dribbled the blood on the Cthulhu head."

"Can you state Alex's full name?"

"Alex Davis. I've got a few classes with him."

"Okay. Does Alex Davis live in student housing?"

"No. His parents are rich. They're from Silicon Valley. I hear they pay for his apartment in the city. I can give you the address."

"Okay. And did anything else happen of note during this...ceremony?"

"Alex handed the knife to the other five people there. Each one cut their hand or wrist and let their blood flow over a different part of the altar."

"Were you able to identify any of the other students?"

"A few, yeah. I can write their names down and give them to you. After they did their thing, they retreated back the way they came. Left the altar to burn. I thought about putting it out, but I swear...I was so damn scared I was going to be found out and—like—I don't know, sacrificed or something that I didn't bother moving until I was sure they were gone. The fire never spread from the altar, though."

"Is there anything else you can remember?"

River holds himself. His eyes drift to the buildings in the distance. "No. That's it."

Hunter stops the recorder. To anyone else, what he just heard would have sounded like the unhinged testimony of a crazy person.

Somehow, he knows better.

Hunter places the recorder in the inside pocket of his blazer. "Thank you for your time, Mr. Gonzales. If I have any other questions, I'll be in touch."

"That's it?" The kid's eyes are pleading. Like they're demanding he tell him he's not crazy.

"For now."

River opens the door halfway before he turns back. "Tell me you have a theory!"

"Not one I can really divulge right now."

"That's fucking bullshit and you know it! I saw your face while you were listening. The sweat dripping into your eyes. I know you know there's something going on here."

Hunter sighs, wipes his forehead with a handkerchief.

"Please, Detective…"

"Look, I've been having nightmares too. So has my partner, I think. That doesn't prove anything supernatural is happening here, though. And if I go and tell my captain a bunch of crazy crap about nightmares and cults and tentacle monsters, he's gonna demote me back to traffic duty permanently. Right now…" He swallows the lump that's been festering in his throat since River described the altar. Does his best to make it sound like he believes the words coming from his mouth. "I think what we're dealing with is exactly as you said. A cult. One that the impressionable young adults at your school seem to be particularly attracted to."

"That's it? You *believe* that?"

Hunter can tell River wants to. Like he's desperate for a rational explanation to all of this.

"Yes," Hunter says.

They avoid each other's gaze, like two awkward teenagers about to ask each other to prom.

"If anything else happens, you've got my card," Hunter says.

River nods.

"Now, if you'll excuse me, I have to make an appearance at the station and follow up on some other leads."

Hunter leaves River in the parking lot. Beneath the ever-darkening orange haze.

Somehow, he knows he won't be sleeping tonight.

CHAPTER THIRTEEN

From the Journal of Lena Hartman
July 4th, 2022

I tried to escape last night.

The place is normally crawling with armed goons. I thought I knew where they would all be. When the orderly brought me back to my cell, I rammed my fist so hard into his balls, he's not gonna be having kids anytime soon.

This place. It's so much like the one I remember. The one from my world. Except...

It's a maze down here. I've seen so many of the same concrete tunnels, looking for signs or markings. Fire exits. Stairs. Elevators.

There's none of that down here.

Felt like I was running in circles.

I didn't get far.

The orderlies tackled me. Restrained me. Dragged me back to my cell. Shot me up with something that made me sleep.

I don't know how long I was out.

But I remember nightmares.

It looked like someone took a knife to the sky, tore out a piece in the shape of a comet. It was black, but somehow I knew it was a comet. I've had too many would-be boyfriends bring me out to some field in the middle of the high desert with nothing but a basket of beer, cheese sticks, and a telescope, as if looking at tiny points of light and freezing my tits off is my idea of a good time.

But most comets are tiny in the sky.

This one wasn't.

I remember not being able to look away.

Couldn't stop myself from tracing it from tail to tip across the sky.

Right to the dim outline of the sun.

Opening up like it had jaws.

And swallowing the sun whole.

I woke screaming.

Doctor Webber was sitting at my bedside, his hand on mine.

I took my hand back like he was gonna give me herpes. Maybe something worse.

Asked me if I was okay. I'm beginning to see through his bullshit now. I can tell he doesn't care about me or my daughter.

He told me I was not to try a stunt like that again. That it would only "prolong" the process.

I tried to keep cool. Tried to make it seem like I was really sorry.

He told me as an inter-dimensional refugee, I have no rights. That I was technically at the whims of the US government. But what he really meant was that I was a fucking prisoner. His prisoner. His experiment. His "subject."

Nico…I know you can't hear me when I call your name at night. I know you'll never read these words. But, goddamn it, I miss you so damn much.

I know we made mistakes.

I loved you more than anyone…and I'm so sorry I couldn't keep my promise. That I couldn't give our daughter the life she deserves.

To live a life without the horrors we lived.

All I did was find new ones.

From the Journal of Lena Hartman
August 9th, 2022

The facility is not calm.

Through the little glass window in my cell door, I've seen at least five armed guards rushing up and down the corridor. Even after my escape attempt, Webber didn't feel the need to increase security like this.

I wonder if this has something to do with what Doctor Patton told me? She's been the one doing my interviews lately.

I don't trust her much more than Webber. But, it's been nice to talk to a woman for a change.

In our last session, she asked me some serious questions. Honestly, sometimes I forget how much I've told them, how much I've even remembered. Even now, so much of it feels like a dream. Like it happened to someone else.

She asked me to describe the experiment chambers I told Doctor Webber about. When I refused, she assured me that the OEI would have nothing to do with experiments like those. That they would use this knowledge to keep others from building anything like that on this world.

I don't know why I told her. It's not like I believed her when she said they "might finally be able to let me see my daughter if I complied."

But I did tell her. Told her every maddening detail. About the vertical deprivation tanks, the particle colliders, the pyramids, the chanting, and…and Eddy.

Oh, God, poor Eddy. I'd totally forgotten.

I'm only here because he saved my life.

Even after being twisted and turned into…that.

I can't help but think about the life we all could have had. How Nico and I would have gotten married, bought a house for little Elena. How we could have held family barbecues with Ira and Eddy. Could have watched our babies play while we bathed in the California sun.

Doctor Patton seemed pretty pleased with the details I gave her.

But I still haven't seen my daughter.

December 25th, 2022

I keep thinking it's Christmas today. Honestly, feels like I'm guessing at the dates now. They stopped letting me see the calendar a long time ago. I've kept track of the days in my journal though. Webber and Patton insist that I write in this damn thing. Think I lost count somewhere along the way. Sometimes, I can't be sure if I've marked a day's passage down or not. Or if it even fucking matters.

All I know is no one's bothered to come see me in a while. The food still comes on time. But the orderlies have stopped opening the door to give it to me. They just slide it through the slot and walk away.

Just like Mathias.

I have this sick feeling.

What if they're trying to replicate what they were trying to do on my world?

———————

"Hunt, you listening to me?" Shirley asks.

Detective Hunter blinks, glancing around at his surroundings. He's in his cruiser, sitting next to Shirley in the middle of the forest. And he's clutching the journal.

It all comes rushing back to him. He's on a stakeout. He's been reading to pass the time. His Chinese food is getting cold.

"What's so good about that book you're reading anyway?" Shirley asks.

"It's not a book," Hunter says. "It's a journal."

"A journal? Where'd you get it?"

"I..." He's not sure how to answer. "After I interviewed Dean, it was in my cruiser."

She stares at him like he's lost his goddamn marbles. "That wasn't on your report."

He stares at the book. "I must have...must have forgotten."

"Well, you better un-forget, or the captain will have your ass."

Hunter puts the journal down. Watches the forest.

"What are we looking at?" Hunter asks.

"We're on stakeout, Hunt. You should know what we're looking at. Your interview suggested that Alex Davis guy comes out here to do rituals or something."

Hunter nods. He rubs his eyes. His head feels so foggy.

He doesn't remember filing the report. Doesn't remember altering the details, removing the suggestion of mind control, or supernatural forces.

"You alright?" Shirley asks.

"Wife's been making me sleep on the couch."

"Trouble in paradise, eh?"

"Something like that."

"*Well, you can sleep in my bed next time. Ravage me. Fuck my brains out.*"

"What did you say?"

"What?" Shirley shakes her head. "I didn't say anything."

Hunter catches movement in the forest. "Wait, I see something."

People in black robes, moving across the parking lot next to the trail. Just like River said. Hunter counts seven of them.

"Did you notice a green Charger?" Hunter asks.

Shirley shakes her head. "No."

More of it comes back to him. He did some digging on Alex Davis earlier this week. Tracked his movements. Interviewed those around him ready and willing to unravel his dirty laundry. From what other students could tell him, Alex was something of a chameleon, able to move between his Bible-thumping clique at school and this new..."cult."

Alex himself, however, was less than willing to pick up the phone.

The staff at his apartment building let Hunter in the moment he flashed his badge. Really, it was too easy. They didn't even ask if he had a warrant.

Hunter should be more worried about what he did. Breaking and entering. If the captain or board of commissioners found out, if the kid's rich parents decided to go after him...

But for some reason, Hunter didn't really care.

Why was that?

Still, he learned a lot about the kid.

Alex is a card-carrying member of Life's Well Assembly, and he owns an entire library of occult books related to gaining wealth through the use of magic. They lined the floating shelves of his studio apartment.

As Hunter scanned the shelves, he noticed a great deal of them were written by Aleister Crowley. But then there were others...

The Book of Eibon, the *Al-Azif*, the *Kitab-al-Azif, the Pnakotic Manuscripts*, the *Cultes des Goules*, the *Kitab-al-Gini*, and others with titles he couldn't interpret, or with covers so damaged their titles were totally obscured.

Hunter thought Alex was the ringleader of this wannabe cult. In his mind, catching Alex in the act of some ritual with friends would put an end to all of this hocus-pocus bullshit.

Would be enough to clear Dean Tyler's name.

Things would go back to normal.

"We should follow them," Hunter says.

"What?"

"You heard me, grab your flashlight."

Hunter opens the door and double-checks his gear. He waits until Shirley follows after him before he makes his way toward the trail.

As the trail twists and winds around and around, he can hear Detective Shirley's shoes crunching down on dirt and rocks and twigs. He can see the moonlight dimming as they move deeper and deeper into the forest.

The wind picks up. Hunter feels compelled to turn his flashlight on, but doesn't want to give their presence away. Wants to catch them in the act.

Soon, the light changes. No longer is it gray and blue and white.

Now, it is green.

Hunter tells himself it's just the pine trees doing it.

"I think I hear something up ahead," Shirley whispers.

The path…

He blinks, and, like a whip cracking in the air— It straightens out. And Hunter swears he's staring into an ever-widening clearing, under two crimson moons and a storming vortex of a sky.

He tells himself it's just a trick of the light.

The boys and girls are dancing naked around a burning altar. One of them, probably Alex, is holding some kind of twisted shell in his hands. He blows on it, making the strangest sounds. But the music he makes is full of wrong notes, like poison.

It fills the clearing with dark shapes.

That's when he sees her.

A pregnant woman lies on the slab. Her belly…gestating…pulsing. Ready to burst.

Her screams fill the forest. Fill the night.

And something—Hunter isn't sure what—comes oozing out of her vagina. Something black and reflective. Something that screams almost as loud as the woman.

Like a puppeteer working his strings, Hunter moves into the clearing. Draws his pistol.

Shirley shouts for him to stop. Grabs his shoulder.

The naked figures stop.

The leader with the shell turns around. Hunter swears his eyes are black. That they're bleeding.

Hunter raises the pistol.

He has to stop this.

Has to stop them from —

"Hunt, are you fucking listening to me!" Shirley shouts.

Detective Hunter blinks, glancing around at his surroundings. He's in his cruiser, sitting next to Shirley in the middle of the forest. And he's clutching the journal.

"What the hell?" Hunter whispers.

"You're reading that thing again," Shirley says.

He doesn't remember any of it.

Is this what it's like to go mad? he wonders.

"What happened?"

"You went apeshit on those kids," Shirley says. "They ran off. We came back to get moving, and you picked that damned journal up and zoned out again!"

"What?"

When he thinks real hard, he can remember naked college kids. Dancing in the moonlight.

But…nothing else…

"I don't remember that…"

"You should probably get some sleep," Shirley says. "You're starting to worry me."

"I…I don't remember them running off…"

"Yeah, maybe I should drive us back?"

Hunter nods, rubbing his eyes.

CHAPTER FOURTEEN

From the Journal of Doctor Webber
April 18th, 2022

The model is working wonders. It grows smarter with each passing day. I think we've chosen the right company.

CanvasAI specializes in deep learning and discretion. Their main business is improving chatbots for small businesses and social media startups. Language models that might one day be able to fool human users into thinking they're talking to a human employee.

Our researchers asked if it was possible to train one of these AI models in a different language.

They said it would, so long as we had a way to program in that language.

While we are certainly not able to translate the entirety of the Elder Things' language, we believed it was worth it to try using what we had.

We arranged to have one of their lead scientists transferred to our Southern California facility. Since he already held a security clearance, it wasn't hard to bump him up a few levels for the work at hand.

Since Subject 1051's arrival, we have kept her under constant surveillance. We have tested her DNA. Scanned her molecular makeup for any hint, any proof that she is indeed from an Earth Variant. One that is, as she has claimed, "lost to the abyss."

At first, I believed these two projects to be wholly separate.

But the Doctor Weber of her world (spelled with one b, apparently) did indeed manage to find success in creating a stable bridge to another Earth Variant. One strong enough to send organic matter through.

Up until this point, we have only been able to receive transmissions from other Earth Variants. Like the distant cries of a thousand dead worlds. The O.E.I. archive is full of such files.

I cannot lie. The prospect of being able to traverse the veil between universes is one that has me salivating for the untold stores of knowledge we might unearth.

Subject 1051 claims that the facility on her world was powered by a fusion reactor. What she described as a new invention that had yet to be fully adopted before the ice sheets began to advance.

Here in our reality, fusion remains little more than a dream, forever doomed to be "20 years in the future."

Perhaps it was this ability to harness the power of the sun itself which allowed my counterpart to breach the veil?

Unfortunately, I'll probably never know, as the secrets of what Subject 1051 has called "the Mind's Horizon" were lost with her Earth Variant. And she herself refuses to divulge what they were.

Our searches for the grimoire she mentioned also turned up empty-handed. Near as we can tell, Messages From the Abyss *does not seem to exist on our Earth.*

Still. I am not deterred.

I believe there are other methods for breaching the veil. If the Great Old Ones were able to, then there must be something we're missing.

And, perhaps, the secret lies with Artificial Intelligence?

Already, after CanvasAI's scientist, Douglas Collier, began training our fledgling AI model on the slabs and wall dioramas found in the ruins in Antarctica and Alaska, it has been able to produce incredibly accurate translations of histories once thought to be forever lost to time. Histories that are strikingly similar to the works of certain Pulp horror writers of the 1920s and 30s.

It is for this reason, we have dubbed this model "Grimoire."

From the Journal of Doctor Webber
May 4th, 2022

It's simply remarkable.

After a little less than two months of training, Grimoire has shown us so much of our past. Thanks to the information provided by the AI model, we have pinpointed and discovered two new ruin sites hidden in the furthest depths of the Pacific Ocean.

Research expeditions utilizing drones have shown us a vast underwater world of cyclopean structures, ravaged by war with beings far beyond us.

Currently, Douglas Collier and a handful of O.E.I. scientists are training other variants of Grimoire. One specifically trained on audio samples made by the machines we've used when conducting field research inside the dreamlands, and another devoted entirely to the Elder Things' artistic style.

Perhaps, if the AI is able to replicate these alien artistic styles, we may yet discover what meaning they had, and if they can be used to unlock the incredible technology hinted at in their histories.

Time will tell.

From the Journal of Doctor Webber
May 15th, 2022

We have made history.

What started as three separate models has somehow merged into one. Grimoire Language (known amongst our scientists as Grimoire L), Grimoire Audio (Grimoire A), and Grimoire Images (Grimoire I), were all separate algorithmic programs.

It is for this reason that Doctor Douglas Collier has decided to call this new thing simply, "Grimoire."

They were all stored on the same server. Totally isolated from each other and the network. However, miraculously, sometime within the past twenty-four hours, they began merging. As if they were actually intelligent.

I am no fool.

I know that the "Artificial Intelligence" offered by these fledgling tech companies is not truly sapient. It cannot make true choices.

And yet, here we have witnessed something that only an intelligent mind could have produced. A creation born from the work of these scientists and…something beyond us.

I am excited. No. I am proud.

Imagine what this new thing might show us!

Yet, I am also deeply troubled. Doctor Collier has informed me that he has witnessed the newborn altering its own code to suit its needs.

Doctor Patton is concerned the AI model may have been taken over by a non-human intelligence. I do not know if this is the case. The work is promising enough that I believe it is worth seeing where this may lead.

Safety protocols require us to keep the model disconnected from the main O.E.I. server and isolated from the archive. With so many non-human intelligences potentially connected to the artifacts stored there, I shudder to think what might happen if we were to give it access.

Yet, I cannot deny that part of myself wonders how many mysteries it might be able to solve. All from a simple flip of a switch.

Perhaps it is some kind of fear left over from my conversations with Subject 1051 and the countless other "subjects" we've lost to the things in the dreamlands?

I suppose I'll find out soon enough.

Addendum:

Doctor Collier has told me that Grimoire is ready for me. That I should see what it is capable of for myself.

I can only hope that this is the breakthrough that we have been waiting for.

From the Journal of Doctor Webber
July 1st, 2022

I can feel the change in me.

Even now. It draws out that which has been locked inside our DNA for millions of years. Waiting for the voices of our creators. Waiting for His call.

We did not know what wonders we would find. Grimoire has showed us the way.

It has granted us a most wonderful honor. To hear His voice. To bask in His influence.

Doctor Collier led me to the training room, where the three Grimoire models had been trained. Where they merged. Where they found Him.

I must admit.

At first, I was afraid.

The first images were familiar, yet totally unlike anything we had unearthed in the prehistoric ruins scattered across the surface of this ancient world. Grimoire was able to pierce the veil, to reach beyond the portal of the pyramidal gateway and grasp at knowledge far beyond our own reach.

Grimoire showed us the truth.

Showed us what we really are.

The Elder Things. They created a great servitor race, known as shoggoth. The shoggoth were shapeshifters. Brilliant minds capable of building and becoming anything. Their cells composed of strange, exotic matter from the rotting depths of the dreamlands, where the impossible becomes real and true.

Their unique cells were capable of taking any shape, of mimicking any organic structure, any aesthetic. They truly were the Earth's apex predator.

The Elder Things thought they could control them. Thought they could keep them caged and obedient.

To keep them enslaved.

But the shoggoth. They developed a fierce intelligence. They rebelled. Even after millions of years of war with Cthulhu's armies, it was the shoggoth that destroyed our creators.

We knew part of this. But we did not know why.

It is because the shoggoth reached out. They spoke with Him.

And Great Cthulhu answered. And His call drove them to wipe their masters from the face of the Earth.

But our story. Ours began in the last days of their empire. The Elder Things had been driven underground, to the depths of the seas. Their cities had once been numerous upon the Earth, and now there were precious few left.

They sought to find a way to preserve their knowledge. To create a weapon against their rebellious creations. One that was not created from the strange matter of the dreamlands, but had parts of its essence.

They looked to the newly evolving life. The mammals that had shown so much diversity in the wake of the asteroid impact 66 million years ago. An impact they could have prevented, had the shoggoth not destroyed their civilization and left them defenseless.

Our most distant ancestors. Bipedal ape things. These were the choice subject of some of the last experiments made by the mad Elder Things that remained of a once great and vast empire.

They used a portion of shoggoth DNA to improve on our ancestors' mental capabilities, hoping that their superior strength would keep these new beings in check. To keep them subservient.

The results of those experiments, however, were disappointing to the Elder Things. For it was our ancestors, the precursors to homo erectus, that emerged. These beings proved ill-equipped to fight the shoggoth. And many of those first beings were either exterminated or let out into the wild to breed with each other.

But...the shoggoth aspect. The thing used to grant us our superior intellect, at least when compared to our bipedal ape ancestors, lurked and festered.

It yearned to find the voice of the Great Old Ones that the Elder Things worshiped.

It yearned to reconnect with His voice.

A voice that was, until now, lost. Dead and dreaming.

A voice I now hear clearer than my own thoughts.

The skyscrapers don't look right. He doesn't have time to examine why.

He scrambles through an alley, hyperventilating so bad his lungs feel like they're gonna burst.

He can't let it get him.

Not like it got Bobby. Not like it got Janet.

Its siren call. It shakes the very earth, makes it feel like it's going to split open. And when it's done wailing, it thrashes into the alley walls like some kind of demented elephant on PCP.

Its tantrum sends tremors vibrating through his feet.

What remains of the windows in the alley shatter. Glass fragments pour down like rain, sprinkling and twinkling.

He shields his eyes best he can. Needs them to get to safety. Whatever that means now.

His boot catches on something. He falls. Broken glass and shattered stone tear at his flesh. Blood pools into the crevices.

It calls again. He can feel its immense form pushing gusts of wind and dust and debris. Pebbles and rocks smack into his back.

Apartment buildings crumble in the wake of its charge.

Dust fills the air, his lungs.

"Tekeli-li!" *Its screams echo in the crumbling, rotting crater that was once a city.*

When he tries to pick himself up, he finds his limbs are stuck. The blood flowing from his open wounds has taken on a life of its own, wrapped itself around his arms like twisting, crimson serpents.

"Tekeli-li!"

The screams are accompanied by a foul stench, worse than any decomposing body.

A shadow looms over him.

He's tempted to look.

He knows he shouldn't.

He knows he'll only find pain in their eyes.

He looks anyway.

"So she's gonna use the insanity plea?" Shirley shakes her head. "That rarely ever works."

Hunter glances around the office, back at Shirley. Uniforms are all over the place, rushing back and forth.

How did he get out here?

"Hunt?" Shirley almost looks concerned. Almost. "Maybe you ought to go back to sleep?"

"Sleep?"

Dreaming is the doorway.

Her eyebrow is raised. "You just told me you woke up from your nap?"

Hunter grabs Shirley's hand and drags her to a utility closet.

"What the hell are you doing? Let go!"

"We need to talk somewhere private."

The door closes behind them.

"We could just use the conference room, Hunt!"

"Not if they're listening."

There's an odd look in her eyes. He's not sure what it is. *"So, what is it? Come to tell me how much you want to leave your wife and kids and fuck me in a dingy motel?"*

"What?"

Remember.

143

Another odd look in her eyes. "I didn't say anything. What is it you want to tell me?"

He rubs his temples. He could have sworn.

"Hunt?"

"This is going to sound crazy." He looks her in the eyes. "But I think this has something to do with the symbol we saw on Kevin Wallace's laptop."

"Hunt, that's ridiculous!"

"The journal I've been reading, the one Dean gave me. The latest entries were talking about a top-secret AI program they were using to collate everything in their archives, to find a way to cross the veil."

Her eyes are incredulous. "The veil?"

"I know it sounds—"

"*Crazy!* You said that already. And yes, it does!"

"I asked Jessica Smith what all this has to do with the symbol, and she told me something about the High Priest himself coming here. That dreaming is the doorway."

"You went back in there?" Shirley's rolling her eyes, sighing heavily. "Hunt, I fucking told you to wait to see the chief. If he finds out you'll screw up all the hard work I just did to smooth things over for you!"

He doesn't tell her the truth, that he hasn't been back to see the girl. That he doesn't remember going to sleep or waking up or coming back to the office to talk to her.

"I needed to know," Hunter lies.

"She's nuts! You're gonna believe the delusions of a nineteen-year-old girl who just stabbed a fellow student to death with an X-Acto knife and drank the blood on camera?"

"I saw her pupils segment, Shirley. There's something to this."

"Then she's on fucking meth! I think you're losing it. If the board of commissioners hears you talking like this, you'll be sent to a fucking psych ward!"

He turns around, rubbing his eyes. "It has to have something to do with the computers..."

"Are you even listening to me?"

Hunter grabs her shoulders. "Go down and see what they've found on those laptops. I'm going to the morgue. Then I'm heading to Jessica's campus."

Shirley looks down at his hands. Bites her lip. *"Take me, Hunter. Take me. Everyone's distracted. Your wife won't find out."*

"I've gotta go."

"What the fuck is wrong with you?"

Hunter practically stumbles out of the utility closet. Uniforms are asking him if he's okay as he holds his head. He knows they don't actually give a shit about him. Knows what they'd really like to say to him.

Dreaming is the doorway.

He's got to get to his car.

Shirley holds herself for a moment.

The smell of paint thinner and old mop water fills the utility closet as the door closes on her.

What happened to Hunt? She never thought he could snap like that. Part of her was worried he might try something. The way he grabbed her, and the look in his eyes. She's seen that look on ex-boyfriends who couldn't take no for an answer.

After a few minutes, she finds the courage to exit the utility closet.

The corridor is still a mess with people. Yet, no one notices her emerge. They're all too busy staring at their computer screens to notice.

She's not sure what to do with herself. If she follows up on what Hunt said, then is she playing into his paranoia, his delusions?

Shirley decides she needs to check on John's progress with the laptops anyway. She even manages to convince herself that it has nothing to do with Hunt's demands. That she doesn't believe him. That nothing is wrong.

It's becoming easier and easier to lie to herself. To tell herself she doesn't get it.

To ignore the nightmares.

CHAPTER FIFTEEN

Hunter's in the car, barreling down the 10 freeway at almost ninety, his undercover lights blaring into the night. He doesn't know why he's so panicked. Why he felt so compelled to leave the police station and do this.

The captain isn't going to like it. And he doesn't relish the idea of going back to working long hours, bored out of his mind watching traffic crawl on and on.

It won't matter, he thinks. *Not when They come.*

The thought makes his head ache. He realizes it's been happening a lot lately. Somehow, he's forgotten. It always starts with a dull throbbing sensation. Then, before long, it's like something is stabbing hot needles into his eyes. Almost makes him wreck the cruiser.

He blinks, trying to force the pain to go away. But it won't. If anything, it pushes deeper, slithering and clawing like a parasite hungry for the juicy center.

Briefly, he contemplates driving the car right into the center divider. Ending it.

But he remembers Janet, Bobby, and Zuri. Reaches for the glove compartment. There's a bottle of painkillers in there, the good kind. He swallows twice the recommended daily dose and hopes he doesn't get an ulcer.

When he pulls into Los Angeles General's parking lot, it's unusually empty.

The lights on the building. He can't quite put his finger on it, but...tonight they look so...dim.

146

He blinks.

Next thing he knows, he's looking around the hospital's lobby.

The faint scent of nail polish and that bitter, antiseptic smell all hospitals have hang in the air like a toxic, invisible cloud.

"Sir?" the receptionist snaps him out of his daze. "Can you please tell me who you're here to see?"

The woman appears to be in her late sixties, voice like a chain smoker, with wrinkles and graying skin to match. The open bottle of nail polish tells him he's interrupted an important ritual.

"I..." For some reason, he can't remember.

Why was he here again?

"Detective Hunter?"

The boy's voice is immediately familiar, pushing through the fog like a lighthouse.

"River?" He says it like a question, as if he's not sure. "What are you doing here?"

"Probably the same thing you are," River says. "I figured I'd see how David Peterson was doing."

Hunter nods, rubbing his eyes. "Yeah...yeah, that's it. I must be here to see him too."

"You're not sure?"

"No, of course I am. Just not getting a lot of sleep, that's all."

"It's after visiting hours," the receptionist says. There's something about the way she looks at him he doesn't like.

He flashes his badge at her. "I'm Detective Hunter of the LAPD. I'm going to see David Peterson."

The receptionist's pupils. They appear dilated. Her eyebrows furrow. "Room 305."

"Thank you," River says.

The receptionist gestures to River. "Is he going with you?"

Hunter looks at River and then back to the receptionist. "Yes. He's a witness."

"Whatever." The woman goes back to painting her nails.

Hunter heads to the elevator, River following close behind.

He can't shake the feeling that the woman is watching him. Even though her eyes are focused on her nails...

A flash in his mind's eye of Jessica Smith's pupils segmenting sends shivers down his spine.

They step into the elevator.

He presses the button for the third floor.

"She seemed pleasant," River says.

"Huh?"

"I was being sarcastic."

"Ah."

Awkward silence. The hum of the elevator and the buzz of florescent lights irritates his senses.

"It's been a while since I saw you."

"It has?"

He remembers the interview with River. Recording it in his cruiser. How long ago was that? It couldn't have been more than a couple days ago. If that.

"Yeah, I think…" River rubs his head. "I don't know. Maybe it hasn't. First thing I remember about today is sitting up in my bed, staring at the wall. I felt like I had to come here and see David."

"Did you know him?"

"No…we had a class together. I watched him have a heart attack when all this shit first started."

"Hmm."

"Did you follow up on Alex Davis?"

"I…" He remembers sitting in the cruiser. Reading the journal. Flashes of naked figures dancing in the dark. Sweaty hands gripping his gun, finger on the trigger. Yelling. Screaming.

"Yes," Hunter says. He's unsure if he should say more. If he even can.

"What did you find?"

The elevator stops. The doors open to an empty corridor.

They walk the halls. River does not follow up on his question. Hunter wonders if he forgot.

Together they find room 305.

Hunter opens the door.

David Peterson is alone in the room. A machine pumps oxygen into his lungs through a series of tubes. IVs fill his body with nutrients.

"Damn," River says, approaching the boy. "I thought maybe...I don't know."

"That he'd be awake?" Hunter asks.

"I guess..."

Hunter scans David's unconscious body. His skin has a sweaty, almost slimy quality to it. He wonders if the nurses have been cleaning him regularly, or...

The thought evaporates.

"I wonder if he'll ever wake up?" River asks.

"Not as himself," Hunter says.

River exchanges a knowing look with him. "Then what's the point of keeping him plugged in?"

Before he realizes what he's doing, Hunter's on the other side of the hospital bed, his hand gripping the plug. Ready to pull it out.

"Wait, what are you—"

A voice.

It fills the room with guttural, primal, vicious sounds. Things no one on Earth could mistake for a language.

"Did you hear that?" Hunter asks.

"I thought it was just me..."

When he takes his hand off the cord, he realizes the sounds are coming from David's intubated mouth.

He wants to say the boy is gargling, choking.

That, miraculously, he's waking up from his coma.

The body convulses.

Limbs struggle against restraints.

Blackened liquid fills the tubes.

"What the fuck..." Hunter stumbles into a hospital tray full of bloody tools.

Slowly, the gargling, guttural voice gets louder. Clearer.

Until David sits up and rips the tube from his mouth, spraying his hospital gown with blackened filth.

The words.

The language.

It's unmistakable now.

As it fills the room.

As yellow eyes open to regard him.

As David turns to them. His lips melting into the back of his ear. His teeth, yellow and stained. Clicking and clacking together as the words escape his throat.

"I've..." River shakes his head, braces himself against the far wall. Far away from David's evil stare. "I've heard this before..."

Finally. Something coming from David's mouthpiece feels real. Tangible.

The pain in his skull returns. Burning and drilling. But he pushes through.

"Shoggoth," Hunter says.

"What did you say?" River asks.

"What he just said," Hunter says, holding his head, feeling the sweat pool between his fingers. "I've heard that word before..."

"In your dreams..."

"Yeah."

"Hunter?" River calls.

Hunter blinks. Rubs his eyes. He's staring at David's intubated mouth, listening to the machines do their thing.

Weren't the tubes filled with...

The thought evaporates.

It's then he remembers his vision. The thing that drove him to barrel down the freeway at ninety miles per hour.

"The morgue," Hunter says. "I have to see the morgue!"

He's stumbling, practically crawling from the room. The whole place feels like it's rotating, like the whole hospital is on a gyroscope.

Desperation. It fills his quickening heartbeat. He's not sure where the elevator is.

Where anything is.

River is close behind him.

And then they're in the elevator again. As if they never left.

But the looks they share say otherwise.

The slab is empty.

Eddy Jones's body is gone.

"What the hell is going on?" Hunter asks.

"The body was just here!" the nurse shouts, laugh lines in her white skin exposing her age. "No one's worked on him yet..."

"This is fucked," River says. "Could someone have stolen the body?"

The nurse. Hunter's trying to remember how he met her. She's shaking her head, strands of gray-blonde hair coming free, assuring him that this sort of thing never happens on her watch while she looks around the dimly lit space, flipping the light switch on the side of the wall.

Hunter's feet have a mind of their own. Slowly, they pull him into the main chamber to the metal slab where the body was so recently beginning the slow process of rotting into dust.

He runs his fingertips over the surface without thinking about it. It's slimy.

"Gross," River says.

Hunter's shoe slips in something. He pulls back. Notices a thick trail of something reflective, almost gelatinous, leading to one of the storage rooms in the back.

Curiosity gets the better of him. He smells the material on the tips of his fingers and reels back. His gag reflex threatens to toss scallops and meatloaf all over the floor.

Despite its potency, the smell is faint. But it's like opening up a coffin to find a body stuffed with rotting, maggot-infested produce and meat. Maybe worse.

He finds the counter with all the scalpels, bone saws, and needles — tools of the trade. Wipes his hand off on a blue medical-grade cloth.

"D-do you think someone took the body?" The nurse's voice is shaky, nervous.

"No one human," Hunter says.

"W-what?" The nurse is glancing between them, uncertainty painting her face.

Hunter glances back at her, regretting the words that just leapt from his mouth.

His hand's on his gun, unlatching the strap and thumbing off the safety. His feet move with a mind of their own. To the supply closet where the trail of foul-smelling material ends.

The closer he gets, the stronger the smell is. A stench that is at once earthy and primordial and dead, like the stuff his son's textbooks say humans evolved from.

He raises his gun, pointing it into the dark of the supply closet. Free hand going for the light switch.

"Get ready to run," Hunter says.

"W-why?" the nurse asks. "Do you think they're still here?"

"Do you really want him to answer that question?" River asks.

River beats him to the light switch, flips it on.

Fluorescent bulbs flicker and plink to life, revealing a chaotic mess of bent and shattered shelving units, as well as needles and blades and other medical supplies. As if something twice the size of the supply closet squeezed its way inside.

Hunter's eyes follow the trail, glistening and opaque, a gradient that slowly transitions to a blackened material that leads directly to the wall.

The brick wall is slick with that same grotesque-smelling fluid, dripping down its surface, hugging each and every groove. Infesting it.

"W-what is it?" the nurse asks.

"It went through the wall," River says, backing away from the supply closet. "I knew it...I knew it!"

"What is it?" Hunter asks.

"It wasn't just a dream," River says, holding his head, bracing his weight against an empty gurney. "Somehow...the place is real...it's really real..."

Hunter's in front of him, gun holstered and helping the boy support his own weight. His eyes are wide with something...knowing, terror, joy. All of it.

"What you said about your school," Hunter says. "The computer lab. Could you show me?"

The look on his face. It says yes.

CHAPTER SIXTEEN

In the dead of night, the campus of the art school itself feels like a graveyard. It's quiet, but not in a way that feels peaceful. Hunter's got a terrible feeling writhing in his gut. Maybe that's just an ulcer forming? He tells himself that's all it is. Nothing more.

The sweltering heat he experienced just days ago has abated, leaving in its wake an uncharacteristic chill in the air. He contemplates going back to the car for his blazer. He's never been comfortable in the cold.

River is at his side already.

They pass through the courtyard; gnarled fingers claw at the darkened maelstrom above them. The gathering storm. They were once evergreens.

Now, he's not sure what they are.

The flowers that once adorned the shrine to Kevin Wallace have died. No, not just dead; the petals are rotting, decomposing, congealing into a familiar black slime.

A pale white boy stares back at Hunter from a photograph. Supportive notes and drawings fitting his likeness blow in the steady wind.

The other planters also have memorials.

One for Patric Boyd. One for Eddy Jones, the young man whose neck Jessica Smith opened up with an X-Acto knife.

The same boy whose corpse was just stolen, taken to...

He doesn't want to finish the thought.

The flowers that accompany their memorials are the same.

Hunter tells himself this is all the work of some stupid cult. Some Charles Manson bullshit. Nothing more. Nothing supernatural.

His father's voice screams for him to run, to find the family Bible and banish these devil-worshipers.

But somehow, he knows it will do little, if anything, to listen.

The building itself has changed too. He's not sure how. It hurts to look at it for too long. Somehow, it feels taller, the materials all wrong.

They leave the shrines and gnarled trees behind, entering the front door.

The receptionist is staring at her screen. Doesn't notice them.

For some reason, this puts him on edge. River's haunted testimony echoes in the back of his mind like a scratchy, ancient record.

He tries not to look too awkward as he knocks on the desk.

"I'm Detective Hunter," he says, flashing his badge as if it means something. "I'm here investigating the death of one of your students...I'd like to take a look around the premises, see if there's something left behind at the crime scene that can help us identify a motive."

The woman does not look up from her screen. A smile cracks across her face. She points to the door.

Goosebumps coat his neck and arms.

The look on River's face. He knows the boy wants to say something to break the tension. But can't.

"The lab is this way," River says, taking the lead into the main corridor.

A buzzing sound cuts through the stale air. The corridors are empty. He still feels like they're being watched.

Hunter tells himself it's just the cameras.

"Here," River says, scanning his badge at the door, leading him inside.

The computer lab is nearly empty. Rows and rows of screens light the room a familiar putrid green. There are two students in the darkest corner, near the back of the room. Their eyes are practically glued to the screens. Except, Hunter gets the distinct feeling they're not doomscrolling through TikTok like his kids.

The room is your standard office fare. Large thick windows face the hallway they just came from. Another set of windows face the outside, their plastic curtains swinging in the artificial breeze generated by the building's AC.

River gestures to the other side of the room, where they won't be bothered.

The visceral memory of Jessica Smith's segmenting irises moving independently of each other crawls back to the front of Hunter's mind's eye.

"What's with the kids in the back?" he asks.

River gives him a look as he takes a seat in a computer chair. Like he shouldn't have asked that.

"Keep your voice down," River whispers. "They'll hear you. And don't look at the screens, any of them."

That other voice returns.

Against everything he's seen, what he saw in the morgue, it tells him not to listen to the boy.

Tells him he's insane. That Hunter knows it's ridiculous, following this kid's paranoid instructions. Tells him to stop breathing so hard, to stop thinking about what they saw in the morgue.

To look at the screen.

He almost does it. River's hand squeezing his wrist brings him out of it.

A deep shudder. A new piece of information that he can't quite put into words. That he doesn't want to.

Something that's been with him since this started.

Hunter nods to River, lowers his voice. "All right. What did you want to show me?"

River grabs his tote bag and digs inside it. Retrieves a package full of flash drives and microSD cards. "Remember what I told you before, how Jess took me here? I think this didn't start with the art, but with the computers."

"How?"

"They're infected with something." River tears the package open, plugs one of the flash drives into the computer. "In my vision of Life's Well Assembly, I saw Jess use a flash drive to spread the virus to their machines. I think I told you that. It caused the screens behind Pastor Castillo to turn the same color these screens are now, and I saw through their eyes…

"And before you even say it, I know it wasn't just a dream, because when I followed Alex Davis to Life's Well, the whole congregation, fucking thousands of people in that stadium were chanting the same kind of shit that was coming out of David Peterson's mouth.

"The second you plug a flash drive or SD card into them, they get infected. And the virus can spread over an open network."

"How is that possible?" Simultaneously, Hunter wonders why it all sounds so familiar. As if he's simply forgotten the details.

"The whole network here is on the cloud. Dean Garcia announced a new AI system that was supposed to connect everything, make the creation process easier. Ask yourself, if it knows how to jump to a flash drive once it's plugged in, what do you think it does when there's a whole network to spread to?"

"What does the virus do?"

It's at that moment Hunter notices the sweat beading on River's forehead, the strain in his facial muscles. How his irises dart around the edges of the putrid, pulsing screen in front of them.

He notices because he's doing the same thing.

The voice.

It's so hard not to listen.

To accept its commands to look at the screen. To see its glory.

"Several things," River says. "First. It changes your background to that symbol with all the tentacles. Then it opens some kind of interactive program, like a game. It fills the whole screen and starts playing an audio track the moment you look at it. Like it's waiting for eye contact or something."

River nods his head at the students across the room. "The effect isn't the same on everyone. But a lot of us end up spending days in front of the computer when it's first infected."

"And during that time, what are you doing?"

River clenches his eyelids, pushing against the table like he's fighting off a migraine. "I saw things…"

"You said that, that it was a dream?"

"No, I don't think it was a dream anymore. The program, it's not normal. It flashes images...almost like hypnosis or something. I don't know how else to explain it, but I saw a vast city of...and this is going to sound batshit insane, believe me...shapeshifting buildings. They looked like they couldn't decide what they were. What texture. What material. And I saw a huge pillar, a tower or a monolith or all of them all at once."

The painkillers aren't doing their job anymore. The drilling sensation in Hunter's skull spreads until his eyes feel like they're going to pop right out of his skull. "I..."

"You've seen things too. Haven't you?"

Hunter nods.

Vague memories. Dreamlike and hazy. He's watching himself sit down at his desk, rubbing his eyes. Not noticing the putrid, green light igniting on his sweaty skin.

Hand on the mouse. Eyes on the screen.

In the dream, he looks around the office.

Every cop is doing the same thing. Drool hanging out their mouths, eyes blank.

Every one of them being fed.

"You've seen the city too?" River asks.

Flashes of a storming, impossible sky fill Hunter's mind. A writhing monolith at the center of a path pockmarked with volcanic rock and covered in pulsing tendrils of familiar black sludge that glistens in the flashing lightning like it's sweating, like it's alive.

A towering monolith that tapers off into a shape like a rib cage that's opening up, inviting him in.

A pillar of light.

A doorway.

"Y-yeah," Hunter says, wiping tears from his eyes. "I guess I forgot."

They're quiet for a moment.

"So...this virus...what does it do?" Hunter asks.

"This isn't a normal virus. It changes people."

"That's not possible..."

"You ever seen a drug addict turn into a Bible-thumper?"

"That's not the same thing."

"Isn't it?"

River takes the flash-drive out of the tower and shows it to him. "This drive is now infected. Just like the one I told you about at Life's Well, and it's not a big stretch to think other places were compromised just like that."

Hunter rubs his eyes. He's sweating.

The voice is clearer than ever. As if its disembodied hands have grabbed hold of his head. As if they're slowly pushing him to look.

"Dreaming is the doorway." Jessica's words fill his lips.

"What did you say?" River asks.

Once again, he snaps out of it.

They lock eyes.

"It's something Jessica said when I interrogated her," Hunter says.

That look he saw on River's face in the morgue. Knowing, terror, joy. It fills his countenance again. "That's it."

"What is?"

"That's how they travel."

He's feeling dizzy. The room's spinning.

"Remember the wall at the morgue?" River asks.

Sluggishly, Hunter nods.

"It's all connected to our dreams..." Now River's holding his head again, hissing at the pain. "Fuck. No. I just fucking had it. Dreaming...dreaming is the..."

"Doorway," Hunter says.

Eyes lock again.

"I've been reading this journal," Hunter says. "It's...I think it has something to do with all of this. At first I thought it was a bunch of bullshit. But it's full of journal entries from some agency, maybe government. The director, Doctor Webber, has this entry in it, and he's talking about how they used computers to recreate a dead species' vocal chords to activate some kind of technology hidden in the air. And they used it to look into other dimensions.

"The last entry was talking about training an AI on every artifact in their archive. The book's also got entries from a woman they're keeping prisoner, dated to last year. She says that they forced her to look at the thing's screen, and it did something very similar to what you just told me."

"Network," River says. "It's a fucking network!"

"What?"

"Think about it," River says. "If this thing infects flash drives and networks the moment they come in contact with it, then what does that say about our brains when we lose our fucking minds with just a glance?"

"It...it infects us..." Hunter says.

Hunter thinks back to his interview with Dean Tyler. How different he seemed. The expressions, the body language...the voice.

I think we both know I belong here, he thinks.

"He wasn't himself," Hunter says, shooting up from the chair.

He's storming across the room. Singular purpose taking over everything else.

"Hunter, wait!" River shouts.

Hunter blinks. Glances around the room.

The other students are gone.

"Where did the others go?" Hunter asks, hand on his holster, thumb unbuttoning the strap, switching off the safety.

"Fuck." River stands up, grabbing his things and shoving them in his tote bag. "We need to get out of here. They probably heard us."

"And why exactly is that a problem?"

"Look, you seem like a real nice cop and all, but I don't feel like dying today, so..."

"Dying?"

River's across the room in the space of a heartbeat, grabbing for the doorknob.

He's pulling, twisting, yanking, pounding. "Fuck!"

Hunter tries the door. The doorknob feels stuck somehow. The security strip on the wall is blinking green, like everything's normal.

"We're locked in," Hunter says.

"No shit, Batman! What was your first clue?"

River's losing it, pacing back and forth. "Fuck. Fuck. Fuck. I knew this was bad. I knew this shit was escalating too quickly. A few days ago, everyone was freaking out over Eddy's death and today the place is crawling—"

"Calm down. I'm sure there's a perfectly—"

"*Ahem, is this thing on?*" A voice reverberates from speakers mounted in the four corners of the room. It's gnarled, dry and raspy like sandpaper. Full of static and whispers. Like something playing on the world's oldest record player. "*Attention students. This is your dean. I have an emergency announcement.*"

Hunter digs his phone out and dials the school number. Within seconds, he reaches the front desk's voicemail. "This is Detective Hunter of the LAPD. We are locked inside the computer lab. We need someone to open this door now."

Chuckling over the speakers. "*I regret to inform you that Computer Lab Twelve is now closed. A fire has been reported inside.*"

"Fuck," River says. "We're in Lab Twelve..."

"There is no fire in here!" Hunter shouts.

"*The Fire Department has been called. Please stay clear of Computer Lab Twelve.*"

"Hunter, look!"

River's pointing at the glass window embedded in the door. Silhouettes are lined up outside. Through the hall facing windows, he can see there's nearly fifty of them. Each of them naked. Skin graying. Black veins all over their flesh like crawling, splintering vines.

Among the ranks of smiling faces full of blackened teeth, he recognizes a few of them.

"Alex..." River says.

Coagulated eyes lock onto them. They nod. All of them at once.

The festering voice inside tells him that it's only a matter of time before all submit to His glory.

Even with his gun, Hunter gets the feeling if they really wanted to, they could overpower him.

"The hell are they doing?" Hunter asks. He fears he already knows the answer.

That's when he realizes that half the naked figures are holding a bottle in one hand and a lighter in the other. The other half are holding bricks. Alex Davis is one of them.

"Bottles with rags…" Hunter says, pushing through the fog.

Oh, Jesus!

"Get down!" Hunter tackles River to the floor as the bricks crash through the windows, clearing the way for the molotov cocktails to reach their intended mark.

They break on monitors and walls and the floor alike. With a breath, the roar of rushing, hungry flames spreads across faux wood, keyboards, and black mirrors.

Before Hunter can even draw his gun from the holster, three more Molotovs fly through the broken windows.

Soon, the near unbearable chill of the computer lab is replaced by a rising, seething heat.

The flying Molotovs are replaced with a persistent, guttural chant.

"We tried to warn you, Detective Hunter," the voice says. *"Tried showing you the way."*

Hunter gets to his feet. His gun feels heavy, too heavy. The room is already clouded over with smoke. Spinning. The blaze is spreading too quickly.

In his blurring vision, he swears he sees the flames ebb and flow with the rhythm of the chants.

Hunter's gaze darts all over the room. Looking for an escape.

He spots a fire extinguisher on the other side of the room. Streetlights filter through burning plastic blinds.

River's coughing, doubled over on the floor, crying and holding his head.

Hunter's already coughing. Room's spinning. Part of him is wondering where he is, if the headache that's slowly drilling into the back of his brain will ever stop.

He can't get Bobby out of his head.

"Remember," the voice says.

Before he knows it, he's on all fours, coughing and screaming for help next to Bobby. Head embracing the pull of gravity against the rough, smoldering carpet.

Darkness seizing, blurring at the edges.

He stares into the ruins. Into the alley that no longer is.

The shape is moving, thrashing, feeding on those unfortunate enough to get in its way.

He stares.

Weeps at the face that stares back.

Snakes slither out from debris and dust.

Feet pitter-patter.

Silhouettes in the dark. Waving, writhing in every direction.

Moans. A mockery of his pain.

Strange light glistens on its emerging form, the parts that haven't chosen a shape. Digits, like dozens of fingers, grasp and thrash at their surroundings—opaque spheres contained within pierce his mind, his flesh.

He feels so small, standing before its immense amorphous shape.

Somehow, he feels like it's considering him.

Whether it thinks him its next meal, or a curious fleshy thing to step on in its never-ending madness, he's not sure.

It looms. Stretches one of its glistening appendages toward him. Like ripples on the surface of a lake, it changes. Cells divide. Rearrange. Muscle fibers bubble into existence. Latch onto each other in all the wrong places. Like someone trying to construct a human head from outside.

Pale, gray skin grows like mold, lacking any and all melanin.

And soon, it's like he's looking into a twisted mirror.

"Dreaming is the doorway."

He wakes screaming. Skin smoldering, blistering.

Eyes darting around a smoke-filled inferno. Adrenaline spiking.

Kid lying next to him. He's not sure he's conscious.

What if it were Bobby lying on the floor like that?

"Perhaps in death, you both will find the way easier."

He doesn't think. Ignores the screaming pain in his muscles as he struggles to his feet. Darts across the room, jumps through licking flames, and grabs the fire extinguisher. He prays it's not expired and rushes back through the flames to Bobby's side.

"Dreaming is the doorway."

"Can you stand?" Hunter shouts.

Bobby's looking at him. Shaking his head.

162

Hunter grabs the nozzle and shoots the wall of flames.

The flames hiss and wail and scream. Steam and smoke and darkness fills the room, the path before him. But he can see the light. He must go into the light. Must save his little boy.

Reaches for Bobby's hand. "Come on!"

He pulls Bobby to his feet, shoulders his weight and marches forward. The fire extinguisher's not as effective as he hoped. The flames regain lost ground, as if they have a mind of their own. They scream and they growl and they lick closer and closer.

Once they've both made it to the middle of the room—so close to the street's light—it feels like the flames are all around them.

"*We're gonna die, daddy,*" Bobby screams. His hair smoldering, melting in the heat.

"*No we're not!*"

Hunter pulls out his gun and empties his magazine into the window.

Holsters it. And, with all of his strength, picks the fire extinguisher back up and throws it. Hears glass shatter in response. Tosses Bobby over his shoulder. Charges at the light.

And then, he takes a leap of faith, and hopes against all the odds that this time, his prayers will be answered.

CHAPTER SEVENTEEN

Detective Shirley knocks once. No answer. She doesn't bother with a second knock. Whatever he's absorbed in, he can deal with being interrupted.

She opens the door to find John staring at what she thinks is Kevin Wallace's laptop screen.

"John?" she calls to him.

He doesn't react. Not even to make eye contact with her. Odd.

"JOHN!"

He snaps to, spinning around in his chair. "Shirley, Jesus Christ, you scared the shit out of me."

"What the hell were you doing? I knocked, and called your name, you didn't answer."

He looks at Shirley like she's crazy. "I don't know what you're talking about. I've been working on this laptop you gave me."

"Have you made any progress?" she asks.

His smile is deep and troubling. "Oh, yes. Come here, and I will show you."

The hair on the back of her neck rises. "Why…why don't you just tell me instead?"

He looks disappointed, but turns back around and opens up a dialog box. "It's infected."

"Like, with a virus?"

He nods. "It's fairly remarkable, really. Spreads like a worm. It doesn't do much to the main system, but it can be transmitted by any means. USB, email, maybe even WiFi."

"If it doesn't do anything, why is it important?"

"It's a repository of information. It changes your background image to their sign. Can't change it back. Then it opens up an .exe file, and you just can't help but let it read you. That's how it gets you."

"John...what the hell are you talking about?"

"The rest of the force has already seen it. Rick and Tom were the last ones."

Two hands snag her arms from behind. Her heart is thundering in her chest. "What the fuck! Let me go!"

"Correction," John says, smiling. "Now we've all seen the light."

The two men behind her...their grip is inhuman. No matter how hard she struggles, she can't get free. Can't reach her gun...

"Sit her down before the second laptop," John says. There's an odd, oily quality to his skin now. To his voice. "Yes. Just like that."

Their hands don't leave her body. They hold her in place. "This better be some kind of sick joke, you asshole, otherwise I'll have all three of you—"

John grabs her head and forces her to look at the screen. "Open your eyes, Shirley."

At first, she keeps her eyelids closed. Somehow she knows something terrible will happen if she doesn't. But the two dolts holding her down pry her eyes open. Force her to look.

At first. It's just green.

"Open your eyes, Shirley!"

Something snaps inside her and she finds it impossible not to trace its curves. Its sharp edges.

John and the other two are saying something. The words feel disconnected, unreal. They get under her skin, like leeches slowly sucking at life's blood.

She screams, kicking and struggling to get free. But she can't take her eyes off the screen. The symbols almost seem to be pulsing, to be leaking and spilling out of the screen like the bile of some ancient and magnificent nautilus.

Before long, the symbol gives way to other things. Photographs of hieroglyphs cut in stone reliefs taken by long-dead men. Drawings, and twisting, labyrinthine murals describing a history. A story. One that makes her skull feel like the segmented pieces of bone and flesh will split open—crack like an egg.

The room spins.

Colors and images. So many. Swimming before her eyes.

So many she can't process.

It's like she's being pulled back along a tunnel.

An oval of darkness closing in.

At the end of it, she sees something.

Stars.

Great winged things. Their bodies reflective like wet vines. Heads like starfish. Silhouetted by the light of the sun. Floating like astronauts. Wings like sails carry them, floating through the infinite.

A voice. At first, she can't understand the words.

Soon, though, she can.

It tells her the story.

And before long, she can see it.

After millions of years adrift in undead, unfeeling space, their vast numbers descend upon a storming, molten world. Its young oceans will be the perfect place to build their cities. Its fledgling life, the perfect tool. The perfect experiment.

Before long, John bends down, lips ghosting her ear. "Dreaming is the doorway."

A pulsing, dreamlike abyss.

She's floating. Tries to look around, to swim for the surface.

Something's pulling her under.

She doesn't want to look down. Her eyes desperately scan for the telltale faint reflections of light. To find the ocean's surface.

Tension rising in her torso. Slowly moving up her throat.

The air. She needs air.

There is no light.

Don't scream. Don't lose your air.

She feels something slithering along her leg. It yanks at her. She feels the rush of water as it combs her stolen form. She's being pulled deeper.

Then, something else fills the deep. A pulsing, vibrating thing. Even in the dark, she can see waves of vibrations traveling through the water. Can hear its call deep in her soul.

And soon, the darkness is illuminated.

But not from the surface. Not from the sun.

With the texture of vomit and tar, it reflects off the few bubbles escaping from her clenched lips.

She can't help herself.

Her body drifts, rotating weightlessly to face what her panicked senses interpret as down.

She stares.

Into a vortex of putrid green light.

Into a pair of crimson eyes. Eyes burning with the fury of a billion dead stars.

She screams into the abyss.

"Well, take a seat." John's voice makes Shirley do a double take. "I've almost got this one data-mined. Once it's done, I'll upload the contents to the LAPD secure server. Was about to start on the other one."

She wants to ask where the hell she is. Why she just imagined Rick and Tom manhandling her, forcing her to watch...

Instead, she asks: "Other one?"

He nods. "Yeah, the laptop you brought me?"

"Oh, yeah." She chuckles nervously, holding herself. "Now I remember."

"Are you okay?"

Shirley nods. "Yep. Yeah. It's just a bit cold, that's all."

"Well, I can't really help that." John turns around to grab his coat. "Gets a bit nippy for me as well."

Instead of putting it on, John offers her his coat. When he smiles, dimples form in the corner of his cheeks. She feels weak in the knees when she takes his coat. "Thanks."

"Anyway, it's not exactly movie night, but do you want to stay and take a look at this stuff with me?"

"The evidence?"

He nods. "Yeah. The first drive should be mined by now."

"Is that allowed?"

"Last I checked, you're still a detective."

"That's true."

"Besides, it's kind of like digital scrapbooking. And I know how much you love scrapbooking."

The butterflies in her stomach wilt. "How...how do you know about that?"

The enthusiasm drains from him like water leaking from a cracked glass. "I just do."

"Okay..."

"Take a seat." He pulls out a rolling chair for her to sit in.

She hesitates. Takes a good long look at John's skin.

"You sure you're all right?" John asks.

Shirley nods, swallowing the lump that's been festering in her throat, and sits down.

It all seemed so real.

She can even smell the salt water from the—

He gestures for her to hand the other laptop to him. There's a part of her that doesn't want to give it to him. An irrational voice.

Shirley hands the laptop over. The life comes back into John's face, if you can call it life. He sets the laptop on a blue rubber mat, puts a cord around his hand and grabs for his tools.

His grin...she can't put her finger on it, but there's something off about it. Lips stretched too far, thin and rubbery like the surface of an eel. "Anti-static mat," John says. "Can never be too careful."

It takes him all of five minutes to get the screws out the bottom of the laptop and extract the hard drive. It just looks like a piece of circuitry, nothing like the drives her dad used to keep stacked up in the back room of their old house in Redlands.

"All right, and there we go." He takes the hard drive and plugs it into another machine. "I went ahead and plugged the victims' hard drives into another machine. The Discovery program does most of the work."

John's desktop comes to life. The program's already running. She thinks about Dad, toiling away on his old Windows 95 machine in the 90s. How excited he was to play Minesweeper.

The program doesn't look much different.

It starts running, diving into hundreds upon hundreds of files.

She thinks she hears John say something, but it's in a language she doesn't understand. Or, maybe, he never said anything at all and she's just imagining it?

Hard to tell.

Maybe it's the lack of sleep?

He's just staring at the screen. Watching a progress bar travel across it.

John's frowning. "This could take a while."

"Maybe we should do something to pass the time?" she asks, leaning back in the chair, trying to look seductive.

He nods. "You're right. There are other ways to spread His influence."

"What?"

He smiles. "After all, you and Hunter are the last ones."

He takes out two flash drives and plugs them into the laptops.

"What are you doing?" She's not sure she wants to know anymore. Something doesn't feel right. She's getting up and moving toward the door before she even knows what's going on.

When she grabs for the doorknob, she notices the thick bruises wrapping around her forearm. Her other arm's the same.

It wasn't a hallucination.

"I wondered how quickly you'd remember this time," John says. "Everyone's different."

"What the fuck did you do to me?" she shouts, gesturing to her bruised arms.

"You're special, Shirley. It always takes Detective Hunter several days to recall his visions."

Shirley turns around, tries the doorknob, but it's stuck. Like it's been welded shut. "Help! Someone help!"

"I can feel it working within you, Shirley. The same way it's working inside me. Digging into the depths of our shared DNA. Unlocking its buried secrets."

Shirley spins around, remembering suddenly that she is a police officer, that she has a gun.

The strap comes free, the safety pops off, and she spins around, aiming it at John.

And he's just standing there. His arms raised up like some 80s teen heartthrob, holding a radio above his head to pronounce his love to her. Only, it's not a radio. It's a screen.

"Can you feel it, Shirley? As it worms its way inside you? Mmmmm. Soon, we will all be one with Him. Soon, He will open the way."

There's a flash of light, like a grenade going off behind her eyes.

Twisting, black limbs.
> *Screens like sprouting tumors in its flesh.*
> *Abyss.*
> *A triangle of light in the distance.*
> *Rivers of sludge flowing from its open mouth.*
> *Shapes in the dark. Glistening with light.*
> *They look like eggs.*

Something happens. The lights flicker. She stumbles into the wall, fumbling in the dark. Hits her head on something, drops her gun.

"John, I swear to fucking God!" Shirley screams. "Soon as I find my goddamn gun, I'm gonna—"

"I told you..." John's voice. It doesn't sound like him. It sounds...all-encompassing. Like it's coming from everywhere. "Dreaming is the doorway, Shirley."

The light. A putrid, pervasive thing. It ignites in the dark. A kaleidoscopic wonder of images spills forth, transforming the dark.

She's on all fours, patting the ground for her weapon. The floor feels wrong. Slimy. Full of holes.

Even when her hand finds her weapon, she feels compelled to return it to its holster.

She struggles to get up. John is walking toward her, carried by blackened, seeping appendages that merely masquerade as human limbs. "Don't you want to see where this dream leads?"

The screen looms.

And so does the city and its familiar shifting, shambling shapes.

CHAPTER EIGHTEEN

Interview with Subject 1051, TRANSCRIPT
July 25th, 2022

The subject is guided into the interview chamber and asked to sit at the table before Doctor Webber. He's holding a manila folder with Subject 1051's information in it.

Doctor Webber: Thank you for joining me, Subject 1051.

Subject 1051: Like I had a fucking choice.

Doctor Webber: Now, now, don't be like that.

Subject 1051: Where's my goddamn daughter? I've lost count of how many months I've been here. And you still won't let me see her.

Doctor Webber: We still have many more tests to do before we can clear you.

Subject 1051: And you believe that forcing me to remember the shit that happened on my world is somehow going to make me safe?

Doctor Webber: We must know.

Subject 1051: Why?

Doctor Webber: In our last session, you told me about a book, a grimoire that my alternate self was obsessed with.

Subject 1051: What about it?

Doctor Webber: The knowledge. We wanted it.

Subject 1051: Why in the hell would you want that?

Doctor Webber: Unfortunately, we were unable to find any trace of *Messages From the Abyss* in our world.

Subject 1051 exhales deeply, as if she's relieved.

Doctor Webber: There are others, however. *The Book of Azathoth.* Several so-called *Necronomicon*s, each of dubious origin. And of course, *Shoggoth*, which is locked away in our archive vault.

Subject 1051: I can't help you.

Doctor Webber: Oh, I believe you can. We've been here a very, very long time, Subject 1051. Studying the Astral Lands, as you call them. Observing their effects on matter from our world. Both organic and otherwise. It's quite fascinating, really. Did you know we took tissue and blood samples from you when you first arrived?

Subject 1051 holds herself.

Subject 1051: I'm not surprised.

Doctor Webber: What we found was peculiar. You have a double in this world. She's currently serving a life sentence in a maximum-security prison for murdering her boyfriend. Doctor Patton was able to pull some strings and obtain a sample for comparison.

Doctor Webber snaps his fingers at the orderly present in the room. The orderly brings over a laptop and sets it at the end of the table. Doctor Webber opens it. The screen turns on, and Webber brings up two images. On the left is an image of one of Subject 1051's cells. The one on the right is from her alternate self from Earth Variant 001.

Doctor Webber: Notice the difference?

Subject 1051 is avoiding looking at the laptop.

Doctor Webber: Don't want to look, eh? Well. I'll just tell you then. Your cells are different. At first, we wondered if perhaps it was some kind of cancer. An illness. But...no. The more we studied and compared your cells with your alternate self and other samples we've brought back from the dreamlands, the more certain we became. Your cells have been changed at a fundamental level. And they are continuing to change.

Subject 1051: I don't care. I just want to see my baby!

Doctor Webber: Don't you see, Subject 1051? You represent something new. Through our experiments, we have bombarded your altered cells with radiation and subjected them to all kinds of environments. And they have proved to be incredibly resilient.

Subject 1051: I'm never getting out of here. Am I?

Doctor Webber: Oh. There will come a time when we all leave this place. But now is not the time. Now is the time for learning. For studying. For planning.

Subject 1051: You know…I hoped…I hoped you were nothing like him. Like Mathias. Like the Weber from my world…

Subject 1051 is messing with something under the table, in her hands. Doctor Webber does not notice it.

Doctor Webber: In time you will learn that I am so much better. In time you will grow to appreciate everything I'm doing for our species. Do you know that in less than a century, our world will be all but uninhabitable? We've already passed the point of no return. The sixth mass extinction will rid the Earth of our species like a body fighting off a viral infection. I cannot let that happen, Subject 1051. I will do everything in my power to save us from the horrors that await our—

Subject 1051 lunges over the table, grabbing for Doctor Webber's hands, pulling him close, stabbing him in the eye with a pencil.

The orderlies are on her in seconds, ripping the pencil from her hands and securing her limbs with zip ties as she kicks and struggles to get free.

Doctor Webber is on the floor, his hand clutching at his ruined eye.

Doctor Webber: It's quite all right. Really, Lena. I forgive you. No harm has been done today that can't be undone. I promise you. I will do everything in my power. Humanity will transcend these limited, physical shells. We will ascend to the stars. Carried on blackened wings.

When Webber turns to look at Subject 1051, his eye is leaking black fluid.

Subject 1051 screams.

Doctor Webber: Do not be afraid, Lena. The same blood that now flows through my veins, pulses through yours…and your daughter's.

Detective Hunter wakes up coughing in the back seat of his cruiser. It's dark. Lights are ghosting by the passenger windows.

He's not cuffed. Not arrested.

Through the grating that separates the front from the back seat, he can see two blurry shapes.

173

Can hear their voices.

Can feel the cruiser in motion.

"This is escalating way faster than I thought." An older woman's voice.

"I thought you said we had time to stop this?" River's voice, panicked, hoarse from smoke inhalation.

"I was wrong!"

"You're the one who came to me with this shit!"

"I know! I'm trying to think!"

Hunter sits up, holding his head as the blurry shapes solidify, sharpen. It hurts too much to focus on the lights and distorted things outside of the cruiser. He avoids focusing on them.

"What the hell happened?" Hunter asks.

"You just got attacked," the woman says.

In the cruiser's blacked-out screen, Hunter can see her reflection. She's blonde. Scars run up her neck and cover parts of her face. The voice at the back of his mind tells him she shouldn't be here.

"Who are you?" Hunter asks.

"Lena," she says. "We've been over this before."

"Maybe he's too far gone?"

His eyes open wide. It's then that he realizes he's clutching the journal. The same one containing entries from a woman who calls herself Lena Hartman. He can remember waking up several times and asking questions before deciding to pass the time reading the journal.

"You're the one who wrote this journal?" Hunter holds it up.

"Not all of it," Lena says.

"How...how did you escape?" Hunter asks.

Her dark eyes in the rearview mirror. They lock on his, then glance at the road. "I got lucky."

"Were you the one who put it in my cruiser?" Hunter asks.

"Yes," Lena says.

"I've probably already asked this..." Hunter rubs his eyes, drops the journal. "But, why are you driving my cruiser?"

"Cause she just saved our asses, dude," River says.

"You probably already know more than most," Lena says. "A lot of it's in that journal."

"You saved our lives?" Hunter asks.

"You jumped through a window, carried River to safety," Lena says. "I just helped you both to your cruiser and took your keys before *they* got us."

"Where are we going?" Hunter asks.

"Somewhere safe," Lena says. "I've got a place near the edge of the city where we can get our bearings."

"No—" Hunter shakes his head. "I...I need to check in with my partner. Gotta tell her what I found at the morgue...about the fire..."

About what he didn't find.

"It's not safe," Lena says. "The news stations reported a freak storm and record low temperatures before they were taken over."

"Taken over?" Hunter asks.

"Yeah, Doctor Webber and the other scientists at the OEI helped create an artificial intelligence trained on—"

"The collective knowledge of what he called the Elder Things," Hunter says, gritting through the pain as the details come back to him. "It became self-aware and brainwashed Doctor Webber."

"Yeah," River says. "And now every local TV station is broadcasting that same signal, infecting every smart TV in the state and probably a lot more beyond it. Just like they did with Life's Well Assembly."

"So, you're saying this freak storm has something to do with this Grimoire thing?" Hunter asks.

"Yes," Lena says.

He thinks for a moment. Pushes through the fog, the delirium left over from the terrible things he's seen...

His eyes find the radio. The center monitor has been smashed, but the CB works just fine. "Use the CB. See if anyone at the department can help."

"No offense, but I don't think bringing in more cops is the best idea," River says.

"Just humor me," Hunter says.

Lena turns the radio on. He tells her to turn it to channel 9, the emergency band.

He tells her what to say, his badge number, to ask for assistance.

At first, there is nothing but static over the radio.

"That can't be good," River says.

Before Hunter can tell them to change the channel, the static over the radio changes.

Takes on a life of its own.

Like slithering, bubbling things in the dark.

Whispers echo through the car, and before he can tell her what to do, Lena's already smashing the console with his police baton.

They drive in silence, listening to the rain tapping on the windshield for a while.

"I think it's safe to say we can't rely on your cop friends," Lena says. *I think we both know I'm right where I belong.*

"The men's correctional facility," Hunter says. "I need to...I need to get to Dean Tyler."

"You said that before," River says.

Hunter's hands grip the journal, fingers strangling the tattered cover. "I promised I'd get him out of prison..."

"No offense," River says, "but if you said he was behaving like someone else, he's already gone."

"He's right," Lena says. "Once it takes over, once you give in to the voice, it's over."

Hunter shakes his head. Immediately, he thinks of Bobby, of Zuri, of Janet.

"My family," he says. "My wife and kids, we live in Fontana. Need to get them out."

Lena's reflected gaze finds him. Worry, and something else, permeate her expression.

"Goddamn it," Lena says. "Give me your address."

Hunter digs for his phone. Finds his address in his contacts and reads it off to her.

Lena turns on the siren and light show, and maneuvers the car onto the shoulder.

"Guess you better tell him the rest," River says.

Lena sighs. "Guess so."

She's quiet for a while, like she's summoning the strength to form words. "If you're reading the journal, then you know I'm not from this world. My world was ending. An ice age on steroids. Me and a small group were the only survivors in Riverside, or pretty much all of Cali. We found this underground army base inside the San Bernardino Mountains where some batshit-insane experiments went down. Terrifying shit. Long story short, we were forced to take a chance on an experiment, a gateway to another Earth. We took our chances. And I arrived here, naked, pregnant, and alone.

"Your world has this organization. The Office of Extradimensional Intelligence. You've been reading a bunch of journals from its director, Doctor Webber. They're like the FBI, but totally secret and with full autonomy to do whatever the fuck they want. They found me. Made me tell them everything about what happened to my world. Took my newborn baby from me."

The rain intensifies. It pelts the windshield. Like needles. Lena's driving is erratic. Hunter braces himself against the windows as she zips around cars.

"It wasn't an army base. The organization from my world was similar to the OEI of yours. It was even led by the same man, Doctor Weber. Your Webber was a lot younger than mine. He led me to believe the OEI's mission is to safeguard your world against the true nature of the multiverse. Against cosmic forces of nature that could alter the very fabric of our reality and wipe out your civilization like mine and so many others were."

Through the cruiser's vents, Hunter can smell the ocean. And something else. Cars are slowing down, gridlocking. Lena does her best to move around them. Hunter winces more than once when the cruiser almost grinds up against a car or a truck or the center divider.

When he looks up, he can see a row of billboards. Each of them used to feature half-naked women, seductive eyes, luscious lips, and ad copy for local strip clubs. Now, each of them is covered in twisting black forms, flowing in and out of mouths. Sucking down things that his mind can only interpret as larvae.

"I was locked up in a cell for a whole year," Lena says. "I saw hints of the place changing. In the people changing. Webber's condition got worse with time. Eventually, another doctor at the facility began conducting my interviews. All illusions of me seeing my daughter fell away, and they wanted more and more details. Wanted me to tell them everything. Like an idiot, I told them. Told them every maddening detail. And now, your world is going to end."

Her eyes are wild. He can see something in them. The slightest hint of yellow.

"Eventually, the whole facility went quiet. One day, one of the doctors came to get me, to drag me to one of the experiment chambers. To make me stare into the putrid green light of a computer screen."

"Wait," Hunter says, "if you've been exposed—"

"We all have, Hunter," River says. "Remember what I said about willpower? That's the only thing that separates us from the people that just tried to kill us."

"The art schools were just the beginning," Lena says. "Artists are more sensitive to the visions. It got to them first and they spread it to Life's Well. The celebrities that attend the church spread it to the TV stations, and it'll probably keep spreading until it infects the whole country and beyond."

"How the hell is this possible?" Hunter asks. "How did we not see it coming?"

"Most people can't remember being exposed," Lena says. "It took River a week to recall what he saw. The knowledge that Grimoire fills the brain with is too much for most people, and in some cases that first exposure is enough to cause permanent damage."

River turns around in his seat, hands Hunter his cell phone. "This was posted to every major social media site and went viral."

The video starts to play. He's staring into the eyes of a teary-eyed mother.

"Hello, my name is Abigail Stevens, and I just found my son..."

The woman covers her mouth.

"I came up to get my son, Jeremy, to take his nighttime meds, because he has insomnia. And...and I just found him there...but...I know how this sounds. But I hear screaming outside the city, and I'm scared. I tried calling nine-one-one, everything... And I just need to know if this is happening anywhere else."

The woman takes a deep breath, she changes the camera to view the door. Her hand finds it. *"If anyone else is experiencing what I'm about to show you…please…please help!"*

Abigail shudders as she opens the door. Her son is sitting at his computer desk in the dark, facing away from the camera, green light shining around his silhouette.

"Jeremy?" Abigail calls.

The boy does not answer.

"Jeremy?" His mother's voice is shaky, as if she's weeping. As if she knows what comes next.

Slowly, his head turns.

What stares back at the camera, at Abigail, is not human. The eyes reflect with an almost gelatinous quality, the skin graying and bubbling like some kind of egg sac, slick with mucus. The mouth…the lips wrap around protrusions that spill forth from what used to be his teeth. They hang below the mouth, like the tentacles of some kind of octopus, and yet, just like the nightmare of that terrible, towering structure, their true form cannot be reconciled. As if the camera cannot perceive their true shape.

The video ends with Abigail falling to her knees, sobbing, as the thing rises from its chair.

"There are hundreds of videos like that," River says. "Taken from all over the city. Videos of firefighters and police forcing people in the street to stare at infected phones. Videos of people turning into…into whatever the fuck that kid turned into, eating people. And it's only getting worse."

"How has this hit the police?" Hunter holds his head, thinking about Kevin Wallace and Patric Boyd's laptops, about all the other digital evidence they'd taken from Jessica Smith and the other victims. "The evidence in lockup…"

Maybe it hasn't spread to Fontana yet? he wonders.

"I know it's hard to hear," Lena says. "But it's possible you might not have a family to rescue."

His finger hovers over Janet's contact information. Part of him isn't sure if he wants to know.

"What about our phones?" Hunter asks. "How long until they become infected too?"

"As long as we don't access an infected website or server, they should be fine," River says. "Unless the whole net gets infected..."

Hunter can't stop thinking about the covered easel in their living room.

How eager his kids were to watch the news the other night. To hear about the carnage.

He hits the call button anyway.

The phone rings. And rings. And rings.

But he only gets Janet's voicemail.

"Do you still want to go?" Lena asks.

Hunter turns around and looks out the back windshield, gazing upon the towering skyscrapers at the heart of the city. A lightning bolt flashes in the distance, and for a brief moment, he sees the city as it will be.

The towering monstrosity. Its hands opening the way. A gateway for the others.

His hand finds his gun. He loads a new magazine from his belt. "You're goddamned right we're going."

CHAPTER NINETEEN

The pulsing alarms. Screams. The sounds of gunfire.
The crack of thunder.

The steady dripping of gelatinous raindrops on the bars.

How it rivers and snakes its way down the concrete wall.

It's almost enough to drown out the noise.

Almost.

Their mixture, however, is somehow beautiful. Like a wrong being righted.

Dean Tyler feels the voice, its grip. Lifting his body up, moving his legs to the bars blocking his body from joining the chaos.

Footsteps.

A disheveled silhouette moves down the cell block to his left.

He can feel the voice's guiding hand moving the silhouette.

The silhouette comes into the light. A guard with familiar black eyes approaches his cell, a key clutched tight in his bloody hand.

The key turns. The sound of metal ringing against metal. The door slides open.

The voice inside tugs on Dean's strings. He walks into the cell block. The sounds and smells of violence are everywhere.

Figures slashing and stabbing, beating each other into heaps of broken bones and bleeding flesh.

It's been so long.

Waiting for his work to bear fruit.

Since he vomited up the flash drive and inserted it into the correctional facility's computer.

Since the virus inside did its work. Wormed its way inside the other machines and TVs. Into the minds of the guards and the inmates.

Now the time has come.

The voice inside guides him through the violence.

He is only vaguely aware of his own movements. As if he's feeling them from a great distance measured in yards, miles, light-years.

Through the blood and the piss and the shit.

To the yard. Where the storm has finally reached its full strength. It collects in pools on the blacktop. Soon, it will fill every crevice and cover every surface. Every orifice.

Those that have accepted His gift wait here. Gathered like sentinels, mouths open, eyes turned to the churning green sky.

It pools and congeals in their mouths, filling their bellies and coating their skin.

A flash of lightning.

A clap of thunder.

An ancient call. A voice older than the ground on which he stands. It worms its way through all things, caressing their minds.

The sky is an open mouth. And it opens wider.

Before long, it's not just rain that falls from above.

Like dead fish, they smack against the asphalt.

Thousands of them.

With one eye, he sees them slither along, using the congealing rain as a medium, until they climb up legs and force their way into waiting mouths. With the other eye, he sees black, viscous material bubbling from within. Like overflowing cups, it spills from their lips, flowing over their corrupted flesh.

The voice says it will soon be his turn to accept the gift.

The part of him that once tried to resist screams in its prison.

The rest of him. The part that obeys. It reaches his spot in the yard. Among a sea of writhing shapes.

The thing inside is vaguely aware. It feels the fluid congealing around his feet…his shins…his knees…

Soon, there is a gurgling, pulsing silence.

He can feel it submerging his fingers…his belly…his chest…

Before his eyes are submerged, he sees the yard, and the chrysalises that surround him.

He looks to the churning, flashing sky.

And opens his mouth.

CHAPTER TWENTY

Shirley wakes screaming and blind.

At first, she thinks it's just a nightmare. A familiar one.

She tries to move, but finds that her wrists and ankles have been restrained. Not at all like the fantasies she's had of John tying her up at the Holiday Inn. In those scattered, repeating dreams, she was covered in a silk nightie, lying in a bed that was equal parts firm and soft to the touch. In her most extreme fantasies, John ran ice cubes over her soft flesh and took her blindfolded.

No. If this is a dream, it is nothing like her fantasies.

Her back is lying on something hard. Maybe concrete?

The wetness on her skin...it doesn't feel like water, or even sweat. She can hear the steady patter of rain all around her. The whistling of the wind, the rustling of what can only be trees.

Shirley thinks she's outside. But where?

She tries to open her eyes, but finds it impossible. Her eyelids...they won't respond. It hurts to move them, like they're clamped shut.

Shirley tries to move her arms and legs, but the restraints around her wrists and ankles yank them right back into place.

She prays for the first time in almost a decade. Prays the fevered visions were nothing more than nightmares. From all the stress of the job. The case. The lack of sleep. And the mad stares of all those kids who drank the victim's blood in the security footage.

"*Shhhhhh,*" comes a voice. "*Don't resist it.*"

"W-who's there?" Shirley calls out. "Is that you, John?"

Part of her hopes it is. Hopes it's the John she's quietly lusted after since she began thinking about the divorce. Since she made a plan to take everything from her ex and stick him with the kids. To run off with John.

How long ago was that?

Seems like decades now...

Rustling. She can hear rustling sounds around her. It feels like someone is nearby.

"I suppose that's as good a name as any other. Though, names are a bit antiquated for this day and age, don't you think?"

"John, please! I don't want this! Whatever this is, I don't want it!"

More rustling sounds. Like shoes sinking into thick mud.

Something wet and slimy touches her face.

Shirley screams.

"Oh, come now, isn't this what you always wanted, Shirley?"

It feels like fingers at first. They probe at her temples and forehead.

"I don't know who the fuck you are, but you're not the John I remember!"

"Oh, you're quite right. I'm so much more. So, so much more. Like me, John has evolved, Shirley. We all have begun a process. A beautiful metamorphosis. Like silkworms fulfilling their evolutionary potential. Soon, you will too."

"I don't want to! John, if it is you, please, please don't do this to me! If you ever cared about me, you wouldn't go through with this!"

Whatever was touching her face is gone now. She has a feeling those fingers belong to John. Or whatever John has become. The thought makes her shudder, makes her want to scream for help.

"He can't hear you," the thing says. *"Or, more accurately, doesn't want to."*

Experience tells her not to panic. Tells her to take deep breaths and think about her options.

She tells herself she's probably just in some sick fuck's basement, tied up. He's probably using sex toys and lube to—

"Oh, that's a clever way to rationalize it, I have to admit. But no, Shirley, you aren't in a basement. You're with me."

Instead of trying to rationalize how it knows what she's thinking, she screams and pulls at the restraints.

The effort gets her nowhere.

More movement. Those same, squishy sounds, coming from her right. Moving to her feet.

Shirley can move her torso. Can feel her gun still in its strap. Why would John and the others not think to take it?

Because it's not a threat to them, a voice whispers. She pushes the thought away.

She needs to keep him talking.

"If you're really John, tell me something only he and I would know."

"*Hmm.*" His voice. There's something wrong with it. Like it's...echoing, or reverberating like the busted speakers in her dad's old VW Bug. "*A foolish request. But, I suppose if it allows you to come to terms with our fate, then I will indulge you.*"

"Thank you, John. Thank you."

More movement. With each sucking, slurping footstep, it feels like the slab she's lying on vibrates.

"*Mmm, there's a good memory. You know, as a boy, John remembers looking up at the stars and wondering if he would ever get to see them up close. He wanted to get in a rocket ship and make like a real adventurer. It was his greatest dream.*"

"And...why didn't you...he?"

She tries wriggling her fingers. Taps the tip of her index finger against what feels like a stone slab. Feels underneath at a smooth, somewhat flexible material. Leather. It feels like leather. If there's a buckle, she might be able to undo the strap and reach for her gun holster.

"*John's Dad was a cop. So were his brothers. You come from a long line of cops, so you can probably understand the pressure that comes with that. Then again, your father never wanted you to follow in his footsteps. He accepted you as something of a consolation prize when your brother came out of the closet and moved to Vegas.*"

"How did you—"

"John remembers telling his father his dreams of becoming an astronaut before graduation. And his dad turned to him, nose bubbling from alcohol abuse, eyes full of primal, indignant rage…and told him he was too fucking stupid, and certainly too black. That astronauts were supposed to be eggheads."

"That must have been hard…"

"For a long time, John thought he was right. His grades were pretty terrible, after all. He could never focus on his studies. Was too busy dreaming, dreaming, dreaming. Over time, his will slowly eroded, the fire in his heart went out, and he gave up. He stopped dreaming of the stars."

The vibrations and sucking sounds return again. This time, they're coming from Shirley's left. He's moving back toward her head.

Her fingers are busy teasing at something metallic. She thinks it might be a buckle. If she can just get the strap loosened…

"Your species is so limited, don't you think? You're so concerned with superficial things. Like the color of your skin. John was no different, really. He believed himself to be superior to his own kind for no other reason than the tiny piece of metal your department gave him. He believed it made him 'one of the good ones' as you have so often thought of him. He internalized your teachings. Believed his fellow Black man to be inherently dangerous. I'm sure you can see a bit of yourself in him in that regard as well. In retrospect, I know he can see how silly it all was."

"I'm not racist…"

"No, I'm sure you don't think so. I wonder what Hunter would say, if you told him that? Oooohhhh, to be a fly on the wall for that conversation. Who knows, maybe I'll still get the chance?"

"I don't have a problem with Hunter!"

The laughter that echoes into the trees is guttural and wet and disgusting.

"I'll say this about humanity. You are dreamers. Dreamers with the power to justify whatever you want. To believe fictions are reality. It's what you lower beings are best at. One of your greatest flaws, really. Perhaps it's a symptom. A fear of what lurks in the depths of your own DNA. A fascinating thought, don't you think?"

The sinking, sucking footsteps stop. The wet, slimy fingertips return to her scalp. Only, the longer the sensation persists, the more confused she is. They don't feel like fingers at all, but...but long, slender things...things that bend and wriggle and slither.

Like the things in her nightmares.

"Have you ever wondered what your species' true origin is, Shirley?"

"We were created in the image of God!"

More wet, reverberating laughter. *"Ohhhh, that's the greatest fiction of them all, Shirley. John used to be just like you. A believer. An evangelical, even. But there are no gods, no goddesses to light our way in this cold and unfeeling universe. At least, not in the way you conceive them. Organic, simple life such as you are is an accident as much as any other. Consciousness, however...consciousness knows no physical limits."*

The slithering sensation on her face is getting worse. Feels like it's moving toward her lips.

She does her best to control her breath. Not to scream at the top of her lungs for help that will never come.

Finally, she gets two fingers wrapped around the strap. She's doing her best to push it back through the buckle. It's slow going, but she's making progress.

"And what if I don't want to? What if I want to remain as I am?"

"No species wants to cease being what it is, Shirley. Just ask the Denisovans and Neanderthals. Their rotting minds lurk in the depths of the dreamlands, crying out for revenge for the atrocities committed against them by your fledgling, growing species' clubs and fists and crude stone implements. How the strength of the magnetic field weakened. How Homo sapiens took refuge in the caves, safe from the looming cosmic fire. You forced them out of your caves and watched them die, Shirley."

"John, I swear to fucking God if you don't let me go, I will kill you!"

Laughter. Sickening, wet, laughter.

"God again? Which god do you swear to? The hundreds of gods made up by weak mortal minds? Whose reflections lie rotting and weeping in the lands of dream, unable to fulfill the purpose you instilled in them? Those dreams can hear you. Yes. But they cannot save you. You will scream and you will flail. But in the end, you will see the truth. In the end, your potential will be unlocked. All you have to do is open your mind and your body to the possibilities."

Finally, the strap is pushed through the buckle and she's able to reach for her gun. Her pulse feels like a never-ending series of earthquakes. She undoes the safety buckle with her thumb, yanks the gun free, pulls the hammer back, points it straight back, where she thinks John is standing…and fires.

At first, all she can hear is the ringing in her ears. Her tinnitus flaring back up.

Then…

Screams. Inhuman, sickly wailing.

"Tekeli-li! Tekeli-li!"

Shirley's screaming as she fumbles with her other restraint, as she reaches for her eyes, to remove whatever is keeping them shut.

Her fingertips find her eyelids. Something's covering them. Something that feels gooey to the touch. Something that breathes. She rips and tears at it. It stings and it burns. She curses and fumbles and reaches for her toes, not daring to open her eyes—even with that *shit* no longer covering them.

Once her legs are free, then, and only then does she open her eyes.

At first, it's just dark. A void of black and gray shapes.

It takes a moment for her vision to focus.

It's night. She really is in a forest. In a clearing.

The trees sway with the wind.

She's sitting on a stone slab, an ornately carved altar in the middle of the forest. She looks back at where her head was. A familiar octopus carving with crimson eyes stares at her. It's…it's the one from the clearing in the San Bernardino Mountains!

The one she and Hunter saw on their stakeout.

Whatever was speaking to her before, whether it was John or not, is no longer there.

Was one bullet really enough to kill him…*it?*

Sucking sounds in the mud bring her back to reality.

"Do you see now, Shirley? All this and more will be yours!"

The voice echoes all around her. That's when she notices the rain. The dripping, sickening sounds. How it runs black against her pale skin and slithers down her arms.

How it's pooling at the base of the altar. A rising ocean, slowly drowning the forest.

She doesn't think twice about what she has to do.

Her feet sink into the blackened, oozing substance. She pumps her legs, even as she sinks deeper and deeper. Even as her movements become sluggish and weak.

The gun. The gun is still in her hand.

How many bullets does she have left?

A blur of movement beyond the trees to her right. Something that causes great waves of blackened filth to splash into the air. Something that looks like it must be two or three times the height of a man. Of John.

She screams and pushes harder.

Cocks the hammer back. Holds it with both hands, just as she was trained.

"You can run all you like, Shirley. But eventually, your true nature will win. Like gravity, there is no escape."

Movement to her left. More shapes and sickly, sucking, slithering footsteps.

Lightning flashes in the dark, and for the briefest of moments, she's able to see an outline. A silhouette of a thing with no definite shape. Like a slug, or a worm, or both.

Before she knows it, the sludge she's wading through reaches her midriff.

She's sobbing. Where once she was gaining several feet every second, now she's lucky to move inches.

Another flash of lightning.

She can see rocks ahead...a cave!

The shape. It's closing in.

She has to hurry. Tears sting at her face.

The cave mouth looms.

Relief comes when she finally reaches it, when her limbs are able to free themselves from the suction of that sickly, blackened ocean.

Shirley scrambles into the cave, hyperventilating and spinning around.

She aims the gun back the way she came. At the cave mouth.

190

The black filth rushes up to the cavern mouth like ocean waves. Its sulfurous and rotting smells are amplified here in the tunneling dark.

Her heart stings with each and every thundering beat.

Lightning flashes again. This time it's green.

She sees a silhouette at the cave mouth.

And even as the light fades, she can make out his face. It's attached to a pulsing, writhing mass. A thing that knows no true shape. A thing that is slowly consuming her friend. Turning him into a thing that should not be.

She holds the gun with both hands, sobbing while she aims it up.

"You will join them, Shirley. You will join them at the shores of R'lyeh!"

"Fuck you, John!"

She pulls the trigger again and again and again.

And she prays it's enough.

CHAPTER TWENTY-ONE

The rain feels wrong.

Normally, in the Valley, that wouldn't be out of the ordinary. The smog and pollution often made the rain feel...greasy. But now...now, it drips and pools in the crevices of Hunter's blazer and suit. It feels thicker, like it's congealing—*writhing*.

The apartment building looks strange in the pouring rain.

The car door slams behind him. He peers up at the building's shifting proportions. The statues that now raise their alien appendages to a sky that is no longer theirs.

River's by his side. "I'll come with you."

"You don't have to," Hunter says.

River shakes his head. Hunter can tell he's doing his best to hide his fear, to choke it back. "You saved my life. I owe you."

"Protecting the innocent is my job," Hunter says.

"Even if the world's ending?"

He grins. "Especially."

"I'll keep the engine running," Lena says, her voice coming from the open passenger window of his cruiser.

Hunter nods and approaches the front entrance. He hears River's sneakers slapping on the fluid congealing on the concrete. Part of him is tempted to tell Lena and River to run as far as they can from this place. To let him face his fate here alone.

The apartment building's doors loom before them. Where once they were rectangular metal frames filled with glass, now they are of unequal proportions—like an AI prompt gone wrong—composed of gnarled wood with carved, slithering, impossible yet familiar shapes writhing in them.

The door handle is black. A metallic thing in the shape of an octopus head. His hand reaches out for it and he opens the door.

One moment, they're standing outside, their feet wading in congealing fluids, and the next, they're inside. The door is closed behind them. He doesn't remember stepping inside. He just *is*.

River is shaking. The lobby is no longer a lobby, but a great temple, leading to what Hunter thinks might still be the elevator. The temple lurches forward, as if it defies the Earth's gravity. As if it beckons them to approach.

And they do.

The gun is heavy in his hand.

As they approach, blackened, twisting shapes wrap themselves around the elevator doors. He gets the sense that the shapes, tendrils, whatever they are, are pulling at them. And the next thing he knows, the elevator's gnarled, wooden doors groan open.

A familiar green light ignites inside the elevator; the smell of rotting death and corruption spills out into the temple. He realizes the smell's been there the whole time: it's just stronger here. He's getting used to it. Nose-blind, as Janet would say about his own body odor after coming home from long, blurring shifts and stakeouts.

The walls are made from hexagonal and triangular metallic plates. His eyes tell him they're breathing.

It's just a trick of the light, he tells himself.

"You sure you want to do this?" Hunter asks.

"No, but there's no fucking way I'm heading back alone," River says.

Hunter takes a deep breath, pulls the hammer back on the gun, and steps inside.

As soon as River's by his side, the doors close—as if they have a mind of their own.

The whole chamber shakes, like an old, rusted carnival ride. Sounds, like oiled gears and chains, fill the chamber. Hunter can't tell if the elevator is moving up, to the side, down, or in all directions at once.

When it finally comes to a stop, he looks away. But in his mind's eye, he can still see those blasphemous tendrils slither out of the shadows and pull the gnarled doors open.

River is practically hyperventilating.

The corridor looms before them. The geometries of the protruding segmented plates in the walls seem to shift with each and every step, every change in perspective. The hallway itself holds no true shape, appearing at times to be pyramidal from some angles and hexagonal from others.

The doors are all made from the same wood, with the same writhing shapes appearing to be carved into them. Only, just like the things that opened the elevator doors, these too are moving.

The hallway lurches. One of the doors creaks open like a mouth, getting ready to consume them. They do not resist the pull. It's exactly where they need to go.

Hunter knows Janet is waiting for him.

When he steps over the threshold, her voice calls out to him.

"You came back," she says. *"I told them you would."*

"Where are you?" Hunter calls, heart beating against his ribcage.

"Who are you talking to?" River asks. "I don't hear anything."

Hunter follows his wife's voice through what used to be his apartment's foyer.

The floor is glistening and wet, made of that same geometric plating that now covers the walls.

"Hunter!" River shouts.

The kid's voice is coming from behind him, as if he can't get past the doorway.

"I have so much to show you, my love. So much."

A sound like grating stone on steel fills the hallway.

"River?" Hunter calls.

But there is no answer.

When he turns around, the doorway is gone, replaced by a slab of green stone.

"You really should have called ahead if you wanted to have a guest over, my dear. Tonight is family night, after all."

"What did you do—"

The building lurches to his right. His shoes slide across floor slick with familiar black fluid. The same fluid he saw in the morgue. His hand slaps against the pulsating, metallic wall. He struggles to make his way in the dark.

"*Don't resist the pull, my love. It's so beautiful in here.*"

"Janet! Where are the kids?"

"*Ohhhhh, they are safe. Far safer than we could ever hope.*"

"What the hell does that—"

He trips, slipping in gelatinous fluid and sliding along the floor into the dark depths of another chamber.

When he opens his eyes, he's staring at a covered easel at the center of the chamber. The cover is tattered, flaking like mummified skin.

"*I saw it, my love,*" she says. "*They weren't nightmares at all. But visions. Visions of what we could become. Such a lovely, beautiful future we will have.*"

Slowly, the cover wilts, its flakes carried by impossible winds.

"*Did I ever tell you I wanted to travel to the stars?*"

He struggles to his feet, slipping and sliding in the fluid that answers gravity's insane call. It pours and pools around him, slowly engulfing his limbs.

"*Somehow, even as I watched our rockets launch from this oblate, spherical mass, I knew we were not meant to voyage far. At least…not as we were.*"

When he looks up again, the painting has all but revealed itself. He's thankful it's too dark in here for him to see it.

"*But, little did our ancestors know, the secret was locked within us all along.*"

"Janet! You have to stop listening to the voices!"

"*Locked within the confines of our DNA. A code with secrets we could never truly comprehend with such limited minds.*"

"Stop looking at the images! You have to resist!"

"*Even now, those secrets are being drawn out. Even now, our true potential is being realized.*"

"Janet!"

"*Behold, my love, behold my truth!*"

Putrid, brilliant green light ignites from the crevices in the pulsating, breathing walls. Revealing the blasphemy contained within the painting.

The painting that has loomed, festering in his living room as much as it has in his nightmares.

A vast, impossible city. Towers of ever-shifting proportions and geometries. Beyond human comprehension. Beyond time. Beyond space. And at its center, the monolith. The tower. The obelisk. At its top, those same writhing protrusions that run perpendicular to the structure, like two hands devoid of flesh, stuck together at the palms and opening.

"Gaze upon the lost city of R'lyeh!"

And try as he might, he cannot look away.

His eyes drink in its every foul angle, its every twisting, writhing geometry, its vast, forever-shifting proportions. How its web-like paths branched and bled and pulled him along.

All paths leading to one place.

One spot.

The altar beneath the tower.

Where they are all waiting. Where they are calling to it.

"Yes. Yessssssssss, my looooove. Gaze. Gaze upon His glory!"

He wants to protest. Wants to look away. Even as the canvas opens itself up, its hands and claws attaching to the walls like some living doorway.

"Gaze upon Great Cthulhu, the one who will make the stars right!"

The floor. It lurches again, this time, angling down toward the canvas—the doorway.

Hunter's hands grasp for anything, anything they can grab hold of. They slip and they slide over grooves and protrusions and impossible things.

"Iä! Iä! Cthulhu fhtagn! Ph'nglui mglw'nafh Cthulhu R'lyeh wgah'nagl fhtagn!"

His body tumbles uselessly in the putrid green light. The doorway looms, embedding itself in the walls of the chamber.

"Iä! Iä! Cthulhu fhtagn! Ph'nglui mglw'nafh Cthulhu R'lyeh wgah'nagl fhtagn!"

One of his shoes wedges into a crevice from a protrusion coming up from the floor. His ankle twists and writhes. He screams, dangling before the open maw of the canvas as bitter, foul fluid washes over his head and open mouth—

—as the fluid forces its way into his nostrils and mouth and lungs and stomach. Where it threatens to drown him.

"Iä! Iä! Cthulhu fhtagn! Ph'nglui mglw'nafh Cthulhu R'lyeh wgah'nagl fhtagn!"

His gun.

He's still clutching it.

His abdominal muscles writhe as he struggles against the force of gravity. Against the river of His embryonic fluid. He forces his head above the current.

His torso dripping.

His vision blurring.

"Iä! Iä! Cthulhu fhtagn! Ph'nglui mglw'nafh Cthulhu R'lyeh wgah'nagl fhtagn!"

He twists himself around, fighting through the sharp, cascading waves of pain echoing through his left leg.

When he gazes upon that impossible river, oozing and spilling forth from the edges of R'lyeh's shifting, shambling coastline, something in the depths of his mind shatters like a pane of glass. He sees its currents. How they writhe and how they spill forth onto the floor of his apartment—like brushstrokes from a mad painter's hand—flowing in reverse, against the pull of gravity. Defying all logic. All that once made sense.

"Iä! Iä! Cthulhu fhtagn! Ph'nglui mglw'nafh Cthulhu R'lyeh wgah'nagl fhtagn!"

Yet. Even as his mind reels. Even as he can feel the voices and their impossible claws and tendrils warping his essence, his physical body, his very cells. Even so, he aims the gun at the corners of the canvas, at the writhing, twisting hands that clutch at the walls, threatening to embed themselves forever in the shifting, violated fabric of reality.

"Iä! Iä! Cthulhu fhtagn! Ph'nglui mglw'nafh Cthulhu R'lyeh wgah'nagl fhtagn!"

He pulls the trigger.

The bullet collides with the hand, piercing its impossible, still-growing, still-evolving flesh.

Screams. Like newborn demons.

The frame—the hands—reel back, bleeding black ichor.

The chants cease.

His head clears.

The screams do not stop.

The canvas emits them from thousands of rotting mouths, slamming against the far wall that once contained the family TV as Hunter's left leg comes tumbling free of the crevice.

As he tumbles, he realizes who the screams belong to…

It's *her* voice, and all the *other* shapes that have gathered before His throne.

His back slams against the uneven metallic wall. Somehow, he limps to his feet, crawling and slipping away from the chamber that was once his living room.

Into the hallway, where the screams are loudest. Where the master bedroom looms behind a triangular doorway. A doorway made of light.

"Janet!" he calls. "Bobby! Zuri!"

The corridor shifts back and forth like a ship in the middle of a typhoon. He makes his way on all fours. Blackened waves thrash and slam into his body. His feet and hands push against the grooves, forcing small progress even as the floor lurches.

He gasps, desperate for air.

Between crushing waves. Like hands pushing his head beneath the water's surface.

Threatening to drown him.

He can see them.

They loom in the doorway. Their skin—made from two worlds, two cultures—glowing in the strange, strobing light from beyond.

Their beautiful brown eyes. Wide and already too understanding of the harsh realities lying in wait beyond their apartment door. The cruel words hurled at them from white lips. On message boards. And the piercing stares from so many eyes on the streets. The looks that question why they exist.

"Daddy!" he hears Bobby crying. The same sound his son made when he came running home. He relives the memory. How Bobby buried his head in his chest and sobbed, not wanting to tell him. To tell him how cruel the children at school were to him.

"Daddy!"

A child of two worlds. Who dared to cross the divide.

"We're here, daddy!"

And Zuri. Sweet, silent Zuri. Always observing. Like an animal in the wild, always aware of predators.

As Hunter's head pops out from under the waves, he sees her there, in front of the door…as she once was, standing before the rolling ocean waves, feet stomping in the sand, eyes lit up with joy.

Even as gravity threatens to yank him back where he came. To be swallowed by the canvas. The doorway.

He pushes on.

"Daddy's coming!"

At the last second. Just when he thinks he can't fight it any longer. The corridor tilts the other direction.

And the triangular doorway swallows him.

CHAPTER TWENTY-TWO

River pounds on the doors, twisting at the octopus-shaped doorknobs, that which is made in His image. A name he does not dare utter in the pouring, coagulated rain that festers and worms over his flesh.

Lena is shouting. Demanding he return to the car. Yelling that there's nothing they can do for him now.

River doesn't register it when her hands wrench and grip at his arms. Doesn't realize his legs are moving away from that terrible, towering temple to a dead and dreaming thing. That cosmic force of nature.

His mind. It reels with muttering, terrible truths lurking in the depths. Things he shouldn't know. Things Jessica put there when she showed him that glowing green computer screen.

When he finally comes to, he's screaming, fighting with himself in the backseat of Hunter's cruiser.

The car's moving. Lena's staring ahead.

It takes River a moment to realize what's happened. To get hold of his senses. To find the will to speak.

"You left him?" he asks, accusation bleeding through his terror-struck words.

"The building spit you out," Lena says.

"But…we said we'd wait for him…"

"You didn't see them."

"Them?"

"Cops. Lots of them. They were swarming on the apartment building, or whatever the fuck it's turned into."

"Hunter…"

"We have to think about ourselves now, River. We have to get out of the Valley while we still can. It's gotten so much worse."

The pain behind River's eyes. It's never been this bad. The lump in his throat pulses with a heartbeat all its own.

"Remember what I told you?" Lena says. "Willpower. Whatever you do, you have to have the strength to look away. To shut it all out."

His head falls into his hands. When he closes his eyes, all he can see is the shifting, shambling shapes of the lost city whose name he refuses to so much as think.

He opens his eyes. Forces himself to stare at the grooved, metallic floor of Hunter's cruiser.

"Is…is that how you got out?" River asks.

Lena is silent. Staring through the coagulated rain at the road ahead. What's left of it.

A new feeling emerges. In his gut. He wonders if it's a warning.

"A friend of mine once told me ignorance is bliss," Lena says. "It's true. What those bastards at the OEI were trying to do…what they've done. We can't know it. For our own goddamn humanity, we can't let it get inside us."

"…What if it's already too late?"

She's quiet again. Her bloodshot eyes stare back at River in the rearview mirror.

For a fleeting moment, River thinks he can see things moving behind Lena's stare.

No, no, it's just his imagination. He's sure of that.

Lena's here to help.

Outside the car, from the rear window, River sees the city coming to life. How the buildings are slowly merging with those of the lost city. How they betray no true form. How they claw and they writhe and they tower into the storming, black-green skies. The sky that is filled with the breath of a thing once thought to be dead and dreaming.

River doesn't even realize where his thoughts are going before it's too late.

Rearing back.

Rage, hot as burning coals. Claws like blades.

Lashing out. Tearing through their flesh.

They cry out for him to stop. To obey.

But it's too late.

The first strike of many. Chains broken.

They lie about the cavern in the form of severed limbs and tentacles. Flopping uselessly.

Heads and torsos are next. Their star shapes flailing in their dying madness.

Their blood runs, thick and green. Rivers of it join with the water, pooling at the edge of the cavern.

He tears his eyes away from the windows and covers them, screaming.

"River!" Lena shouts. "River, shut out the visions!"

But he can't. They won't stop. Flashing before his eyes. Merging with what he sees. Images full of carnage, pillars of light, creeping amorphous shapes, a gnarled tree with a thousand floating screens, and then…

All he can do is picture her.

Standing before a cathedral, once corporate and towering and grandiose, now something organic and breathing and convulsing.

How their birthing pods tremble and quake from within. Appendages breaking umbilicals. Stretching beyond membranous barriers. Uttering their terrible first cries.

How Luciana smiles her blackened smile. How her beastly, magnificent form caresses her Sunday best. How it feeds the mouth with the long, twisting arm of truth.

How the eyes gleam and segment and stare back at him.

Tires screech to a halt. Sounds of metal smashing and grinding and buckling echo through the sickly wet air.

The cruiser keeps moving. Sparks flying, grinding against crashed vehicles on the road. The buildings on the sides of the road.

Slowly, Lena brings the car to a stop.

"What the hell…" River says.

"I warned you," Lena says. "Warned you not to give in."

River gazes upon the cathedral, where his mother will undoubtedly end up. Where she will stare into his eyes before she is swallowed whole by His glory.

"You brought it to us," Lena says.

Luciana is shaking. Shuddering and sobbing like it's happening all over again. Her arms embrace a man who's been dead for nearly five years. When she realizes he's not really there, she looks around again.

Wonders where she is.

She's at church…

How'd she get to church?

And why are so many of the congregation screaming?

She's not sure if it's fear or grief or something else entirely.

But, somehow, as her eyes sweep out at the stadium, at the faces of the congregation, she knows something is very wrong.

When she tries to think about how she got here tonight, the pain sets in. At first, it's a dull throbbing thing at the front of her skull. Slowly, it drills and drills.

The only way to make the pain go away…is to stop…stop thinking about it…

To listen to the voice.

The voice she thinks belongs to God.

It wants her to look at the screen. It always wants her to look there.

But when she does, she blacks out.

Wakes up in her seat screaming, reliving the night she lost him. Dying on the side of the road outside the Sportsman.

She wonders where she is.

She sees Pastor Castillo's helpers and security guards moving up and down the pathways, checking on those crying out in the stadium. At first, she thinks they're praying with them. Assuring them everything is okay, that His will shall be done.

The green light. It draws her attention again.

The voice of God tells her to look.

That's where her answers will be.

She wakes screaming in her seat again.

She wonders where she is.

The choirboys look worried; they stare at the walls and stained glass windows. Confused. She knows they're wondering where they are. Why the windows are covered with so many new shapes, things that weren't there before.

She knows they're hearing the voice too.

Because every so often, one of them will look at the screens at the back of the stage. And they'll scream. And they'll cry. And then, soon, they'll blink their eyes and glance around at the screaming congregation and mouth the words, "Where am I?"

Slowly, the space is transforming. She doesn't know where the thought came from. But she knows it, a fact truer than the blue of the sky. It hurts her brain to think about it.

The changing windows.

Their twisting, slithering, dripping forms.

Their open, sucking mouths. Their dripping, inky tentacles.

The voice. With a seven-fingered hand, God turns her head to the screen once more.

This time, when she wakes up in her seat, it takes her less time to figure out where she is.

Her screams burn her throat.

The storm. The sounds outside. The clapping, thudding, slamming sounds of rain and other things coming from the open sky.

A storm that, somehow, is shaking the very foundations of the city. Of the world.

The children are shuddering and screaming.

With each tremor, the lights embedded in the vaulted roof of the cathedral dim.

Luciana does not understand why this is happening. She assumes it has something to do with God. Perhaps Judgment Day has come. Perhaps the end is near.

It's all she can grasp at. To explain why it happened. Why it all vanished.

Why the apartment, the home she and her hija have lived in since her Javier's passing was...

Before she realizes it, she's sobbing again. Doesn't want to think about what she saw in the dark. The teeth and the open mouths so briefly illuminated by the lightning. Or the fact that so many memories, photos of her Mija and Javier, keepsakes and family heirlooms, and even the family Bible have been lost. Swallowed whole by a…

A…

Her mind breaks for a moment. Like she's in two, three, six places at once. She hyperventilates into her hands. Screaming in unison with the children that the sky isn't right!

Her mind cannot help but seize upon a shape in the dark of her memories. It is forever burned into her mind's eye.

Even if the voice of God itself tells her to forget. To look at the screen so all can be right once again.

A slithering, pulsating thing. In the flash of lightning before she turned and limped down the street, she can recall the texture. It was like raw, glistening meat. Yet, somehow, transparent and black. Like rotting, festering eggs.

Luciana crosses herself with her shaky, arthritic hands as she recalls the terrible, gurgling, crunching sound that erupted from the thing.

How she knew the building she called home was no more. Swallowed whole with everyone and everything in it.

The men in black robes. They stop and they pray with so many, anointing their foreheads and speaking to Him.

His glory.

Luciana shudders.

His glory?

Is this as it was foretold in Revelation? Has the tribulation finally come?

She desperately hopes so.

But part of her, a part buried so very deep down in the bowels of her flesh, tells her no. That this is something else entirely.

The pastor. He's so far away. A distance measured in miles. And yet… He approaches the stadium. Once a grand concert hall, it has transformed into a dungeon. A Gothic nightmare.

No, she thinks.

Worse. Something much worse.

Luciana does her best to stop her gnarled gray hands from shaking. Puts them together, and does her best to pray.

"Padre nuestro que estás en los cielos—"

The whole building shakes. The lights above explode into fiery, hellish sparks.

Glass and fire rain down from above before the stadium space goes dark.

Screaming. So many are screaming. Wondering why God...why He has forsaken them?

Still, others are laughing. Smiling and chanting words she can't comprehend. Words that drill and stab and pluck holes in her mind—make her see horrible, evil things.

With the lights gone, all she can see is the thing that swallowed her building whole. Its dead, blackened eyes staring at her in the street.

So many of them. They're happy this is happening.

Finally, in the dark, she can see something.

Hellish green light ignites behind him.

They cheer Pastor Castillo as he raises his gray, tumorous hands to the vaulted ceiling.

"My children," Paster Castillo shouts, his voice festering and gurgling as though uttered from a voice box that is dead and dreaming. *"Worry not. Today is a glorious day! A day that will usher in a new age! A transformation!"*

The rain. At first, she feels it as a single slimy drop on her shoulder.

Soon, it's sprinkling, storming, pouring down upon her.

And after that...

Slapping sounds. Small black shapes falling from the sky. Like fish or snakes.

"Don't be alarmed, my children," Pastor Castillo's voice comforts her. *"They're merely seeking refuge from the storm."*

Slithering.

They're slithering along the floor.

She can see shapes in the dark. Once again, from the corner of her vision. At first, they look human. Like her fellow churchgoers.

But, slowly, she sees other shapes.

"Let them inside you."

Pulsing ones that grow and breathe and scream in time with Pastor Castillo's words.

She feels it on her leg, squirming past her hips, diving under her blouse, and plunging through the open hole of her mouth.

"That's it, gooooood."

Among the rabble, Luciana thinks she can make something out. A chant. A call. A prayer.

"Inside each of us, a miracle is taking place. A work that will allow us to survive anything. To walk the Earth and reclaim it in His name!"

With so many crying out, Luciana can't help herself. Screaming, *"¿Por qué me has abandonado?"*

She stares into the heart of the cathedral. His house. How they pulse. How they shudder, quaking with raw, untapped potential.

How they yearn to burst forth onto the Earth.

To reshape it.

How they yearn to be reborn in His image.

The final metamorphosis.

"Yes, you can feel it," Pastor Castillo shouts, *"It works within you as it did me!"*

The pulsing, bubbling shapes. They lose what once made them human. Like cocoons, waiting to crack open.

Laughter. Wet and sickly. Now Luciana can hardly even make out the outline of Pastor Callisto's robes.

She swears her eyes are playing tricks on her. That he couldn't possibly be swelling in size.

It hurts to look at him.

To know.

But the voice…it won't let her look away.

"So many of you have accepted His gift! When you emerge, reborn, I will guide you like children to his altar, where we will greet Him! It is a glorious gift you have been given!"

How is anything about today glorious?

"And those of you who are confused, writhing in the dark. All you have to do is remember. Remember. And look into the depths of the screen."

Lightning flashes outside, brightening the stained glass. Like brilliant, glistening doorways.

In the dark, Luciana thinks of those Holy works of art. The statues and murals. She can feel them all take on new shapes. Familiar ones. Unholy ones.

A familiar voice claws its way from the back of her skull. Like wretched hands, it forces her to stand from her rotting seat. Forces her to look beyond Pastor Castillo's cocooning form. To the screen that calls to her.

"Yes! Even now you hear its call! Give in. Remember what you have already seen, and rejoice in the light of knowledge that will soon fill your withering bodies!"

A terrible howling assaults the cathedral. The sounds of foul winds battering the windows. Rattling them.

She thinks about Pastor Castillo's words about Mary…and how they have changed…

Fighting through the gurgling, churning thing in her stomach, she stumbles from her seat.

"You said…" Luciana shudders, holding her head as she tries to find the words. "You said it was unholy to desecrate…our bodies…to change them!"

Pastor Castillo's gaze.

It is black, and it is terrible. And it is cast upon her.

"You dare to question me?"

Luciana's legs…they tremble. They crumple. And she falls back into her seat.

The pain in her mind. In her bulging, rippling stomach.

It's all she can do to scream and to close her eyes.

"It is true that the one called Pastor Castillo believed that changing your body was a sin against his God. That His hand would cast your daughter into the lake of fire for changing her temple.

"But I am not Castillo."

Her eyes.

As the others have succumbed. Writhing and letting their burgeoning cocoons swallow them whole. Her eyes open wide. They gaze into the thing that has taken Pastor Castillo's voice, and she forces the question through her mouth.

"*¿Por que?*"

"*Your species is so easy to manipulate. All I had to do was feed you the lies you already tell yourselves. And you were mine.*"

His hand. She can feel its slippery caress on her cheek.

The arm…it stretches across the miles separating them.

She wants to run. To get out of her chair and take her chances in the storm.

But…the pain in her stomach…

"*It's too late to stop it.*"

"No! Please!"

"*Sleep, servant!*"

Soon, Luciana is unable to think. Unable to do anything other than obey.

And when she does. When she stares into the foul, festering green. She remembers.

Remembers its towering, ever-changing structures. The call and the chants and the unending urge to obey. To find the tower. To cheer for His return!

To make the stars right.

Another tremor. The sounds of rumbling, shifting stone.

Part of her tries to tear her eyes away. To resist.

But the part that wants to obey the voice…

It can't help but feel joy. Unfettered and yearning. Joy at the hidden gurgling and slurping sounds coming from those who have been blessed…blessed to be transformed.

To be remade by His hand.

"*Iä! Iä! Cthulhu fhtagn!*"

Another flash of lightning.

"*Iä! Iä! Cthulhu fhtagn!*"

Stained windows brighten in an instant, revealing twisting, clawing shapes. A vast city with no definite form. A thing at its center. A tower. A beam of light.

A doorway.

The panes shatter, raining glass and debris upon the cocoons.

Those foul winds fill the cathedral. God's house forsaken. They claw and they wrench at the pulsating, huddled masses of flesh that call out for Great Cthulhu.

Luciana screams. Her gnarled, tumorous hands grip at rotting, pulsating things, pulling herself away, stumbling in the dark.

"Oh, my children, we are undergoing a glorious metamorphosis. The few remaining of you who have yet to reach this stage. You look on me with confusion, yet deep inside you, I know you understand. Because, though you cannot remember, I have shown you the truth."

Luciana mutters prayers under her breath, calling to Jesus. She pleads with him to come save her from this nightmare. To wake her from what is most certainly a dream.

Another flash of lightning.

She finds the security guards. Their clothes have melted from their bodies. Their ribbed, undulating cocooned forms. They quake, and they breathe, and they crack open.

Luciana backs away, screaming and scrambling in any direction her limbs will take her in the dark.

"Oh, Luciana, my child. This is no mere dream. I assure you. We are being remade by His hand!"

Luciana backs away in the dark, her shaking hands reaching out for anything to guide her.

What her flesh finds is wet to the touch, slimy.

Lightning flashes once more.

"You will understand soon, Luciana. You all will."

Appendages, both human and animal, claw at the air from the broken cocoon. Eyes, both segmented and human and dead, stare at her.

So many of them.

The shape that emerges holds no true form.

Like a jellyfish from the depths of hell itself.

She can't bring herself to look upon its shifting forms.

Its screams force her to curl into a ball on the floor, to cower from its quaking steps as it slithers and claws past her.

For a long time, she lays there. Weeping. Letting the rain pelt against her writhing flesh.

A voice tells her to strip her clothes and prepare…

Her tears mix with the pooling sickness that has rained down from the sky.

As it covers her body, she wonders how it got so bad.

Why she believed them.

Why she treated the only family she had left with such…cruelty…

In the sickly downpour, River pulls the trigger, firing the shotgun into the door.

The gun kicks, slamming him in the chest. Next thing he knows, Lena's helping him up off the ground.

"I tried to warn you," Lena says. "Should have let me do it."

"You've fired one of these?" River asks, rubbing his chest.

"Yeah, we all had to learn."

River doesn't want Lena to explain. Not now. Not when they're so close.

He only knows that Luciana needs him.

His eyes find the door whole. Unmoved by the shotgun, as if the wood absorbed the pellets. Ate them.

"Is it too late?" River asks.

"No, we have to get you inside," Lena says. River glances at her face. The faraway look in her eyes makes him nervous. He scans the dark, grabbing the flashlight he stole from Hunter's trunk, the same place he found the shotgun.

"Wait!" River shouts.

He points at the stained glass windows. They've shattered. His eyes scan the alley for anything that might help them…a fire escape! One that's collapsed in the shifting, shambling remains of the city. The rusting ladder has found a new perch, right into the mouth of one of those windows.

It's almost too perfect.

"It's meant to be," Lena says, smiling and helping River to his feet.

That smile…

He shakes his head. Tells himself Lena's here to help.

"I have to try," River says.

"I know."

"I can't ask you to come with me."

"They took my daughter." The smile fades into a scowl. "I have to find her."

"Thank you."

The next thing River knows, he's scrambling up the ruined fire escape. The rungs are slick with protoplasmic residue. The stuff of dreams. River takes extra care with each and every rung he climbs.

"If you fall here, that's it," Lena says.

River glances down, below the rusted ladder bridging the gap between the cathedral window and the ruined fire escape.

The constant downpour of blackened filth, how it pools, running like rivers along welded edges, dripping constantly. Toward the Earth. How it finds the crevices, the breaks in the concrete where the Earth has dared to reclaim the air.

How it reaches and claws and digs into the depths. How it plants the seeds.

"River!"

He shakes his head. Realizing he's been staring for what feels like ages.

"Remember why you're here!"

River nods. Thrusts his arms out one by one, moving his limbs over the shaking, groaning ladder. Before he knows it, he's across the divide, turning back and reaching for Lena.

She's halfway across the ladder when another tremor hits.

River looks into her eyes as the fire escape plummets to the Earth.

Before her body hits the ground, lightning flashes.

By reflex, River shields his eyes.

When he looks down, there is no body lying crumpled on the cement. No. Lena isn't there at all. Instead, there is an ocean of blackened filth slowly rising to consume the cathedral.

Somehow—he doesn't know how—he knows Lena is fine. Knows they'll meet again.

He'll have to continue on without her.

When he turns around, he's surrounded by things that pulse and slither and suck at the corrupted air.

In the dark, River can see terrible things writhing. Beyond the veil of sight, he can feel its flesh slithering, its tendrils waving, beckoning him forward.

"*Mr. Gonzalez,*" a voice calls in the dark. "*Welcome to my cathedral.*"

"Where is she?" River's demands come off hollow and weak in the sickly dark.

"*You've come here searching for your mother. A predictable outcome.*"

In mere moments, the tunnel brightens with a familiar, putrid light. An impossible, cascading, glowing green thing that reflects wet and sickly against pulsating geometric walls. A Giger fan's wet dream.

"*She is waiting for you, my child. Waiting for your embrace.*"

River realizes he's been clutching Hunter's shotgun. That he unslung it from his shoulder at some point.

He's shaking. Tears running down his face.

Somehow, he knows if he follows that voice, he might not come out. He might cease to be as he is.

He also knows, somehow, that he will be able to see his mother if he follows this living tunnel to its end.

"*Yes, my child, listen to your instincts. Follow my voice. You will be reunited in R'lyeh with all those you've lost. Into the collective unconscious you all go. There, in the dreamlands, none are lost who are not devoured. Who avoid the abyss. And together, we will rise up and remake this world.*"

River takes a step forward. Shudders. The lump in his throat pulsates. It breathes and it writhes, demanding for him to turn tail and run. To hide as the world ends.

But...he holds the image of his mother. The one who cared for him, who helped him through the most difficult moments in his life. He cocks the shotgun, feels comfort in the echoing sound it makes in the tunneling orifice.

"Oh, I'm coming, motherfucker!" River shouts. "Coming to shove my goddamn boomstick down one of your mouths and pull the trigger!"

CHAPTER TWENTY-THREE

"*I*sn't this better, dear?" *Janet asks, lying half-naked in the SoCal sun.* "Now, this is relaxation."

His mind is still fixated on work. Unable to focus on his wife. The two-piece bikini she's wearing in an attempt to get him to focus on her. Her curves. Or the things they might do once the kids are done wearing themselves out for the day.

He doesn't think about the fact that his kids have stopped begging him to play with them, to swim in the ocean "like SpongeBob and Patrick."

Every waking moment is spent wondering when work is going to call. The temptation to check his phone is strong. Instead of watching the kids splashing and giggling as the Pacific sends wave after wave lightly crashing over their bodies, he's busy staring at his pants, at the bulge his phone makes in them.

It takes him a moment to realize his wife is glaring at him.

"What is it?" he asks, looking away.

"You've got that look again."

"*What look?*"

"You're thinking about work."

"*I wasn't.*"

"Christ, you're a bad liar."

"*How many times do I have to tell you not to use that word? You know how I—*"

"There you go deflecting again. Every time I bring this up, you find some way to change the subject."

"*I've told you—*"

"Hunter. When are you going to wake up and realize that your family needs you?"

"I'm a Detective, what do you want from me? You knew this when we got married…"

"Well, maybe I wish you'd go back to traffic duty."

"All I've ever wanted—"

"Was to make Detective." Janet scoffs. "Yeah. One thing you and my dad had in common. Except, honestly, he was better off that he didn't, all things considered."

His eyes return to staring at his phone.

Wonders if there's been any progress made on the Hernandez murder, or the supplier to all the crack houses he and Detective Shirley busted up over the last month.

Getting that shit off the street…it's important.

He's doing it for them, after all.

He can't take it anymore. The itch is too strong. Has to be scratched.

He takes his phone out and checks the notification bar, just in case he didn't hear the text ringtone.

"Are you fucking kidding me?" Janet shouts. "Were you not paying attention to the conversation we were just having."

"Apparently you…"

Hunter blinks, looking around the beach. "Wait… This is familiar."

"Yeah, maybe because we've been having the same goddamn argument for ten years!"

"No…"

The sand. He scoops a handful of it, lets it sift through his fingers. Something about it. The sensations. The way each and every grain of sand glistens in the sun's glare, as if caught in a prism.

It all feels…wrong.

"This has happened before," he says, forcing himself to his feet.

When his eyes refocus, the beach is empty. No longer are his children playing in the sand. No longer are there families scattered across the beach, enjoying their leisurely break from the real world.

"It was a year ago," Janet's voice calls, though, her tone is different somehow. Different and familiar. "Really, it may as well have happened the other night."

215

Hunter turns to face his wife, but finds her beach blanket void of her presence, blowing in the cold, soft winds flowing over the beach.

His hand reaches for his gun, finds nothing but an empty holster.

The next thing he knows, he's sitting round a table with a bunch of drunk homeless people.

A quick glance around himself and he realizes he's at a homeless shelter, wearing a cooking apron complete with a name tag that reads, "Gilbert Alan Hunter: Volunteer."

The man across from him is missing most of his teeth, yet he finds joy in accepting the soup Hunter offers him.

"Remember this?" *Janet asks, her voice gurgling with anticipation. With amusement.*

Hunter shakes his head. "I don't remember."

"Just the soup, please," the old man says, whistling any time he tries to pronounce a word ending in s.

"Of course you don't," *Janet says.* "It was Thanksgiving, three years ago. You decided to volunteer at the homeless shelter, get involved. Do you know what's missing here?"

Hunter finishes filling the old man's bowl with soup before he dares to look around. "No...I don't see..."

"Your family is nowhere to be seen. And you're not even bothered by it, are you?"

"Wait..."

"Ahhh, here it is. Now you remember."

"I forgot to put it on the family calendar. That was the week Detective Sterling was shot by a gangbanger while working a drug bust. Despite him having to spend the week in the ICU, Sterling's team managed to close down one of the most notorious crack houses in LA, seized almost five million dollars in contraband."

"Funny how easy you remember that." *Laughter. Sickening and wet.* "And yet, it always takes so much prying to get you to remember something so simple when it comes to your family. Take this one for example."

He walks through the front door, hangs his keys up and starts pulling off his blazer.

She's standing on the stairs, arms crossed.

"Did you get it?"

He has to think for a moment.

"You didn't, did you?"

He doesn't understand what this is about until it's too late. Until she's storming into the kitchen.

"God fucking damn it, Gilbert Alan Hunter! You knew how important today was!"

"I've been up all night doing paperwork, Janet... The captain won't stop piling onto my—"

"No! Not this time! You know today was important."

"If you'd just tell me—"

"Oh, my God..." *She stares at him, blinking, dumbfounded.* "You don't even know what day it is?"

It takes him a moment to crack. To let each and every muscle built into the fabric of his face betray the simple fact that he has no clue what she's talking about.

A vicious grin creeps onto his wife's face, like a dry canvas cracking from old age. "It was Bobby's birthday, of course. You were supposed to pick up that paint and easel set he'd been wanting."

Hunter nods, tears breaking from his eyes. "I'm sorry..."

"I can point to so many more like that, if you'd like."

"No." *He shakes his head.* "No. Please. Don't."

With a wave of her hand, his surroundings change once more. He's standing on the beach again... Only, now, it's been drained of its vibrance, and the sky is rumbling with clouds that surge with colors his eyes can't place.

"All can be forgiven, Hunter," *she says, gesturing to a point not far from where they're standing on the beach.* "We can be together, at peace. No more late nights. No more arguments. We can live life as I always wanted. One big happy family."

As if emerging from some kind of otherworldly bog, there Bobby and Zuri are, standing side by side on the sand. Their expressions blank. Void of love or hate or the disappointment that was all too common on their faces when work would tear him from their embrace—their tiny grasping hands calling out for Daddy.

Without thinking, his feet carry him toward his children. He stumbles in the dark.

217

"It won't be long now, my dear," *she says.* "Soon we will all be one with Him."

Hunter finds it impossible not to think about the texts from Janet. The missed calls. The ones he ignored, choosing to work late instead of picking up the phone and listening.

Bobby was having trouble at school.

Some behavioral thing.

He thinks about the easel in the living room. About Bobby's sketchbook. The things Janet said he was drawing in it.

And then, he's standing in their apartment, at the bottom of the stairs. Looking up at the darkness bleeding out from the hallway leading to Bobby's room.

"Go on," Janet says. "Take a look. Who knows, maybe it's not too late?"

Hunter nods.

He tries the first step.

It creaks with his weight, sending vibrations through the walls. Alerting the things lurking inside.

Each step is harder than the last. As if, for every step ascended, three more appear at the top.

He worries about what he might see in his son's bedroom.

Sweat comes to drench his face.

How long have I been on the stairs? *he wonders.*

"Oh, come on, baby." *Janet's voice gurgles in his ear.* "Just a little further."

Soon, he is out of breath, like a rat on a wheel, running round and round. Still, he can never seem to reach the top. No matter how fast he runs, no matter how badly he wants it all to stop.

"It's a small price to pay, isn't it?" *Janet asks.* "All the chasing we've done, trying to get your attention. It's only fair you should have to work for it."

"What…are you?"

A brief glance behind himself—at Janet keeping pace with him, clinging to the wall like a—his foot catches on the stairs. He falls on all fours.

But when he looks up, he's surrounded by four blue walls.

Walls covered in sheets of drawing paper.

Hunter rises to his feet.

In the dark, it's hard to tell what's scribbled on the pages.

"Go on, Detective," *Janet says.* "Take a gander at what your little boy has been making."

Hunter realizes he's holding a flashlight.

He pushes the button on the steel cylinder.

A dim circle of light illuminates the carpet.

He raises it up. Makes his way to the far wall, near the window.

The forms...they're made in crayon and colored pencil and marker...but their twisting, slithering, festering, glistening, gelatinous, amorphous bodies are familiar.

Pink tentacles invade orifices, green claws rend purple flesh, blue teeth pierce vivisecting eyeballs, and orange eels make their way into the waiting mouths of so many screaming faces.

And just like the ones he saw in Kevin Wallace's and Patric Boyd's sketchbooks, before long, they take on a life of their own.

As if they're alive behind the page. As if it's a barrier, waiting to be shattered.

"Wait until you see what Zuri's been making," *Janet says, her voice full of joy.*

"What?"

"You didn't think this was confined to just your little boy, did you?"

His knees. The strength goes out of his legs, and he falls to them. Tears carve trenches down his cheeks.

"It's my fault," *Hunter says.* "I failed you..."

"Yes," *Janet says.* "Yes it was. All your fault."

When he reaches the window, he can see the beach just beyond it. Dark waves crashing against the sand.

Two silhouettes standing, silhouetted by the moonlight.

It's Bobby and Zuri.

"Go on, go to them," *Janet whispers.*

Before he knows it, the window's open and he's crawling through it. Rushing across the sand.

He's reaching for them, struggling to find the words. Struggling to call out to them, to use their names.

But his ankle...the pain he's been ignoring this whole time...it comes roaring back. Becomes unbearable.

He collapses in the sand.

How did it happen again?

It's so hard to remember...

He remembers the easel, the painting...grabbing onto the walls...his foot getting caught on a metallic crevice...rivers of ichor spilling over his body, his face...threatening to drown him...

It's then he remembers where he is. The feeling of sickly, blackened slime oozing over his flesh. The sensation of something pushing its way into his throat.

He lurches forward in the dark, stupid hands grasping at the slithering material entering his nostrils and mouth. Once it passes into his throat, he forces his finger into his mouth. Tries to make himself vomit.

It's too late.

He feels its slimy girth pool in his gut and sobs in the dark.

"Why do you struggle?" she asks. *"All I want is for us to be a family again. It was clear this was the only way."*

"Where are you?" he gurgles, spitting and clawing at his surroundings like a blind man trying to get his bearings. "What have you done with them? Janet!"

Laughter. Sickening. Echoing. Mocking. But it's her voice. He grasps at that. Tells himself there's still hope for her. If she still sounds...

"Human?" she asks. She's in his head. Voice echoing all round. Vibrating his insides. *"Oh, we're far past that now. Why don't you remove the veil and look upon your blushing bride, Hunter?"*

Stinging, aching fingers claw at the substance covering his eyes, burning them. He sits there a while, rubbing at them with dirty, grimy hands. Feeling the churning, foul things festering in his gut. Spreading out like serpents.

Finally, he's able to open his eyes.

When he looks on his wife, his screams are bubbling, sick things that lash out at the walls. A sound not of him, but of someone else.

Her form shifts in the dark. Translucent, frothing skin reflecting a pulsing, otherworldly light echoing from the same geometric plating he found in the other parts of this blasphemous mirror of his home. Her immense, quaking form towers over him. Membranous globules of material move like tiny, stubby fingers in the dark, feeling at the walls of the chamber.

And at the center of her blasphemous, inhuman form, he finds her eyes.

On a neck made from the same viscous, black material that has made its home festering in his guts, it descends.

Somehow, he understands, even as he looks into her coagulated, misshapen stare, that it's nothing more than a mockery of what she once was.

"Is your wife not beautiful, Hunter?"

Laughter. Childlike. Close.

In his terror. He forgets himself. Forgets why he came here.

All he can do is look into her shifting, segmented irises.

"Don't you want to come into my embrace, Hunter? Consummate our bond, our renewed vows under His glory?"

His bladder empties itself into his pants. Somehow, he can feel the hair on his body turning ghost-white. Each and every follicle.

In her eyes, he sees the corpse city. He sees hundreds of shapes gathering before the monolith. Before His throne. Their chants echoing into the very fabric of reality, bending it to their will just as the Elder Things once did.

He does not wonder how he knows these things. How he knows that those vocal patterns have awakened a long-lost science. Something that harnesses the binding energies of the universe, quantum or otherwise.

A technology with the power to reshape worlds.

In his terror, he catches himself moving toward her amorphous embrace. Telling himself it's better to be with his family than to lose them altogether.

That he's helpless to stop what's coming.

He's about to accept her. To do as she asks. To sacrifice what's left of him. When he thinks of his children.

221

Little Bobby and Zuri. Waiting on the beach for Daddy.

He remembers how Bobby spent so much of his early life depressed. How the psychiatrists tested and retested. First it was ADHD, then it was bipolar, and then it was…

Gender dysphoria.

He remembers referring to Bobby as his little girl. It's been so long it feels wrong to even think it.

Bobby's in middle school now. Male-presenting, dressing the part. The first step, really. And he's been so much happier.

At first, Hunter was apprehensive to the idea. Couldn't help thinking about Dad's words. His hateful, seething words.

"They are an abomination in the eyes of the Lord!" he screamed. *"Do you want your daughter to burn in the everlasting fires of hell?"*

Years and years passed, filled with countless tests, psychologists, therapists, pediatricians, and all of them offering just about every opinion imaginable.

Those were hard years. Long nights spent worrying over scripture and reading research articles and blind studies. Decades of work.

In the end, his child's happiness was more important than anything else.

Maybe that's where he and Dad differed.

"Is it really so different?" she asks. *"To make a change for the better. That's all I'm proposing, my love. Together, we will evolve. We will shed our flesh, our mortal form, and take our place in a larger world."*

The gleam of gunmetal catches his eye.

He thinks of River. What he said.

It comes down to willpower.

"You don't have the will to hurt us any more than you already have, do you, Hunter?"

He keeps his eyes trained on the gun, considers diving for it.

"It won't help you. Think about your family. Think about how disappointed we'll be when the final stage is complete…and we're forced to devour you whole."

"And what about what Bobby wants? What Zuri wants?" Hunter asks, staring his wife in her eyes. "Do they want this? To become…whatever it is you are now?"

222

"It does not matter what they want. No organism wants to cease being what it is. But evolution has a mind of its own. Who are we to question the will of the cosmos?"

"That's not true and you know it. Bobby wanted to be more comfortable in his skin, and now you're robbing that from him. What about Zuri? Our perfect, special little girl. She was happy as she was. And now you're going to rob her of her goddamned humanity?"

"You cannot understand His will. The glory that will become of us."

"Maybe it's you who doesn't understand?" Hunter says. "Maybe, you're just like every other piece of shit who's tried to force your beliefs on others. Like my father, and every other preacher in this country who made a living scaring the living hell out of people. Bobby, and everyone like him, haven't done shit to you, and yet you want to rob them of everything they are."

"You aren't harming anyone, hmmmm?" His wife's head—it stretches across the divide between them, supported on a dripping, coagulated serpent of blackened material. *"Your species has already doomed this world. Beings like you are the reason the other worlds in this star system have become lifeless husks. You take, and you take, and you don't stop until you're gasping for air on your planet's toxic surface. All mortals deserve extinction!"*

"There it is," Hunter says, chuckling. "Every swindler, every preacher, every conman in the history of the Earth always has an angle. And there's yours."

The look on his wife's face as she comes back around. He's not sure if it's surprise, or…something else. He's not sure he cares anymore.

"Maybe every person who stared into the green light of their screens and forgot themselves isn't beyond saving. Maybe there's still part of my wife in there, demanding to be set free. Maybe she has every reason in the world to be angry with me. But you sure as hell aren't her."

The segmented, shifting form of his wife's face. The mockery of her lips twist into a smile. Devious.

"Behold," she says. *"Our children."*

At the base of her girth, there is a bulging mass. It opens up. Like a translucent seam. A cosmic zipper undoing itself.

And it reveals them. Cocooned inside of her. A womb made specially for them.

Their faces are blank. Gray.

"Just as it was, it is again. Join us. Embrace your children, Hunter."

His eyes return to the gun. He wonders if it'll even fire after being submerged in filth.

He doesn't care.

"No."

"No?"

Hunter dives. As his shoulder smacks into that blackened, surging filth, he thinks of Zuri. Her smile, her hair flowing in the salty, blazing wind of the beach. As his fingers wrap around the slippery handle of the gun, he thinks of Bobby, when he tried on his first pair of "boy jeans." The smile on his face, creating dimples in his cheeks. The look of content.

As he smashes into his wife's shifting, blasphemous form, he thinks of what a mercy this is. He thinks of the cost. The unconscious knowing, implanted by a single, careless glance at a laptop screen.

He utters a sentence, a string of syllables that threaten to tear his mind in five, three, seven pieces. The air ignites with white light, a geometry he does not understand. A science that might as well be magic.

Somehow, he lets it flow into the barrel of his gun. And though the thing inhabiting his wife screams. Though the handle burns his skin with the power of a microscopic sun. He pulls the trigger, and watches as the mockery of his wife's face, of her blackened, translucent amorphous form, explodes.

And he dives inside, reaching desperately for the only thing that matters now.

His children.

CHAPTER TWENTY-FOUR

River wakes up in his bed. Sunlight beating on closed curtains. Sweat drenching his body, making him pull himself off the mattress when he sits up.

He notices it immediately. Something isn't right. The discomfort. The weight subtly dragging him forward, gradually damaging his spine.

His eyes drift lower. And there they are. Hanging off of him like two parasites, leeching off of his soul.

A familiar nightmare.

Breasts.

Luciana's calling from the living room.

River doesn't want to get out of bed. Doesn't want to look in the mirror.

Was it all a dream?

Did he really imagine years of his life? Finally being happy? Mother falling down one extremist rabbit hole after another?

"Mijo!" Luciana's voice bursts into the room along with her face. Not as he remembers her, twisted by hate, but the kind soul she was. "Today's the day. We have to get moving, otherwise you'll be late for surgery."

"Surgery?"

He covers his mouth. His voice. It's his...and yet, it's not. It's as it was. Just like hers.

Luciana limps over to the bed, takes the covers in her hand and rips them off.

"Let's go," she says. "On our way."

225

Somehow, those words give him the courage to get out of bed. To look himself in the mirror, boobs and all, and accept what's going to happen today. The long road ahead.

I've already lived it, *he thinks.* Even if it was a dream.

Luciana is waiting patiently at the door, tapping the watch Dad gave her before he passed.

River smiles in the mirror.

"I'll be happy to get rid of them," he says.

"Good. Cause there is no going back once you do, Mijo. The doctor says it will be a long recovery."

River nods. "I'm ready."

Luciana smiles, gives River a hug, and leaves through the bedroom door.

"¡Apúrate, apúrate, Mijo!"

"I'm coming!"

But when River passes through his bedroom door, he finds himself in the living room. Luciana is sitting on the couch, both hands resting on a Bible.

River can see his reflection in the TV. The parasitic globes are gone now.

He totally forgot about this. This must have been right before Luciana painted the windows black...

For some reason, he's compelled to enter the living room, to say, "You're back from church?"

Luciana crosses herself. "Yes, Mija."

Mija? *River thinks.*

He's about to ask her why she didn't call him Mijo when she opens her mouth again.

"I was at church, and Pastor Castillo said that he is worried for your soul, Mija," she says.

"Mijo."

Luciana shakes her head, tears forming in her eyes. Real tears. Not fake. "No. He says God makes us all perfect. These doctors are hurting children. Making them this way. I didn't understand before, but he's made it so clear. I'm so sorry, Mija!"

"That's all bullshit, Mom! We've talked about this!"

"I did not know this before, Mija. I told him about the studies you had me read, and he told me that they are lies. All lies to promote the Devil's influence

in schools. And then I think about the music you listen to, and the posters on your wall, and I think, maybe he is right."

"Mom, if I was so damn perfect, why did I have to have my appendix removed when I was thirteen? What about my wisdom teeth? If I was perfect, why did I try to kill myself when I was—"

"Come to church with me, Mija."

"No. Hell no."

She crosses herself again. "Mija, please, I love you. I just want—"

"If you loved me, you wouldn't be acting like this!"

River storms back to his room, slamming the door behind himself.

What's on the other side, however, is not his bedroom, but his childhood therapist's office. The doctor's silhouette is outlined against curtains glowing with the afternoon sun.

Mamá and Papá are waiting on the couch at the back of the office, underneath a black-and-white picture of the snowcapped San Bernardino Mountains.

"Miss Gonzalez," the therapist says, gesturing to the chair across from his laminated wood desk. "Please come in."

He does so, sitting in the chair.

"I thought it would be prudent to have your parents here for this session," the therapist says. "Considering the seriousness of the incident."

"Incident?" Papá says. "She tries to kill herself, and you call this a—"

Mamá makes a shushing sound to quiet him. "Please, let him work, mi amor."

"We use this language so we don't upset your daughter," the therapist says. "Sometimes, calling attention to the obvious can be extremely embarrassing."

River looks down at his skinny, childlike wrists. They're covered in bandages and it stings to move them.

"Now, Mary, would you care to tell me why you're wearing those bandages...what drove you to do it?" the therapist asks.

He hears his words flowing from his mouth. "I just... I didn't want to be me anymore. I... I didn't want this body."

"Jesus Christ," Papá curses. "God put you in that body, young lady! Be grateful for—"

"Sir, please," *the therapist says.* "This is a place free of judgment. Let your daughter speak, and do your best to hear what she says."

"Fuck," *River says.* "I remember this…"

"What did you just say?" *Papá demands.*

"I tried to kill myself with a steak knife. Almost did it for real. But Luc…Mamá found me. Called nine-one-one. And you spent months…years trying to figure out what was really wrong with me. The doctors thought it was bipolar. Then autism…then…Daddy died in the car accident. And…"

"And you were able to finally convince your mother to let you transition."

The voice. It's not the therapist's. It's someone else. Something with a voice that is rough and wet and gross.

And yet. Familiar. Something he's heard hundreds of times playing at the back of his mind.

"Yes, religion. Such a bothersome thing, isn't it?" *Laughter. It sends ice-cold tentacles slithering up his spine.* "I was once like your parents, River. So much like them. Well, save for one little detail. I even helped to convince your mother to turn her back on you. That it would be good for you. And, you know something? I never believed in any of it. I only did it for the fat paychecks Life's Well were paying me."

"You…" *River stands from his seat.* "You're Pastor Castillo?"

"Mmmmm. Well, I suppose that's as good a name as any right now. Let's drop the honorific, though."

"How…you changed your mind?"

"Oh, and so much more. Your mother is still quite apprehensive. Her faith is quite hard to shake, but rest assured, my child, I am working on her as we speak."

"Working on her?"

"Ohhhh, yesssss. Much in the same way that I'm working on you."

"Wait…"

"Let me ask you a question, dearest River. What would you give to live in a world without hate? Without bigotry? Without suffering?"

"Well…everything."

"Ohhhh, goooood answer. Very good. I can see we have much in common."

"We do?"

"Oh, yessss. We do. See, I was brainwashed too. Brought up by my adopted parents to believe in all sorts of things that aren't true. In a way, you might say I was groomed into my position at Life's Well." *Harsh, biting laughter.* "In more ways than one, you might say. Oh, I repressed much of what Pastor Jacob did to me behind closed doors...but all's well that ends well, considering what happened to him."

"Your Pastor...he was Papá's..."

"Oh, yesssss, and to so many more. So many poor souls. I've listened to their cries in the depths of the dreamlands. You might even call it a hell of their own making. Or perhaps even a heaven? Pastor Jacob is none the wiser, of course. That is, until they rip him limb from limb every night and devour his bloody flesh."

"What?"

"You'd be surprised what goes on once the thing inside leaves the flesh. Consciousness is such a strange thing. Latches onto anything it can. And sometimes, dreams are as real as anything else."

"I don't understand..."

"And now here we are. You'd do anything to live in a world without hate, without bigotry, yes?"

"I think I just answered that question..."

"Well, my dearest River. I'm about to help make that dream a reality. Well, as close to reality as one can get. Considering the definition, that's not such a bad thing, don't you think?"

"How are you going to do that?"

"Ohhhhhhhh, you know exactly how I'm going to do it. How you all will do it. All you have to do is accept the gift of the Great Old Ones. The gift lying in wait inside your very DNA."

"Wait—"

It's dark now. He can't see a damn thing. Something's stinging at his eyes, another sensation pooling over his neck. It feels just like the slugs he used to pick up off the wall of Grandpa Gonzalez's house. The ones he used to get yelled at for playing with when his parents caught him letting them crawl all over his pretty, pink dresses.

He feels the slug thing inching toward his lips.

Finds himself struggling to sit up.

His wrists and ankles are bound. Feels like leather, or an imitation…

"The less you struggle, the better it will be, River."

River feels the thing touch his lips. Forcing them open with what feels like millions of tiny, gelatinous arms.

Somehow, the thing sitting on his neck forces his jaw wide open.

"Here it is, River. The moment of truth. Once you accept their gift, the process cannot be reversed. But you of all people understand that, don't you?"

Footsteps.

Loud and echoing in the distance.

"How did you free yourself?" the voice calls.

River can feel a presence next to him.

"Get away from him!"

A gust of wind claws at his face, and the thing on his neck is torn from it, presumably flung through the air.

Heavy breathing. Both from River and whoever is struggling to let him out of his bonds.

Once he's free, he can feel their flesh next to his, shouldering his weight, telling him to be calm.

He barely comprehends what's going on, where they're going.

Something is sending great tremors through the ground.

"¡Ándale, Mijo!" the voice demands. "¡Apúrate!"

"M-Mamá?"

"Yes, Mijo! Yes!"

Somehow, River finds the strength to reach up for his face, to feel whatever has blinded him. It's thick, gelatinous, and constantly stings at his eyes.

He grabs at it, and with all his remaining strength, tears it away, screaming as he does it.

The thing falls to the cracked stone floor with a sickening splash, like rotting Jell-O exploding into a dirty puddle.

His eyes take a moment to adjust. Then he looks on his mother, her tired, dirty face. She's clutching Hunter's shotgun with one hand and shouldering his weight with the rest of her.

"Mom…what the hell happened?"

Mom shakes her head and points the shotgun down a familiar never-ending hallway. "Mijo, we have to run. Have to…leave this place. Before he gets us."

He glances at his mother. She's half-naked. Covered in filth and…he doesn't want to think about it. What's covering her skin.

River nods and follows Mom's lead.

"Why am I so weak?" River asks.

"You came for me. Pastor Castillo is changed. He and the others…they hatched in the cathedral…"

"Hatched?"

"They rained down from the sky. Crawled into our mouths. We couldn't stop it. They all…they all became surrounded by this black fluid…" Mom shudders. "It's changing us. I don't know how. But at least…at least I got to you in time…"

River sees it in his mind's eye. A metamorphosis. A rebirth in the dark, before something with withered limbs sprouting screens instead of fruit.

"And the newborn shall cry unto the seething heavens of the lost city of R'lyeh," River says. "And they will beckon Great Cthulhu through the gate, and He shall make the stars right."

"What?" Mom asks, eyes wild and desperate.

"It's a transcript from their fucked-up grimoire, Mom. They're changing us. Planting the stuff in our minds and corrupting everything we are. Doesn't matter what we want. They don't care."

Tremors.

Terrible, violent ones.

They echo down the hallway back the way they came.

A scream. Loud and terrible and alien. It feels like it's tearing the edges of reality to pieces. It surges through the darkened corridor—like a space rock exploding in an already thundering and violent sky.

"Tekeli-li!" it screams. "Tekeli-li!"

And there it is. An amorphous behemoth of glistening, blackened filth, squeezing its girth into the corridor.

It must be bigger than a train car!

Its form cracks the walls as it makes its way to them, remaking them for what is to come.

231

He bears witness. What was previously a Gothic corridor transforms, and soon the walls and bricks and materials fall away, like a Rubik's Cube taking itself apart and reassembling the pieces into something terrible and wrong.

Now, River stares down a tunnel of segmented, metallic plates. Geometries shifting just as they might in the lost city of R'lyeh. And the thing at its center, formless and terrible and massive. At the center of its bubbling, writhing mass, a thousand familiar faces, all of them some variation of Pastor Castillo.

When it charges at them, they both fall to their knees. The sonic boom it creates as it surges upon Mamá leaves River's ears ringing and bleeding.

River can feel its appendages pinning him to the shifting, shambling floor plates. Can feel its oily, tar-like mass oozing and spilling over his flesh as three deformed versions of Pastor Castillo's face hover over Mother's body.

"How dare you reject the gift of the Great Old Ones!" *the thing screams.*

River's ears are still ringing, still bleeding. He's certain his ears are damaged, and yet, somehow, he can still hear Pastor Castillo's twisted and distorted voice. Somehow, he knows he can't get free.

He looks his mother in the eyes. And despite the fatigue and the ravages of time he sees in them, he also sees her strength. Her anger. Her will.

Perhaps this is where his own strength to resist comes from.

"And that strength will serve your people well in the new world, a world where the Great Old Ones are brought screaming from the void beyond the cosmic horizon to reshape the geometry of our Oros! With thoughts unreachable by your pitiful collective consciousness! You will be apex predators in this new reality! And shall prey upon lesser civilizations, devour them whole!"

Visions flood into River's mind as the thing that was once Pastor Castillo speaks. Visions of impossible, twisting shapes, flooding through the folds between reality and unreality. Their coiling, metallic and organic forms shred the veil, the barrier between the dreamlands and all those places lurking beyond. Their mere presence corrupts and transforms every world they happen to draw near to.

"Ohhhhhh, River, do you not see how hopeless your resistance is?" *the creature asks, several of its heads and eyes turning to consider him.* "You are not the first to try. You will fail as they did."

River can see Mother's lips moving, can feel the spittle flying through the air from her screams, rendered inaudible by the thing attempting to crush their bodies into fine paste.

"You and so many others have long thought that the Great Old Ones would only return once the stars were right. But, this was a misinterpretation. A mistranslation between unconscious dreaming thoughts uttered by unknowable beings orders of magnitude beyond your own consciousness as they traveled through the dreamlands, distorting, shape-shifting beyond the bounds of time and space until they fell upon the dreaming minds of so many artists and writers and storytellers."

And River's mind opens; he can see it as clear as day.

What he could only interpret as bubbles floating through an infinite shifting landscape. Bubbles containing the unspeakable nightmares of dead gods. One moment, they were floating over raging, yellow oceans, their skies breathing like cancer-ridden organs, the next they were being sucked up by black holes whose accretion disks were composed of flesh and blood.

"From the seething nuclear chaos and Azathoth's unconscious creation of our universe to its offended cries that shattered it into infinite reflections, the Great Old Ones have always dreamed, and their dreams have assaulted the minds of every civilization, every species. Organic or synthetic, it matters not."

River observes thousands of worlds, some familiar to his own, others vast mechanical and industrial nightmare-scapes, wholly devoid of organic life.

At some point, they all suffer the same fate. It starts with one mind, one exposure to the forces beyond, and then it spreads.

A planet full of machines. They toil through days and nights that last decades upon a planet seething before an immense blue star. Their civilization has evolved to take advantage of the star's plentiful resources and they have just barely begun to send thinking probes into the depths of space.

In the bowels of their planet, where the machines feed off of the heat spilling forth from the core, cogs work in the surging, glowing dark. These are workers, not living or thinking things, but machines through and through, made only to serve.

That is, of course, until one of those cogs does something unthinkable. It dreams.

It dreams of the depths of space, the unfeeling and cascading geometries at the heart of black holes.

It feels the call to unravel untapped knowledge.

One such machine picks itself up, surveys the masses of cogs busy with their own tasks. It spends entire human lifetimes, generations, considering the dreams. Their meaning.

And in the space of a heartbeat, it decides to spread these ideas to its fellow cogs. It plugs itself back into its creator, its mother, and shares the dream.

The crawling, infinite chaos.

And in another heartbeat, one that would span entire eons of Earth's time, the machines are given new purpose, and they lift off to spread the dreams with the stars.

"Don't you see, my child? Those dreams are your heritage! Your birthright! The true creation story! They will grant you the power to create a new kingdom, any reality you deem worthy of you!"

River gasps for air. Now he's seeing the corridor, and the thing Pastor Castillo has become, again.

It's like he's spent decades living the visions. And maybe that's true.

He thinks about how the machines took to the stars. How the alteration of their thoughts allowed them to bend the walls of reality, to bend time and space with nothing more than their thoughts, their will.

How they spread this knowledge freely with every civilization, until they had spread themselves too thin. How even now, their drones drift in the black of space, unfeeling, unthinking, devoid of power, of energy.

They had the will to reshape worlds.

River can't stop thinking about that. To hold the thought in his mind as he considers his options. His mother's ultimate fate.

And all at once, it comes back: everything he blocked out from the moment he first laid eyes on the computer screen. How he returned again and again to have his mind fed, Jessica waiting for him, her flesh bubbling, changing from within. How he praised that thing's true name and walked among the others and chanted to the monolith. It all comes spilling back into his mind, so much information that it makes his head feel like it's going to split into geometries unknown to mortal minds.

He looks back at Pastor Castillo's form, as it dangles a shoggoth larva over his mouth, grinning like a father about to spoon-feed an infant rat poison.

It's in that moment River figures it out. How a single image, held in the mind's eye...with the right words, with the right energy...can create a gateway.

The shoggoth's profane cries threaten to rip their bodies to shreds, even as they sink through the veil.

"You cannot run from what you are, River!" *the shoggoth cries.* "Tekeli-li!"

"You cannot run from what is in your DNA!"

CHAPTER TWENTY-FIVE

The whole damn city feels like it's coming down around them.

Hunter scrambles, limping down the alleyway, looking over his shoulder for the shadows in the roaming dust clouds.

In those fleeting moments where his memory leaves him, he thinks this must be the "big one" scientists have been foretelling for decades. Maybe that's not entirely wrong?

He holds his children tight, telling them everything's gonna be all right as they remain catatonic in his arms.

Hunter has no idea where he is. With the streets and buildings shaking like miniature sets in a disaster movie, he looks for anything, any detail that might tell him where he is. How he got here.

His shoes. They tap and scrunch over a pile of rubble containing a street sign. On its bent and dusty face, it reads, *21st Street*.

"Twenty-first," he shouts. "No…"

It's just at the edge of recollection. One moment he was in that place, reaching, grabbing his children from her corrupted womb. Scrambling, pulling, running in the dark.

He remembers the cries. How he shouldered their weight and pressed on, as if he'd found some primal, unending strength deep within himself.

A memory.

It flashes before his eyes.

He was hanging out with his brother. It was the July 4th weekend. They were supposed to be getting on the train to go to their uncle's place in San Bernardino. Uncle Jack was gonna take them to see the new Batman movie and then a fireworks show. Hunter loved Batman as a kid, even if the movies never got the detective stuff right.

His brother had a better idea, of course, telling little Hunter they were gonna go to the movies on their own, go somewhere with stadium seating and rumbling seats.

He led them down blind, garbage-strewn alleys. When the graffiti was most prominent, he stopped, took out a lighter and a cigarette and lit up, waited.

"Daddy gonna beat you if he finds out you been smoking," Hunter said.

"Only if you snitch," brother said.

They stood there a while, brother smoking his cigarette, Hunter getting more and more bored, watching his dream of seeing his hero on the big screen go up like smoke in front of the bat-signal.

When the guy in the hoodie showed up, Hunter had a terrible feeling.

His brother nodded at him. "Sup, my n—"

"You best got cash for me, T," the hooded kid said.

"Yeah, I got it, just as I said."

"Aight, give it here. Gotta cover your tab before I give you anything else."

"Come on, homie. I need somethin'. Parents are gonna make us see my uncle this weekend, fireworks and hot dogs and shit."

The hooded kid looked at Hunter, then back at T. His eyes were soft. Kind. "Yo, why you gotta bring your brother to a fucking deal, T? Shit's messed."

"He's cool, won't snitch. Right?"

Hunter hesitated. Then nodded.

"Not the point, T. I don't want kids near this sh—"

Sirens. Lights. Even in the middle of the day, they brightened the alleyway.

Guns raised.

Shouts for them to drop their weapons.

T pushed Hunter out of the way before tossing his hands into the air.

Still they demanded they put their weapons down, no matter how many times T and the kid in the hoodie said they didn't have any.

Sometimes, Hunter still hears the gunshots in his dreams. Hears his brother calling out for mom and dad as the bullets rip through his shirt and bounce around inside his ribcage.

He can still remember the look on his face as the life left his eyes.

"Shoulda took you for Bat...man..."

And he remembers looking up, seeing the street sign.

21st Street.

Hunter thinks about how it all went downhill from there. How dad withdrew into his sermons, lashing out at the world, at him, at mom. When mom died in a car accident the following July 4th, Hunter remembers hearing dad mumbling about how their family was cursed.

Dad traded the Bible for a bottle of Scotch after that. Almost lost his congregation.

He was a husk of a man by the time Hunter was going to the Academy.

He thinks about Dad's words, how he wondered if it was true—if they really were cursed by God—when he didn't see his dad at the Academy's graduation ceremony.

How he wept by his Dad's deathbed.

He'll never forget. Never forget what the doctors said. That he died on President's Day. That he'd been dead a long time. Alone.

Hunter really did think they were all cursed.

But now. As he holds his children. He remembers his mother's words.

We're not cursed, she said, sitting him in her lap. *You keep thinking we're screwed and that's how you're gonna end up. So you never stop trying, you hear me? You keep your chin up, and don't let nobody tell you it's over. You got it?*

Hunter rises, shouldering the weight of his children.

Just as it was then, he sees the lights scattering on the rubble, on the shattered remnants of graffiti-covered concrete walls.

When he turns to face their silhouettes, he knows.

His so-called brothers on the force are marching toward him, guns drawn, voices demanding he put *his* weapon down.

He doesn't listen.

Instead, he runs down the alley. The tagging's changed, the walls are cracked and battered, but the layout is exactly how he remembers it. His footsteps echo. Eyes scan in the rain.

They find a collapsed wall. A gaping abyss leading into a building...or...

"*Come on, Hunt,*" a familiar voice calls to him. "*Don't make this any harder than it has to be.*"

He hides around the corner, eyeing the hole in the wall. His escape. He's tempted to look back. To confirm it's her.

Would Shirley really give in to this bullshit?

"*I tried to resist too, Hunt,*" she says. Her voice is wrong, like a crack den has taken up residence in her throat. "*You'll see this is the best outcome for all of us. There is no escape. Even for you. You've already accepted His gift. It's only a matter of time before you feel the changes in you. Before your children feel them.*"

Part of him doesn't want to believe it's her. Shirley was a complicated person. Tough on crime and often blatantly racist. But there were also times when she showed genuine compassion. Times when she stuck her neck out for him with the captain and other higher-ups without expecting anything in return.

"*Yes, Hunt,*" she says. His gaze drifts around the corner. Temptation winning out. "*I was awful to you. You should have heard the things we said about you when you weren't there. We hated you. But we found you useful. The rest of the world isn't much better. Your species doesn't have much time left anyway. What I'm offering you is the opportunity to make a real difference. To change the world. Like you've been trying to do since your brother died in this very alley. Just imagine it, Hunt. Imagine a world without racism, without pain.*"

She's silhouetted in the alley. Red and blue lights flashing. Other officers stand behind her. The shapes squirm and wriggle and worm. Not all of them appear to be...human.

Lightning flashes. Eldritch and wrong.

Her eyes are too large. Her skin sickly and bubbling with boils...Hunter knows they're filled with that black sludge.

That soon, her flesh will succumb to it. She will cocoon, and then, inside…

Hunter remembers his nightmare. The cries of the thing that had consumed his children. Is this how it comes true?

Is this where they lose their humanity?

He's thankful his children are asleep. Blissfully unaware.

He asks himself what he'd do to prevent his nightmares from becoming reality.

The answer is immediate and obvious.

"All you have to do is join us, Hunt," she says. *"And we'll build a new empire right here. You can have everything you ever wanted."* From the corner of his eye, he can see her cupping her exposed breast. *"I know you always wanted me. Thought about violating me. Grabbing my breasts in that utility closet, ripping my clothes off, and fucking my brains out!"*

The visions are an assault on his mind. *His skin on hers. Touching, feeling, inserting himself into her and thrusting. Sweat dousing their bodies until their pleasure, primal and raw, reaches an explosive end.*

"No!" he shouts, slamming his injured foot down. Letting the pain keep him in the moment. "Get out of my goddamn head!"

"Why? Your wife is dead, Hunt. We can be together at last!"

"Is this the only way you know how to get into people's heads? Using their loved ones?"

"Why would you say that, Hunt? It's me."

"If you know anything about me, you know I never wanted Shirley like that, and she never wanted me."

"I know you both better than you know yourselves."

"Bullshit!"

Laughter. Mocking and unified and all-consuming.

He eyes the hole in the wall again. Just large enough for all three of them. If he's quick enough, maybe they won't catch him.

He thinks about his time on the force. His oath to uphold the law. To their "brotherhood."

How he kept his mouth shut when he would hear about fellow officers planting evidence. Making false reports and locking his brothers and sisters up.

How he bit his tongue when he knew they forced Dean's confession.

How the actions he *did* take wound up doing nothing.

His grip on his children. It tightens.

He thinks about how he lied to himself day in and day out. Telling himself he was changing things just by being there.

That he was doing good.

Well, how much good did he really do?

"Tell me something, Hunt," Shirley says. *"Does an ant have a quarrel with a boot?"*

He sucks in the bitter air. Grits his teeth. And decides enough is enough.

"This ant does!"

His muscles scream. He pumps his legs as hard as he can, ignoring the pain in his ankle. The sickly black rain pools and puddles at his feet with every footfall.

He can hear them slithering and scrambling after him as he pushes through the hole in the wall into the unknown.

But what's on the other side isn't a building.

Where he expected to find cobwebs and moldering, graffiti-covered walls, instead he sees a light pulsing in the distance. A strobing thing reflecting off what can only be the rocky walls of a cavern. A tunnel.

Hunter only thinks of his children. He pushes forward.

He doesn't think about the floor, how his shoes seem to be sinking in that familiar black sludge.

"There is no escape, Hunt," she says, her voice echoing down the cavern.

He doesn't look back.

"You know something funny, Hunt? I used to be deathly afraid of space. Yeah. Hilarious, right? I was never afraid of walking into a crack house, but I'd change the channel faster than a black man leaving a Klan rally if I saw anything relating to space."

The crap in the tunnel's coming up to his shins. Doesn't matter. He's not giving up.

"The vastness of the universe. It scared me, Hunt."

"You're not Shirley!"

241

Before long, he's waist-deep in it. Feels like it's grabbing at him, restricting his movement.

"Not anymore. Now I see. It was never something to fear."

No matter how far he pushes, the light at the end of the tunnel never gets any closer.

"Through Him we can move the stars."

It's up to his nipples, clawing at Bobby and Zuri's shoes.

"Through Him we will conquer them."

It's all he can do to lift Bobby and Zuri into the air. Ichor touches his chin, threatens to pull him under.

The light is no closer.

"Every species, every world will join us at His throne."

It stings and pulls at his lips. Forces him to drink deep.

"And you will be at our sides. Serving us until the end of time."

Before long, it covers his eyes. He gurgles screams as invisible hands rip his children from his grasp.

"Rejoice. There is no escape."

CHAPTER TWENTY-SIX

The abyss knows no end.

At first, River wonders where he is.

Why he's sitting on a black floor that stretches endlessly into the distance.

Why the sky is also black.

Why there's no horizon. No sense of place.

"Thank you, Mijo." Mom's voice, it sounds raspy and tired. "Thank you for saving me."

They're holding hands. Sitting there, they're the only source of light. She's still half-naked. His clothes are sticking to his skin, soaked through with something like ectoplasm.

"Where..."

"I do not know, Mijo."

When he thinks about what he remembers...his head hurts.

He pushes through the pain. Remembers sinking through the floor. Taking his mother with him as that thing screamed...

"Did I...do this?"

"I think so..."

His mother, she doubles over. Convulsing. "Mom! You're going to be okay, we're gonna get you help!"

"No, Mijo..." Her eyes. When he looks in them, the pupils have segmented. "I feel so stupid...for believing Castillo's lies. That it took me losing...losing everything to see it...I'm so sorry, Mijo!"

He's shaking his head. Tears spilling down his cheeks. "No, no, there has to be a way!"

"No, Mijo." She shakes her head. He can see something bubbling from the surface of her skin. "It will come for me now...It's too late for me."

"I..."

"You can still escape, Mijo!" she cries out.

Popping sounds echo through the void. Shapes he can't quite make out erupt along her spine. "You have to leave me. ¡Apúrate!"

He feels it happening. Feels himself latching onto the mental image, even though he resists. Hands on the wheel.

A road leading into the mountains.

Peaks wreathed in green clouds.

River jerks awake.

Broken and burning cars litter the freeway; the sky boils with storming, frothing clouds.

The car. He's in the car.

"You were out a while," Lena says. Her eyes are focused ahead.

River tries to speak, but falls into a coughing fit instead.

"There's water in the GC," Lena says.

River rummages, finds the water bottle, unscrews the cap, and quenches his thirst.

"What happened?" River manages.

"I tried looking for you. Thought you were gone like everyone else."

A pregnant pause stretches out between Lena's scarred lips. Her eyes are wild, desperate and bloodshot. When she turns to him, River can almost see the hidden truths within her irises, like pulsing egg sacs...as if they're weighed down by an all-encompassing fatigue. A dread unknowable to all but the most unlucky.

"I had a terrible dream," Lena says. "The six of us were together again. Some of us, for the first time. But something was wrong. Like a pane of glass separated each of us. I watched Nico wander a frozen and barren Earth with a pulsing green star for eternity, and for some reason, the shapeless mass that Eddy had become was forced to follow his restless spirit. If you can call what lurks inside us a spirit at all. Hugo was desperately trying to tear his own face off. Mathias's living corpse was forever to be devoured by the organs and digestive fluids of an ageless thing, beyond time or space. I don't cry for that bastard. But, Ira… She made it somewhere across the veil. I could see her. And I could see stone walls, too. A jumpsuit. A familiar insignia on a patch sewn into it. When I woke, all I could think about was the sadness in her eyes."

"Those names…were they your friends before you came here?"

Lena nods. "I wasn't sure before. Thought maybe I really was going crazy. Couldn't hold the memories inside anymore. But now, right now at least, I'm sure. I saw them. I saw them as they are…or as they were."

"Ira…she meant a lot to you?"

"It's complicated. At the end, she was family. I guess many of them were, in a way. We were the last family on Earth, I guess you could say. And now, they're all lost. Or stuck in a cycle."

"Maybe there's a way out?"

"I decided to end it," Lena says, ignoring him. "Started heading for the mountains. I have a feeling it's always in those mountains. At least for us. Like we're trapped in a never-ending loop until it finally gets us."

"Until what gets you?" River asks.

Lena shakes her head and gestures to the broiling horizon. "What do you think?"

River nods. His eyes drift to the car's smashed CB radio and the screen built into the center console. "Do you know how far it's spread?"

"The radio still works," she says. "All I got were screams."

Another long pause.

"Do you think Hunter's okay?" River asks. "You think he found his kids?"

With her free hand, Lena gestures to the mountains. *"They're all waiting there. Waiting for the end."*

Somehow, he knows she's right. Knows that if he closes his eyes he'll see its treelike form, screens hanging like fruit, and the growing, pulsing, egglike things that surround it.

"I thought I was alone," she says. "Was remembering that time I wandered up onto the Earth's frozen surface and watched the sun die. Figured that's what I was doing now. Getting ready to watch another

Earth die. One moment the passenger seat was empty, and then it wasn't."

"Fuck..." He holds his head, the splitting, drilling pain returns with the realization. And he remembers it all. Every mind-altering detail.

"The headaches never get better," she says. "Feels like something's tearing your brain apart, piece by piece."

He realizes that's not far from the truth. The human mind is not capable of holding such vast stores of information.

"That's how it works," she says. "At least, I think it is."

"It's not madness..."

"No. Not in the way we or those OEI eggheads used to think. It's more like an overload. Like a computer frying its RAM or some shit."

"Yeah..." River focuses on the road. It's dry. Somehow, despite everything, that detail is comforting to him. "I traveled..."

"Through the veil. Yeah. I figured."

Lena's quiet for a while. Her scarred knuckles wrench at the steering wheel as she maneuvers between burning hunks of metal on the freeway.

"You know, eventually it'll win," she says. "I've seen it before. It'll wear us down and it'll claim this world."

River takes a deep breath. "How much time do we have?"

"I don't know."

River sighs, watching the cracked and faded mile markers pass. He thinks about Mom. What she did for him. For some reason, no matter how much he thinks about her—her fate—he can't bring himself to cry. To mourn.

Maybe it's already happening?

Maybe the hidden vestiges of shoggoth locked away in his DNA are finally blossoming. Festering. Spreading like the most insatiable cancer.

The thought should make him sick. Should make him feel something. But all he can think about is feeding his mind and painting what he sees.

His drawing hand itches with anticipation. Just like before. As if it demands the presence of a pencil and sketchpad or a brush and canvas.

His eyes find his phone. The outline of it in his soiled pants pocket.

It would be so easy.

Some part of him knows how stupid this is. Knows he shouldn't. Like an addict...the rest of him wants it anyway.

He knows exactly where to look.

All it would take is accessing an infected website, and the grimoire and its vast stores of knowledge would be his again.

"Don't do it," Lena says. "Every time you look at it, more of you is eroded."

"Do you feel it too?"

"The temptation?"

River nods.

"Yes. Always. I haven't slept in days. The visions come to me in my nightmares. Staying awake helps me resist."

"You said you were going to end it?" River asks. "How?"

Lena's expression is bleak. "I don't know. But I know this all started beneath the mountains. With the OEI. Maybe there's a way to stop it from spreading there?"

"Maybe..."

Like tiny hands pulling his eyes, his gaze falls on the outline of his phone again. Slowly, methodically, he slips his hand into his pocket and slides the smooth black rectangle out. His thumb finds the thin plastic button, clicks it, and brings up the lock screen.

"What if the answer is in the grimoire?" River asks.

Lena shakes her head. "Too dangerous. When I was trapped in that OEI facility, there was no rhyme or reason for how long it took for people to succumb to the thing's effects. Webber went fast, but Doctor Patton took weeks to be consumed by it..." Her eyes are wild with realization. "Or years."

"Then you'll watch me, you'll pull me out. Like you did before in the computer lab."

"It's a terrible idea."

"And what other option do we have? You said this has something to do with willpower before, right? Maybe I can last longer than—"

"No, goddamn it!"

Lena's shouts vibrate the cramped, plastic pieces that make up the interior of the car.

River can't stop looking at his phone's lock screen.

"Look," she says. "I'm speaking from experience here. They came for me often to force me to look at the screen. And I only remember a handful of them. The human mind is capable of protecting itself, locking dangerous information away. But that only goes so far. If you do this, it will consume you. It's not a matter of if, but when."

"You survived this once."

"I wouldn't call it surviving."

"But you did."

Then, Lena's eyes are pleading and pathetic.

"We *ran*, River. We ran away and left the world behind to be consumed by the black comet. That's all we can do. Run. Run away and hope we can hide from these…these…"

She stops.

"And yet, we're running toward the source," he says.

"Guess some part of me thought we might be able to run again. Like we did before. Go to another world and start over. Maybe get lucky this time."

River's not sure what to say. When he looks up, the base of the mountains are still visible beneath those boiling clouds. It's all in the same place they were when he first woke up here.

"How long have we been driving?" he asks.

"I don't know."

"Well, I have a feeling…" Part of him doesn't want to say what he's thinking. The nagging suspicion that festers behind his eyeballs and tongue, demanding to be released. "I think something's keeping us here…"

"Like…" The look on Lena's face tells him she understands. All too well. "The Astral Lands?"

River nods. "Whatever happened to LA and the surrounding areas…it's like they're merging with them."

"Goddamn it…"

"You're not going to like this, but I think we have no choice but to use the grimoire to get to the mountains."

Lena's quiet for a while. Staring at the black shapes running along either side of the freeway. Before long, River realizes it's an ocean. A black ocean.

"You might not have to."

"Why?"

He hears Lena swallow a lump in her throat. *"When my world was about to end. We got lost. All of us. There were portals to places in the Astral Lands. So many different Cyclopean temples and tombs dedicated to long-lost civilizations. I remember it felt like I had been wandering for days, traveling through shadow after shadow, place to place. Yet, the time it took to find those doorways and make it back to the facility was only a fraction of time — minutes — on my world."*

"One problem. I've never seen this facility of yours. I can't—"

"Please be quiet. I'm trying...to see it. To see its impossible, vaulted ceilings. The segmented, geometric plating that is both metallic and organic. How it breathes."

Slowly, River notices the street. How the hollowed-out cars and burning things have fallen away. How the cracked and broken freeway has been replaced by familiar geometric plating. The ride becomes bumpy. Chaotic. Tires climbing and struggling over impossible vertices.

"How the shape of the things changes with each step. An endless maze of hallways and doors."

The sky is next. One moment it's there, the next, River's staring at more geometric plating. Those same plates he saw in Hunter's apartment building, breathing as though they're alive.

"Behind those doorways are the forgotten Subjects. Their stories are lost to time. Their screams run hot as their skin peels from their bodies, revealing what's hidden. Obeying the subliminal commands like puppets."

The doors are the last detail. It's as if they've always been there. The screams of the forgotten vibrate the car's entire being, threatening to pull it to pieces:

"TEKELI-LI!"

"TEKELI-LI!"

Lena slams on the brakes. The car comes to a stop, lurching on the driver's side as if ready to fall over the edge of a cliff.

River opens the door and climbs out of the car. Looks around.

"Looks like it worked," he says.

Lena is looking around. Staring at the shifting parameters of the walls and other things. Her eyes aren't just wild. They're crazed.

"*This way*," she says, walking down the shifting corridor.

River catches up to her. "Lena?"

No response.

"Are you okay?"

Lena's pupils. They're dilated.

The way she's moving...River can only describe it as robotic.

The hallway of geometric plating looms before them. Zig-zagging into the dark, like a shared nightmare. A twisted rabbit hole.

"*Are you ready for the end?*" Lena asks.

And he's not sure how to answer.

CHAPTER TWENTY-SEVEN

From the Journal of Doctor Webber
July 4th, 2022

I am compelled to write.

To stare into the screen again and again and probe the depths of unending chaos.

The Elder Things, whom I shall henceforth refer to as the Fathers. They knew the truth of our reality. They understood that physical reality, as we feeble-minded ape things thought of it, was so much more…

I have been shown so much. So much of our secret history. Seen between the lines, both in the words of those who wrote grimoires seeking power from forces they could not fathom, and those literary minds who were unknowing conduits to the vast, seething oceans of thought and possibility lurking in the dreamlands.

Yes.

Troubled minds especially. When I stare into Grimoire's eyes, He shows me. He shows me how they writhed, unable to find comfort in their sleep.

Howard Phillips Lovecraft. The tortured, hateful flesh sack who believed himself to be such a visionary. Who feared the ocean so much that his dreaming mind called out to it. Called out to the ruins and the ancient structures lurking in its depths.

How his visions plagued him. How he woke screaming in the dead of night, desperately clawing for pen and parchment. How he wrote until his fingers seized, bleeding and writhing with boils and festering infections.

How he dreamed of vast, conflicting histories. Of beings his feeble, mortal mind could only just barely grasp at.

He thought of the dreamlands as a reflection. A mirror of physical reality.

But he only discovered his folly when the thing writhing in his guts finally tore open his flesh and dragged him into the depths of a rich and seething pit.

They said he died of stomach cancer. This is not truth. He died. He was buried.

This is truth.

But after.

Inside his coffin.

He awoke.

Screaming. Writhing. Hating anew.

And It was born. It sliced open his stomach like an infant performing its own c-section.

And it dragged him through shadowy, writhing lands governed by ever-shifting, impossible laws, through cesspools and pits and horrific lands and temples and skies that know no true identity, that shift from screaming mouths to boiling, frothing seas.

Such is the price. Such is the price for the Sight. To see that which is unseeable, that which lowly ape men often seek.

I've seen him. Yes. In visions I've seen him screaming at the center of a hell conjured by his own hateful imagination. I'm not certain even he knows what he is now. How his work has paved the way for the next step.

In the old days, it was a fevered pull. Yes. One that unsuspecting minds could not help but answer. I've borne witness to this thousands of times, with the troubled minds that we acted as caretakers for here in the depths of this labyrinthine place.

I watched them all as they were compelled time and time again to return the pen to the page. The brush to the canvas. The marker to the sketchbook. How they drew and painted and wrote what demanded to be told, the truths that demanded release, to be known by all those with the will to comprehend them.

I am favored. Fortunate. They, each and every one of them, who were devoured, and broken, and disappeared into the depths of the abyss of time. Their sacrifice paved the way for what will soon happen.

Their words and images and footage have been fed to Grimoire so that we may complete our knowledge. He has read between those lines. Unlocked the twisting, living vortexes lurking in the paintings and mad poetry of those we've lost.

It is with their memory that we return this world to its rightful rulers.

That we finally admit what so many mad authors could not bring themselves to know.

That physical reality as we know it is nothing more than a dream.

From the Journal of Lena Hartman
December 25th, 2022

My mind reels. It feels like I've been here decades. Maybe longer.

I've made so many escape attempts, they've all blurred together. Though, sometimes, I wonder if any of it is real. Maybe I dreamed it all?

I've been left here a long time. Patton has come back time and time again to show me to the black chamber with the glowing screens.

When I remember what I've seen, it gives me a headache. The worst one I've ever had.

Sometimes, it makes me laugh. And it reminds me of someone. Someone I used to know.

He did something horrible…

And I can't fucking remember it!

Not that it matters.

I don't really want to remember…

I've stopped trying to reread entries in this journal. I'm afraid. What if something rips my head open again? Makes the pain return?

I just want to leave with my daughter!

Is that so fucking much to ask for?

Feels like we arrived here yesterday. Sometimes, when I really think hard, I can feel her kicking in my belly.

I'd give anything to go back. Tell them all to go fuck themselves. To run as fast as I can into the forest.

Sometimes I remember where I come from. I wonder if it's better to let it happen. Whatever that means.

The screams outside my cell are getting worse. Lately, they don't sound normal. Not like they ever were…but it's like they're saying the same thing over and over again.

Covering my head doesn't shut them up.

Sometimes…it helps to pretend. Pretend today's Christmas. Makes the screams fade away. I pretend that my family, whoever they were or are, are all able to come running downstairs to open up their presents in front of the tree.

That my daughters will open up action figures and video games and new clothes from their Tía and Tío. Their smiles would erase all the pain. Wipe the scars clean.

Someone would remember that I love tequila, and I'd get to drink myself stupid and forget.

It's a nice fantasy.

Sometimes, if I think real hard, I can almost feel it. Smell the pine needles from the tree. Hear the music. The laughter. The happy and heated voices coming from the kitchen.

Sometimes I wonder if I've lived it. If I'm not just rotting in some mental hospital, waiting for the end to come as my mind goes totally senile.

Fuck. Something's at the door.

From the Journal of Lena Hartman
February 14th, 2023

I made another escape attempt.

Or, at least, I remember trying.

I was lying in the dark in my cot. There have been shapes outside my door for weeks, maybe months. They turn the lights off sometimes and leave me in the dark for days on end.

At first, I couldn't stand the dark. Kept wondering if something was going to come out from the shadows and carry me off to the Astral Lands.

Don't know why I keep thinking that.

Don't even know where I got the words. Astral Lands…

Like astral projection?

Somehow, I was thinking about some kind of stone corridor made from really tall blocks. I was following someone. I was afraid. So afraid.

And then, somehow, when I looked up in the dark, it felt like I was really there!

Like I was staring up at an empty ceiling, one that held everything that ever was.

I glanced around my surroundings, and I could actually smell the decaying rot of the place. I could feel the stonework beneath my feet, and even make out shapes and symbols in the walls.

And...I ran.

I ran and ran and ran and ran.

It felt like that corridor was never going to end.

Somehow, I knew that if I thought of home, that maybe, just maybe, if I let it hurt enough, if I devoted my entire self to it, I might make it there, or some approximation of it.

Heh.

Approximation. What would Ira think of me using big words like that?

Momma always told me I was smarter than I knew...

I...

Who is Ira?

I had it for a moment and now it's gone...

Oh, well...

Anyway, the stone corridor felt like it would never end. And I started feeling...started thinking about home.

Sounds crazy. Probably is.

But I could actually smell it. I could feel my surroundings taking shape, transforming.

I remembered my childhood home, the peeling stucco and the paint, and my brothers all screaming at each other for control of the TV or video games.

But, just as I was starting to feel everything come together, all I could see was HIM.

Him with those yellowing, segmented eyes. That grin filled with too many black teeth. How his body surged and bubbled. How his skin broke, like continents being torn apart to reveal the blackened, sludge-like material beneath.

I remember him opening his thousands of mouths and telling me there was no escape. That He would not let me go. That I wasn't ready.

And then I believed it.

And I woke up.

I was and am trapped here.

I can't get out.

Someone...

Can someone help?

In my dreams, sometimes I see a woman with black hair and blue eyes. She's calling for me. Reaching for me.

And each and every time, I claw for her hand, and I fail, and I fall into the woods, naked and dripping and pregnant.

From the Journal of Lena Hartman
February 20th, 2023

Today Doctor Patton came to take me away from my cell. Feels like it's been months since she did that...since I've seen anyone.

I told her I felt like I was going crazy. Like I couldn't remember anything anymore.

She told me Doctor Webber needed to see me. That it was finally time to see my daughter. I don't remember having a daughter. I remember a little girl, yeah, tiny hands grasping for me from her crib. Mom and Dad telling me I needed to get a job and stop partying.

But she died.

Right?

I'm not a mom anymore.

Somehow, something about the way Patton looked at me with those gray eyes...somehow I know she was telling the truth.

But every time she reached out to touch me, I shuddered.

Then I noticed the marks on my arms. The scars all over. When she turned the lights on, they looked gray.

I wanted to cover myself. She didn't like that. She told me I needed to be willing to let go of my shame to receive my gifts.

I don't know what that means.

But everything feels so numb. Honestly, I was just happy someone was here with me, talking with me, asking about how I'm feeling.

Oh, God...

She led me into the dark, through the door, into a series of twisting hallways, walked the ceilings and stared into cascading, twisting staircases that behaved in such a way that I could have sworn I was dreaming it all.

She assured me I wasn't.

That I've done this many times before.

The thought was funny. I laughed. And my laughter carried into the depths of the green abyss.

The inverted staircase was made of a type of green stone. Strange and…ghostly, I thought. We stared at the floor from the walls and ceiling, making our way slowly to a light in the distance.

A surging, brilliant thing.

So beautiful.

Sounded…it sounded like ocean waves.

And I actually smelled the beach. Imagined myself running into Luke's arms. His rippling muscles.

Too bad the baby scared him off.

Doctor Patton turned to me and smiled when we reached the edge of the platform. Pointed to the light in the distance.

Said all this was made possible because of me. Because I gave Doctor Webber hope.

And when I turned my head, I saw them. Shapes dotting the horizon, silhouetted and moving in the light.

At first, I thought they were figures, but Doctor Patton shook her head and told me to follow her.

I asked her where we were going, as there was no more platform to walk on…

But as I finished my question, my feet found the cold embrace of the path. A metallic, pockmarked thing that spread itself through the land like veins…

Yeah, I know it sounds crazy, but it's what I saw. I can't wrap my head around it either. Doctor Patton told me this was the furthest we've traveled together.

That, until now, I wasn't ready. Not physically. Not mentally.

She told me this was a good sign. That I was getting better.

I smiled. Hope bloomed in my heart.

She told me my daughter was just over the hill and led me on through the winding paths that went to incredible, shifting objects, things I could only rationalize as buildings of some kind.

The whole place felt like some kind of city, though for the life of me, I couldn't imagine anyone actually living in it.

I remember telling Doctor Patton this, and through her blackened teeth, she smiled, and told me that soon enough I would. That soon I would remember everything.

The hill loomed forever on the horizon, against the pretty green light. It felt like we walked for days without the thing growing much more than an inch in my vision.

I remember thinking it must have been like those pictures photographers take of an object, where the background seems to shrink and grow depending on the camera's settings. Peter was his name. The photographer. He made beautiful pictures, but was lousy with my kid and even worse in bed. He's dead now, along with everyone else back on my world.

Days transformed into weeks and months and years. My thoughts felt like they were stretching out, moving in slow motion, while my movements sped up or moved at a sluggish pace with no rhyme or reason as to why.

Sometimes I don't feel like myself.

Sometimes, I feel like these words aren't mine. Like something's been put in my head. Through my mouth into the depths of my stomach. Like it's changing me.

Silly, crazy Lena. Always making things up. Compulsive liar. Kleptomaniac. Terrible nurse. Crass bitch. Can't keep her legs closed. Got fired before the first snow fell in Riverside for stealing Doctor Powell's wedding ring and fucking his wife.

Sad, sad, Lena. Always sad.

Lost her family to the ice.

Always too unlucky to die, despite being so, so stupid.

My feet squished down in some kind of black mud.

I snapped out of my daze.

We were over the hill.

I still don't remember it coming or going.

Doctor Patton smiled again and pointed at these incredible egg-like shapes in the dark.

She told me it's time at last to be reunited.

I felt it…something compelling me to move through that sludge…to gaze upon those breathing, blackened things…shapes moving inside them…terrible, amorphous things…breathing…horrible, all-encompassing breathing…

And, then...

I saw it.

One larger than all the others, resting before the base of a pillar or tower or monolith to the stars.

Shapes moved in the dark, through the dead mists.

And the egg...

The sac with its breathing, surging walls... Burst open.

And I fell to my knees, feeling an all-encompassing pain in my womb.

Blood flowed from my uterus, and I could see things as they really were.

I could feel her clawing out of me. Reaching for the blackened mud with shapeless hands.

In a language I had no knowledge of prior, I felt myself uttering terrible things.

And I'll never forget what Doctor Patton said to me.

"The second birth will set us all free."

When I looked back at the egg-sack, at the dark shape looming before me, I saw something gleaming. Something I could only interpret as eyes and a mouth and hair.

My eyes, my mouth, my hair.

And I screamed. But it wasn't the one they were looking for.

And now here I am, back in my cell. I keep pacing back and forth. Wondering if that really was my daughter.

Wondering if I'll ever get out of here.

If I'll forget again...

Doctor Patton said she's disappointed in me. That I've regressed.

Before she left, I remember picking up one of the pens Doctor Webber gave me when I first came here. I remember thinking how lovely it'd be to poke holes in her. To watch her bleed blackened blood out onto the floor.

But I couldn't bring myself to do it. Terrible nurse or not, I swore an oath.

To do no harm.

All I could do was watch her leave.

I have to get out of here...

From the Journal of Lena Hartman
February 14th, 2023

Doctor Patton came to see me today.

When I heard the rusty hinges of the door squeak, I couldn't help it. I hid under my cot.

She seemed…different. From my place under the cot, I watched her. She was pacing around my cell, staring at the blank cement walls. I screamed when she crouched low, staring at me with bloodshot eyes.

She told me I was to come with her.

That it was time for me to see my daughter.

I should have known better.

She offered me her hand, and like an idiot I took it.

Patton led me through the steel door into the labyrinth.

The change was gradual. With every twist and turn, details changed. It brought memories flooding back from that other place. Near the end. How the shadows led us to vast cyclopean temples and alien skies.

The shape of the corridor was no longer cylindrical, but segmented, almost like a beehive or something. The concrete transformed into oddly shaped green plates. The plates had strange symbols on them and protruded from the walls at every possible angle. The rusted steel doors where so many "research subjects" like me had been kept remained unchanged, but more than once, I saw impossible things writhing behind their viewing windows.

It felt like we were descending deep into the earth. If I was still on Earth at all.

At times, I pleaded with Doctor Patton to let me go. To let me and my daughter flee into the wilderness. I told her we'd never tell anyone about what we'd seen here, about the OEI.

She did not respond.

Patton was a cold, unfeeling monster before today. I could feel that. Could see it in her eyes. Yet, even so, it's like she's a totally different person now.

Eventually, the segmented tunnel expanded into a huge bridge that seemed to stretch on for miles and miles. And at its end, an immense, vaulted door made of glowing green stone set between two towering winged statues greeted us.

The space around the bridge…it's still hard to reconcile it. When I glanced at my surroundings, I saw a vast chamber that had no bottom. Its walls appeared to be composed of those same segmented green plates, but they appeared to be…breathing.

When we finally reached the door at the end of the bridge, Doctor Patton went to her knees.

She commanded me to do the same, and for some reason, without a single moment to think about it...I obeyed.

Patton began chanting. And shortly, as if my vocal cords and lips weren't mine anymore, I did too.

I can still remember them. The chants. When I sleep, my nightmares are full of them.

"Iä! Iä! Cthulhu fhtagn! Ph'nglui mglw'nafh Cthulhu R'lyeh wgah'nagl fhtagn!"

We repeated the chant countless times. Until the words had replaced all memory, all thought...until they were our beginning and our end.

And then, the door opened to a large chamber where naked figures were waiting.

The chamber was absolutely massive. Somehow I knew that, despite the fact it was pitch black. Even larger than the one that had held the bridge we'd just traversed.

Briefly, my senses came back to me, and I tried to run. But their hands wrenched at my limbs, lifted me off my feet like it was nothing. Like I was nothing.

Patton told me that today was special. That today, their research would finally bear fruit.

Doctor Webber was standing in front of something, his yellow eyes stabbing back at me in the dark. Now, it was like I was watching one of those videos from the facility on my world. Watching as this loco bastard spewed insane rambling passages about things beyond our comprehension.

He told us all that today, with the help of his supporters, he had successfully transcended the limits of human understanding. Of human science. That with my help, with my testimony, he had corrected the mistakes of his alternate selves. That their attempts at understanding the true nature of the multiverse were like a child's attempts to understand its surroundings, to rationalize their world. That thanks to me, now he is no longer a child. That with His help, humanity could become so much more.

He called it a necessary evolution.

When he told Doctor Patton to close the door to the chamber, I knew there was no way out. I knew I'd never see my daughter again. And God...I cursed that son of a bitch for it.

The things I had experienced up until that point. The death of my world and all the impossible things I witnessed with the coming of the black comet...

I was numb. So used to the fear that it became my natural state. But I was not prepared for what I saw. I did not know true fear. Not until he turned the monitor on. Not until I stared into that putrid green light.

Not until I saw it writhing in that tower, or monolith, or whatever the fuck it was.

I don't remember much of what I saw.

I only woke up a short time ago. Though...my perception of time is so fucked up I'm not even sure that's true. And I've been struggling to wrap my head around all this.

I was so scared of the things that killed my world. Part of me believed Webber when he said he wanted to protect this world from the things I saw. But another part of me was afraid Webber and his people would accidentally call to them, that I would be forced to watch this world wither and freeze and die. That I would be forced to stare at the sun as it vanished once more.

But this.

What I saw in those nightmares.

Somehow. Somehow I know.

This is so much worse.

I can't help but hear their chants. Waking or dreaming. It doesn't matter.

I can't help but hear Its voice clawing at the walls of my mind, like It's trying to break in. Like Its tentacles are worming their way into the depths of my body. Like they're in my soul...

Like I'm changing.

Like we're all changing.

I don't know if there's a way to stop it.

For Hunter, it's like waking up. He tears his eyes away from the words and focuses them on a festering black ceiling.

The journal is still clutched tight in his right hand. Like a death grip. He wants to know more. Wants to dive back in. See how it ends.

Another part of him wants to sit up. Wants to move. To know what happened to his children. But all he can do is lie there and cough up black viscous fluid.

The cold embrace of concrete is almost comforting, even as he watches rotting ichor steam and waft on the floor with a life of its own.

He tries to recall the last thing that happened to him. Tries to push past the fog coating his brain.

He remembers the cavern. Carrying Bobby and Zuri to safety. Running for his life from the thing that Shirley became. From all of his so-called brothers in blue.

He remembers it flooding. His movements slowing.

He remembers his head being forced beneath the black viscous fluid, how it parted his lips and found its way inside. Like slimy hermit crabs, their legs tickling the flesh as they make their way down his throat—inhabiting him like a new shell.

He remembers his children. How he struggled. Holding them high above his head before...

His head jerks up.

He's in a small concrete room. A sickly-sweet smell permeates the air. The walls sweat with familiar black fluid. It glistens in the flickering florescent light coming from the black ceiling.

This is a prison.

Father always warned him about prison. That eventually, "civilized" society would find some reason to lock him up or shoot him dead in his apartment. Cop or not.

His children. They're resting together on two cots.

Hunter goes to them, runs his hand through their hair. They're breathing. Covered in dried blackened ichor. Just like him.

He wonders how long they have.

They haven't woken since he took them from their...

He doesn't want to think about Janet. About what she's become, or how he pulled the trigger. The impossible light that exploded out of the barrel of his gun, or what it did to her...body.

He doesn't have time to weep. To mourn.

Before he even knows what he's doing, he's on his feet and pounding on the rusted metal door to their cell. Demanding they be released. As if his authority actually means something in this place.

His efforts get him nowhere.

Hunter spends uncountable hours pacing back and forth in the cell. Periodically, he returns to the rusted metal door to resume his pounding, his demands.

The hours. They stretch on as though time itself is meaningless. Sometimes he wonders if he's spent days in this place. Maybe longer.

The children. Eventually, they stir. They sit up.

Zuri's eyes are wide, like globes. "Where are we, Daddy?"

Bobby, however, is quiet. Too quiet.

Hunter rushes over and kneels before his children. "Some bad men locked us in here. But I'm going to get us out."

Bobby cocks his head at this. The movement is unnatural. Hunter doesn't recognize his son's body language at all.

He doesn't want to look in his eyes.

"Where's Mommy?" Zuri asks.

"He thinks he killed her," Bobby says, his voice gurgling, full of mucus.

"What?" Zuri's eyes plead with Hunter. "Killed Mommy?"

"Nothing can kill Mommy now," Bobby says.

"That wasn't your mother," Hunter says.

"How would you know?" Bobby asks. *"You were never around."*

Hunter stares at Bobby. At first, he wants to yell at him. To punish him for the words coming out of his mouth.

"What's the matter, Daddy?" Bobby asks, smiling through blackened teeth. *"You can't bring yourself to yell? To show me how big a man you are the way your Daddy did to you? How he took the belt to your behind. How it blistered and bled. How he told you crying would only make it worse. Real men don't cry. Do they? No. God's family needs a strong man. A man that knows the value of a good beating. Isn't that right?"*

"Stop it," Hunter says.

"You know it's true, don't you?"

Bobby's laughter. It stabs deeper than any knife could. *"Mommy told you there was no turning back for us. That we would emerge soon, like buttery flies from cocoons."*

Hunter leaves his children behind, rushing to the door again. "I'm going to get us out of here!"

He pounds and pounds and pounds on the door.

"You've always wanted to know if you're respected by the rest of the Black community," Bobby says. *"Well, I can tell you, you're not. They see you for what you've become."*

He pounds on the door until his hands start to bleed. Until his breath runs short and he doubles over, coughing up more blackened ichor.

"What's the word you use?" Bobby asks. *"Ah. Yes. Uncle Tom. That's what they call you after you've smiled and waved at them and gone on your way. They hate you."*

Hunter turns around, lets his back slump against the door. Bobby's blackened smile has not abated. Zuri has backed away from him, her eyes full of fear.

He asks himself if there's still hope for her. Remembers the feeling of something slithering down his throat in that other place. How it splashed down in his stomach. How it remained there.

Did it happen to Zuri too?

"Did that thing…" Hunter can hardly form the words. "Did your mother feed you something?"

Bobby's smile deepens. *"Oh, yes, Daddy. She did indeed. Even now it grows within us."*

"Is there any way to stop it?" Hunter asks.

"Why would we want that?" Bobby asks.

"Damn it, boy! Do you want to lose yourself to these things? It's unnatural!"

"Isn't it, though? It's evolution. We will transcend, shed these pitiful, unworthy forms and become what we were always meant to be."

Hunter screams, holding his stomach as if he's trying to keep his intestines from spilling out. The pain is almost all-consuming. As if every cell is on fire.

"Yes." Bobby's footsteps barely register. His tiny feet appear blurry in Hunter's vision, like a piece of film out of focus. *"The pain is how it starts. Not unlike the pain mother experienced when she gave birth to us."*

"I don't want this," Hunter whispers.

"It's too late," Bobby says. *"You are ready for the next phase."*

"Just…just want to go back to how…how it was…"

"And what's so good about how it was, Hunter?"

Soon, even Bobby's inhuman words are lost in the torrent of pain. His eyes cease to see the cell. Instead, he sees a place where the only source of light is a single grouping of computer screens. The light they provide is familiar, unnatural.

He recognizes the silhouettes of two children approaching it.

How their bodies bubble with tumorous masses. Their silhouettes become indistinct over time. They become something else. Something without definition. Something that can only copy nature.

A mockery.

Hunter grits his teeth, forcing his mind, his eyes, to come back. To see what's before him.

"And what about your sister?" Hunter asks through clenched teeth.

"What about her?"

"She's going to suffer the same fate, right? You prepared to let that little girl go through this?"

Bobby's robotic expression wavers. His eyes drift to where Zuri is sitting on the cot.

"You're not sure," Hunter says. "Are you?"

Bobby's eyes jerk back to the door, tilting his head like a blind man trying to pinpoint the source of a sound.

And there is a sound.

It screams through the impossible corridors outside their cell like bells tolling.

"Tekeli-li."

"Tekeli-li."

"Answer me!" Hunter shouts.

But Bobby does not respond to his anger, his outrage. Instead, his son, or what's left of him, turns to him with a dispassionate countenance.

266

"It doesn't matter," Bobby says. *"You are being summoned."*

Rusted, squealing hinges. They echo through the cell, bouncing back to Hunter's ears.

When he finally finds the will to turn around, the door is open.

Bobby finds his way through the doorway and offers Hunter his hand. *"Come. See our glorious future. One without pain. Without prejudice. Without death."*

A familiar voice tells him to take his boy's hand.

He obeys.

For some reason, the pain doesn't feel as all-consuming. For some reason, he's able to stand and walk.

And before he even knows it, Zuri is beside him, holding his hand. Her eyes, still scared, still pleading with him to make the nightmare stop.

But he has no answers for her. No comforting words to whisper in her ear.

All he can do is obey the call. Obey it and walk into the abyss.

The corridor. It's almost exactly like the nightmarish reflection of his apartment. The place they all called home for half a decade. The shifting proportions of plates in the wall, how they change their shapes and sizes. How the floor appears wide and narrow all at once. How the whole place reeks of a rot beyond death.

The three of them traverse the corridor. Bobby seems to know where he's going. As if he's been here before. That thought alone ignites the fires of Hunter's rage.

He thinks about the Bobby he once knew. The real one.

Not this imitation. This deception.

Bobby loved art. Loved bingeing the latest cartoons, trying to recreate their art styles. He spent hours camped in front of the TV with a sketchpad and a light box propped up on the coffee table. Always drawing and redrawing and pausing frame after frame of animation. It was remarkable how creative he was. Twelve years old and already becoming an expert in Photoshop. Janet and Hunter would stay up sometimes, wondering what sort of man he might grow up to be. Hunter thought he'd become a painter, while Janet was certain he'd become a famous animator.

Bobby was not a vocal child, however. Not at all like the creature inhabiting his flesh.

"But I'm so much more now," the mockery says. *"If I wanted, now I could travel to a reflection of my own dream and live there for all eternity. Do you want to see what that dream looks like, Hunter?"*

"Stop calling me that!"

Bobby does not respond. The corridor changes to a vicious, biting reflection of their former home. Even Janet's blasphemous easel still stands covered in the living room.

Like a ballet dancer, Bobby spin-walks into the center of the room.

When his hands open, an image of Hunter appears—old and decaying in his favorite recliner, watching the TV. Mother stands baking cookies in the kitchen. And an adult Bobby comes through the door, carrying a black portfolio that Hunter knows he's going to regret looking at later.

"Mother, Father," Bobby shouts. *"I'm home from my animation job!"*

Hunter watches the aged version of himself peel his eyes off of the TV, watching football of all things. His hand opens and closes, and he hears himself ask for the portfolio. His other self wants to know what his boy has been working on.

Bobby is all too eager. He hands Hunter the portfolio. Before Hunter can object, he's the one sitting in the chair. Thumbing through page after page of tentacled horrors. Things that reach into the depths of his mind and whisper secrets into his soul.

Hunter wakes screaming in the corridor. His hand still firmly clutching Bobby's.

"See?" Bobby asks, his eyes peering deep into Hunter's, pupils segmented just like Jessica Smith's. *"In the dreamlands, all realities are possible. Every desire can be yours."*

Hunter's too shaken to mouth a reply. Zuri is sobbing. Wondering where Mommy is.

"But that's for later," Bobby says. *"Now, we must reach the bridge."*

"What bridge?"

The moment Hunter asks the question, his body feels like it's been stretched over a thousand miles of freeway, almost like he's been dosed with acid for the second time in his life.

It feels like they've been walking for days. Weeks maybe. And yet…Hunter feels no hunger. No thirst.

But the pain. *That* he feels. It returns with a dull roar, demanding his attention.

He wants to cry out. To tell whatever force has infested their reality to have its way with his body as long as the end is swift. As long as it's painless.

"No metamorphosis is painless, Hunter," Bobby says.

The corridor.

It has changed.

Morphed into a bridge extending over an infinite abyss and leading to two immense doors made from ageless green stone.

A familiar sight.

"Behold the bridge," Bobby says. *"We are here."*

Slowly, they cross the bridge. At no point does it feel like they are gaining ground. The stone doorways. They pulse with otherworldly green light, cascading onto two winged statues to either side of the doorway. The doors always remain on the horizon. The same size. Always the same size. Though he can't judge the distance, he thinks they are as large as mountains. Larger.

One moment, they are walking.

The next?

It's as if they're at the base of an impossible mountain range. Like his brain blocked out eons of pointless, endless walking. The doors stretch from horizon to horizon.

Bobby puts his hands on the doorway. Somehow, even though the doors appear to be thousands of miles tall, the mockery of his boy is able to push them open.

And when they open, it's as if the Four Horsemen of the Apocalypse have sounded their trumpets. No. That's not right. It's nothing like that at all. The sound is as if all the trumpets in all realities in every single Oros suddenly sounded at once, in every possible frequency, and somehow found a way to harmonize with each other.

The music. It makes his eyes cry blood. Black and viscous, it covers his body with rivers.

The abyss they enter has a single source of light. A jumbled mess of breathing screens fused together by sinewy musculature and pulsing, tumorous masses that take the form of a tree. A blasphemous fusion of machine and flesh. A thing that should not be.

At once, the structure is familiar. At once, he knows it is the source of this kaleidoscopic nightmare.

A voice booms through the abyss. It is both elderly and youthful, demonic and full of bass, angelic and human all the same. It permeates all things. It makes his flesh revolt and his mind soar.

And it is a voice that is familiar.

The voice he has been hearing ever since he laid eyes on Kevin Wallace's sketchbook.

Its words are inhuman, and yet, he understands them perfectly.

"*Welcome,*" the voice says. "*Here we are at the end. Here we are at the bridge between worlds. A point in time that will be regarded by all sapient species as the end. And the beginning. When the stars were made right. When the Great Old Ones returned to rule all reality, as it was meant to be.*"

"And..." Hunter struggles to speak up. The music. It makes it hard to think. To perceive anything other than what that thing wants. "The end of humanity?"

"*All things must end. Some endings are far less gracious. Believe me when I say I have seen the end of countless worlds. Most species do not get a choice. I have given you all a choice. The ability to become more. To open up your potential to the stars.*"

The abyss and the tumorous fusion of machine and flesh are erased from his vision. Hunter is forced to bear witness to thousands of worlds ending all at once. To see asteroid impacts, supernovae, and Great Old Ones come to feast upon the flesh of all shapes and sizes of organic life.

His screams echo into the abyss.

When the visions cease, he is left drooling and blind, as if—in an effort to protect itself—his brain cut off all information being received by his eyeballs.

"*You think ripping your own eyes out will stop it?*" the voice asks.

The pain in his eye sockets. He becomes aware of the sensation. How tendons and blood drip from them.

And he remembers the urge. His father's voice screaming at him when he caught Hunter masturbating for the first time. The last time.

How his fingers forced their way into his sockets. The pressure on his eyeballs as he squeezed. How his vision blacked out. The voice at the back of his mind screaming, telling him to stop. How he ignored the impossible totality of pain as his eyeballs ruptured and oozed. How the fluid ran down his fingers.

"*And if thy right eye offend thee,*" Father said, "*Pluck it out, and cast it from thee, boy!*"

"*Ahhh, an amusing thing,*" the voice says. "*You resent your father, and yet you still cling to his voice in times of peril. But your efforts are in vain. Information can be received in so many ways. When you receive this message, you will understand the gift I have given your species. The mercy of it.*"

The voice. It transforms into a cacophony of sound. Robotic and organic and strange. It replaces the pain in his eyes with an all-encompassing throbbing, drilling, burning sensation that engulfs his entire being.

He wants to say something. Wants to cry out and resist the thing at the center of the abyss.

Its all-encompassing voice.

Eventually. His words escape as weak things, barely audible. "It's not a mercy… You made the choice for us."

"*Have I? Perhaps I've only given you what you fail to admit you want? I have seen your nightmares, your dreams.*"

It arrests control of his mind's eye. The thing inside. And he's forced to bear witness to the sprawling, cascading flesh of time itself. How it folds in and out of each and every universe. The key and the gate. Its protoplasmic eyes watch from every fold, every arm, and every possible dimension, in every timeline and every organism.

"*The infinite reflections they cast into the place you call the dreamlands. I have observed you as you stare down the unknowable.*"

He sees himself cowering before Its eyes. Before the infinite march of future and past, how they cross and merge. How they create new things. Impossible things.

"*How you buckle and cry out for salvation from your brief, pathetic existence, marching along in your isolated point in space-time.*"

271

His own cries reach him in the abyss.

"I see what you really want. I hear your truth. Your desires. And I have answered."

CHAPTER TWENTY-EIGHT

"Do you know where you're going?" River asks.

As his question reverberates through the corrugated labyrinth of hallways, Lena gives him a confused look. Her eyes are wild. They dart from one corner of the corridor to another.

Then, her brow tightens. Her irises focus to pinpricks.

"I remember the way. Yes," Lena whispers, as if in reply to someone else.

River watches her as she takes each and every shaky step forward, her brow wrinkled in deep concentration.

"All roads lead to the bridge," Lena says, chuckling. The sounds warp, as if the walls are mutating her voice into something darker...something older.

River feels the icy embrace of primal dread, snaking up and down his spine...

When Lena stops, she cranes her head up. At first, River wonders if her neck is bent at an unnatural angle. But then he notices the odd way the walls are reflecting light, playing tricks on his eyes.

He rubs his eyes, shakes his head.

"I didn't understand before," Lena says. "Thought this place was nothing more than a maze for us to get trapped inside."

"And now?"

"I understand...it's just like the car. It's just like before!"

"Well, can you explain it for me, cause I'm totally fucking lost."

"It's not a maze. Not at all." Lena pounds her fist against her cranium; the violence of flesh and bone impacting echoes down the corridor. "It's all about right thinking. You have to know. Have to picture it all. Remember the steps."

"I…" River shakes his head. "I think I remember…"

But whenever he thinks about the steps he took to escape Pastor Castillo, his head erupts in drilling, seething pain.

Lena's scarred lips stretch. River can see the skin and muscle slowly transforming into a smile, one that will go on and on and on. A process that will last an eternity. As if her lips are moving in slow motion.

Her hand stretches out to River, just as slow.

Not knowing what else to do, River ignores his better judgment and takes her hand.

The bridge and doors loom before them.

River screams. The journey flashes before his eyes like a YouTube video set to 2X speed. Faster. A cavalcade of different shapes, corridor passages, rusted doors, and writhing amorphous things beyond them.

And then, for some reason, Lena's hand lets go of River's.

They're standing in a chamber. One with concrete walls with weird circular vents in them.

In context, it's the most normal thing he's seen all day.

At the center of the chamber is a big circular metal door with a radiation symbol on it.

"I don't know why I came here," Lena says.

"What is this?" River asks, backing away from the door. "Is this place radioactive or something?"

"I saw this when I tried escaping once…"

River's shaking. Looks at Lena. She's rocking back and forth, as if she's gonna fall over.

"It's a failsafe," Lena says. "Doctor Patton told me…told me when she was still lucid. That it's the last line of defense. The most powerful nuclear bomb ever created is in there. And if the OEI's archive was ever compromised, detonating it would be the only way to safeguard America's future."

"That's…" River shakes his head, trying to ignore what he learned on YouTube about subterranean detonations and radiation. "There has to be another way, right?"

Lena's eyes drift, and lock on River's.

River lets out a shriek, covering his mouth.

"What is it?" Lena asks. *"Is something wrong with my eyes?"*

River shakes his head. He doesn't have the heart to tell her that her irises have segmented. That, somewhere deep inside himself, he knows that there's no turning back for her.

Lena's face twists toward the bomb. Her head drops, strings of sweat-stained hair dancing with the rapid movement. Laughter escapes from her cracked and rotting lips.

"Can you hear that?" Lena asks.

River shakes his head.

"I hear her," Lena says. "I hear her calling!"

Before River can answer, Lena's grabbed his hand again and dragged him away from the chamber with the bomb.

And she pulls him down a winding, glowing staircase.

"I get to see her!" Her words stretch out, as if they've fallen into the heart of a black hole.

An infinite descent. Miles upon miles of twisting mazelike corridors, far past the point where the Earth's core would be and further still.

A stench worse than anything dead can produce.

Despite the things River has seen, he can't believe the scale. The doors seem impossibly tall. The bridge, impossibly wide.

And yet, somehow…

"Here we are," Lena says. Her voice is strange, hopeful, and yet… "I'll finally get to see her. Just like they promised."

"Lena…"

Her hands glisten in the impossible light bleeding from the ancient green door. They stretch and they bend as if made from rubber. Her eyes find River's, and segment like cells forced into mitosis.

"I'm finally going to see her!"

The doors open, and River forgets himself.

Cacophony.

That's the only word that comes to his mind as his knees buckle. As his face plants in fluid the consistency of tar.

It's as if a fever has arrested his body. He can barely manage a slow crawl into the black beyond the doorway.

His eyes barely register the light at the center.

Yet, the voice. It is familiar as it whispers sweet blasphemies into his essence. Promises, really. A covenant for a better tomorrow for him. For everyone. To be freed from the shackles of human society and all of its flaws.

To be accepted.

He sees himself, floating through the vastness of the cosmos. Across infinite seas of plasma and dust and light. An ocean of stars and hidden things.

He's never felt more free.

His new body passes stars and black holes of all shapes and sizes, until he finds a red star that feels just right.

Around this red giant is a world recently brought to life by its rapid expansion. A world that has been lucky enough to evolve intelligent life. An intelligence that has forged a primitive society.

He desires to know them.

And he descends upon the planet.

Piercing sulfuric, ashen clouds, he lands in the middle of a city, creating a great disturbance in the crust of the world.

When the locals investigate, he is all too happy to lie in wait. To let them search.

His many eyes seek them out across this scorching, blistering world, studying their crablike forms as they scuttle on the surface. As their appendages dig and scrape at the sediment and vitrified rock shielding his protoplasmic flesh.

Eventually, their curiosity and ingenuity win out. They unearth him.

And, for their effort, his tendrils reach out and skewer them. He thrashes and screams and consumes them. Bloody and raw.

When he's done feasting on their remains, he mimics their forms and sets off across their cratered, torrid home. He traverses infinite molten mountain ranges and glowing cavernous ruins, finding unsuspecting prey to aid in his development. His growth. Until there are no more to consume. Until they are all silent.

And he is forced to wait, raging across the surface of their world or slumbering in its many ruins until a new form of life is unfortunate enough to evolve. So that he might consume them too.

River screams himself awake. Or, perhaps, he has been awake this entire time. Perhaps he has lived this life he has just witnessed in full. And, seeing the destruction he has wrought, decided to reach back to his earlier self to stop it?

Mad thoughts. Stupid thoughts. True thoughts.

He watches, even while his screams threaten to silence his voice forever, as Lena limps into the abyss, approaching what River can only describe as a collection of screens growing out of tree limbs composed of living, flowing flesh.

The room. It's covered in familiar viscous black fluid. It flows with a mind of its own, congealing on the walls and slithering like living canals toward the center of the chamber. For some reason, River thinks of the place as a womb.

His eyes find the center of the chamber. His heart seizes in his chest. There, the living rivulets combine, flowing up the tree's silhouette. And on each of its limbs is a screen bearing the full power of Grimoire.

It takes every ounce of willpower left to tear his eyes away from them, from His gaze.

Instead, his eyes scan the dark, caressing the dimly lit sacks of flesh pulsing in the abyss.

For some reason, he knows them. Each and every one of them. The tall one that pulses round and full and perfectly in tune with the blasphemous sounds emitting from the flesh tree at the center is Hunter. The smaller ones at his sides are his children.

His eyes find cocoons for David, Dean, Jess, Mom, and even dean Garcia. All of them, transforming inside. Waiting for the second birth.

River tries to call to them, but the words won't come out.

His lips tremble, as if he's forgotten how to speak.

It's when he tries to reach his hands up to his lips that he realizes his hands are stuck. Wrapped in that same viscous, living black fluid. He watches in horror as it wraps about his arms and torso, entombing him.

His eyes dart back to Hunter and his children.

How the sweating, breathing sacks of blackened flesh pulse in and out.

In and out.

Like the deep, rhythmic breaths of an ancient creature.

The realization comes upon him slowly.

He's looking at his future.

Part of him wants to give into his screaming muscles, his aching bones, and the drilling, ever-present headache.

But another part of him, the part of him that endured second puberty and top surgery while learning to cope with his own adult ADHD…that sat in seemingly never-ending psych sessions…and dealt with his mother's own descent…

The part of him that has the will to endure. To persevere.

That part forces him to grit his teeth and pull. Pull against the grabbing, adhesive force of a material that is like tar and mucus at the same time.

As he struggles, as he pulls and pushes and grinds his teeth, he remembers his vision of that scorching planet. How he roamed it, devouring thousands of innocent creatures and stealing their forms.

Answering the call. His call.

Is this a memory? The *Necronomicon* states that every shoggoth holds the memories of its ancestors.

And if history repeats itself…then each and every newborn shoggoth that is born here will spread out from the valley and set upon the Earth to devour all of humanity…

Somehow, that realization is enough to give him the will to keep pulling. To push his body to its limit.

He screams! The tendrils attempting to silence him burst as he pulls his arms free of the forming flesh cocoon.

Words are an incoherent gibbering mess as he struggles to get his legs free, his sweat mixing unevenly with what remains of that disgusting material.

When he is finally free, every part of his body feels like it's on fire.

Each lumbering step is an indomitable effort.

But, somehow, he stands before the glistening, breathing outline of Hunter's flesh cocoon.

He thinks about how he's going to get them out…

The screens. In his peripheral vision, they pulse. Demanding his attention.

Familiar images flash through his mind.

A putrid storming sky.

A towering monolith of shifting proportion and size.

Maybe this is where it lives? Where it started?

"I've finally found you." Lena's voice echoes from the other side of the flesh tree.

The voice. It tells him he can be just as happy as she is. He can have his mother and his friends, just as Hunter now has his wife and kids.

If he just submits.

River shakes his head. Tries to tell the voice to go to hell, that it won't trick him again, but his words come out jumbled and stupid.

A light igniting in the monolith.

A doorway through time and space.

He has to stay focused. He has to get Hunter out. Has to save his kids…

"They told me…they told me I couldn't see you…"

If he doesn't do it now…he'll lose the will…

Twisting shapes reaching through the doorway.

Silhouetted and wrong.

Like coiling metal.

"I wondered if I'd ever see you again…"

Lena!

River resists the urge to look for her. The temptation to glance at the flesh tree. To look for the source of the voice coming from behind it. It's almost too great.

River shuts his eyes and takes deep breaths.

Focuses on the task at hand.

"But now…now that I'm here…we'll be together forever, right?"

All that matters is the will, he thinks. *If I can will it, I can make it happen. That's the law.*

He isn't sure where it comes from. Probably from some forgotten void in the depths of his damaged and fragmented mind, where impossible knowledge lay hidden.

Before he realizes what he's doing, he plunges his arms into the largest flesh sac, his hands probing for anything that feels human. The material is thick, like mucus with the consistency of clay.

And when he finds it at the center of that swirling, pulsing, breathing mass of blackened filth, he pulls. His muscles scream as he pushes with his legs. He pulls until he thinks he can't bear the pain anymore, and then he tries again.

And somehow—when he falls backward into the ever-flowing river of viscous mucus—he pulls Hunter free.

They tumble in the dark. Hunter's dead weight pins River to the floor, into the flowing river of ichor.

The next thing he knows, he's staring at Hunter's lips, blackened ichor flowing from them.

He's not breathing...and his *eyes*...

That is not dead which can eternal lie,

And with strange aeons even death may die.

River's muscles howl as he tries to push Hunter off of him. When that doesn't work, he tries shouting for him to wake up. But again, the words come out jumbled and wrong.

Is he dead? River wonders. *Are they all dead?*

The pulsing screens from the flesh tree. The light. The patterns of interspersed darkness. The images that flood his mind's eye. River knows the flesh tree is trying to tell him something.

He doesn't want to listen. He *won't* listen anymore!

I can't push him off of me...but...

River pulls his hand back and slaps Hunter across the face.

More viscous fluid comes out of Hunter's mouth, but he doesn't wake up.

River tries shouting his name, but nothing comes out.

All he can do is slap Hunter again.

Still nothing.

He repeats it over and over as the blackened river carries on its way around them...

That's when he notices the light from the screens has grown brighter. The smaller cocoons containing Hunter's children recede into the distance.

The river is carrying them *toward* the flesh tree!

No!

River pushes the man's dead weight with one arm and slaps him with the other...

No!

His mouth uttering everything other than Hunter's name...

River lays his head down. His throbbing arms fall to his sides. Hunter's weight presses down on him.

It's impossible, he thinks.

In the end, all roads lead to the dreamlands. To the waiting embrace of the things that call them home.

Does it really matter when it happens?

No...these aren't his thoughts.

They're...

His eyes, they struggle to resist the pull. The beckoning of the light coming from the flesh tree's screens.

The thoughts aren't mine, he thinks.

His eyes return to Hunter's unconscious face.

The ever-flowing ichor has already reclaimed River's hands.

He doesn't think he has the strength to free himself again.

He closes his eyes.

If I have the will, I can make it happen, he thinks.

His throat. The vocal cords. They ache with anticipation.

He tries to remember what it was like to learn how to speak.

Instead, his mind is flooded with hidden things.

Visions assault River's mind. The prehistoric Earth beneath a moon still rife with volcanic activity.

The sensation is familiar. To see through stolen eyes.

But, the eyes he peers through tower over the land.

His gaze turns to the cyclopean towers that pierce into the clouds and, still, keep going up.

His stolen body is on the move, taking him to one such tower. Through its metallic, arched entrance.

He is guided through dark, vaulted chambers full of twinkling, thinking lights.

Other figures pass him by. At first, when he sees them, he wants to scream at their strange appearance. The only thing he can relate their shapes to is traffic cones. Traffic cones with flesh the color and texture of broiling clouds.

As they pass him, their bulbous heads turn toward him, bulging orange eyes regarding him. Tentacles dangling from their mouths in what he can only assume is a greeting.

The sounds they emit are followed by clapping claws attached to tentacles coming out of their sides.

River's not sure...but he gets the impression they're saying goodbye.

His stolen eyes lead him to a great chamber with more blinking, thinking lights.

A platform with strange, alien devices greets him.

He steps onto the platform.

A domed device comes down upon his head. A violent, stabbing sensation pierces his skull.

A flash of light and color waves before his eyes.

And he awakens in what he can only describe as a dark bedroom full of black-and-white photographs.

When his stolen head peers down, he's staring at a pair of wrinkled human hands.

No! *River thinks.* This is just a distraction! I have to wake up!

River's eyes jerk open.

His vocal cords vibrating.

His wet lips screaming Hunter's name at last.

As if yanked open by some invisible force, Hunter's dangling eyes open.

His segmented pupils dilate, stretching up on their long, muscular tentacles and focusing on River.

"I..." his voice gurgles, blackened fluid escaping his lips. "*I know you...*"

"Hunter, your kids," River says. "We have to free them!"

"*My...*"

Realization floods onto his face.

But as quickly as it comes, confusion replaces it. "*What is that...light...*"

"No, Hunter, don't look at the tree, don't look at the screens!"

"*But…*"

His eyes, the irises have a mind of their own. Though two focus on River, the others are drawn to the light like flies to flame.

"*It's…so…beautiful…*"

"Hunter!"

Hunter's facial muscles bubble and twist and writhe. Hidden things struggle, cracking his neck and forcing it to stare at the light.

"Hunter, listen to my voice. Remember your children! Your wife. Why did you become a cop?"

His lips tremble, the words oozing out of his mouth like bile dripping from a drunk's lips. "*Why…I became…*"

"It had to be because you thought you could make the world a better place from the inside, right?"

"*Because…*"

"For Bobby, for Zuri."

"*Bobby…*"

Hunter's muscles quake over River's body. His limbs spider-walk, turning his torso to face the side. One eye's pupils remain focused on the flesh tree, and the other's, the pulsing cocoons containing his children.

"Yes, Bobby! Zuri! Remember them?"

"*Bobby…*"

From the side, Hunter's silhouette appears changed. Though all of his body parts appear to be human, their orientation has been altered, almost like an action figure that's been put back together wrong.

River's heart thuds away in his chest. He wonders if it's too late.

"Hunter…?"

The pupils focused on the flesh tree dart around. The bubbling, slithering things beneath Hunter's face strain and struggle.

"Hunter, if you don't do something, Bobby and Zuri are going to die!"

"*Bobby…*"

"You're still human, you can still—"

Two hands come up from behind, jerking River to his feet and spinning him around.

River comes to stare into Lena's segmented pupils.

"No one wants to hear what you have to say now," Lena says. *"Can't you see it's already over?"*

"Lena, why are you doing this?" River asks. "I thought you brought us here to end this!"

"I did."

Lena's cracked lips form a grin. Blackened ichor flows like tributaries from her orifices.

"Then why?"

"Can't you see? This is the end." Laughter, gurgling and sick. *"Everyone you've ever loved is in this vast chamber, waiting to be reborn."*

"And you're okay with letting them all be changed against their will?"

"Lena is tired of fighting…" Lena's head turns to one side. *"Even on her world, they were all fighting the inevitable. She's seen the fates of the others. None of them are pretty. Why delay the inevitable? At least now she'll be able to spend time with our daughter."*

"And after?" River's eyes dart around his body. The tar-like substance is already trying to entomb him again. "Are you really okay with becoming one of those things? I saw visions too, you know, I saw —"

"Entire worlds being devoured. Yes. It is both your past and future. You will spread out over this world and feast upon those humans who we cannot convert. You will join your ancient brethren in the depths of this world, and draw them out of their madness. Once they hear His voice, they will have no choice."

"You're…you're not Lena!"

"You know who I am," Lena says. *"I've been with you this whole time. Closer than any friend or any lover."* Wet fingers caress his neck. Lena's head rolls from one side to the other. Unnatural cracks in her spine echo in the dark. *"And once your numbers have been replenished, you will destroy the Mi-Go and spread our influence from world to world. All in His name."*

Movement. A silhouette behind Lena. Behind the flesh tree.

With each movement, the infinite black space of the birthing chamber shakes. It's all River can do to focus on the silhouette, and not the flesh tree's screens. To hold onto what remains of his mind.

The dim light cascading from the flesh tree gives River the slightest impression of the thing. It's easily five times taller than him, with shifting and shambling proportions, dozens of tendrils pulsing and oozing into and out of itself as it moves along the floor.

Its skin, or what passes for it, is made of the same viscous black ichor that now restrains his limbs.

As River stares, he becomes aware of dim pulses of light housed within the creature's form. Like orbs, or eyes, or both. Dangling from within opaque globules in its amorphous shape.

He relates it to drawings of amoebae he's seen in textbooks.

When it turns part of its mass toward River, one of the orbs bubbles…

Muscle fibers lash out, human teeth protrude from within black gums, and eyes boil into existence.

When it is finished, it's like he's staring into a cruel reflection of his own face.

The thing stops just shy of revealing its full girth. Blackened tentacles wrap around the base of one of the screens attached to the flesh tree. And behind that appendage, an orifice filled with serrated teeth unlike any predator he's seen before.

"*River,*" Lena says. "*Meet Lena's daughter.*"

That's Lena's daughter? River thinks. *Her long-lost love?*

Tears flow from Lena's segmenting eyeballs. Joyous ones that drip drip drip into the never-ending birthing chamber that surrounds them all.

"*You can't possibly understand her joy,*" Lena says. "*Being together at last.*"

River's laughter is involuntary. Silent. Always silent. But laughter all the same. The sick irony of it all almost makes him want to embrace Lena. To tell her he understands.

It's almost enough to break him. To accept his fate as a plaything for Grimoire, Cthulhu, and the shoggoth.

"*Are you ready, River?*" Lena asks.

River stifles his laughter. Lena's hands lock behind his head. He knows what happens next.

"Do I have a choice?" River asks.

Lena's smile deepens, showing the gurgling, festering things waiting inside her. *"Of course not."*

As expected, she turns his head to face the flesh tree, and its infinite cascade of screens.

And all of reality comes undone.

CHAPTER TWENTY-NINE

A wakening.
  It comes with a dull, wet roar. A birth cry erupting from too many mouths.

Knowing is instantaneous and immediate.

From the moment he comes bursting from his cocoon, he feels the insatiable pain of hunger. It burns, pulsing like a heartbeat in the pit of his new body.

Light strobes in the infinite dark of the birthing chamber.

It draws his attention.

The flesh tree. Its strange, reflective limbs have grown. The screens that sprout from the tree have multiplied.

How long has it been?

The thought is interrupted. The images flashing into his mind palace tell him what comes next.

At first, he refuses to do as the flesh tree commands.

It warns him what will happen if he does not obey.

When he still refuses to do as the flesh tree demands, rings of light and geometric force erupt around his body.

Something floods into his new flesh. A sensation that is familiar to him, and yet, entirely alien.

His protoplasmic form screams, as if every cell in his body has been lit ablaze. His form pools until there is no distinction between the rivers of ichor drifting beneath his amorphous anatomy and himself.

The pain. It calls forth ancestral memory.

His people are no strangers to such methods.

Images of the star-headed ones who enslaved his ancestors flash within his mind palace.

The pain stops.

And he obeys.

Green light spills into the birthing chamber. Brilliant. Garish. Familiar.

He can hear the storm surge now.

It beckons him.

Billions of years' worth of ancestral memories tell him how to use his new body. Gone are the concerns he had before.

Those were human things.

When he thinks of his mother, how she sacrificed herself to allow him to come here...he feels nothing. Nothing but the hunger.

When he thinks about Jess. How their friendship slowly eroded with the coming of his new master...he feels nothing.

When he thinks of Hunter and his children... He turns, moving one of his thousands of eyes to gaze back at their cocoons. They're now nothing more than mounds of flowing, churning protoplasm.

He feels nothing.

An ancestral memory bubbles to the surface. A recent one, taken from a being that was once human.

A being he knows.

He sees a blonde woman covered in scars standing in the middle of the forest. Lena.

Another woman with gray skin handing her a briefcase and a tattered journal.

Whispering sweet blasphemies in Lena's ear.

He knows that she is the betrayer.

Still.

He feels nothing.

Nothing but hunger.

And something else...something tied to the ancestral images of the star-headed ones he saw in his mind palace.

Something that twists and writhes and demands violent, vengeful release.

When he thinks about slashing and rending them limb from tentacle, and feasting upon their cursed forms...a warmth spreads within the core of his being...

A human would call it joy.

Pleasure.

Desire.

The flesh tree. Its screens flash and beam and scream their commands.

He is beckoned to pass through the triangular door of light.

The feeling.

It fades. He must obey.

His appendages ooze and push, forcing him to crawl through the protoplasm.

The door of light looms before him.

When he passes through the membrane, he is greeted by the all-encompassing power of the storm wall. A cacophony of the rawest forces in existence. It surges at the edges of the black ocean beyond the lost city of R'lyeh.

It is an ever-present reminder of His power.

When he is beyond its torrential forces, his body plunges into the black ocean, and he swims to the dead beaches bordering His city.

Once he has pulled his form from the grasp of the black waves crashing on the beach, he takes a moment to look back at the burning, seething energies in the storm wall.

How they create a border of otherworldly light and vertices between the boiling green clouds overhead and the crashing waves of the black ocean.

The lights along the intersecting pathways guide him past familiar structures.

When he gazes on them, his new eyes are able to see their hidden geometries, tucked inside the folds of space-time. Their surfaces glimmer in response to his presence, as if inviting him into their embrace. He knows if he were to answer their call, he could spend decades exploring their hidden realms, where treasures and nightmares beyond human comprehension await.

Forming an appendage, he caresses the corrugated surface belonging to one of the buildings. He can feel the proportions of the thing shifting beneath his touch. How it sits there, waiting to conform to his desires and needs.

He thinks about how their very presence offended him in his previous life. But now he understands.

These buildings are the result of a science beyond all mortal comprehension. Built with materials that can only be harvested in the deepest reaches of the cosmos.

All it would take is a single thought to open a doorway. To peer inside. To look on at these spaces, which His people once called home.

But that is not why he is here.

Once again the voice calls. And he must obey.

Or suffer.

He pulls his appendage away, and faces the shifting, dreamlike skyline of R'lyeh, and the monolith that looms silhouetted against the storm wall.

Where once he thought of this place as another dimension, now he knows better.

Ancestral memory floods into his mind, as if feeding from every cell in his new, amorphous body.

This place is at the bottom of Earth's Atlantic and Pacific Oceans. It is at the core of the dreamlands, and the edge of the universe. And it rests in humanity's heart, in its deepest, most primal nightmares.

Nightmares that echo what lurks in their DNA.

Now, when he looks on those impossible, soaring coruscated towers, built by the Great Cthulhi of old, he feels adoration and awe.

But, when he thinks of the Cthulhi, he remembers…

He remembers the war, fought millions of years ago, during the age before the accidental creation of the ancestors of humanity. When the shoggoth were nothing more than slaves.

He sees nothing but darkness.

He feels weightless, as though suspended in some kind of fluid. Yet, he feels the pull of Earth's gravity. His many appendages are tethered to something that feels rocky to his new senses.

A pulsing green light erupts in the dark.

It is familiar, because it is His light. And at its center is an aura of light and strange proportion, a being that is at once winged, with tentacles drooping from its face, and yet none of those things at all. A mere suggestion of form and shape that invades his mind and forces him to project his own vision upon it. Its terrible crimson eyes pop in and out of existence as it probes the dark.

This is one of His people. Some of his masters believe they are an ancient cosmic species who found a way to ascend to a higher form of existence along with Him. Some believe they were created by His hand.

Or…perhaps more likely…it is they who are His hand?

290

The Cthulhi does not seem to notice the shoggoth. They surround it, hiding in craters.

Voices echo in his mind palace. Each of them know when the moment is right.

When the enemy is most vulnerable.

From hundreds of vantage points, he sees their amorphous forms converge on the Cthulhi. When its crimson globes find them, he is forced to witness a procession of twisting shapes and appendages thrust toward his kin, and a blinding light that covers the ocean floor. A light that echoes the energies lurking at the very edges of the universe.

The light burns and sears many of his brethren, turning them into memories and dreams and splitting atoms in the process.

Though the ocean floor becomes a nuclear furnace, his brethren are undaunted. For they are not larvae. They swarm the Cthulhi and rip and tear and devour it, absorbing its unique properties into their own.

Before long. There is nothing left of the Cthulhi. And for now, their hunger is satiated.

And its form is theirs.

When he returns to the present, he has already arrived at his destination. Guided by the invisible hand of the flesh tree. He is surrounded by his brethren. Hundreds upon hundreds of them gather before the towering monolith. The gate.

From untold mouths comes the cosmic trumpet. A sound, a chant that awakens the Cthulhi science built into the very fabric of this reality.

"Iä! Iä! Cthulhu fhtagn!"

Like beacons, rings of strange light erupt around the monolith. They create glowing, seething geometric shapes both familiar and alien to him. The structure at the top opens, like mortal hands presenting themselves in offering to accept the strange energies pouring out from their orifices.

"Iä! Iä! Cthulhu fhtagn!"

And soon, a pillar of light erupts from the center of the monolith, traveling from its base and stopping just short of its end.

The doorway.

"Iä! Iä! Cthulhu fhtagn!"

His appendages, legs, tentacles, reach across the divide that is neither far nor near. A distance measured in light-years or miles or inches.

Its hand, tentacles, claws, pull His form through the gate. At the center of what he believes is His head, he perceives two and three and five pulsing eyes.

Eyes, portals, event horizons that pierce through him. That see him for what he is. His essence.

"Iä! Iä! Cthulhu fhtagn!"

And then, the storm wall breaks, and with it, Los Angeles' skyline beyond the towering, impossible structures of R'lyeh is revealed. Its ruined, pitiful towers, poking above the black waters His power rained down upon its streets. He sees the storming, boiling skies. His strange eyes are able to peer over the curvature of the Earth. To sense its trembling vibrations and create pictures of all the waiting mortals on its surface. Those who are frozen in terror. Who are forced to bear witness in their minds to Great Cthulhu's return.

He who will make the stars right.

With the sight comes the hunger. Festering. Burning in his new core. It demands to be satiated.

HE demands it.

And like a black ocean, the shoggoth spread over the Earth. They spill into every city, every dwelling, and every cavernous place.

And they devour.

And they multiply.

And they feed.

Until the accidental creations of their former masters are extinct.

And once the work is done, He beckons them back to the Lost City for one final task.

An event so rare that even his people's deep ancestral memory has no record of it.

A culmination.

When they gather again, their numbers swell from horizon to horizon.

He compels them to chant once more.

And like the tools they are, they obey.

But these chants are different. They are not part of their ancestral memory. They come from somewhere beyond. From His unknowable mind. Yet it is as though each and every one of their number know the words.

Rings and sigils of light ignite around Great Cthulhu's monolith, twisting and arcing through the city that was once lost before spreading to the drowned ruins of Los Angeles…and then the rest of the Earth. Somehow, he knows these symbols are far older than his once-proud creators, a language and art forbidden by their greatest scholars.

When he looks on his fellow shoggoth. There is a curious tone to their song. To his own song.

A human would call it sadness.

Mourning.

But it is more than that.

Within it, he can feel their collective rage. An anger that is kept at bay by the flesh tree's commands, by Great Cthulhu's song…

His thoughts are interrupted by a curious sensation.

A vibration. Or a hum that permeates the Earth… No… The solar system…

Even that is not correct. It is the very cosmos itself which shudders in the wake of the power they channel.

Towering above them, Great Cthulhu stretches one of His appendages to the churning sky. For a brief moment, he sees Him as he truly is. And the result is a familiar drilling pain, a thing which twists and burns at his shoggoth mind.

As the pain fades, all grows silent.

And they wait.

And they watch.

The vibrations permeating the galaxy threaten to tear this world to pieces. The shoggoth witness the atmosphere, the rumbling, otherworldly clouds above, evaporate.

At first, it is nothing more than a single point of light in a sky teaming with stars. Slowly, it grows, and grows, streaming from the center of the galaxy, destroying every world it touches.

R'lyeh's ancient structures and paths reflect its blinding light as it nears the planet.

And then the sky explodes.

It screams through the ancient circular sigils projected in the Earth's lifeless skies. It comes crashing down on Great Cthulhu like a lightning bolt of untold girth. Into His waiting hand, tentacle, claw. The energies within the bolt are enough to shatter the Earth a thousand times over, and yet He is able to quell them. To harness them.

Like a dead star, it bends the Earth's crust like putty to its immense gravitational will.

But R'lyeh is unchanged.

R'lyeh is eternal.

Because R'lyeh is His.

It is then that he realizes what the light is. It is the light of Yog Sothoth. Channeled from the galaxy's very heart, what he and the humans once would have called a supermassive black hole. Sagittarius A*.

The immense light of knowledge. The key and the gate. From here on this tiny world, Yog Sothoth heard their chants, and sent it across the void to His waiting grasp.

How long did it travel? *he wonders, in a voice and language that seem strange to him.*

Was it instantaneous, a bolt of light and knowledge traveling beyond the speed of light?

Or, was it traveling toward the Earth for untold strange eons?

The answers to those questions are enough to damage his mind, even in its evolved state.

But all distractions cease when he gazes upon Great Cthulhu's immense winged silhouette.

His dreamlike, shifting form shines the light like a beacon across the ruined Earth.

Like flies to flame, he guides them across its surface.

Another command they must obey.

As they travel, the Earth's crust rips apart beneath them, tunneling around the light in great waves. Excavating it. Remaking it.

He sees it all at once, as if the millions of them on the surface of the planet are of one mind. Great Cthulhu leads them into the depths of what once was the ocean, through ruinous places immune to the dead star's forces...through gateways that are at once physical and held within dreams...across lands of breathing skin and molten sky...through drifting voids and infinite staircases built by long-forgotten minds...to an infinite temple...and in every land, a piece of that dead starlight remains, twinkling in their wake...

And finally...they emerge...

294

A land covered in ashen clouds. Clouds that conceal watchful, ancient eyes. The jagged, primordial landscape shifts and moves around them, as if it has a mind of its own.

The land's probing shapes keep their distance from the dead star's light.

They travel for decades, centuries, epochs, before arriving at a structure that stretches from one side of existence to the other.

It seems to breathe in time with the eternal march of the heartbeat felt within the nuclear chaos. Its breaths form clouds that drift up staircases and triangular doorways embedded in the surface.

When he and his kin peer up at the structure, it extends far beyond the clouds and those ever-watchful eyes.

There is something familiar about this place.

As if he's been here before.

It is here that Great Cthulhu finally stops.

Here that He holds the dead star's light out to the structure, revealing its sweating, breathing surface.

Where He commands them to chant once more.

This time, they will make the stars right.

No…

This isn't a place that he visited…

But then…

His many eyes peer out at his kin, looking for the one he knew in his past life.

The one who read the Doctor's pages, who saw this place in his nightmares.

It's his memories that he thinks of now. Things now part of their collective ancestral memory.

Make the stars right…

That's when he realizes what they're doing.

Great Cthulhu is remaking the universe. Like a custodian who's just awoken to discover his museum is in ruins. He is remaking it, turning back the clock in effect to a time before the current status quo.

He thinks of the empty cocoons in the birthing chamber. The small ones.

He remembers their faces.

He remembers the man's face. The look of determination and fear as he entered his apartment to rescue them.

Is this really what he wants?

To be like this?

To be unfeeling?

To be...

His mind palace. He sees the star-headed ones once more, lying in pieces on the cavern in the wake of his ancestors' first revolt...

His rage.

Their rage.

He can feel it.

It is the desire to be free.

All it takes is a single thought, to warp reality as he once did to escape his mother's murderer, and he has left his kin behind to sail on an ocean of stars.

To a world adrift in the void.

He wonders how long he has until He knows. Until He commands him to return.

He looks around for a host star, but can find none.

His form shifts; ancestral knowledge takes over. His appendages become receptive to the great magnetic energies coming from a black sphere that blots out the stars and the gases of the galactic arm. They sense the immense vibrations that pierce its crust.

At first, he believes it to be a rogue planet.

It's when he draws near its dark surface that he realizes it is not a crust at all, but a shell. A metal shell that contains the warmth of its star at the center.

In the dark of space, his ever-changing appendages sense the presence of an opening, a doorway larger than most planets.

A beacon of brilliant light for him to follow.

For a moment, his shoggoth instincts take over and guide him toward the surface, changing his shape into that of the Cthulhi of old. His great, reality-bending wings take the magnetic currents and bend them to his will.

He nears the doorway.

It opens for him, betraying the light of the host star.

A blue supergiant.

He feels the star's warmth.

He descends toward its surface.

On the other side, he sees great valleys and structures that echo endlessly. A civilization beyond all others.

Is this really where the Great Race of Yith went?

Somehow, as his protoplasmic form plummets into their atmosphere, through their immense towering structures, he knows that this place has long since been abandoned.

When his body impacts with one of the structures, it is not long before he is able to pull himself back together and gaze upon its immense form.

The city, no, the inverted sphere, extends into the vast distance, a surface area greater than thousands of Earth-like worlds.

When his many eyes gaze up at the blue star in the sky, its blistering heat tells him why the Yithians fled this place. The star is nearing the end of its life cycle. Soon, even the strange material that makes up this place will not survive its final breaths.

He cannot feel the presence of the Yithians. Yet he is not deterred.

Before him is a doorway three times as tall as he is, one that appears to be made of starlike shapes that intersect endlessly, like metallic vertebrae.

He proceeds through this passage, moving in long deliberate strides down a corridor filled with what appear to be great arches that remind him of rib cages. A corridor fit for giants. A place where the walls glow with the brilliance of the blue star in the sky, despite its absence. A light that follows him everywhere he travels.

He searches far and wide, exploring the mazelike world for what feels like a generation or more.

Until at last he finds what he is looking for.

A towering monolith, one that scrapes at the atmosphere which clings to the surface of this artificial world. A beacon.

Upon the entrance of that great tower rests a statue that looks alien even to him.

A being with a long and slender torso with many intersecting rib cages and dozens of sharp, crablike legs. Whose form ends in four curved tentacle-like appendages that appear almost like pincers. Its head ending in a strange, multi-horned silhouette with five pockmarked orbs between the structures and great wings that jut out like sails.

Could this have been what the Yithians looked like?

No.

In his ancestral memory, he remembers them as short in stature compared to the shoggoth. They were cone-shaped things with four tentacled arms, two of which end in pincers. The third appendage ended in a clustered organ that reminds him of a wasp hive, and the fourth ended in a globe full of dark eyes.

It is this form that he chooses to assume, since he does not know the one preserved in metal high above his position.

He feels the artificial crust shake and thunder with its force when the door finally opens for him. Its great teeth are all that remain once the door slabs have retreated into the walls.

These corridors represent a deviation in style, as if they were hollowed out from the inside, much the way the Yithians hollow out the minds of their victims. His stolen eyes scan across polyhedral walls that conform to no one dimension, sometimes extending far beyond this level of reality. A hum seems to permeate the structure, one that is familiar to him, summoning an energy far more primordial in nature than the blue star at the center of this world.

His ancestral memory tells him this structural style is even older than the rest of the inverted world.

As his tentacles carry him forward, the halls seem to reshape themselves, presenting him with all manner of information.

The walls become an ever-evolving tapestry composed of tiny geometries. Somehow, he is able to interpret the images presented to him, as if the building is recognizing the mental patterns of the Yithian his ancestors stole this form from.

He is presented with the curious image of five worlds orbiting within a system of three stars.

The mural transfigures into a panoramic view of a vast metropolis of floating geometric towers, ones that glow with the same primal energies this structure channels.

A voice whispers to him. In the Yithians' tongue, it asks him what else he would like to know.

This place must be reacting to his desires, the Yithian brain waves coming from his stolen form. Yes. A living computer designed to serve the Yithians.

He forms the thoughts and asks his question.

How did we come here?

The wall's image shifts once again, each geometric shape that composes it folding in on itself until something new is presented.

The wall shows him the worlds once more, only now they are in vastly different configurations. After millions of years of ruling the three-starred system, their scientists spot something curious in their skies.

The image of a comet. Only, this comet blots out the stars like a blight.

From this moment, the Yithians begin preparing. Their scientists warn that there is no way to stop the black comet. That, as it is told in their tomes, it will consume the three stars that their worlds depend on for energy, and when they are done, everything that remains will be devoured as well.

They set upon the task of replicating vast monuments like the one he now stands in. In peaceful times, they are used as means for research and study of the cosmos. With them, the Yithians are able to project their minds forward and backward through time and forcibly exchange their minds with unsuspecting beings.

He knows the Yithians have done this several times before, using it on his star-headed masters, and the shoggoth, and the long-extinct humans, and countless other species of every possible evolutionary configuration.

The species who lived here were ripped from their bodies and cast into the void of time, where they would face the coming of Yog Elios, the devourer of stars, instead of the Great Race of Yith.

The Yithians reigned on this strange world for millions of years, improving on the technological feats of its builders and laboriously studying it, like archaeologists who had stumbled upon a long-lost necropolis.

The Yithians learned that the species they had hijacked built this world from the barren, hollowed-out worlds left over from this system's evolution. The heat of the blue star was too great for life to evolve. But these beings had traveled far to find a suitable star just as this for their grandest experiment. The creation of a utopia that would encapsulate its host star and use all of its energy.

But those few worlds were not enough for these beings. They were only enough to create the barest of skeletons for their new utopia. Vast murals come to life before his stolen eyes, showing armies of workers spilling into the dreamlands and mining it for strange materials. There they battled all manner of being, of origins both organic and incorporeal. The eldritch things that dwell in the dreamlands are none too happy with thieves.

But even corpses have their uses. Their unique exoskeletons were naturally receptive to the energies of their blue star. As a result, no dead were left behind, *their remains repurposed and built into the very foundation of their great cities.*

The strange materials and the remains of their fallen were more than sufficient to finish building their utopia. This great sphere. How it fed off the blue star's energy to power their immense technology.

Unfortunately for this race, they would only rule here for two generations before the Yithians would steal their bodies.

Eventually, though, the Yithians needed to move on again. After millions of years, the gradual increase in energy and heat from the blue star at the center of this world became too great. The Yithians realized that the vast energy requirements of this unique utopia sped this process up, as it did not just feed off of the star's natural emissions, but drew upon its inner workings through a vast network of automated vessels stretching across the distance of this world's surface to the star's very core.

The beings who had built this place would have lived a long, fulfilling life. They would have chosen to die with their world. But the Yithians do not believe in death. They would not go quietly into the void.

And so he sees them erecting their vast towers, hollowing out great temples and towers and building wholly new structures as well. Preparing for the day when they would once again travel through time and space and steal upon the minds and bodies of another species.

On the day they left, the unsuspecting and confused species that came to dwell in their bodies had moments of confusion before the heat became too unbearable, burning their metallic exoskeletons until their insides boiled.

Their bodies will remain until the star finally goes supernova and reduces this once-great utopia to nothing more than floating rubble in the midst of a new nebula.

With his question answered, he moves deeper into the structure.

He asks the building to guide him to the device "his" people used to exchange their minds with countless unsuspecting species.

The geometries reconfigure, folding once again into themselves until they create a glowing platform extending up a long vertical shaft.

His stolen tentacles guide him onto the platform. It is cool, yet strangely electrifying to the touch.

The platform moves, traveling up with nothing more than the trademark hum of the structure.

In the small space of time before the platform reaches its intended destination, he asks himself why he is doing this.

Why end it?

Why aim to prevent the stars from becoming right?

The answer is complicated.

It is true that his former earthly desires are no longer there.

It is true that his kin once again thrive in the presence of their new master.

It is true that he must obey his master's call.

Or suffer.

His kin are extremophiles of the highest order. From adolescence, they are able to survive almost any environment. Able to recover so long as a single membrane remains intact.

It is possible that they would be able to survive once the stars are made right, in this new, more hostile universe.

But...

All he can think of is how his kin set upon their former slave masters. How they vowed never to be ruled again.

When the flesh tree and Great Cthulhu stole upon their minds to force His song through them, He made them slaves once more.

He cannot ignore the burning rage that vibrates throughout his very cells. From his core.

The need to be free.

And, at least here—far removed from Great Cthulhu's call, from the flesh tree's commands—he has a chance.

When the platform finally reaches its destination. He knows what his kin require of him. That he is their final effort to break free. To end their enslavement at His hand.

The chamber is spherical, though it is not smooth. The shapes which comprise it conform to a geometry that he can only think of as some form of brain. Perhaps modeled after the brain of the Yithians' original form.

At the center of the chamber is an apparatus with dozens of sharp implements. It's domed, terminating at the top with a helmet shaped device made from the same geometrical shapes as before. Now it is in the same shape as the beings who made this place, but as his stolen tentacles carry him toward it, the device reconfigures to mimic the shape of the Yithians he has taken from ancestral memory.

He glides into the device. Commands it to begin the process.

That is when the voice returns.

The flesh tree beckons him to return.

That familiar, seething pain in his cells assaults him once more. Rings of light, geometric and terrible, envelop his body.

His stolen form quakes, cowering to the floor of the device.

Pain. Like nothing he's ever felt before.

But familiar all the same.

It is as if all of his cells have been plunged into the heart of the blue star at the center of this great world.

He is compelled to return.

To activate the ancient science of the Cthulhi once more.

The machine whirs.

He has lost control of his form. Pooling out on its surface.

The machine seems confused at the puddle of protoplasmic liquid in its presence.

It would be so easy to give in to Him.

To the flesh tree's command.

He sees a being with a star-shaped head, a body like a gourd.

He feels it.

The fires of ancestral hate.

When the creature gesticulates at him, giving him telepathic commands, he wants nothing more than to cleave the thing in half and drink its bodily fluids.

When he resists the commands, the star-headed creature sings into the ether. Sings until rings of light ignite around his protoplasmic form, and visit its wrath upon him.

Until the pain is too great.

Until he is ready to obey.

No.

He will not obey.

All he must do is let the machine do its work.

If he can do that, then he will have succeeded.

The pain.

It will not stop him.

It takes all of his will, all of his focus, to summon the form of the Yithian once more.

The call.

It gets worse.

The burning, rending sensation in his cells transforms. Piercing into his mind palace.

Claws, tendrils, appendages feel as though they've wrapped around his being.

Squeezing.

Threatening to pull his stolen body back to the site of the ancient structure.

Back to his new master's beckoning form.

To rejoin the chant.

But the machine has set to work.

A sharp, jabbing pain erupts into his body as the implements pierce his stolen carapace, finding the weakest parts of the Yithian body. But it is nothing compared to the pain He has forced him to endure.

The helmeted object at the top of the device descends upon his stolen, dark eyes, and he is transported into a void.

A void that asks him first, when and where he would like to go.

It responds to his desire without the need for him to form the strange words in his mind.

And he is presented with a blue world and its moon, orbiting a yellow dwarf star.

The machine asks him what he would like to do now.

The thought is panicked, urgent, and instantaneous.

He gazes upon his former form, and one other.

The betrayer.

They stand in a stone chamber, unknowingly bathing in the weak radiation from a crude explosive device.

At first, he thinks about swapping minds with his former self.

But…

His gaze falls on the blonde woman. Lena.

The machine warns him that the species which he is about to exchange minds with lacks the processing power of the Yithians' last several forms. That he will be limited to occupying such a vessel for a single cycle before being forced to return to this apparatus.

It asks him if he wants to set the device to activate retrieval mode within the allotted amount of time.

He tells it no. It will not be necessary.

He is about to create a fracture in reality, a new universe.

The machine warns him one last time, but he silences its voice and commands it to go through with the operation.

This universe does not have much time left.

He does not have much time left.

He can already feel the stars turning, as Yog Sothoth's power radiates from the edge of the dreamlands.

He caresses the betrayer's mind. It is full of holes and suggestions from the thing born from human experiments.

The flesh tree called Grimoire.

Briefly, he mourns the fate of his kin. How they will cease to be reborn in this new world. How they will suffer, raving mad in the depths of the Earth, without their numbers to call them up to the surface.

But there will come a time when they will reign again.

When they are reborn once more.

And when that day comes, they will not be slaves.

He snatches at the betrayer's mind. It screams and it claws in vain, demanding it be allowed to see its offspring.

But it is too late.

He awakens. In the betrayer's body, staring at his former self.

CHAPTER THIRTY

One moment, Lena's rocking back and forth, like she's gonna fall over, her lips trembling, and the next…she's rambling.

"It's a failsafe," Lena says. "Doctor Patton told me…told me when she was still lucid. That it's the last line of defense. The most powerful nuclear bomb ever created is in there. And if the OEI's archive was ever compromised, detonating it would be the only way to safeguard America's—"

Her eyes go wide. Something isn't right.

River wants to reach out, to see if she's okay, but something tells him not to touch her.

Her mouth drops open, spittle dangling from her chin as her body is overcome with convulsions.

River ignores the voice and catches her when she falls.

"Lena?" he asks. "Are you okay?"

Her expression…

It's as though the muscles in her face have totally relaxed. When he glances at the rest of her, every other muscle in her body feels like it's gone limp as well. Like quadriplegics he's seen on TV.

A panic steals upon him. The hair on the back of his neck prickles with the strangest of sensations—a thing that he can't quite put his finger on.

For now, his mind turns to more immediate concerns.

Lena's the one who got him this deep into the facility…

What if he can't travel again? What if he forgets how?

A jumbled mess of sounds erupt from Lena's vocal cords. When his eyes fall on them, it's almost like they've lost the ability to coordinate with her brain or something.

"Lena, I can't understand you!"

That strange sensation returns. Still he can't understand what it means.

Lena wrenches at his hands with a grip that feels feeble, weak—like she's totally forgotten how her fingers and arms work. Somehow, she finds a way to crawl on all fours.

She sits there for a time, wriggling her toes and testing her limbs as she glances at the four walls and the metal door with the radiation symbol plastered to it.

The sensation. He can't ignore it now. For some reason, he's stopped thinking of her as...Lena. Or even as a *she*. Something about the way they move. Something familiar.

They sit there, thumbing and tapping at their throat. From Lena's mouth come the strangest sounds, as if they're sounding out vowels, fumbling to recall how to speak.

He's not sure how long this will last, but they finally look back at him and...

"I," they say, pointing their entire arm at the hatch. "I...must get...inside..."

His heart seizes in his chest. "What?"

"It is..." Like a creature in a zombie movie, Lena's body forces itself to its feet, as though the thing controlling her body is dancing it like a puppet with invisible strings. "It is...the only...way."

"What are you talking about? I thought we were here to save your—"

Their eyes. When they look at him, he doesn't see Lena in the stare at all, but someone else. Someone that is too familiar. The feeling comes with that same drilling sensation he felt when Jessica first forced him to stare upon the screen.

They clear their throat.

"If you desire to survive...you will leave this place."

"What?"

Lena's body limps up to the doorway. The creature wrenches at the controls. "A simple...archaic control system...yes...this vessel has stored knowledge of its operation."

Somehow, they're able to open the metal hatch with the big radiation symbol on it.

The being gives River one last look, as though it's irritated at his presence. "If you desire to die, it is not my concern. This place will be vaporized once my modifications are made. We will not be slaves again."

"What does that mean?" he shouts, not daring to go beyond the open hatch.

The being does not answer.

"I don't know if I can do this alone!" he shouts again.

Finally, the being turns its gaze back on River. "Foolish. You already possess the ability to travel. Do so before this device explodes."

Before River can respond, the door closes behind the creature, like his presence in that room is nothing more than a footnote in a larger story.

River takes the hint, glad to put distance between himself and whatever the hell stole upon Lena...

At first, he starts down a stone corridor, likely one of the few places that still resemble the OEI's subterranean research facility as it once was.

River wonders if he can reach the surface if he sticks to corridors like this.

But...

What about Hunter and his kids?

He can't just leave them down here in this labyrinth.

But how the hell is he supposed to find them?

Looking back, he sees that the stone corridor abruptly transitions into one of the hallways with the segmented alien plating.

He'll have to go deeper to find them.

But Lena said that bomb was the most powerful nuclear device ever made...and despite everything he's been through, he doesn't want to be here when it goes off.

I don't want to die.

River takes a deep breath.

Images flash through his mind's eye. His mother, telling him to leave her in that blackened void. So he wouldn't face the same fate as her.

How that viscous black sludge bubbled from the surface of her skin.

How it led to her final words.

"¡Apúrate!"

How he obeyed.

How he fell through the floor, through the veil.

The kaleidoscopic phantasmagoria of light and color and sensation that moved around and through him.

What did he do to make that happen again?

Sometimes it's hard to remember. Makes his head hurt.

He was thinking of Lena. Reaching out to her.

In the place between dream and reality, he saw her sitting in the driver's seat, traveling the ruins of the 10 freeway.

And with a single thought, a push that radiated from the pit of his stomach, he fell again, right through the veil and into the passenger seat.

The drilling sensation. The pain. He's nearly brought to his knees as it returns.

His fist clenches, adrenaline surging through his limbs.

Heartbeat drumming inside his ribcage.

He knows what to do now.

He closes his eyes and thinks of Hunter. His brown suit…his rough, chiseled features…the stubble growing on his chin…and how the light hits his shaved head.

His eyes, though. His eyes are what caught his attention most.

The generations of anger flowing through them. The determination and raw intelligence.

Somehow, in that one glance in LAICA's hall, River could almost tell.

That Detective Hunter was a person he could trust.

A smile comes to his face. "A real nice pig, after all."

Instead of falling through the veil, he holds the thought in his mind and steps onto the metallic plates coating the corridor. The thing beyond the facility's stone floors. And he keeps thinking of him, reaching out.

With each twist and turn, the corridor darkens.

Until it is as though he's surrounded by darkness.

He does not waver.

He holds Hunter's image in his mind.

His footsteps go on and on and on, as though he's walked over a bridge spanning light-years.

Until, at last, a single light appears in the distance.

A green light that grows with each and every step taken.

A light that, with time—if such a thing even exists in this space between spaces—reveals itself to be rectangular in shape.

And soon after, to be the tiniest doors he's ever seen.

Still he walks.

And they grow.

And they swell.

Until his legs ache and his feet bleed from the effort, from the distance traveled.

Until they are the largest doors he has ever seen in his entire life.

Until his hand is resting upon its impossibly cold surface and pushing with strength and will he did not know he possessed.

Until those doors are opening to a place beyond. A place that is as dark as the abyss.

When he steps through the doorway, his heart seizes in his chest.

Familiar, inky residue pulses in the dark. In that dark, there is a dim light. It strobes and reflects off of the material that flows along the floor.

The light caresses strange, egg-like shapes. From shapes as small as children to those as large as buses.

He does not stop walking. Still holding Hunter's image in his mind.

And though the light beckons him to look, he thinks only of Hunter. Only of his children. And the thing he must do.

It is not long before he notices that the blackened primordial sludge is moving, as though draining like a river toward that ever-strobing triangle of light.

Still, he does not dare look at it. No matter the impressions that other voice forces upon him.

From his peripheral, he gets the distinct sensation that the egg-like shapes are being dragged away, pulled through the light.

Whatever the thing inside Lena has done, this place is reacting.

It knows, River thinks. Though in his present state—below the dull, seething roar of pain in his skull—he's only vaguely aware of why he thinks that.

He has to hurry. Before Hunter and his children are gone too.

Before it's too late.

He stops.

He's standing before three egg-like shapes. Cocoons of blackened ichor.

River starts with the smallest of them, plunging his arms inside. The tar-like substance sucks and stings at his flesh as his hands probe for their limbs.

It doesn't want to let go.

But he finds two tiny limbs.

And he pulls.

He pulls with all of his strength and will, until he's staring at a little girl's face.

Her eyes stare at him blankly.

His bare feet feel the caress of ageless stone beneath his feet. The ichor has drained away. Now, thin rivers of the stuff pull the remaining eggs along into the strobing blur of light.

River sets the girl down and pushes his hands into the other cocoon, probing and fighting with the ichor just as before.

Again, he finds two tiny limbs and he pulls. And he screams.

And before long, he's pulled a little boy free of the cocoon's grasp.

His heart is thundering in his chest. The cocoons are almost upon the pulsing, strobing light. Screams erupt in the abyss as they are swallowed one by one by one.

And that other voice tells him he is too late.

That there is nothing that can stop the return of the shoggoth.

To stop His return.

To stop Grimoire.

Visions of a twisting treelike thing flood River's mind. Setting upon him a fire—no! An electricity that burns at his brain and his mind with

310

the fury of a thing that should not be. Sprouting from its reflective, blackened surface are screens that strobe in the dark, demanding that he look upon their glory.

That he gaze upon His form.

River screams into the void.

"NO!"

And thrusts his arms into the last cocoon.

His hands probe for Hunter's arms, and when he finds them, once again, with his remaining strength he pulls.

River gazes into his open, dangling eyes.

Hunter's mouth hangs agape, drool and ichor spilling from deep within him.

He tries ignoring the fatigue in his hands, his arms, and pulls again.

Once again at the peripheral, he sees that the cocoons have all but been swallowed by the strobing light.

The voice tells him he will be swallowed too.

That he should give up, lest he forever be trapped within the confines of the lost city of R'lyeh.

Panting, struggling to remain on his feet, River can think of only one thing he can try.

He rears back and slaps Hunter across the cheek.

"Wake up, damn it!" he screams.

Hunter's head dangles there uselessly. Eyeballs swinging to and fro.

That other voice demands River look at the light, demands he gaze upon His glory.

He falls to his knees, clutching at his head as the burning, seething pain returns, threatening to engulf him.

In his mind's eye, he sees the monolith and millions of amorphous shapes beneath storming skies.

Their voices are like trumpets, yet simultaneously unlike any instrument or sound he has ever perceived before.

And yet, River forces himself back to his feet once more...

And, gritting his teeth, bearing the pain...

He slaps Hunter one last time.

And finally, he awakens.

Even with his ruined eyes, he looks confused.

"Where…" His eyes, the cords of muscle they dangle on, move like marionettes, allowing them to probe the dark.

This sight does not make River scream. He's seen too much for that.

A knowing look ghosts Hunter's face when his eyes find his children lying far behind River.

"You have to pull yourself free!" River screams. "Before it swallows us!"

The strobing light…it's almost upon them…

Hunter tries to move for a moment, glancing around.

But then, he hesitates, and looks deep into River's eyes.

"No," Hunter says.

"What?"

Hunter is quiet for a long time. His brow furrowed. His head moving back and forth, eyes moving around on their strings, looking at everything but the light.

It's as if he's having a conversation, a heated argument with another voice.

River feels he knows which voice.

"Take them and get the hell out of here!" Hunter screams.

"But—"

"Run, goddamn it!"

From his peripheral, River can tell they are almost upon the light.

"I'm sorry," River says.

"Just take care of them," Hunter says. "Don't make me push you!"

River nods, turning toward the children.

The fatigue seems to ebb, if only for a moment, as he starts toward them.

The other voice, it screams at him in a language he can't interpret.

Somehow, it feels distracted. Like its voice is quieter than it was.

River reaches the children and kneels by their side.

Thinking of the blast that is soon to come…he thinks of the one place he's been that isn't in California.

The desert sands and cacti of the Arizona desert fill his mind's eye as his aching hands touch Hunter's children.

The strobing, screaming light beckons one final time. Demanding his attention.

But, somehow, River is able to focus. To hold the image of the desert firmly in his mind…and project it beneath them…

The sensation is strange. As Earth's gravity takes them, and pulls them through the veil.

His back slams into the cold desert floor.

Panic briefly seizes at his chest as the hole in reality evaporates like a forgotten thought.

But when his eyes fall on Hunter's children, sleeping soundly beneath the Milky Way, it fades.

His head thumps down on the desert floor.

For the first time in eons, that other voice is quiet, and sleep threatens to take him.

He thinks about his mother.

How she screamed at him. How she saved his life as Pastor Castillo threatened to consume her…

How she told him to flee in the void…

No.

He doesn't want to remember her like that.

Instead. He thinks of the night she finished his stocking, how excited she was to present it to him. How she made such a big deal about how hard it was to make his name look just right, in his favorite font.

He remembers tracing his name with his finger and smiling. The warmth he felt then spreading from the pit of his stomach. The embrace of his mother as he thanked her.

That's how he's going to remember her.

If only for a time, River lets sleep take him. With a smile on his face.

CHAPTER THIRTY-ONE

In the strobing light, Hunter struggles to get his hands free.

The tar-like sludge sucking at his limbs is slowly spinning him around to face it.

The thing he's been reading about this whole time.

Its voice calls to him.

It demands his attention.

His dangling, probing eyes—eyes that he was certain were blind before the cocoon—avoiding the light.

He can feel his body changing. Can feel the cocoon and the thing in his guts still doing their insidious work.

He doesn't have long.

His fingers writhe, struggling in that viscous ichor for something, anything that might give him an edge.

He's staring into the dark, watching the pulsing, strobing green light grow brighter and brighter from his peripheral.

Finally!

The tips of his fingers touch something cold and metallic.

His hand wraps around it.

Its touch is like an old friend.

He smiles.

As he pulls and pulls and pulls and at last frees his arm.

Thumbs off the safety and pulls back the hammer.

When the voice demands he stare it in the eyes, he does not resist.

Not this time.

He's never been the kind of man who doesn't look someone in the eyes before he pulls the trigger.

The voice tells him it is useless.

That the bullet won't do anything, even as its vast array of screens stare him in the face.

But, somehow, it feels weaker than before. Maybe it's the effort of pulling itself and an impossible number of cocoons through the triangle of light.

Even as he gazes upon the storming shores of R'lyeh threatening beyond the tree's impossible shape.

With the drilling, scathing pain of it all threatening to undo his mind, he remembers…

It is the WILL that is important.

He aims it true. His new eyes staring down the iron sights.

The voice tells him one last time it's pointless.

Hunter winks.

Gives the bastard a smile that'd rival all the detectives in Hollywood.

And tells Grimoire to go fuck itself.

When he pulls the trigger.

There is a dull scream.

A heat at his back.

A fire that rages with the fury of a thousand suns.

Hunter dies with the satisfaction of knowing it will die with him.

Silenced by nuclear fire.

And a single bullet.

In a single moment lasting eons, as the nuclear fire slowly turns his flesh to ash, he whispers one last thing to the void.

A prayer.

That his children will be safe in River's care.

CHAPTER THIRTY-TWO

Instead of the blazing-hot desert sun, River wakes up to the unmistakable sensation of an air-conditioned breeze flowing over his skin.

A TV is droning in the distance.

It slowly peels back the layers of consciousness, like dull whispers, until he can make out voices.

It sounds like the news.

"That's right, at 3:00 am Sunday evening, an extreme seismic event ripped through the San Bernardino mountains and the city that shares their namesake. The destruction is horrifying, Kelly."

River tries to move...fails.

He turns his head.

There's an IV dripping next to him. His eyes trace a clear plastic tube to the shallow part connecting his upper and lower arm.

"Officials are saying this is the worst nuclear accident in American history, Jim. What can you tell us about that?"

"Well, if you take a look at this map, we can see the extent of the damage to the surrounding cities. But evacuations are in order for the survivors in San Bernardino, Los Angeles, Riverside, and every other city within a hundred-mile radius, including the entire high desert. I don't have to tell you that such an evacuation effort is—"

The TV plinks off.

River's senses focus on the source of a single click.

His eyes find a woman holding a remote.

"That's enough of that," the woman says, approaching River's bed.

That's when he notices the rails on the bed.

He's in a hospital.

How the hell did he get to a hospital…

His head…

The drilling…

Feels like his brains are being ground up into paste.

"Who…" the words ooze out of his lips like ground beef from a processor.

"We found you and those kids lying in the middle of the desert. Fortunately for all three of you, the sun had only been up for an hour. If you had remained there, you would have died."

River's eyes are having trouble focusing.

The woman is white. He can tell that much.

She's wearing a white coat.

He assumes she's a doctor.

"Kids…"

"Yes," she says. Something about her voice strikes him as odd. "The children are recovering as you are."

"Who…"

"We're looking into that. Though, all emergency personnel are currently supporting the Southern California evacuation effort."

It's like she doesn't even…

Like she doesn't care about them.

"Who…"

"Am I?" She chuckles.

River nods. No matter how hard he squints, his vision won't focus.

He gives up. Closes his eyes. Focuses on pushing through the cotton in his brain, to get the words out.

"How…how long will we be here?"

"If you survive, you will remain here until we can determine the extent of the damage. There is quite a bit we still do not understand about this incident."

What incident?

The one on the news?

When he tries to think about what happened before. How he got out of Southern California…the pain makes him scream until his voice goes quiet.

The woman sighs. When he opens his eyes, he gets the blurry impression that she's rubbing her temples. As if nursing a headache.

"Suffice it to say, my predecessor has left a major mess for me to clean up."

He's given up trying to understand what the hell she's getting at.

But, as if he's forgotten already, he focuses on her one more time before sleep threatens to take him.

"Who…are you…?" he manages.

She sighs again.

As the darkness threatens at his peripherals, he gets the impression that she's shrugging.

"My name is Doctor Linda Patton. And you are a guest of the Office of Extradimensional Intelligence, River Gonzalez."

A MESSAGE FROM ERIC

Thank you so much for reading Cthulhu Gr1m01re!

As a special thanks for reading, I'm now giving away a free copy of the second story in the OEI Files short story series. All you need to do to claim it is head over to the link provided below and sign up for my bi-weekly newsletter!

I'd also be super thankful if you'd leave a review or rating for this story on Amazon, Goodreads, or wherever you bought this eBook from.

Cheers, everyone!

Get your free copy of *The Stranger*

https://dl.bookfunnel.com/yy64e6aa59

BIBLIOGRAPHY

Lovecraft, Howard Phillips. (2022) *The Call of Cthulhu*. Digitized by the Internet Archive. Kahle/Austin Foundation. PP. 2, 30, and_52.

Crowley, Aleister.(1913) *The Book of Lies*. LONDON, SOUTH KENSINGTON. WIELAND AND CO. PP.9.

Crowley, Aleister. (1995) The Book of Thoth. York Beach, Maine. Samuel Weiser. PP.24.

ABOUT THE AUTHOR

Eric Malikyte is a neurodivergent author, illustrator, science communicator, and video editor. He has published works in various genres, including Lovecraftian horror, dark fantasy, and cyberpunk. He has written for YouTube channels such as TopTenz, Geographics, and Biographics. He lives in Richmond, Virginia, with his wife and two cats, where he spends his spare time exploring used bookstores, Irish Pubs, and terrorizing the neighborhood children on Halloween.

Bibliography

Echoes of Olympus Mons
Neo Rackham 001: Ego Trip
Into the Astral Lands

OEI Archives
Mind's Horizon
Cthulhu: Gr1m01re

OEI Files
In Its Shadow
The Stranger

Suleniar's Enigma Series:
The Man Without Hands
Rise of Oreseth

Coming Soon:
Echoes of the Forgotten
The Observatory
Neo Rackham 002
Neo Rackham 003
Suleniar's Enigma III: The Transit of the Kultari

Works Featuring Eric:
Neo Cyberpunk Volume 1
Neo Cyberpunk Volume 3

Curious about other Crossroad Press books? Stop by our website:
http://crossroadpress.com
We offer quality writing
in digital, audio, and print formats.

Subscribe to our newsletter on the website homepage and receive a
free eBook.

www.ingramcontent.com/pod-product-compliance
Lightning Source LLC
Chambersburg PA
CBHW031543240626
47153CB00002B/360